Praise for THE APPEAR...

'The most teasingly pleasurabl...
come across this year is *The* ...
The plot is cunningly set up ar... writing a
crime mystery novel which then dissolves into the real thing.
Or perhaps not. The play of appearance and reality
is maintained to a satisfying denouement.'

JOHN SUTHERLAND
The Times, Books of the Year 2015

'I've asked for it to be placed in my
Christmas stocking.'

IAN RANKIN

'In this witty and entertaining story of a crime writer
who has lost interest in his recurring hero…
there is a good deal to relish.'

JESSICA MANN
Literary Review

'It's a brilliant crime novel full of typically British characters,
from the slightly unhinged middle-life-crisis neighbour who
is always 'testing' military combat gear in his back garden;
the slightly sinister ever-watchful tech entrepreneur; the
romantic and fragile rock star; the washed-up kids' TV
presenter with his badger sidekick and the charming crime-
writer narrator who despite his best efforts is never quite
in control. If you like Tom Sharpe you'll love this book. It's
intelligent, quietly sexy and beautifully written. A real gem.'

Goodreads Review

'Uber-clever crime fiction.'

ASKMEN UK,
10 best books of 2015

A NOTE ON THE AUTHOR

John Nightingale was born in Bedford and read English at Cambridge. As a civil servant he specialized in, among other things, fraud and alcohol abuse. He lives in London and Suffolk with his wife and two daughters.

The Appearance of Murder is the first in a series of novels about crime writer David Knight.

He is also the author of *The Sky Blue* Parcel.

Further information is available at Johnnightingale.org.uk

JOHN NIGHTINGALE

THE APPEARANCE OF MURDER

SPIDER MONKEY BOOKS

LONDON

**SPIDER MONKEY
BOOKS**

First published in Great Britain in 2015
by Spider Monkey Books
82 Wroughton Road
London SW11 6BG
spidermonkeybooks.com

Paperback ISBN: 978-0-9933788-3-6

Also available as an ebook
Mobi ISBN: 978-0-9933788-1-2
Epub ISBN: 978-0-9933788-2-9

A catalogue record for this book is available
from the British Library.

Typeset by Chandler Book Design

Printed and bound in the UK by
CPI Group (UK) Ltd, Croydon CR0 4YY

The publisher supports the Forest Stewardship Council® (FSC®), the leading
international forest-certification organisation. This book is made from acid-free
paper from an FSC®-certified provider. FSC is the only forest-certification scheme
supported by the leading environmental organisations, including Greenpeace.

For Caroline, Elizabeth, Victoria & Molly

PART ONE

Friday,
Saturday,
Sunday

Appearance – noun – an act of appearing

ONE

FRIDAY 8.45PM – 10.00PM

I REMEMBER THE MOMENT before she arrived. I had just looked at my watch. Not yet nine and still light. I wasn't expecting anyone. This was the first of the few days of peace that had been so hard to arrange. I could have left the door unopened and kept murder from appearing in my life.

I had swirled the white wine round and round the glass. There was a disconcerting metallic sheen on its surface. I sighed. I was beginning to regret my decision not to go to Norfolk. A week near the sea with my wife's friends was more than appealing. The five children would look after themselves while the adults enjoyed good food, conversation, and doing nothing much at all.

Instead I had left Kate tight-lipped as I had backed out of the holiday at the last minute to sort out my latest crime novel, *Murder is Equal*. It wasn't something I would normally do but it was a question of disappointing Kate or Debbie, my agent. I had spent a considerable mount of energy trying to convince Debbie that I needed more time to rework the series after completing *A Grave Mistake*. She had been as firm in her view that delay would kill the series off but had finally relented.

A string of emails I had sent to Debbie between January and May had indicated that I was back on track, or at least could deliver to the revised timetable we had agreed. But somehow I couldn't finish the book off. Increasingly I had only myself to blame. My wife and sons had started tiptoeing around the house. Kate had offered to take them to their Saturday morning matches. They had both started cleaning their football boots. Yet stubbornly, as the days slipped into weeks and the weeks into months, the book failed to progress beyond page 313, which, apart from feeling unlucky, was also a prime number.

I had told anyone who would listen that the problem was my detective hero. Tom Travis had somehow lost his energy. I needed to find a new angle on him to exploit. Quite what that should be was not so clear. I put the glass down. He could always strike up a relationship with the policewoman who had been hovering indecisively in the background in chapter seventeen. I had been toying with the idea of making her more attractive. That, and getting him to sort out his current case, was what the week was going to achieve.

So that was why I had had to back out of the family holiday. Opening the wine was simply to mark the transition point between family hubbub and artistic solitude and endeavour.

I had promised Kate that I would ignore anything that threatened the book's completion by the time she and the boys returned. But I had also undertaken to try to contact the local builder about the cracked tiles on the roof to see what we could get away with to keep the winter storms at bay. I was a month overdue on sorting anything out, as Kate reminded me as she left, and I had made a call to him, or at least left a message asking him to drop by, before she had driven to the end of the street.

That was why I got to my feet when the doorbell rang. If I hadn't things would have been very different.

To guard against the possibility that it was simply Kate's return to pick up some essential piece of kit that the boys had forgotten to pack I put the wine glass discreetly out of view behind the hi-fi equipment.

I needn't have bothered. It wasn't Kate on the doorstep. It wasn't the builder either. It was a young woman. The retreating summer day bathed her face in golden light. She was tall and slender with reddish brown hair. She would be ideal as the model for the policewoman in chapter seventeen.

'David, David Knight?' she said hesitantly.

'That's me,' I said.

'My name is Perdita. I'd very much like to talk to you.'

The words came in a slight rush. She was nervous about something.

'I'm sorry. I don't…'

I stopped. It didn't seem she was selling anything, and I had a strange sense that she hadn't appeared out of the everyday, but from a dream. Her blue eyes were sparkling, and a slight breeze ruffled her hair. She was wearing black skinny jeans, a cream blouse with an amber necklace and a grey, well-tailored jacket.

'What's this about?' I said.

'If you could spare me a few minutes. I'd be very grateful. It's something you might be able to help with.'

There was a faint tremor in her voice, a hint of vulnerability. She reminded me of someone long ago. But I couldn't think who it was. I opened the door wider.

'I've got half an hour,' I said. 'You'd better come in.'

We stood in the hallway. She looked at me as though she didn't think I was real.

'Can I get you a glass of wine? I'm just winding down for the weekend.'

'Wine would be great,' she said.

'I'm in the sitting room on the first floor. It's at the top of the stairs on the right. I'll be with you in a second.'

I went into the kitchen and stopped. What precisely was I doing? I had promised Kate to keep my nose to the grindstone and shoulder to the wheel. It had seemed better than setting out a more precise plan. But I could hardly hope to cure Tom Travis's lethargy if I refused to help a damsel in distress. I poured myself some water and drank it. Then I got two glasses out of the kitchen cabinet and the best bottle I could find out of the fridge.

Upstairs shadows were beginning to fill the corners of the room. The papers that I had moved from the study in search of a more inspiring work environment were scattered across the coffee table. I put the wine and glasses down and shuffled the papers into a protective pile.

'Is white OK?' I said. 'Should be fairly light and cheerful.'

'That's fine.'

She was surveying the room with unusual intensity. I found it slightly alarming. She looked as though she might be an estate agent, or a mistress appraising her lover's wealth. But she was fooling herself if she was searching for clues about me. At least half of the furniture in the room had come from Kate's parents when they had moved house.

'So?' I said. 'How can I help?'

'It's rather an odd story.'

'Why don't you tell me? I can judge for myself then.'

She smiled and picked up a glass of wine. Then she sat down on the sofa and curled one long leg over the other.

'It's my mother and father,' she said. 'They died in a car crash in Scotland six weeks ago, or I thought they did.'

She stopped. Her last few words had become strangled and she was struggling to control her emotions. Then she swallowed hard and made herself take a sip of the wine. For a moment she didn't seem a confident young woman, but a vulnerable child.

'They left a note with their solicitor; to be opened if both of them died. I don't suppose they were expecting it to happen, but it did. It said that I had been adopted. They'd wanted a child and hadn't been able to have one and an opportunity had come along. They had me registered as their own. They couldn't tell me who my real parents were because they didn't know. But they hadn't regretted what they had done for a moment and were very proud of me.'

'It must have been quite a shock,' I said. 'Do I know them?'

'They were called George and Mary, George and Mary Green. He was an accountant and she worked part-time in the local library. They were both rather quiet and we didn't seem to have any close relations. We were quite well off. I used to think they must have some sort of guilty secret – perhaps they weren't married, or something like that. Sometimes I used to worry that we didn't have very much in common. But I suppose I can understand that now. I'm really very grateful to them. They were always kind to me. It was a happy home.'

Green, I thought. Did Kate or I know anybody called Green? I was sure I didn't. How was I meant to be able to help then?

The golden gleams of sunlight from outside were beginning to fade. I got up and turned on the table lamps and the shadows retreated back to the corners of the room.

Downstairs the telephone rang but I ignored it. I was beginning to find my continued lack of a place in her story unsettling.

'Look, I'm not sure I understand what help I can be,' I said. 'If there is anything I can do I will of course, but...'

'No, no, please forgive me. That's not the end of the story. I had just about managed to get used to the fact that my parents were not who I thought they were when something else happened. It's something that came in the post. That's why I'm here.'

She was reaching into a black canvas bag that she had brought with her.

'It's *this*.'

This turned out to be a black and white photograph. It was a group of five young men in evening dress. There was something familiar about the group but for a moment I didn't recognise what it was. Then I felt the evening air colder on my forehead. I remembered the photograph being taken.

'It's Cambridge,' I found myself saying. 'Five or six in the morning. There were twenty or so of us – dons and undergraduates who wanted to talk about ideas to change the world. This was taken after the annual dinner. It must have been just after dawn.'

I put the photograph on the coffee table and slid it towards her but she didn't pick it up. Instead she got out of her chair and came round to my side of the table and sat down on the sofa beside me.

'Do you know who these people are? I can see which is you and the person at the back, the one who is a bit hidden, seems familiar.'

'That's Peter Parchment. You might have seen him on children's TV. He's done five or six series with a badger called Chorley. The two of them are always getting into scrapes with everything going wrong. They'd go to a laundrette and it would end up flooded or they would be decorating a house but would find they had applied more paint to themselves. That was pretty much what Peter's life was like then as well. The other one you might have heard of is Mark Ryland, the musician. He's the one looking into the distance as though the camera is not really there. As it happens there's a new documentary about him on BBC4.'

'*The* Mark Ryland?'

'That's him.'

'He's dead isn't he?'

'I'm afraid so,' I said. 'Suicide, or an accidental overdose. I don't think it was ever sorted out to everyone's satisfaction. And since he's become famous the theories of what might have happened to him have grown ever wilder.'

'Are the rest of you still alive?'

'Yes.'

'That's good,' she said in a faltering voice. 'I'm sorry. Please forgive me. It was finding out that Mark Ryland was in the photograph and knowing that he was dead. It just came as a bit of a shock.'

'Of course,' I said. 'Very understandable.'

Not, of course, that I did understand. I had no real idea why finding out that one of the people in the photograph was Mark Ryland had had such an effect on her. But then I had no idea why she had the photograph in the first place. I couldn't even begin to place her in any of our lives.

'Are you in contact with them now? I mean do you know where they are?'

I had a horrible feeling that I was being drawn into something. I ran my hand across my forehead. It was cold but little beads of perspiration were beginning to appear.

'I don't understand...'

'This is really very important to me,' she said. 'These are people I need to see.'

'Why?'

'I've got a letter that explains that. It came with the photograph.'

I didn't like the way the conversation was progressing. It seemed to be building up to something that I was certain I wouldn't welcome.

She was searching in her bag, her movements flustered.

'I can't have brought it with me. How stupid. I don't know how I managed to do that.'

'It doesn't matter,' I said. 'You remember what was in it don't you?'

'Oh yes, but I could have sworn I had it here.'

She started a further examination of the bag.

'We can catch up with the letter later,' I said. 'Why don't you just tell me what it said?'

She looked at me. It was an unblinking look designed to fix me to the spot. It succeeded.

'It said that one of the men in the photograph was my father.'

I thought I must have misheard. But I hadn't. Her father?

'Are you sure that's what it said?'

'Yes.'

'Yes, yes, of course you're sure,' I found myself saying soothingly although more to calm my own nerves than hers. 'Of course you are.'

She seemed to be expecting me to say something more. Yes or no would both have been good answers to her implied question, particularly no, I'm not your father, but I couldn't commit to anything definite until I had a moment to think.

'I wonder,' I said, 'have you had a birthday recently or got one coming up?'

'The beginning of next month,' she said, 'the 5th of August. Is it important?'

'I don't know,' I said.

I went down to the kitchen. I made a platter of cheese and biscuits and added a bunch of grapes. It was a little elaborate but I needed time to do a few calculations.

'This birthday coming up,' I said when I returned. 'You're going to be twenty-five aren't you?'

'How do you know that?'

'Just a hunch.'

'A hunch?' She didn't sound as though she believed me. 'Somebody told you I was coming, didn't they?'

'No,' I said truthfully, 'I didn't know anything about you until you came through the front door.'

'Then how?'

My detective, Tom Travis, would have given a rueful smile by way of explanation. I was operating on a different basis – a longstanding feeling of guilt. I'd always had a fear that something would emerge from that period but as the years had gone by I had got used to thinking that bit of the past was closed off and I could relax. It seemed I was wrong.

'A lucky guess,' I said. It was pretty much an accurate explanation but I could see she was struggling to believe me. 'It's a bit complicated,' I added. It was. She looked at me for a moment and then nodded.

'The letter said that you might help and I thought you'd be the best man anyway because you're sort of a detective aren't you? I mean you must be if you write crime novels. That guy you write about, Tom Travis, he's pretty bright isn't he?'

'That's not quite the same,' I said. 'He's fiction. This is real life.'

'I don't know,' Perdita said brightly. 'Look how you managed to deduce my age.' She smiled encouragingly.

I couldn't help feeling her confidence was misplaced. At this stage, faced with a new client and a new problem, Tom would be feeling his adrenalin levels rising to deal with whatever onrush of murder and mayhem he was about to be faced with. I simply felt ill.

TWO

I HAD THE DREAM AGAIN. It was very warm and, if I could just stretch out my arm, I was sure that I could touch her and hold her to me, but then she was gone. She had been here but now she had faded into nothingness like an unrepentant ghost.

I opened my eyes. The morning sun was already bright. This wasn't going to be the moment when I finally remembered who she was. It was the moment that I realised that the dream would fragment and fade, as it always did, and in a few seconds every detail would be gone.

I had put a pen and a notebook beside the bed in case a solution to who was the guilty party in *Murder is Equal* came to me in the early hours. I grabbed it and started writing but even as the first words appeared I was reduced to capturing generalities. *The dream again. The woman. Who is she?* I took a deep breath that sounded like a sigh and felt my heart beating far too fast.

My wife had once told me that on average everyone dreams for six hours every night but most people are hardly aware of this parallel existence at all. Dreams aren't brought on by eating too much cheese or exotic food, it's just that if you over-indulge you are more likely to wake abruptly and remember something of what has happened, although generally you won't be able to remember more than the last fifteen minutes. The first part of the plot will always be held back and you'll just get the ending.

I would have been satisfied with an ending that told me who the woman was. But that, from the evidence of today's repeat, was always going to be denied to me. Even now I could only really be sure she had appeared again by looking at the words written on the pad.

When I had finally fallen asleep the night before I had been convinced that there had been something familiar about Perdita that I'd hoped a night's sleep might help me discover. Instead the dream woman had appeared. I stretched. I needed a shower and a coffee. I also needed to do something about Perdita who was returning mid-morning with the letter. I had promised to come up with a plan to help her. In the warm light of a summer morning it didn't seem as straightforward as it had the night before. But I had had to say something. Kate wouldn't relish the idea that I had a long-lost daughter. The matter needed sorting out before she returned.

I had made a copy of the photograph Perdita had brought with her. It was on top of the bedside cabinet on Kate's side of the bed. I reached across. It hadn't changed miraculously overnight. Peter Parchment was still partly obscured and Mark Ryland was gazing into the distance. I was there too, in the middle. Then there are the other two.

Stephen Angell is looking purposefully into the camera aware that a photograph is being taken and ensuring that he projects his own sense of certainty into the future. He had started his first company, Angellic Entertainment, when he was still an undergraduate. Peter and Mark had been his first signings and Peter was still on his books, his chaotic career as a children's entertainer still somehow in being. Stephen hadn't been so effective with Mark. He'd managed to get him to make a couple of records that were now regarded as masterpieces but he hadn't been able to get him out on the road and build success in his lifetime. Somehow Mark had slid into the darkness and none of us had been able to save him. It was Stephen's only failure in a career in which everything else he touched turned to gold. Over the years he had progressed from being a promoter of artists, rock concerts and festivals, to becoming a technology guru and businessman and a lot of other things beside. He'd also married into old money and old land.

On the left of the photograph John Hazlitt seemed distracted by something that was happening to one side. It was probably not something but someone, and not someone but a woman, and probably a pretty one. I met up with him once or twice a year for lunch where he would give me a debriefing on his latest entanglements. He was invariably optimistic and invariably disappointed. He seemed better at understanding the odds in investment banking. This at least provided him with the finance necessary to support one ex-wife and son and offspring from other liaisons. Over the past few years he had had more relationships than Tom Travis had solved murders and showed no sign of slowing down in his search for the perfect mate. If there was an odds-on favourite to be Perdita's father it had to be John.

In the kitchen the answering machine that Kate had bought, before we married, was flashing green. It was the size of a small breeze block and about the same weight, and, as far as I could see, indestructible. I remembered the phone had rung the night before. I pressed the play button.

'David? You're not answering. If you remember you did promise the boys about six hours ago that you would ring and wish them goodnight. Anyway it's too late now and I don't think they particularly noticed. I imagine you're concentrating on the book. Do get it finished and then we can get back to normal. I still think you need to move the relationship between Tom and Julie on a bit. He could become much more vulnerable if he really fell for her. Why not think about it? And do remember to contact the builder won't you? We can't afford anything to go wrong with the roof. Good luck finishing everything off. Miss you. Bye.'

Kate's tone wasn't quite as warm and affectionate as usual but she had put in a couple of weeks' hard grind in chambers getting her commercial work into good order so that she could take a week off. She hadn't been so impressed with my own preparations, or lack of them.

Eventually she had reluctantly agreed a house free of distraction offered the perfect opportunity to sort out a final version of *Murder is Equal*. In particular I could confront Tom's complete lack of urgency in identifying Crispin Cruickshank's murderer.

I looked at the clock on the kitchen wall. After last night I had other problems as well. I wondered if anything Perdita had told me the night before provided any clue to identifying her real father. She had studied theoretical physics at university and then decided that her vocation wasn't the missing matter of the universe but medicine. She was in her fourth year of medical training. She had been particularly upset about Mark Ryland but, as Tom Travis would have told me, that didn't mean anything. Mark was the only one of us who was dead.

The BBC4 documentary about Mark had been shown again a week ago. I had recorded but not yet watched it. It wasn't clear what another film about him would add. It was twenty-five years since his death. There wasn't a great deal of material to fill another sixty minutes. There was no live footage, there were no concerts, and no interviews. Just the voice, the lyrics, and that inexplicable fingering that nobody else could quite do. He used to have a complex tuning system for the strings of his guitar. Sometimes a low string would be tuned higher than the string above. It all added to the sense of impeccable Englishness emphasized by the distinct and sublime voice.

I switched the television on, located the recording, and pressed play. His music was reassuringly haunting as a camera sped along green country lanes with high hedges, with a lilting voice at home in England, as the countryside darkened into night and a car's headlights picked out the branches of trees bent over the road.

Mark had composed songs of extraordinary originality and beauty. Knowing his music was like being part of a secret club that admitted you to a sight of a new and vulnerable version of heaven. Over the past decade the music had appeared in commercials and as little snatches in any number of television programmes and films so that his genius, cut into bite-size pieces, was omnipresent on the world's electronic airways; background healing for a restless generation.

I spread a copious layer of marmalade on the toast and poured myself another cup of coffee. I shouldn't be focusing on Mark. In his time at Cambridge, and in the years until his death, I had never known him to have a regular girlfriend, although women were invariably attracted to him, as much by his distance as his closeness.

I pushed the coffee cup to one side and propped up the photograph that Perdita had brought with her against the jar of marmalade. There we all were, in our final term, five years before Perdita was born. I wondered who it was who had attracted John Hazlitt's attention. I looked along the faces and stopped at my own. The young Knight is square on to the camera, unblinking, neutral, my natural freeze when faced with committing my image to posterity.

I got up and poured myself the remains of the coffee. I needed to get a proper sense of perspective on what Perdita had told me and a tactful plan for establishing which of us was her father. Neither task was entirely straightforward. I needed a second opinion. Luckily there was one at hand. Jerry Davis lived three minutes away.

Jerry and his wife Faith had moved into number 1, The Grove, ten years before. From the gate at the end of our own garden it was fifty yards across a triangle of urban woodland to the back garden of their house. In the decade they had been there they had dug out the basement; added an annexe at the back for Faith's exceptionally fit sixty-five-year-old mother to occupy in a couple of decades' time; put in solar panels; changed the colour of the paving stones in the drive which seemed to them too pink; and bought a flat in Nice. Even more threateningly everything in the house was immaculate. Paintwork gleamed, dust had been banished, and nothing was ever more than a millimetre away from its ideal location. In the same period Kate and I had managed a new shower for the bathroom and a re-decoration of the boys' bedrooms. Our only excuse was that they didn't have children who had a magnetic attraction to grime.

Jerry was in engineering. Faith was a government lawyer who was pretty much as busy as Kate. The great thing about Jerry was that he was never stumped, whatever the problem or issue he was faced with. What seemed to me to be a problem that required scheduling into the future Jerry regarded as something that should be sorted out today, whether it was a loose washer or a career change.

He went abroad a lot but had compensating spells between jobs, sometimes a week or two at a time. If Jerry was home we tended to fit a lunch in during the week. Our respective legal spouses found it difficult to meet up once a year despite their best intentions.

I hadn't told Kate before she left for Norfolk that Jerry had the week off. I also hadn't said that Faith was away on a residential leadership course for government lawyers in Edinburgh and was leaving early to visit one of her sisters in Glasgow. I looked at my watch. She should already have left. I had envisaged three days or so of monastic abstinence and work on getting Tom Travis into shape before a guiltless mid-week celebration of progress. I did, however, need to get the Perdita situation under control. Besides, Jerry had a consultant role on the Tom Travis books, and advised me on any equipment or gadget issues Tom might have.

He was a notoriously early riser and greeter of the dawn. He was bound to be up. A foolproof plan for dealing with Perdita was no more than a few minutes away.

I reached over the fence in Jerry's back garden and pulled the bolt back. The gate slid smoothly open. The rear part of the garden was studiously overgrown, a continuation of the city woodland outside. Jerry had told me this was the most expensive part of the garden to maintain, as Faith had never quite settled on a firm view of what wildness should look like. I pushed on through the undergrowth to the annexe at the back of the house where, in the absence of any imminent threat of occupation from Faith's mother, Jerry had installed a desk. This was where he spent the early hours of the day so that there was no possibility of him inadvertently waking Faith, who, Kate had once told me, invariably slept three hours longer than he did.

I can't remember why I didn't knock on the door. I think it was because I suddenly realised how one of Crispin Cruickshank's six nephews and nieces could have got into the cabin he had securely locked from the inside. It was one of those shafts of inspiration from the unconscious mind that had been sadly lacking in sorting out the problems in *Murder is Equal* thus far. Anyway the upshot was that I found myself simply opening the door and walking in.

The main part of the annexe where Jerry had put his desk consisted of a large garden room connected to a small kitchen, a bedroom, and a bathroom. There was a large mirror on one wall, which faced the bedroom. I stopped. There was a reflection of a woman in the mirror but it wasn't Faith.

For a moment I thought I might be in the wrong annexe attached to the wrong house. I have a notoriously bad sense of direction. I had once entered, in error, the kitchen of a terraced house in Buxton in a snowstorm and engaged in conversation a surprised woman who, in retrospect, had borne no resemblance to the wife of the friend we were visiting.

I hadn't made a mistake today though – at least not in terms of place. Whether I had crossed the other great English taboo of an unannounced arrival was another matter.

The woman was lithe, young, naked, and, as far as I could tell, perched on top of a man. Perched was hardly, now I come to think of it, an adequate description. There was considerable vigour in her movements and a rhythmic shaking of her firm breasts that was curiously hypnotic.

As far as I could see the man's muscular arm and leg could easily be Jerry's. Jerry must be forty but he kept himself in shape. As the woman jerked backwards all doubt was removed. There he was, eyes strangely transfixed. I backed away. It wasn't a situation where there was an adequate conversational opening.

I took a series of delicate steps backwards, opened the door as silently as I could, and retreated into the garden. There was no reaction from inside and I must have been almost back to the wilderness section when I realised there was something behind me, and not simply something, but someone. I half turned and nearly fell. I pushed my arms out to support myself only to find that I was clutching at a body behind me. A pair of arms arrested my fall. They were a woman's arms.

'David? Do be more careful.'

'Faith. I thought you were in Edinburgh.'

'Clearly I'm not. Whatever are you doing David?'

Faith was really rather wasted as a desk lawyer. She should have been a barrister. She would have made any witness quake with her razor-sharp questioning. In fact she might manage to paralyse them into immobility. Having experienced her forthright manner before I wasn't quite as affected as a newcomer might be but I noticed I hadn't managed to speak.

'Well?' Faith said sharply.

'Wrong garden.'

Faith looked bemused.

'Ben Horne at number 3,' I said. 'He promised to lend me some pruning shears. The long-handled ones. I'm going over to collect them. Bit early I know but I think he's going out later. But it's the wrong garden. I must have been on autopilot. Thinking about my novel. I've finally worked out who the murderer is.'

'That's good. About time I imagine. So who is it?'

'What?'

'Who did it? Kate told me you had had some difficulty in deciding. It's time you sorted it out. Kate said she thought you were suffering from writer's block.'

'Not entirely writer's block,' I said. 'More too much writing, or more accurately re-writing. I have a lot of branching possibilities that are difficult to control. I also need a new angle for Tom Travis, maybe even a weak spot.'

'Why?'

'Kate said he needed more edge.'

'If Kate says so I'm sure he does.'

I took a step back. Faith was wearing immaculate white jeans, and a pale cream jacket with a beige blouse that had an elegant neckline. On anyone but her they might have been described as casual. She was very trim, full bust, narrow waist; a sort of female wasp approaching middle age in prime condition.

'It's the third garden along,' she said.

'What is?'

'The Hornes. Your shears.'

'Of course it is.'

'That's that then,' Faith said briskly.

I held my ground for a moment and then nodded and headed back towards the garden gate. There wasn't anything else I could do.

THREE

SATURDAY 8.00AM – 9.30AM

I'M NOT SURE I AM at my best in a crisis, certainly not somebody else's. Faced with the necessity for action I tend to slow down. In times of stress I like to draw up in the car, turn off the engine, and not get out.

Immobility wasn't an option in the present situation. I could feel Faith's eyes boring into the back of my head as I left the garden. After remembering to turn right in the direction of the Hornes I ambled forward until I got to the back gate of number 3 where, using a Tom Travis stratagem, I dropped to one knee apparently to re-tie my shoelace but in reality to glance behind me. A figure in cream and white was exiting from Jerry and Faith's garden at speed and a moment later it had disappeared altogether. I got to my feet, made a play of not being able to open the back gate to number three, and then headed off towards the common to get my thoughts into some sort of order.

If I had to put money on any couple being rock solid in their affections for each other it would have been Faith and Jerry. They had been together for twenty years, since they were students. They had met at a party that both of them had only decided to attend at the last moment. Even then if it hadn't been for a winter storm and sudden lashing rain Faith would have left before Jerry arrived and their lives, as they told the story, would have been unfulfilled. Instead they talked into the night and dismissed all other suitors, theoretical and real, from their minds until, at dawn, they had decided on a lifetime's commitment. Ever since then, as far as I could see, they had remained touchingly in awe of each other and their mutual good fortune. Their careers had prospered. Elements of Faith's large family appeared in London on regular occasions for parties, particularly her younger sisters and their husbands and children. It looked like domestic bliss. Faith was one of the few women I knew who wouldn't really ever flirt with anyone, even in the most minor way. It wasn't that she wasn't an attractive woman. It wasn't that she didn't like men or hadn't flirted in the past. It was just that she was totally in love with Jerry. I had thought the feeling mutual and lasting but it didn't seem it was going to survive into its third decade.

Maybe Tom Travis could work out what was happening but I couldn't. Or perhaps I simply wasn't prepared to make the obvious, and pretty much *only*, deduction about what I had just seen – a man dealing with a mid-life crisis by having a fling with a younger woman.

By the time I had got back to the house and brewed myself a stronger cup of coffee I found that there was one unexpected upside to Perdita's appearance and Jerry's fling. The suspects in *Murder is Equal* had suddenly sorted themselves into the innocent and guilty. It was clear to me, and it would be to Tom, that Isabelle had murdered Crispin

Cruickshank on his yacht in the Mediterranean. It would take a bit of retrofitting but only from Crispin's meeting with the art dealer in the taverna in the old town. Isabelle, after all, had been the only one of the six nephews and nieces, or indeed of the family as a whole, to appreciate Crispin's interest in the *Quattrocento*. Only she would have any idea of the immense value of the collection of Italian art that he had been able to amass.

The perfect surprise ending lay before me, so perfect that it seemed that it had always been there. I could also see the possibility of opening up a real chink of emotional vulnerability in Tom by developing his relationship with the young and attractive insurance investigator, Julie Pearson, who had already made brief appearances in *Killing Spree, The Terminal Man* and *A Grave Mistake*. It was an idea that Kate had suggested. I spent fifteen minutes hastily making notes, took a deep breath, closed my eyes and counted to five. When I opened them again the plot still lay precise and clear before me.

I decided to treat myself to an extra slice of toast, coated liberally with ginger marmalade. I had been telling Perdita the truth when I said I hadn't known anything about her before she arrived but I needed to give her a full explanation of what had happened and why I didn't know whether or not I could be her father.

Twenty-six years before I had been roped into a game of hockey for a team organised apparently by somebody called Marcus who worked for the Midland Bank before it morphed into HSBC. The Bank was short of numbers for a match against a team of architects at a sports ground in Chiswick. It was a friendly fixture and they could provide a hockey stick. More than that, there was a party afterwards.

They put me at the back and told me to stay there and act as a useful block in front of goal.

I didn't hit the ball more than a couple of times but it seemed I had a crucial impact on the match as I stopped what would have been a last-minute equaliser with my head. I was out cold for two or three minutes and when I came round I didn't remember where I was or anything that had happened for months before. A rather cheerful doctor in a hospital consulting room explained events. He had a model of a cross-section of a human head with a rubber brain inside that he gleefully compressed against the side of the skull to illustrate what had happened when the hockey ball had hit me. He said that if the headaches had gone the only real problem was the traumatic amnesia and that the best approach was simply to ignore it. Memory might be recovered or simply lost forever.

I was left with a hole in my memory that stretched for six months before the hockey game began to a few hours afterwards. The beginning of September one year to the end of February the next was a complete blank. I couldn't remember Marcus, or agreeing to play, or anything at all. Curiously everyone still expected me to be able to tell the story of what had happened. So I gathered any information I could from those who had been there. I even went back to the sports ground. In time, as the memories of others faded, I became the acknowledged expert on what had occurred even though everything I knew came from secondary sources.

During the blackout period I had been house sitting for friends of my mother in Kensington, a cushy number that provided me with free lodgings in return for keeping the house in good order and administering a small programme of improvement and maintenance. Although I didn't remember, I had overseen the installation of a downstairs shower and organised new tiles for the kitchen floor. A pile of invoices in a kitchen drawer detailing the work had handwritten notes from me attached to them. I had also apparently earned a living from reviewing books, and teaching adult literacy in a prison. All in all, with subsidised accommodation, I had probably had a happy time.

But there was no regular girlfriend going in to the six-month period and none coming out. It was possible that I might have been celibate for the whole period, but not certain, or entirely likely. I've never been keen on spending a long series of nights alone unless I have to. But I hadn't kept a diary and there was no tear-stained letter regretting that we had to part and, because I wasn't in any regular pattern of employment, no colleagues to confirm what I might, or might not, have been doing at the time.

I looked at my watch. It was still too early to be phoning the boys. I wouldn't be redeeming any brownie points if they had to be woken to receive my morning greetings. Besides I hadn't quite worked out how to pitch the possibilities of additional fatherhood to them. I tried to think of a good conversational opening but instead found myself wondering why there had been such a look of abstract concentration on Jerry's face and what Faith had been doing in the garden. But that, I told myself, was their business. I had a problem of my own that I needed to work out.

Mark Ryland had been alive at the start of the six months but dead by the end. The circumstances of the other three, as far as I remembered them, were not immediately promising in suggesting they might be Perdita's father.

John Hazlitt had started the period married and had
still been married, and to the same woman, at the end.
Given his general temperament and subsequent string of
romances an affair and offspring couldn't be ruled out
but then, at least, he had been fond of his wife and son.

Peter Parchment, his career blossoming, had been
getting together with a woman called Lorna Trevanian
who he was still living with, and Stephen Angell had
become engaged to the beautiful and aristocratic Francesca
Hayter who he had subsequently married. None of that, as
Jerry's recent actions had illustrated, was conclusive; but
admitting to an affair at the time wasn't something that
either Stephen or Peter in particular were likely to want
to do. The simple telephone calls I had in mind when I
had spoken to Perdita weren't necessarily going to sort
anything out.

I went back to the television programme about Mark
Ryland. Middle-aged men in sweaters and jackets were
talking round a long pine table in a large kitchen. There
was a pencil sketch of Mark being handed round to nods
of recognition. The talk was of the good times, Mark
playing for his supper in bars in Nice, and the magnetic
effect his music had produced. But ten minutes later spring
and summer had passed and the camera had moved on to
glummer faces, and the debate on the screen had reached
the question of how distant, perhaps clinically distant,
Mark had become; how he had withdrawn into himself;
how much time he had spent in barely furnished rooms
staring at white walls. Only a Cockney photographer
was rebelling against the orthodoxy of a soul in terminal
decline. During the shoot for the last album, he was
recounting, Mark had been relaxed, communicative, even

happy. This was a view that didn't tally at all with the other descriptions being given in the programme. But then the photographer wasn't being interviewed round a long pine table in an extended kitchen somewhere in a fashionable part of North London, but in the East End.

At least the programme didn't go into some of the wilder theories that had appeared on the net that Mark had been murdered. It shuffled instead between accident and design with drugs playing a larger or lesser role depending on the speaker. Emotionally I was more attracted to the notion that he had chosen to leave the world rather than that he had left it accidentally. As far as I could remember I hadn't seen much of Mark in the last year of his life although, again, I couldn't be sure as his death fell into my black hole of memory loss.

When he had been in Cambridge Mark had kept his life surprisingly compartmentalised and had flitted between one group and another. Sometimes at Cambridge we had talked together long into the night but even that had been mostly in the first two years and not the third. For some reason I had an image of snow flurries in the court and Mark swathed in a long heavy overcoat heading out towards the Eagle Inn with Stephen and Peter.

There was a noise somewhere in the house that jerked me fully into the here and now and away from images of the past. For a moment I couldn't think what it could have been. Then I walked down the stairs to the hall.

A brown paper envelope was lying on the floor. I picked it up. It had been sent first class. I went into the kitchen and sat down. The contents were a single sheet of paper and a photograph. I recognised the photograph. I had seen it yesterday.

I went back to the front door and opened it but the postman had already gone. I took the envelope into the kitchen and sat down. This version of the photograph was much larger, nearly twice the size of the one that Perdita had brought with her.

I pulled the sheet of paper that had also come in the envelope towards me. Someone had typed two words in an italic font in the middle of the page –

Feeling guilty?

As a general proposition it was one I found almost impossible not to agree with but I wasn't feeling guilty so much as nauseous. I felt like a fly caught on a web waiting for a spider to appear.

FOUR

SATURDAY 1.30PM – 2.30PM

'IS THAT YOUR WIFE?' Perdita asked.

She was looking at a picture on the kitchen wall. Kate and I had been in the Scottish Highlands. We had got out of the car at the top of the long sweeping climb to Rannoch Moor. Kate is smiling, hair ruffled in a light breeze. Behind her the bracken is gold and the mountain peaks white and snow-capped against a clear blue sky. Two days later, when we were journeying back from Glencoe, the mountains had become brooding shadows in the grey cloud and shards of mist had darted across the moor's innumerable peat bogs.

I nodded.

'She looks happy.'

'It was a couple of years ago,' I said. I had been happy as well. It had been the last time the Tom Travis production line had been on schedule.

'And are these your children?'

'Yes.'

It was a picture of Oliver and Iain on holiday in France.

'They look like nice kids,' Perdita said thoughtfully. 'How old are they?'

'Oliver is just twelve and Iain a couple of years younger.'

She was running her right hand through her hair as she twisted her head to one side. I had noticed the gesture the night before. Today it seemed more a habit rather than an indication of anxiety.

I had phoned the boys earlier and Iain had told me that Kate had said I hadn't been able to phone the night before because I had been busy planning the end of the novel. He seemed enthusiastic about the explanation he had been given. I'd also had the time to tell Kate that I'd left a second message with the builder and to sketch in my plan for Tom to develop a relationship with Julie Pearson. Kate had softened her tone in the face of such rapid progress but insisted on ending the call by telling me how much she and the boys were missing me. I hadn't managed to say anything to her about missing daughters or alarming messages through the post.

'You were going to tell me,' Perdita said.

I must have looked blank.

'About the traumatic amnesia. Why you can't remember.'

I ran through my story as quickly as I could. I'd told it so many times that I was pretty much word perfect. I couldn't see any particular reaction to anything I said. When she had been looking at the photos of Kate and the boys I had sensed she might be wondering what her relations with her potential half-brothers would be like. I had been more concerned about how Kate would react to becoming a stepmother.

'What do your family think about it?' she said when I had finished.

'We don't talk about it much. It was years before we met and, actually, there's not a great deal to say. I just can't remember. I've managed to work out most of what must have happened but not everything.'

'No, I suppose not,' Perdita said. She didn't seem convinced.

'Did you bring the letter?' I said changing the subject.

She pulled a cream envelope from her bag and took out two folded sheets.

Dear Perdita,

Please excuse me writing to you at what must be a difficult time. But I have some information that you should have as you now know the truth about George and Mary Green.

One of the men in the photograph that comes with this letter is your father. If you want to find out who he was you will need to speak to them.

A Friend of your Mother

P.S. David Knight, the crime writer (in the middle of the photograph), is likely to be most helpful. His address and telephone number are on the attached sheet.

I picked up the second piece of paper. Whoever had written the letter knew where I lived and the house telephone number. Not that that was exactly difficult information to find. I picked up the letter again. *David Knight, the crime writer* – a description that I was perfectly happy to live with – *is likely to be most helpful.* Why? Why would I be likely to be helpful, more helpful than anyone else? I wrote fiction. And why *A Friend of your Mother*?

'When did you get this?'

'Last Friday. I'd gone down to my parents' house in Dorset. Not, of course, that they were my parents but that's how I think of them. There were some clothes I wanted to sort through and bits of paperwork that needed looking at. I hadn't felt like doing it before but I didn't think I could put it off any longer. The letter was there by the front door when I woke up on Saturday.'

'There's no stamp on the envelope, or franking.'

'I thought somebody local had dropped it in. There are a lot of circulars that just get pushed through the door.'

'Is there anybody local that your adoptive parents – the Greens – were close to?'

'I've been thinking about that. I think the answer is no. The local shopkeepers knew them as well as anyone could. They were perfectly hospitable but they didn't really work at relationships so there were little fits and starts of contacts but nothing that was lasting. They didn't seem to want to have close friends, just acquaintances.'

'So there's no one you can think of who they might have confided in?'

'No.'

'Or anyone that might have seen who delivered the letter?'

'The house is pretty much by itself. There's plenty of passing traffic but no neighbours. Somebody might have seen something but I wouldn't know who to ask. Sorry. This letter doesn't seem to tell us anything.'

'I wouldn't say that. Whoever it was who sent it seems to know a fair bit about both of us. Claiming to be a friend of your mother implies that they know who she is as well.'

'Maybe, but I've been thinking. I'm not sure I want to go on with all of this. I mean if it was you, even if you were told who my mother was, you wouldn't remember her, and you wouldn't have any idea of what happened or why. Perhaps I should just run my life forwards. I've got friends, things I want to do, a career. It's pretty clear my mother never wanted me to find her.'

'You don't know that.'

'I don't know that it isn't that. Anyway I'm not sure it's worth going on with this.'

She left the words hanging in the air. I was going to try to argue her round but I stopped. Maybe Kate and I should have had another child, our own daughter, and a sister for the boys. Perhaps I had delayed more than she had. But we had discovered, anyway, that we were too late. Kate had been philosophical. At least we had two sons. Not being able to have a child at all was the real tragedy, genetic line ended, no footprint in the world going forward, no one to love, pick up, and build sandcastles for. That would have been something to properly get upset about, one of the worst things that could happen. Besides it would probably have been another boy, although that wouldn't have been bad. But her words hadn't quite matched the regret in her voice. It would have been easier if they had.

'I don't know what to do.'

Perdita was standing in front of me. I looked into her clear blue eyes. I was sure I had seen them, or eyes like them, before.

'It's difficult, but it's your father you're trying to find isn't it? That's what you need to focus on,' I found myself saying.

I could see Perdita's face reflected in the glass of the kitchen cabinet. Were there any resemblances to the boys? Perhaps somebody else would look at us and say *isn't it obvious?* If we could both stand in front of the mirror in the hall perhaps I could see if we had any physical similarities. There wasn't any getting away from it. She reminded me of someone.

'I can make some phone calls,' I said. 'To Peter, John and Stephen. Perhaps we can work this out quickly. I'll be as discreet as I can. Then if anything comes of it you can decide what you want; and if you don't want to do anything that's fine. I can make the calls today.'

Perdita was running her hand through her hair. 'That would be great,' she said. 'But I don't want to push anyone, I don't want to force people to do DNA tests or anything. Whoever it is has to be happy about it.' She smiled. 'There's one good thing. I'm sure you're the best man for the job.'

'Why?'

'You're a crime writer. I mean you find things out don't you?'

'I only find out what I've thought of in the first place.'

Perdita was not to be deterred.

'I bet if I asked you if you had a magnifying glass...' she said teasingly.

'As it happens I do have one.'

'There you are then. If you could call them it would mean a lot to me. Some friends in the country have invited me there for a couple of days. It would give you time. I could get out of your hair.'

'Fine,' I said. 'Let's speak on Monday.'

I was still basking in the Tom Travis afterglow as she walked away down the street in the direction of the tube. I watched until she was out of sight.

I was loitering on the doorstep when I was aware of another voice.

'David!'

Jerry Davis was walking towards me. I wondered whether he had seen Perdita and then I blinked. I hadn't expected anything Jerry might do could surprise me more than his early morning sexual exploits but I was wrong. A warm mid-summer day didn't seem the occasion for any civilian to don military fatigues.

FIVE

SATURDAY 4.30PM – 5.00PM

TWO HOURS LATER I hadn't made too much progress in contacting the other occupants of the photograph. My chief success was a strangled conversation with Peter Parchment's partner, Lorna Trevanian, who seemed eager to bring the call to a speedy conclusion as soon as I announced who I was. The oblique message I was trying to convey – that there was something urgent that I wanted to talk to Peter about but I couldn't say precisely what it was – seemed to sour relations further. In the end I only managed to get a grudging commitment that she would ask him to telephone me if there was a convenient moment. I finished the call wondering what it was I had done in the past to upset her. She appeared to hate me.

I didn't do too much better in trying to track down Stephen Angell at Rainbridge Hall. Eventually his secretary had taken a message and given me an assurance that he would ring when there was a gap in his schedule. From her tone it didn't seem that it would necessarily be in the next twenty-four hours. John Hazlitt was simpler to deal with. He wasn't answering his mobile, so I left a message.

I had a niggling feeling that there was something I was missing in my conversations with Perdita. I had the uncomfortable sense that I had been forced to change sides. The people I had been friendly with for thirty years now looked like a group that needed to be investigated.

'So is that it?' Jerry said.

He was sitting on the sofa. I had found myself telling him the whole story after I had invited him in. I hadn't meant to be so forthcoming but my normal discretion had wilted in the light of his battle readiness. Besides, provided I could keep the likely disintegration of his marriage to one side, I needed his skills in problem solving. It wasn't just a question of finding out who was Perdita's father, and who had sent the second photograph, but how best to handle Kate.

'So she's a good-looking girl is she?' Jerry said.

'Woman.'

'Oh yes. I forgot you knew her age.'

'Guessed.'

'Guessed, OK. You don't know what you know. I think I get it but even if you can't remember anything extra…'

'I was thinking about that. I get these little flashes. Her eyes remind me of someone. There's also something else about her that I can't quite pin down. The consultant said that my memory might come back at any point. Just naturally, or it could even be another blow on the head that triggered it.'

'Knocking you out is too risky a strategy. I'm not sure it matters in any case.'

'Meaning what?'

'You should consider the negative evidence,' Jerry continued authoritatively. 'You weren't arrested for running orgies in your borrowed house in Kensington, were you? There's no police record or anything untoward, is there? I appreciate you can't remember but the paperwork on that wouldn't have been sorted out in six months, would it? If there's nothing at the end of the period the odds are that nothing happened in it. And you can take it a step further. I mean I know you're God's gift to women but is it likely that you can father a child and the fallout is over before it's born? They wanted to keep it secret because they were just interested in you as a high-class sperm donor? I don't think so. And who were you sleeping with at the time? Somebody must have given you a wink in recent years. Think about it. Who do you know that seems to have carnal knowledge of you but you don't know why?'

'I'm not aware of anyone.'

'Friends then. They would have known who you were going out with even if you were working freelance, wouldn't they?'

'I told you there was no one else in the house. The basement where I lived was a self-contained flat. For the period before the memory loss I used to check the house once a day, or morning and evening if there was building work going on. I imagine that was the pattern I carried on with.'

'What were you doing then? Writing the great British crime novel? You didn't take up with Tom Travis till ten years after that, did you? Anyway there must have been some woman around. Maybe it didn't go too well.'

'I told you, I can't remember.'

Jerry looked unconvinced as though somehow I wasn't trying. Or maybe he wanted an alibi for his activities earlier in the day, confirmation that males were always at it if they had the opportunity. Tom Travis always maintains that any interpretation of a series of events is possible and one should always be wary of jumping to conclusions. From the evidence before me – Jerry's current buoyant mood; Faith's flight from their back garden; Jerry's actions with the young woman – I was finding it difficult to find any alternative explanation other than that he was having an affair. Faith had suspected the truth and had come back to check on him, and he didn't know he had been discovered. That wasn't the tricky part – the really difficult question was what should I do? Tell him he had been rumbled or regard it as entirely his and Faith's business?

'So why do *you* feel guilty?' Jerry said.

'I'm not sure I do. It's that I've always had a feeling that something from that time would catch up with me.'

'Have you told Kate about this?'

'I said I got knocked out and didn't remember much about it. There wasn't very much more to say. I didn't know anything about it except what I had been told by other people. Everything else is pretty much a blank.'

'Almost a no,' Jerry said. 'You need to be careful. Secrets between man and wife can be tricky. Best avoided. Still if it comes up you could always play the *not wanting to worry you* gambit, or *so nervous you would refuse me*, or *thought you might think I was mentally unstable*, that sort of thing. Shouldn't be a problem.'

'So how are you and Faith?' I said. Jerry in an ebullient mood could be irritating.

'Fine,' Jerry said. 'She left for Edinburgh early this morning, around dawn. She's got this leadership course for government lawyers next week but she's staying with her younger sister in Glasgow this weekend. Florence is pregnant again. I thought she and Jack might have delayed things a little after the twins but apparently not.'

'Did you see her off?'

'She took the BMW.'

'I thought you normally drive her to the airport.'

'She decided to drive herself.'

'You haven't had any sort of tiff have you?'

'Of course not.'

'Did she get there all right?'

'She's phoning this evening.'

'And the combat gear?'

'Neat isn't it? Should have been using it on Dartmoor next week for a new course on solving practical problems in difficult physical conditions – building bridges across rivers with just ropes and timber – that sort of stuff. Meant to improve teamwork. The firm wanted some help on setting it up. Now they've been taken over and the week has been cancelled but they've let me keep a couple of the uniforms they wanted to try. I was planning an initial jog on the common as a preliminary trial. You're welcome to join me if you like. The other one should fit you.'

'I take it from your excess of energy that you haven't got anything to do next week?'

'I've got a bit of free time if you want some help. Besides I owe you a favour.'

'Never mind about the car. It was nothing much.'

'Yes it was. I don't know what Faith would have said if she had known who dented the bonnet.'

'It was an accident.'

'Faith likes to have everything in perfect order. To tell you the truth she's so touchy at the moment I don't want to upset her. Saying it was your fault let me off the hook. I hope Kate wasn't difficult.'

'Kate has this view that I'm naturally clumsy. Actually she's been breaking more things than I have recently. The accident was a welcome reassertion of the natural order of things.'

'Still I owe you a large one.'

'Fair enough.'

Jerry seemed genuinely concerned about Faith's equilibrium. Kate had said that she thought Faith had been overworking in the last few months and was looking stressed. It seemed to me that the causes of any cracks in Faith's morale were likely to be personal ones rather than the pressure of government legal business. But clearly Jerry wasn't prepared to come clean about the events of the morning. If he didn't know that both she and I had been observing him there was probably no reason why he should.

'So how's the book?' he asked.

'A few more days' work should get the essential stuff done.'

'Sorted then,' he said enthusiastically.

'Pretty much.'

'So we can move on to the mysterious Perdita?'

'Absolutely.'

'Then I've got a suggestion about this photograph of the five of you that's doing the rounds.'

'Which is?'

'Who took it?'

'What?'

'Who took the picture? Somebody did. It wasn't set up on some tripod on its own was it?'

'Of course not.'

'So it's very simple. You get a photograph that's been blown up from the original or the negative. Perdita gets a photograph that may be the original as it seems to be the right size but may be a copy. All of that is by the by. The key question is who took them?'

'I don't see how that helps.'

'Think about it. The person who sent it to both of you must have got it from someone. Find the photographer who took the original picture and you're well on the way to finding out the identity of the person who sent it to you and Perdita. If you can find out who that person is you can ask them why they are so sure that one of the five of you is Perdita's father. Whoever it is also seems to know who Perdita's mother is. Perhaps the person who took the picture also sent it? This isn't your amnesia period David. Do you remember who the photographer was? There can't have been too many of you milling around at that time in the morning. And if you can't remember surely somebody else in the picture will?'

'It must have been a decent camera,' I said. 'There would have been low light levels. So it was somebody who knew what he was doing. Come to think of it, it's not very difficult, I'm pretty sure it must have been Charles Sotherby. He was around that night. He was a keen photographer even then. He's a professional now.'

'Faultless,' Jerry said. 'I look forward to the deductions in the new Tom Travis. Is this guy still around?'

'I've got his number. I could ring him. But it's a long shot.'

Theoretically it was. Charles Sotherby might not have been in, or might not remember the photograph, or might not have records of what had happened to the others, or might have been unwilling to share any information he had. There were any number of possible difficulties.

'Well?' Jerry said when I got back into the room three minutes later.

'Charles was very helpful. He seems to have a perfect record system.'

'Great. So we've found our man?'

'Not exactly.'

'Why?'

'He sold six copies of the print.'

'But he doesn't know who to?'

'He does.'

'Better and better,' Jerry was positively beaming. 'Whoever bought the prints is likely to be our man. Who did he sell them to? Who is our mystery buyer?'

'I am,' I said.

SIX

SATURDAY 5.30PM – 6.00PM

'APPARENTLY CHARLES WAS TREATING photography as a business even then and was scrupulous about his records. He's got me down as having paid for six copies.'

'Could he have sent them? Could he be Perdita's father?' Jerry said.

'Unlikely. Different inclination. Anyway...'

'What?'

'I remember commissioning something from him. He was short of funds. In all probability these are what I ordered.'

'I take it that means a definite yes.'

'Pretty much.'

'So what did you do with them? If you can remember who you sent them to, we're back with some suspects. With modern technology anybody could easily make further copies that would be pretty much indistinguishable from the original prints. It just means we've got rather more suspects than before.'

Jerry was sounding enthusiastic again and had started to wave his hands expressively. I gathered from his movements that it was a question of tracking each individual down and subjecting them to rigorous questioning.

'There's just one problem,' I said. 'I don't think I did anything with them. In fact I don't recall seeing the photo before. Whatever my idea was I don't remember carrying it through. It was probably one of my lack of application moments.'

I gathered from the look on Jerry's face that he was no more impressed by my application levels than Kate. However he managed to pull himself together with a shrug and started again more slowly. 'So, let's assume you've got the prints he gave you. That means the photographs that were subsequently sent to you and Perdita must have come from this Charles Sotherby guy but have been sent to someone else. He must have printed more from the original negative.'

'Not possible.'

'Why?'

'He said all the negatives from his Cambridge years had been destroyed. They were in temporary storage in a shed in his mother's garden while his studio was being re-decorated. A Guy Fawkes bonfire next door got out of control and the shed was burnt to a cinder along with its contents. Made the local paper apparently. He was interested in me sending the photograph back. He wants to re-build the early part of the archive.'

'Maybe somebody stole the negative and set fire to this shed or whatever it was to hide the crime,' Jerry said triumphantly. 'It's the only logical explanation.'

'Unlikely.'

'Why?'

'The fire was ten years ago.'

'OK,' Jerry said. 'Actually that's helpful. It means the most likely source of these photographs is the prints you have.'

'It looks like it.'

'So where would you have put them?'

'Well, if I have got them, and I'm sure they're not in any of the albums, they're most likely to be stored in the loft.'

'Well then?' Jerry was getting to his feet.

'If they're anywhere they'll be at the back. You can't actually get to the back easily at the moment. Over the years we have piled up a lot of stuff. It would take hours even if they are there.'

'Why?' Jerry said. 'Why would it take hours?'

'We would need to go through everything methodically.'

'We could start at the back. If they were stored away when you and Kate first got here that is where they will be.'

'It will be pretty dusty up there.'

'This military kit is guaranteed to stand up to anything Dartmoor can throw at it. I imagine it can stand up to your loft.'

'I'm not sure I've got a torch.'

'I have.'

Jerry pulled a rubber-cased torch out of a side pocket in his combat trousers.

'Halogen Evolution 3 with supaflood,' he pronounced. 'Should do the trick as long as your loft isn't more than a hundred metres in length.'

'I'll pull the ladder down,' I said reluctantly.

The loft mechanism, which normally stuck, worked with German precision, and the aluminium ladder slid smoothly into position in front of us.

'There's also an attachment to turn it into a miner's

lamp, rather neat,' Jerry said. 'Not that we will need that function I imagine. Lead on.'

I climbed up the ladder into the gloom. As my eyes adjusted, however, I saw that sunlight was filtering through the skylight at the far end. I was about to move forward when I felt Jerry's restraining hand on my arm.

'Just a moment,' he said.

'What is it?'

'I want to look at something.'

The loft was suddenly illuminated in bright white light.

'Remarkably wide beam isn't it?' Jerry said in a satisfied voice.

'Very,' I said. 'So what are we checking?'

'Don't you see? When you and Kate come up here you store stuff over to the left but you never go any further. You can tell that because of the marks in the dust. Over there, towards the back, it looks as though nothing has been moved for years.'

'I think I said that didn't I?'

'This provides important independent verification,' Jerry said. 'Get some police experts up here and they could probably tell you precisely how many years it's been since you and Kate went down that end. I thought Tom Travis was strong on forensic methods. Didn't one reviewer call him the new Inspector French?'

'I don't think that was meant to be complimentary. I think her actual words were *rivalling the dogged persistence of Inspector French in his attention to detail* with some supporting remarks about how out of date unbreakable alibi plots were.'

'Old girlfriend was she? A woman scorned and all that? Personally I like the detail. The Swedish match analysis was pivotal. How do you research all that stuff? It must take months.'

'I only research the thing I reveal. It's sleight of hand.'

'Have it your own way.' Jerry sounded unconvinced. 'Anyway we need to find those photographs. Given that you've had them from your college days they're likely to be right at the back. Over there for instance.'

Jerry was pointing at three stout cardboard boxes against the far wall.

'I suppose they're on my side.'

'Your side?'

'When we first got here we had a side each for anything we wanted to keep.'

'Gold dust,' Jerry said. 'If we move those suitcases and whatever that other stuff is we can get to them easily.'

'They're heavily taped up,' I said a couple of minutes later.

'Shouldn't be a problem,' Jerry had a short thin knife in his hand. 'Ceramic blade. Sharpest you can get.'

The second box offered up a couple of college plates that had once seemed indispensable souvenirs, exam papers, some old essays, the magnifying glass that I had spent an irritable weekend looking for, and, at the bottom, a couple of green shoeboxes helpfully marked PHOTOGRAPHS.

'There you are,' Jerry said unnecessarily.

Five minutes later, pictures of the people in my life before Kate were spreading out on the kitchen table and vying for attention. As in life, and in line with Jerry's promptings, the beautiful received more attention than the rest.

'Who's she?' Jerry said. 'I'm sure I've seen her.'

'Television most likely. She became an actress. She had a part in that new police series a few weeks ago. Put on a few pounds recently.'

'She was certainly something then,' Jerry said with genuine warmth.

I was about to open the second box when the phone rang.

'That'll probably be Kate or one of the boys,' I said. 'I'll take it in the study. You see what you can find.'

'Hello,' I said a few seconds later, breathless from sprinting up the stairs. I didn't know why I had suddenly developed such a morbid objection to having my telephone calls overheard. Perhaps I had a secretive nature.

'David?'

It wasn't Kate or the boys.

'David, it's Stephen Angell. You were trying to get hold of me.'

'Something has come up,' I said.

There was a pause at the other end of the line.

'It's a personal matter,' I found myself adding vaguely, 'Cambridge days and the years after.'

'Dinners? Photographs? People we know?' Stephen asked crisply.

'Yes.'

'Then I know what you're talking about. We can find time to speak tomorrow.'

'Tomorrow?'

'The lunch tomorrow. I'm sure you accepted didn't you? Martina, have you got that list?' There was a rustle of paper. 'You're down as a definite yes.'

'I don't know anything about a lunch. I'm positive I...'

'Never mind about that,' Stephen cut in. 'Can you make it? It's at Rainbridge. One o'clock.'

'Yes.'

'Do you want to bring anyone?'

'No.'

'Good. Nothing too formal. Jacket and tie. Networking lunch really but I sometimes throw old friends into the mix. If anyone asks, you're the next big thing in crime. John Hazlitt should be coming as well. Bye.'

The line clicked dead before I had time to say goodbye. I put the phone down. I wondered what information Stephen had. From what he had said it seemed he knew quite a lot. I felt a strange sense of discontent. Given his desire always to be in control of events there would probably be a solution waiting for me at Rainbridge Hall.

'That was quick,' Jerry said when I got back to the kitchen. 'Trouble with Kate?'

'It wasn't Kate. It was Stephen Angell. He's the one standing on the left next to Mark Ryland. Seems to know about Perdita.'

'Does he? What did he say?'

'Nothing we don't know. But he's obviously got a photograph. I'm going to see him tomorrow at his country pile. John Hazlitt will also be there. That's him on the left. Why are you looking so smug?'

'I might have found the originals,' Jerry said. 'They could be in this. It was right at the bottom. I thought you might like to open it yourself.'

It was a white foolscap size envelope that had been folded three times round its contents. I took it from Jerry and let it unravel itself and then reached inside. It was the photographs. I counted them.

'How many are there?' Jerry asked.

'Five,' I said.

SEVEN

SATURDAY 6.00PM – 8.00PM

'ONE MYSTERY SOLVED THEN,' Jerry said, magnifying glass in hand.

'Which is?'

'Where the photographs came from. It's pretty clear that both the one you received and the one Perdita got have been copied from one of these original prints, presumably the sixth one that is missing. There's just a slight loss of picture definition on the copies. You can see it more clearly on the one that has been enlarged...'

'I suppose so.'

'Have you got a better explanation?'

'No. I've been racking my brains. As I said I do remember ordering some prints from Charles but I don't remember seeing this photograph before. Maybe I just took the envelope and forgot to look inside it. Perhaps I was distracted by something.'

'Sure you trust this Charles Sotherby? How do you know he's not lying?'

'Why should he lie?'

'Why should anyone send you, Perdita, Stephen Angell and presumably your other friends this photograph?'

'Somebody wants to alert her and us to the fact that one of the five of us is her father.'

'Why?'

'Her adoptive parents are dead. Time she knew the truth.'

'But why so elaborate? Why not simply tell her?'

'Whoever sent them doesn't know who the father is. It's a wake-up call to somebody's conscience.'

'If you say so.' Jerry didn't sound convinced. 'But what if it's Mark Ryland? He's not going to get a photograph is he? Wasn't there a programme about him last week?'

'I recorded it. It's on the box in the kitchen. Have a look if you want to.'

'I might just do that,' Jerry said, 'and there's one other thing. Have you got the envelope this photograph came in? There might be some clues there.'

'See for yourself.'

Jerry got up and examined it with the magnifying glass. I was surprised he hadn't got a device offering both light and magnification.

'There's a stamp but no postmark,' I said. 'I thought it was the postman but it could have been hand delivered. I'm pretty sure it wasn't there last night. I don't think it was there either when I went out to this morning to see...' I stopped. It was better that Jerry didn't know where I had been going.

Jerry looked up.

'The early morning sun,' I said. 'Couldn't sleep.'

'Perdita is obviously getting to you.'

'Must be.'

'There's some other mail here.'

'Oh that,' I said. 'It's from my agent.'

'Shouldn't you open it?'

'I have a feeling I know what's in it. The book is months overdue.'

'Whatever it is there's no point in ignoring it,' Jerry said. 'I thought you said you had sorted it out.'

'Hand it over then. I'll read it in the sitting room. I need a private moment if it's another hurry-up letter. Why don't you look at the Mark Ryland programme?'

Upstairs I examined the Coles & Hunter envelope without opening it. It was difficult to deduce anything from its external appearance. Down below Mark Ryland's melancholic pastoral was wafting skywards from the television in the kitchen. I sank into the armchair and looked at the bookcase. Even with several copies of each Tom Travis book on display the series looked insubstantial.

The music downstairs had switched to the lyrical sequence that accompanied the cameras sweeping over the green rolling hills round Mark's childhood home. I was tempted to let it wash over me but I needed to face up to my agent. At least now I had a book where the murderer was known and which a few days' work would complete. I spread the letter out in front of me. It wasn't from Debbie Hunter herself but her assistant, Angie.

Dear David,

Debbie asked me to thank you for the material on the new novel. Debbie was anxious to talk to you personally but she has to get the ten o'clock flight to New York. She wanted to let you know that she was very excited about

the new departure! She said she would be in
contact immediately she returns! I found some
comments she scribbled before she left which I
attach and hope make sense!

Angie

I doubted they would make sense, at least to me. There had been some sort of mix-up. I hadn't sent Debbie an outline of anything new or groundbreaking. I had mentioned thinking about a new novel at the Coles & Hunter Christmas party when she had been stalking me for a firm delivery date for *Murder is Equal*. But that had been a diversionary tactic.

It wasn't like Angie to be this slipshod. Normally she was very efficient – a wafer-thin girl with a first class degree in Sanskrit and a limitless enthusiasm for writers. She probably derived her energy from her daily eating regime that seemed to consist solely of fruit, nuts, and diet Coke.

I picked the letter up again. Looking at Angie's transcription of Debbie's notes would at least identify with whom I had been confused. Debbie had three other crime writers on her books who, judging from last week's Amazon rankings, were all selling considerably more than I. Angie could be confusing me with Leonard Best whose last outing for the emotionally challenged Inspector Jim Breeze had featured two sets of homicidal twins; or Sarah Potter's endlessly stalked forensic pathologist dedicated to the elucidation of sexually motivated crime; or, more hopefully, Dennis Blackstone's classically educated Mathias Penn for whom no allusion was too obscure, no clue too misplaced, but who inhabited a world of rather more readers than the other two.

I took a deep breath. Hopefully Angie had transcribed Debbie's doctor-like handwriting accurately –

> *V. exciting!*
> *Love the concept of 'Murder Unseen'!*
> *New amoral Tom (and Julie) fascinating!*
> *Love the extracts! Muscular!*
> *Could hold back 'Murder is Equal' and sell*
> *together (Angie – we're still waiting for the*
> *final version from David aren't we?)*
> *This is much better!!!*

I put the paper back on the table. Angie certainly hadn't confused me with Dennis Blackstone. Mathias Penn was asthmatic and well on the way to being twice Tom Travis's weight. It wasn't a possible mistake. Sarah Potter's heroine was excluded on grounds of gender and Leonard's alcoholic and erratic Jim Breeze was about as different a personality to Tom as you could get. The new 'amoral' Tom and Julie? Whatever I had decided this morning, and anything that had already been suggested in the books, was only the start of a relationship.

I looked at the rest of the list.

> *The new Ripley?*
> *Film rights to Anco? (I think it's Anco?*
> *Debbie's handwriting huh!).*
> *Un – can't read the rest of the word clearly –*
> *Unaccountable?*

Angie had also attached some comments about the outline of my new novel. The only trouble was I wasn't writing a new novel called *Murder Unseen*. And, even if I had been, it wouldn't have featured an amoral Tom and Julie. I didn't do amoral, particularly in relation to Tom.

I spent a few minutes trying to come up with a halfway plausible version of what could have happened, without success. Then I walked irritably down the stairs with the letter in my hand. I didn't need another problem. I had more than enough of them already.

Jerry was looking at the end credits of the programme.

'I've had a few thoughts,' he pronounced.

I put Angie's letter down on a side table. A few thoughts from Jerry usually meant a plan.

'Which are?'

'As far as I can see when it comes to Perdita one of the five people in this photograph is by far the most likely candidate to be her father.'

'And who's that?'

'Just at the moment, purely objectively, it's you, David.'

'What?'

'Think about it. Look at the circumstantial evidence. Somebody sends out a photograph saying that one of the men in it is Perdita's father. On the information we have the only person who has access to the originals is you, at least in the last ten years. So you seem to be the only one who could have done it.'

'But only some years ago to judge from the dust in the loft,' I said with heavy irony.

'Not necessarily.'

'Why not?'

'You could have taken one of the prints out before you put them up there.'

'But I've told you I'm sure I've never seen it.'

'So you say, but suppose you're suppressing the memory?'

'Why should I do that?'

'You've said yourself you forget a lot of things – six months of your life in one go for example. Perhaps you've got some sort of condition that not only blots out swathes of memory but particular memories as well. If you don't remember having the photograph, perhaps you don't remember making the copies and sending them out.'

'But what motive could I have?'

'You want to know who Perdita's father is. You've just told me that you can't say whether it's you or not.'

'That's crazy.'

'It's what somebody looking in from the outside would think. Just bear that in mind. Maybe you've got an unconscious suspicion that you're the father so you need to find out. Perhaps you know you are but want to be forced to admit it. That's what Tom Travis argues to that American heiress.'

'What American heiress?'

'The one who gets her pearls stolen.'

'I thought I'd taken that bit out.'

'No, it's still in *The Terminal Man*.'

'It wasn't a bracelet?'

'No, pearls.'

'Are you sure I didn't make her an Australian in the end?'

'No. I can find the page for you if you don't believe me.'

'That's OK,' I said as Jerry moved over to the bookcase. 'Perhaps she was an American now I come to think about it.'

'So,' I continued as Jerry reluctantly sat down. 'Where does that get us?'

'You've got a six-month memory gap. You can't remember anything about a photograph you ordered half a dozen prints of, you haven't any idea where the last print is, and you don't seem able to recall what you have written in your novels.'

'I always write two or three versions of a Tom Travis novel, it's not surprising that I can't remember everything.'

Jerry looked as though he was about to argue the point but then thought better of it.

'Maybe you're right. We should go for the concrete. Where's the photograph from which the copies were made? It's a key question. Don't ignore the obvious.'

'I suppose that is a Tom Travis maxim as well.'

'I don't think so,' Jerry said. 'Anyway the point stands. We need to have a running hypothesis on the photographs and adapt it as circumstances change. It's a vital clue. Whoever has the missing one has had it for a reasonable period of time. Nobody has been to the back of your loft recently. One of your six photographs is missing. Let's suppose that's the one from which the copies were made. We need to find out when it went missing. If we knew when it had been taken and who had it we'd be a lot further forward. When did you move in here and put your belongings in the back of the loft?'

'Thirteen years ago.'

'Then whoever took it from you is likely to have taken it before then.'

'Where does that get us?'

'It builds the case.'

'Does it?'

'Yes.'

'OK,' I said. 'That's a building block.'

'There is something else. Mark Ryland, I may have a lead on him.'

'He's been dead more than twenty-five years, Jerry.'

'I know. But I recognised somebody in the film I've just seen – the photographer. The one who was taking issue with the drug-hazed reminiscences of artistic doom that the rest of them were indulging in. I know him. Andy Fontaine. He lives round the corner. He should be having a nightcap in the White Hart later. Usually pops in on a Saturday evening. Bit taciturn but I managed to get him into conversation. If I'm there to introduce you we should be able to pump him for some information about Mark.'

'I didn't know you were a regular.'

'I'm not really. But Faith has been working on Saturday evenings to get up to date before the course.'

'So you go to the pub?'

'It's only been a month. That's where I met Andy.'

'Just the last month?'

'Yes.'

'So how are you and Faith?'

'Fine.'

'No problems then, either side?'

'None. Anyway what about lining Andy Fontaine up? It's a key lead.'

'I don't see why. I'm not sure I've ever met him.'

'He might have met you though.'

'How?'

'From what he was saying on the programme he seemed to have been around at the time of Mark's death.'

'Yes, but...'

'It's two birds with one stone. We can't ask Mark about Perdita's conception and, although we can ask you, you can't tell us anything. Andy Fontaine clearly knows a lot about Mark, he might know something about you. He might know something about Perdita. Why not ask him?'

'I don't suppose there's any harm in it,' I said reluctantly. I was beginning to find Jerry's enthusiasm exhausting. 'In fact I'll look at that documentary again. But you need to change out of that uniform.'

'OK,' Jerry said. 'It probably would be better to be a little more discreet. By the way what was in that letter from your publishers?'

'Nothing of relevance to this,' I said firmly.

EIGHT

SATURDAY 10.00PM – 12.00PM

'ANDY!' JERRY SHOUTED, 'ANDY!'

Andy Fontaine was a short wiry man dressed in a white shirt, blue jeans and a dark blue jacket. That wasn't a surprise. He had been a short wiry man in the television programme. Now a gold chain also glittered round his neck. At Jerry's shout he slowly raised a hand in reluctant welcome.

It didn't seem the best platform for launching a series of questions about Mark's love life twenty-five years before. It wasn't as though I had any basis for starting such a conversation. I couldn't remember Mark ever having any girlfriends, at university or afterwards.

'What'll you have?' Jerry said enthusiastically to Andy when he got to the bar. 'Your ears must be burning. I was just talking about you. Do you know David? He used to be at Cambridge with that friend you mentioned, Mark Ryland, the one on the television programme. Do you want a pint of the usual? Let me get these.'

I might have got it wrong but I sensed that Andy

Fontaine wasn't as certain as Jerry that they were new best friends. He did, however, drain his glass.

'Why don't you two go through to the back,' Jerry said, enthusiasm undimmed. 'It's a better place to talk. I'll bring the drinks through.'

The furniture in the garden at the back of the White Hart was an eclectic mixture of old leather armchairs, sofas, and wooden seats and tables. Four poles held up a circus-like tent that was open at the sides. The moon was full and low in the sky, the night warm to the touch, and white fairy lights were intertwined in the branches of a cherry tree. I sank into one of the leather sofas as Andy gave me an appraising look.

'You don't remember me do you?' he said.

'You were around with Mark,' I said. That was incontrovertible enough – he had been. 'But no, it's a bit of a blur. I've always been terrible at names and faces.'

'You're David Knight.'

He seemed pretty certain about it. Quite what there was for me to say was more problematic. Luckily Jerry chose the moment to appear with three pints on a tin tray.

'They seem to be going for the enchanted garden effect,' he said breezily. 'Could be an improvement or it might be a bit grotto. There's something I wanted to ask you Andy. Didn't you do the photographs for that Mark Ryland album? The one that everybody likes so much now?'

'*Other Days*?' I said. 'Great album! Great artwork!'

'Yeah, maybe,' Andy said with a wave of professional self-deprecation that revealed a gold chain on his wrist. 'Last one would have been better though.'

Last one? There hadn't been a last one. Some out-takes, different versions, but nothing of substance to add to the albums horribly neglected in Mark's lifetime, but endlessly re-issued by Stephen Angell in the last ten years.

'I heard something about that, sounded interesting,' I said casually. It wasn't entirely untrue. I just had.

'What did you hear then?'

Andy was looking at me sharply, and his tone of voice was halfway between a question and a challenge. In the television documentary on Mark's life Andy had been his last defender insisting on painting a picture of a genius still at work, rather than a declining drug-addled victim of his times. His artwork for *Other Days (Than These)* had been superb, Mark photographed against Victorian brickwork on Commercial Road, the world moving by while he remained the solitary observer, the unknown Prince among his people.

'Well,' I said, 'I never really believed all that stuff about him being played out. I mean I suppose he might have taken an overdose by mistake but I wasn't sure it was an inevitable journey down and out. There was new stuff coming. It all seemed a sad waste to me.'

It was one of Jerry's consultancy tricks. Take something that somebody had said, convert it into capitals, and broadcast it back to them. And, of course, now I thought about it, there was another possibility worth floating.

'And then there was that girl…' I continued.

Logic would dictate that there must have been if Mark had any chance of being Perdita's father. Conception would be a month or two before he died. The music press had tried to find a partner for Mark ever since his burst of posthumous fame but had never been able to track anyone down. Might as well go for broke –

'That girl he was with just before his death.'

'Some cookie,' Andy said. He didn't seem to be questioning what I was saying but agreeing with me.

'She sure was.'

'Know what happened to her? You were close weren't you?'

'Lost touch,' I said. I had done – for the last twenty-five years of memory loss at least. 'Mark and I were old friends,' I continued as though that explained everything. 'There were a group of us who met at Cambridge and stayed in contact. You probably know Stephen Angell, Mark's manager. Then there was a guy called John Hazlitt and Peter Parchment...'

'He does that stuff for children doesn't he? Wrecks everything he touches. He's in league with that badger. What's he called?'

'Chorley.'

'That's the one. My nephew loves it.'

'Children tend to.'

'He's doing a degree at Leeds now but he still thinks it's great.'

'Does he?'

'Cult following,' Andy pronounced and then fixed me with a steely gaze. 'So you were all friends together were you?'

There was something in his tone that suggested the answer was no. 'There were always a few tensions between Stephen and Mark.'

For a moment I thought I had hit the wrong note but Andy was nodding.

'He's some piece of work that Stephen isn't he? Some piece of work. He was lined up for an interview for the TV programme but surprise, surprise, he couldn't find the time.'

Andy took a pull at his glass of bitter and then a grimace crossed his face. I gathered it wasn't the quality of the beer that was in question but the sourness of the memory.

'If you'll excuse me,' Jerry said, 'I've just seen somebody that I really need to talk to.'

Andy watched as Jerry got up and hurried back into the bar. It was convincing enough. I was almost ready to believe that he had seen someone he wanted to talk to.

'Yeah that Stephen,' Andy continued once Jerry had completed his diplomatic exit. 'If Mark was depressed he was half the problem. Anyway Mark was on the up. I got a call from him. He sounded a lot more together than he had been. He had material for a new album. Needed some artwork to convince a new record company he wanted to sell it to. Would I come round to talk about it? He looked pale, a bit thinner, but he wasn't away with the fairies anymore. We talked through his ideas. There had been some noise but I thought that was from a different flat. Then she appeared. She was quite something. She was carrying a tray, tea, and a couple of white china mugs. Mark switched right out of talking about the songs and mumbled some sort of introduction and then she was gone and he was back in it again. They weren't just ideas, he had some songs in the bag.'

'But never found.'

'Maybe he didn't have time to make a tape. Perhaps they were lost, perhaps he destroyed them.'

Andy abandoned the intense gaze he had been transfixing me with and surveyed the garden room and its other occupants. None of them seemed interested in us.

'Anyway,' he said, 'I hadn't realised that he had talked to anyone about her. Maybe it was serious if he spoke to you about her. I think he mentioned you. Used to scribble stuff on the notices on the walls in college didn't you? Disagreeing with everyone. Sounds sensible enough. The *new refutations* Mark called them.'

'Did he?'

'If you're the right David Knight – yeah. I reckon you must be. There can't be too many of you running around can there?'

'I should have made more of an effort help him. I always wondered about his death.'

'He overdosed on amitriptyline,' Andy said. 'It cures your depression but makes you suicidal. His skin was going slightly yellow before he died. He must have taken a lot of tablets. Might be that woman. Maybe it was the record that was stillborn. I talked to Stephen Angell about it afterwards. I had some photographs for a new album if he had any new material. I thought he might have wanted to take them off me but he wasn't about to put his hand in his pocket. Didn't want to look at anything. He was launching that domestic spy range in the States; all that surveillance crap. He was getting tired of rock and roll. He didn't have any time left for Mark.'

'So that was the end of it?'

'Maybe. But from what Mark was saying I reckon he'd done some songs. He had a friend who could get him into a recording studio. He could have done something at night and nobody would have been any the wiser. But maybe it wasn't working out, or the songs weren't good enough for him. We were due to meet the day before he died. There was a Greek place off the Tottenham Court Road. We used to go there for kebabs when we were planning *Other Days*. It had good vibes for him. But he didn't show.'

'So that's the last you saw of him?'

Andy picked up his beer glass and took a long sip as though it was a rare wine. Then he looked me straight in the eyes. He seemed to be trying to weigh me in some sort of scale.

'Mark liked you,' he said. 'Bit of an idle bugger apparently but you hadn't given in like the rest of them and you weren't signed to Stephen Angell. That would have been a bonus.'

'So when did you last see him?'

Andy gave me a long appraising look before he continued. 'I didn't hear from him that day, or the next, so I decided to go to the flat. No reply but it was easy enough to get in – he only had a Yale on the door. But there wasn't any sound. Then I saw the door to the sitting room was open. Mark was lying on the floor on his back. He looked like he was asleep. He looked OK, peaceful anyway, but he wasn't breathing. I closed his eyes. Then I left. I've never told anyone. There didn't seem any point. I didn't need the aggro and I didn't know the number of anyone who could help except Stephen and I wasn't about to phone him. I think he was out of the country in any case. As it turned out they found Mark pretty quickly. One of Stephen's guys was doing a check on the property. It was one of Angellic Entertainment's flats he was living in. You probably remember. Anyway I heard that this Fred St James turned up, used to run the roadies for the festivals. Tough bugger. Not somebody to tangle with. He was the one who found the body.'

I nodded in appreciation of the wisdom of these actions.

'Sounds like he ran out of road.'

'He was on an *up*, man,' Andy said. 'The last time I saw him he was definitely on an *up*.'

'That's a dangerous time,' I said. 'Sometimes you think it's getting better and then you get a knock back and the whole feeling of optimism is just blown away and you realise you're never going to get out of the rut.'

'You seem to know a lot about it.'

'I write crime novels. I do a lot of research into causes of death – murder disguised as suicide and vice versa, that sort of thing.'

Andy considered the point.

'I read one about that fat man once. Quite good. That isn't you is it?'

'No.'

'Been on telly?'

'No.'

'Make a lot of money do you?'

'Not especially.'

'Must be a competitive game,' Andy said sympathetically. 'Anyway what were we saying? Suicide? His mother always used to say it was an accidental overdose.'

'Maybe it was despair over the woman you saw. What was she like exactly? I'm not sure I'm not confusing her with somebody else.'

Andy drew himself back into the depths of the leather chair like a spider retreating to the safety of a corner. Then he gave a thin smile. He didn't seem to detect too much of a threat in front of him.

'She had long auburn hair, wide blue eyes, tallish.'

'Anything else about her?'

'That's pretty much it. But you can judge for yourself.'

'What?'

'You can judge for yourself. I've got a photograph of her.'

'You have?' I said.

'I thought I'd take a couple. You don't get girls like that every day. She didn't seem to mind. She knew how attractive she was.'

I felt a faint tingle of fear, a bit like Pandora before she opened the box.

'I don't want to trouble you,' I said.

'No trouble. Do it now if you like. I'm just round the corner.'

'Sounds good whatever it is,' Jerry said moving back towards us and nodding before I could think of a reason to delay for a day, or a year or so, while I could collect my thoughts.

When we arrived outside Andy's front door I was feeling calmer. I must have walked past Eliot Road a thousand times but I had never turned down it. The road was a dead end with six houses on one side and the long brick wall of the Kwik-Fit garage on the other. On the left the small front gardens were awash with shadowy plants.

'Have some of this,' Andy said when we had got inside. 'A toast to Mark.'

He was pouring large measures of fifteen-year-old Laphroaig into glass tumblers that he handed to us.

'Smooth, elegant,' Jerry murmured.

'Don't miss the zesty oak and warm peat-smoke top notes,' Andy said sardonically. 'Or the fresh nutmeg or toasted almonds. Anyway, one for Mark.'

He drained his glass and poured himself as large a measure as before. He held out the bottle but Jerry had only sipped his drink and I hadn't touched mine. He put the bottle down on a table.

'Yeah. Help yourselves. I think the photographs are upstairs.'

'We've hit some sort of nerve,' Jerry whispered as Andy slid out of the room. 'Who is this girl anyway?'

'I wish I knew.'

'What?'

'I just thought that if Mark was the father there must be a woman involved somewhere. I said I'd heard of one. It was a long shot. I didn't expect any reaction.'

'Clever,' Jerry said, 'very clever.'

'I suppose so.'

Andy had a clutch of photographs in his hand when he came back into the room. He spread them out on the table.

'That's her. Wish I could remember her name. Do you know her?' Andy said.

'I'm not sure,' I said, but I was lying. I knew who this woman was. This was the woman of my dreams.

* * *

'I meant it literally,' I said half an hour later as we walking home. 'Literally the woman of my dreams.'

'I always thought that was Kate,' Jerry said irritatingly.

'You know what I mean.'

'I'm not sure that I do. Tell me again.'

'I have this dream about a woman. I think I know her very well, but although she's there in the dream and we're close to each other, when I wake up there's just this fleeting memory and I can't remember who she is. There's a terrible sense of loss. Then after a few seconds I remember I'm married to Kate and everything is fine.'

'Have you tried this out on Kate?'

'No.'

'Sensible enough,' Jerry said. 'Although there's probably some psychological explanation that she could help us with. Not likely to be worth the price though. So anyway, this woman, you've tracked her down at last. But shouldn't she be in the other universe where you don't have Kate to prop you up? Turning up in real life doesn't seem too helpful. I mean it complicates this one and takes away the attractions of the other. Familiarity kills allure doesn't it? Maybe that's why she is so elusive in the dream. Perhaps she's turned into a ghost there and become real here. Tricky.'

'Maybe,' I said. I wasn't really listening. Jerry seemed to be away on a metaphysical fantasy of his own. Something else was creeping into my consciousness. Something I could almost feel. I looked at the photograph. There was my dream woman, no longer elusive or mysterious. No longer a fleeting touch, a fleeing figure, but a captured person, forever young and smiling, who would never be able to escape me again. What was it about her?

'Anyway,' Jerry was saying, 'that's a pretty impressive performance you put on with Andy. Tom Travis-like.'

'There's something else as well.' I said. 'This photograph Andy Fontaine gave me. I can't quite see, oh yes I can.'

'What's the excitement?'

'When Perdita turned up yesterday I thought there was somebody she reminded me of. I couldn't think at the time. Now I know who.'

Jerry whistled.

'You mean it's her.'

'I don't know for sure but look at the cheekbones, the shape of the face, the blue eyes, the hair. What do you think?'

'I'd like to help if I could,' Jerry said, 'but I haven't seen Perdita.'

'Didn't you even get a glimpse of her? She'd only just gone when you arrived.'

'You were staring into space when I arrived.'

'That's a pity. But as far as I can see they could be sisters.'

'So you've found the mother?'

'I think so.'

'So mother and daughter. I'm impressed.'

'I could be mistaken.'

'You don't think you are do you?'

'No,' I said, 'I don't.'

NINE

SUNDAY 10.00AM – 1.00PM

'YOU SHOULD GET PERDITA to give you a photograph of herself,' Jerry said the next morning as he helped himself to toast. 'It's the sort of detail that Tom Travis goes on about. I used to think he was a little pedantic but it's good procedural stuff.'

I nodded.

'If she could send you an image on her mobile then I can get it printed up into whatever size you want. It could be key in all this.'

'I promised I wouldn't contact her until Monday,' I said firmly. 'Besides with one thing and another I forgot to take her mobile number.'

'Not the sort of mistake Tom would make,' Jerry said in a resigned tone. 'You don't detect any traits in Perdita that link her to you, do you? Neglecting to think about the obvious, that sort of thing.'

'Why do you mean?'

'Does she look like you?'

'I can't say.'

'Do you mean you don't want to say, or you simply can't tell?'

'The latter.'

'Right,' Jerry said in a resigned tone. 'Right. What about hair colour? What did you say Perdita's hair colour was?'

'Reddish brown.'

'Not much difference from this woman then,' Jerry said looking at the photograph. 'Not that that particularly helps us. Parents without red hair can be carriers of the gene and have a red-haired child, although we might be able to do something with the colour of the eyes. Anyway I've been thinking. Are you sure you want to go on with this?'

'Meaning?'

'Nothing really. Have you phoned Kate and the boys?'

'Yes.'

'How are they?'

'Fine. I was able to update Kate on progress on the book.'

'Good,' Jerry said.

'Have you spoken to Faith?'

'Not yet. I might phone her later. She's probably out with her sister.'

I wondered if Faith and Jerry were any longer on speaking terms. In normal times if Faith was away Jerry would be in contact on one or other of his devices every hour or so.

'Is the weather in Edinburgh OK do you know? There are squalls forecast for London. Some rogue low-pressure system from the Azores sneaking in. It might be worth checking what's happening there.'

'I imagine she'll survive in mid-summer even that far north,' Jerry said firmly. 'Isn't this Stephen Angell guy you're off to see doing rather well? Hasn't he been in the papers?'

'Both he and his wife have,' I said. 'They're in the *Sunday Times Rich List* each year for a start. Stephen and Francesca Angell – "inheritance, brewing, land, entertainment, and technology." Nothing more one could reasonably ask for.'

Jerry nodded and turned his attention back to the Sunday papers.

When Stephen had married Francesca Hayter, the Hayter family home, Rainbridge Hall, had needed considerable amounts of restoration and the family brewing business had been losing the competitive battle with bigger concerns. Stephen had launched the Rainbridge rock festival on land next to the ancestral home and turned Rainbridge Ales into a premium product. Before that he had launched his own record label, set up a string of music festivals across the country and signed up and promoted Mark and other artists; and got Peter Parchment his break on children's TV. I had spent a happy afternoon on Wikipedia researching the ins and outs of Stephen's business affairs in the mistaken belief that it would free up my unconscious mind to sort out the plot of my Tom Travis novel.

'Francesca Angell,' Jerry said from behind his newspaper, 'isn't she meant to be a great beauty?'

'So they say, but I haven't seen her for years. She doesn't normally come to Stephen's fireworks party at the London house and I've never been to Rainbridge. I don't think I've exchanged more than a couple of words with her.'

'Why no visit to the ancestral pile?'

'There were a couple of parties Kate and I were invited to but for one reason or another we couldn't make them.'

Jerry put the newspaper down and picked up the Cambridge photograph.

'So one of you went on to riches and happiness and worldly success. Not saying of course that the description couldn't fit you as well, just in a more minor key. I imagine their children are spoilt and troublesome...'

'Two boys. Turned out well. Both went to Eton and the college. The oldest one has just got his degree. One is going to be a musician, the other a scientist. There was a colour magazine article on them.'

'It's quite an apple cart to upset,' Jerry said gnomically.

'What?'

'Steve's apple cart. He's got a lot to lose if his wife takes exception to an illegitimate daughter.'

'Stephen. He's never liked being called Steve.'

'Stephen then.'

I looked at my watch. 'It's time to go,' I said.

'I've got a new sat nav you could use.'

'I'm fine.'

'If you've never been there...'

'It's near Guildford, straight down the A3. It won't be a problem. Shouldn't take much more than an hour.'

In the event it took five minutes less. The traffic was light, the outskirts of London wet and dripping in a sudden burst of morning rain. Then, as I got deeper into the countryside, the grey clouds lifted and patches of sun appeared. I found myself humming the opening bars of *Storm Time,* the first track on *Other Days*, joining Mark in wondering why life did seem to be moving so fast.

Rainbridge Hall, the Hayter ancestral seat, was imposing, Elizabethan in part, rather beautiful, and large. It was reached by a slightly winding drive that cut through parkland. Thirty or so cars were parked on a gravel square to one side of the main entrance. Stephen Angell appeared as I got out of the car, the house arrayed behind him. He looked as confident and commanding as ever, if a little greyer around the edges.

'David, welcome to Rainbridge. You should have come before. I can't think how I let that happen, but better late than never. You must bring that charming wife of yours here as well. It's Kate isn't it? I'll get something arranged. People are having drinks in the gardens. I'll need to get back to them in a couple of minutes. We can talk about our bit of business later. Do you want the Grand Tour?'

Stephen had run through the shortened guide by the time we got into the house proper. Rainbridge Hall had been built in the 1590s with stone recycled from the ruins of a nearby abbey. The house had replaced a smaller one that Elizabeth the First, on a grand tour around her domains, had declared was not adequate for her needs. The Hayter-Molyneux family had acquired it at the beginning of the seventeenth century. The minstrel's gallery had some particularly fine carvings by Grinling Gibbons dating from the 1680s. The Hayter-Molyneuxs in the great hall either looked disdainfully down from the wood-panelled walls or lifted their eyes to destiny or heaven. At the end was a modern portrait of a striking and slender woman with green eyes.

'I'm not sure it does Francesca justice,' Stephen said, 'although in many ways it's a remarkable work. But I must go. Do take a look round. Lunch won't be for three-quarters of an hour or so. If there is anything you want to know about the place ask Brown, Francesca's butler.

He's been here for decades. Drinks are in the rose garden. Follow the noise.'

I looked round the crowded portraits on the walls and tried to trace the development of the Hayter-Molyneux genes through the generations. Here dissipation became more pronounced, a thin lip became even thinner, and kind eyes turned to indifference. On another wall the family seemed to be returning to robust health, each generation rosier and clearer eyed than the last. Occasionally there were discrepancies in the ascending or descending patterns of genes. It seemed implausible that the second and third Earls had any genetic connection at all.

I walked out of the great hall and into a corridor of creaking boards. There was a small Zoffany of a child with blonde curly hair and a drawing of a dog. I wondered if the family had ever had their servants painted.

At the rear of the house was a long terrace with central steps leading gently down to a garden where a number of intricately shaped beds in some secret heraldic design were filled with roses. In a circular paved area fifty or sixty people were split into small chattering groups around a fountain. Arches cut into a long yew hedge led to further gardens beyond. Three men in white jackets were moving from group to group re-filling glasses of champagne. I couldn't see any sign of John Hazlitt or Peter Parchment.

On my right a striking woman in an elegant trouser suit, who I had last seen resolutely not answering questions on *Newsnight*, was drinking orange juice with commendable restraint. As far as I could recall she was a junior Trade Minister. A young woman, probably her private secretary, hovered in respectful attendance.

I was edging into the outskirts of the group when there was a ripple of movement through the crowd, which seemed to be parting as though manipulated by some invisible force field. Francesca Hayter appeared in front of me as others receded to a deferential arm's length.

'It's David isn't it?'

Stephen had been right about his wife. Francesca Hayter, or Francesca Angell, was more beautiful in person than depicted on canvas. The artist hadn't captured her enormous vitality. In this light too her eyes were olive green, and sparkled with mischief in her delicately sculpted face.

'Let's get you some champagne, then you can tell me more about Stephen. I'm sure he can't have been quite so brilliant at Cambridge as he makes out. Weren't you a member of that secret society he always talks about that almost didn't let him in? Let's go down this way. There's somebody over there I really don't want to meet.'

She managed to scoop up a glass of champagne like a marathon runner afraid of losing momentum at a drinks break and handed it to me without any loss of pace. Only when we were free of the crowd and the noise of others' voices had begun to fade did she slow down.

'So,' she said, 'do tell!'

'Tell you what?'

'Why you're here.'

'I was invited.'

'Twice I believe. Stephen's office invited another David Knight by mistake. Stephen was very cross about it when you telephoned. Unusually cross, and he doesn't get cross. I wondered why. He wouldn't tell me so I'm hoping you can.'

It was a curiously intimate tone for a conversation between people who had scarcely spoken.

'I'm not sure I know what we're talking about,' I said.

'So it's nothing about this deal Stephen is doing?'

'What deal?'

'Borkmann Industries? Paying Stephen a great deal of money? It's been all over the business pages.'

'I don't know anything about it.'

We were moving more slowly. Francesca was looking up at me, trying to work out whether I was telling the truth.

'You're really quite tall,' she said absently, 'and he didn't tell me you were so serious, or that you had such intelligent eyes.'

There were one or two faint laughter lines on her face but she seemed to be being serious. She also didn't look any older than her early thirties although her real age must have been at least fifteen years more.

We had come to the yew hedge at the end of the rose garden and were following the path round. An archway led through to another garden. The green yew had been clipped so finely that it almost seemed smooth.

To the right, through an arbour, a smaller, more intimate, garden room had been created with a marble statue near the perimeter wall. The three daughters of the God Zeus, life size, were locked in an eternal sensual embrace.

'The Three Graces,' Francesca said. 'It's a modern take on the Canova. Stephen got it for me as a surprise birthday present. He smuggled it in somehow. Legend has it that it was in the middle of the night. According to our butler he must have fixed the concrete base himself. I don't think Brown approves of manual labour being carried out by the non-manual classes, but Stephen apparently swore everyone to secrecy and had them all moved out of the area. I don't actually believe he did it all himself as he says.

But it was very sweet of him. So there they are – Aglaia, Euphrosyne and Thalia.'

There was the sound of a bell being rung in the distance. Francesca looked at me.

'If you'll excuse me,' she said, 'there was some dispute with the chef on Stephen's plan for pudding. They may need somebody to give a ruling.'

She hesitated for a moment to give me a further opportunity to reveal what it was that had brought me to the house, her features ready to break into a smile if I was to come clean.

'I mustn't detain you,' I said. 'If I may I'd like a few more minutes in the garden.'

'Of course. We can speak later.'

I nodded.

A dark cloud crossed the sun and the light faltered as I watched her lithe, slightly boyish, figure disappear into the crowd around the fountain. In her elegant white dress she might have been a classical shepherdess, or on a shoot for *Vogue*. Stephen clearly hadn't told her about Perdita.

I moved closer to the twentieth century version of the Graces, the bringers of joy and goodwill to man and god alike. Canova had made the naked maidens classical but erotic. Stephen's artist had added more explicitly sexual references to the close embrace the young women shared and slightly dissipated the charm of innocent youth. I wondered if Stephen had given the sculptress a picture of Francesa to use as a model for the work. My fingers brushed lightly across Euphrosyne's rounded buttocks. In this version Euphrosyne had turned away from the gaze of the world towards her sisters, her left hand resting lightly on one sister's waist, her right higher under the left breast of a younger, more vivaciously curved, sibling. I took a step backwards. There was something about the piece that was puzzling.

'The more we look at things, the less we see them, sir, or so Matisse once observed,' a voice said. 'For some objects that may be a compensation.'

I turned round.

'I am sorry to disturb you sir, but Mrs Angell wondered whether you would care for some more champagne.'

The man before me must have been nearly seventy but was effortlessly straight backed and authoritative. This, I assumed, was the butler Brown, a living embodiment of the golden rule that between master and servant there should always be a barrier that no intimacy could ever cross.

'I'd love a little more,' I said. 'Thank you. And you haven't disturbed me. It's an interesting piece but I am not sure that I want to look at it any longer.'

'A perfectly reasonable observation, sir, if I may be permitted to say so. Mr Angell often comes to observe the piece but I suspect that is for sentimental rather than artistic reasons.'

'There is something slightly odd about it.'

'It has never been greatly admired sir, although I would say that is a somewhat unjust judgement. It is the position more than anything else. It never becomes animated where it is, which is unsatisfactory for those bringing mirth and beauty.'

'It would certainly benefit from being moved a few feet to the left.'

'I am sure you are right sir and the proposition has been mooted but has never found favour with Mr Angell even though Mrs Angell favours re-positioning. So there it has remained.'

'Unfortunate.'

'Indeed sir.'

Perhaps I was being too hard on Stephen. It must have been extremely difficult to add to the splendour that Rainbridge Hall and its gardens had already possessed for hundreds of years. It would also have irked me to be told I really ought to move my attempted contribution.

I followed Brown back to the rose garden. At the entrance I glanced back. The ever-darkening sky had plunged the Three Graces into deeper shadow, and injected a note of desolation and decay into the setting that shouldn't be there. The young and nubile goddesses seemed sadder than they should have been, somehow frozen, victims of Stephen's romantic haste. I could also feel new flecks of rain, colder than I would have expected for the season. I thought of Perdita and daughters abandoned by their fathers and shivered.

TEN

SUNDAY 1.00PM – 3.00PM

THE FLECKS OF RAIN that had reduced the Three
Graces to gloom turned into a squall, and then a minor
storm, and the guests fled to the orangery where lunch,
in any event, was about to be served. Seven round tables
bedecked with white tablecloths, flowers, and gleaming
silver were set out in a row down the length of the
building with eight chairs around each. Vines were
unfurling along the rear brick wall behind orange and
lemon trees in green wooden tubs. As the skies continued
to darken outside, the men in white jackets who had
been serving champagne appeared carrying candelabra
which they placed on each table so that in a couple of
minutes the gloom of the outside world was repulsed with
bright flames.

I must have said something about the pleasing nature
of the effect to my companion on the left, a woman of
uncertain years but preserved intellect. She assured me
that the use of candles in such circumstances had been a
Rainbridge custom that had survived the installation of

electric light. The great improvement in lighting in the building had been the installation of a glazed roof in the early nineteenth century that provided significant extra sunlight. She also confided that the most recent improvement had been in making the building warmer. Stephen, she said, had experienced great difficulties with English Heritage in getting the insulation in the building improved but had eventually prevailed. Now there was no danger of being overcome by cold draughts even at the extremities of the building.

I looked down the room. Stephen was at the central table talking to the junior Trade Minister. Francesca was expending charm on a man who might have been Korean or Chinese. From time to time I could see her check with the hovering Brown that everything was proceeding to plan. Occasionally her glance rested on Stephen as though she needed to make sure that he too was content.

I wondered why Francesca had been quite so keen to pump me for information on the reasons why I was at the lunch. Something must have aroused her suspicion. Perhaps it was just simply the lateness of the invitation to what was rather a formal affair.

'You must be the crime writer Stephen was telling me about,' my elderly companion ventured.

'Guilty,' I said. 'How did you know?'

'You've got enquiring eyes. I can see you scanning the room. I've always imagined that authors spend a lot of their time observing people.'

'It's rather an awful professional habit,' I said turning back to her. It would have been more honest to explain my actions had nothing to do with fictional aspirations but I didn't want to destroy her illusions.

Francesca was now talking to a solidly built man on her left. There was a curious intimacy in their gestures as though they might have been brother and sister.

'That's Ronald Williams,' my companion said following my gaze. 'He and Francesca grew up together. I always thought she would marry him but perhaps it's a good thing that she didn't. His family used to own the neighbouring estate to Rainbridge but they only have the manor house now. Then I thought the next generation was going to tie the knot. Francesca's eldest, Edward, was very keen on Emma Williams. She was pretty certainly, but I thought there was more to it than just a childish infatuation. Francesca, however, was very opposed. She thought that Edward was far too young to be thinking of marriage. Perhaps part of her didn't want her son to take up an alliance that she herself had once contemplated. It's all rather academic now. His law firm sent Edward away to Australia for six months and the Williams girl found herself another young man who works in the city. I'm sure Francesca had something to do with having Edward sent to the other side of the world. It must be difficult to keep up a relationship under those circumstances if you're young. Perhaps it's best if they can't survive a few months' separation, and yet I do wonder sometimes. But there it is. I really mustn't bore you with an old woman's ramblings.'

'Not at all,' I said. 'It's absolutely fascinating.'

My companion, Francesca's aunt, turned out to be a mine of information on almost everyone in the room including one of the occupants of the next table, a gnarled, balding man in a silver-grey suit. He had enormous hands and skin that had been left out in the sun for so long that he looked as though he had been stained with tea.

He was about six foot four and must have weighed seventeen stone. As far as I could see none of this was fat. This, my companion told me, was Frederick St James, a business acquaintance of Stephen's who appeared periodically at Stephen's luncheons but with whom she had never had the opportunity of a conversation. His principal residence was in the Algarve.

It wasn't likely that Stephen had two associates named Frederick St James, or even Fred St James. This must be the man who Andy Fontaine said had discovered Mark's body. Given the fact that as far as I could see he had only uttered a few grunts during the meal it wouldn't be entirely easy to engage him in conversation even if I could think of a pretext for starting one. Nor was it likely that there was a great deal to be gained that would shed light one way or another on the possibility that Mark was Perdita's father. I wasn't here to find information about the circumstances of Mark's death but events in his life.

It was not until I had finished the pan-fried monkfish that I had a chance to speak to the dining companion on my other side, an overweight American businessman called Blenkiron who seemed intent, for some reason, on establishing what precise role I occupied in the dwindling manufacturing base of the UK. My vague answers about my circumstances, rather than deterring him, as I had intended, only seemed to encourage him into thinking that, as a crime author, I might be a key business contact with numerous *government* connections.

He, Blenkiron, he assured me, was a key man in surveillance, a representative of a mighty global conglomerate that was interested in exploiting technologies pioneered by Stephen's company Angellic View. The British, he explained grudgingly, were world leaders in many aspects of CCTV surveillance. He wondered how many of the twenty cameras that covered the approaches to Rainbridge Hall, the house itself, and the Rose Garden I had detected. When I indicated that I hadn't noticed any at all he at first looked dumbfounded then laughed heartily and launched into a commendably brief but stunningly inadequate analysis of the British sense of humour.

Our relationship was developing so fast, at least on one side, that Blenkiron felt emboldened to discourse on the place of surveillance in the home, particularly in relation to the second, and I gathered much younger, Mrs Blenkiron. At what place the conversation might have ended was hard to imagine but fortunately in a natural pause, while Blenkiron considered his final advice on the control of the female, we were interrupted by a raucous beeping that turned out to be Blenkiron's mobile. This forced him from his seat and into the open air to get a better signal. Luckily for him the rain outside had stopped and the black clouds were dispersing.

'Stephen has a number of diverse business associates,' my elderly companion explained.

I could see the lunch was beginning to break up although Frederick St James seemed fused to his chair, an immovable object. I looked beyond him. Francesca was glancing nervously to one side but the cause of her anxiety was not clear. Stephen's chair was empty and the Minister of the Crown had also disappeared. I checked the empty place opposite me on the table. The place card said that a John Hazlitt should also have been joining us.

I helped my companion retrieve her stick and thanked her for her company. She saw that I was looking at Francesca and then she looked at me.

'They are devoted to each other,' she said authoritatively. 'Francesca would do anything for him.'

'They certainly seem the golden couple.'

Frederick St James was moving away from his table. I had imagined he would pull himself ponderously upright but he seemed to pop to his feet like a cork released from a champagne bottle. I had started edging towards him when I saw that Blenkiron had returned and was making a beeline for me. I hesitated.

'David,' Stephen's voice said behind me. 'There you are. I was beginning to worry that I might have missed you. Why don't we go to the small study? We can talk there. Please excuse us, Hank.'

Blenkiron looked slightly put out and then nodded briefly and turned his attentions elsewhere.

'Sorry about that but I didn't think you'd mind being robbed of his company,' Stephen said as we walked into the corridor. 'We had to slip you on that table for lunch as it was the last place we had. I must say I shall be extremely pleased when he is no longer in residence. But Borkmann won't sign anything unless Hank agrees the figures so we're stuck with him until the deal is done. Here, this is it.'

The small study was only small by Rainbridge Hall standards. An intricate hexagonal plasterwork pattern covered the high ceiling and wooden panelling adorned the walls. In the centre of the ceiling the letters H and M intertwined lovingly with each other in a combination that predated the Swedish clothing firm. Above the fireplace was a Patrick Caulfield painting of a window frame and hanging shade. Squares of grey morning sky were visible through a pale yellow leaded window. A shade in the same pale yellow hung in front of the panes.

'I thought that was in the Tate.'

'It is,' Stephen beamed. 'Watch this.'

In front of me the painting seemed to be dissolving, the colours bleaching into whiteness. For a moment the canvas was again pristine and untouched and then form and colour started to return and the Caulfield window reappeared. This time the sky was black, the leaded window and shade red.

'They're a series of four,' Stephen said. 'That was *Interior: Morning* morphing into *Interior: Night*. You can also have *Interior: Noon* and *Interior: Evening*.'

I could feel Stephen's impatience to demonstrate the full potential of the technology but I couldn't really believe what I was seeing. From a foot away it seemed to me that it was Caulfield's painting on the wall. A canvas mounted in a simple wooden frame. It was unbelievable that it wasn't.

'The canvas has interior lighting,' Stephen explained. 'That can be turned off if you don't like perfection. The memory can store ten thousand paintings. The picture can be reproduced to exactly the same size as the original. Apart from the remote everything is in the block.'

'Impressive,' I said as Stephen switched to *Evening* with its red blood-like sky.

'It should be in full production by the end of the year.'

Evening faded on the canvas and was replaced by a portrait of a handsome, bold-featured woman in blue satin, cradling a pug-like dog in an idyllic glade.

'We do have the original of this if we ever fall on hard times. I must say I prefer this version. That is Caroline Molyneux about 1780 before the great fire here. According to contemporary accounts she had a fine intellect but was lacking in the looks that usually graced the Molyneux family. Reynolds tended to paint flattering portraits so this is probably the best she ever appeared.'

'Fascinating,' I said. 'Although I'm not so sure that a traditional painting works so well with such a simple frame.'

'We're working on that. The enhanced Picture Screen will give you any frame you want.'

'Picture Screen?'

'It's the provisional name of the product.'

There was a knock at the door and a moment later it opened. The man who had been watching me in the dining room handed Stephen a note. Stephen waited for the door to close before he read it.

'It's a message from John Hazlitt. A pile-up on the M25, although I imagine he didn't give himself time to allow for anything that might go wrong. For someone who drives cars as fast as he does, he does tend to be irritatingly late. I thought the three of us should talk. Unfortunately I've got a meeting with some of Hank's more obnoxious colleagues in an hour that I can't afford to miss. So I think we need to press on. John can join us when he arrives. Peter can't come because he's filming but that's no great loss. I think you've seen this before.'

Stephen was pointing to the picture above the fireplace. Caroline Molyneux was dissolving into history and being replaced by five young men in Cambridge who inhabited a different past.

'You've got one of these haven't you?' Stephen said.

'Yes,' I said. 'When did you get yours?'

'Wednesday. It was in the post marked *personal*. There was a letter with it saying that a young woman called Perdita would be contacting me as she had been told that one of the men in the photograph was her father.

Simply that. That's why my office invited Peter, John and you, albeit the wrong you, the same day. I have a lunch here every couple of months. I'm always adding last-minute guests. It seemed the best opportunity to get together to talk and give me cover.'

'Cover?'

'People are beginning to know too much about me and my business, far too much. And I don't want them knowing about this. Can I speak in confidence?'

'Of course,' I said.

'The Borkmann deal is to exploit the technology in the States.' Stephen gestured towards the picture frame, where five young men were dissolving into Monet's haystacks. 'It's potentially the next iPad. We could sell one to every library, museum, art gallery and school in the world before we even think about individual sales. But I need capital to scale up the project. And any number of people would like to scupper or delay it. The Koreans are developing their own version but the market will be totally ours before they get anywhere provided we press on now.'

'So what's the problem?'

'Borkmann Industries. My prospective business partners see themselves as leaders of America's moral majority. An illegitimate child wouldn't go down well as the first item after morning prayers when they look forward to the commercial success of the righteous and the building of the New America. Somebody knows that and has invented this story. That name she's using – *Perdita*, the lost child. Come on. They're playing with me. How many women have been christened Perdita in the last thirty years? Any? How much do you think they want? £200k? £400k? They could have that tomorrow. I'm going to burn through that every day if the plug on this gets pulled. I can't risk that. But why isn't there a demand note? Maybe Blenkiron is behind it? Another little lever to get the price of the deal down. Perhaps that's why they're being so difficult in finalising everything. Yes, that could be it.'

Stephen stopped his progression round the room.

'I don't think it's a plot,' I said.

'Why, for heaven's sake?'

'Because I've met Perdita.'

There was a discreet knock on the door in the momentary silence that followed my remark.

'Mr Hazlitt,' Brown announced as John Hazlitt slid elegantly into the room.

'I'm so sorry I'm late,' John said as the door closed behind him. He was wearing an elegant grey flecked jacket, soft white shirt and carefully cut black jeans that made him look as though he had just come from presenting a design programme on TV. He looked as relaxed as Stephen was tense. 'I hope you got my message. I should have left myself more time. Entirely my fault. I must apologise.'

'You have,' Stephen said brusquely. 'Look, I'm sorry but I'm short of time. Do you know anything about a woman named Perdita or a photograph of us in Cambridge? This one.'

Monet's haystacks dissolved back to the five of us.

'That's remarkable,' John said. 'What was your question?'

'You might have got a copy of that photograph recently,' I said.

'I have,' John said. 'I must say I had a hunch that your sudden summons, Stephen, might have something to do with it. From what you were saying you seem to know more about this than I do. I can just about remember when this was taken but otherwise I'm a little baffled. My photograph came with a typed message – *Feeling Lucky?* I can't honestly say it means anything to me. As to the other half of your question what am I meant to know about this woman called Perdita?'

'Somebody is alleging that one of the people in this photograph is her father.'

'Really?' John said after a moment. 'Do you mind if I smoke? It does calm the nerves.'

Stephen nodded reluctant approval and John Hazlitt extracted a small cheroot from a metal tin and lit it. He took a long puff and inhaled deeply. 'I don't think I've ever heard of anyone called Perdita,' he said.

'Her surname is Green.'

'How do you know that?' Stephen said, half looking at his watch and half looking at me.

'She told me,' I said. 'It's a long story and not for now. We need to cut to the chase.'

'So?' Stephen said irritably. 'What's the chase?'

'It seems to me,' I said, 'that it's very possible that Mark Ryland is Perdita's father.'

'Mark?' Stephen said. 'Why on earth would you think that? I mean he was hardly the type to sow wild oats was he? Besides, how old is this woman? Surely Mark would have been dead?'

'No,' I said, 'he was still alive then.'

'Even if he was, I don't see it,' John said. 'Mark always used to have admirers around him at Cambridge but I can't remember anyone special, and he got a lot more isolated after he left. And Stephen is right. He wasn't one for casual relationships.'

'Look,' I said, 'I'll explain the detail later but I think Mark might have been Perdita's father and this woman her mother.'

I took the picture of the dream woman out of my pocket and passed it to John.

John looked at the photograph and then at me. A puzzled expression was playing on his features. He put the photograph down in front of Stephen.

'I think I know who she is,' Stephen said after a moment. 'I employed her as a temp. Lorna Trevanian, Peter's partner, recruited her. Lorna wanted some help on a festival Angellic Entertainment was putting together in Cornwall. She seemed to fit the bill. She was an Australian doing the European tour. I think she wanted to be an actress and was looking for work until she got a break. I don't know what happened to her after she left. She was rather slender, not the Australian hearty type at all. What was she called? Was her name Jane something? Jane Reddon I think. I can't think she had anything to do with Mark.'

'She was his girlfriend.'

'Are you absolutely sure, David?' John said looking up from the photograph. 'I must say I find your theory surprising.'

'Why?'

'As far as I recall you used to go out with her.'

ELEVEN

SUNDAY 3.00PM – 5.00PM

I THOUGHT FOR A MOMENT that I must have mis-heard what John had said but from the ribald grin crossing his features I hadn't.

'Remember, remember, the fifth of November,' he added.

'Meaning?' I said.

'You left one of Stephen's fireworks parties with this woman. Arm in arm if memory serves.'

'There could have been any number of reasons why we left together short of being an item. Maybe one of us was ill, or I was drunk, or we were sharing a taxi somewhere.'

'You had a glass or two of wine with me but that was about it,' John said. 'When you left with Jane you were more than alert.'

'That doesn't prove anything.'

'I'm not saying it does. Maybe you both decided you didn't like parties. I simply don't know. But you left before the fireworks ended. If Stephen hadn't had some particularly bright fireworks leading up to the finale you would have managed to slip away unseen. I must say I felt more than a slight pang of envy, she was very good looking.'

'Surely you must remember something about it, David?' Stephen said sharply.

'My memory is very patchy after the hockey accident. There's a period of six months when I can't remember anything.'

A look of exasperation crossed Stephen's features.

'I know you had some memory problems but are you saying you can't recall any of this?'

'Not a thing. Look, you can help me on this,' I found myself saying. 'Did I say anything about Jane to either of you?'

Stephen shook his head while John languidly stroked his chin before speaking.

'I think there was some woman around at the time but I never knew who it was. You changed your plans I remember. There was a New Year's Eve party in Scotland and we had planned to share the driving. Then at the last minute you couldn't go. You were a bit evasive about it so the reason was probably a feminine one.'

'I wasn't in a relationship in the following March which is the first part of that year when I have any reliable memory. It couldn't have been long term.'

'It wouldn't have to be would it?' Stephen said. 'It could just have been a fling. She was an attractive woman. Anyway let's get this straight. When is this period when you had memory loss?'

'My memory is blank from the beginning of September 1988 to the end of February 1989.'

'You can't remember anything?'

'That's pretty much it.'

'I'm not sure this is getting us any further forward,' John said. 'What were you saying about Mark?'

'I've got a picture Andy Fontaine took,' I said putting the photograph on Stephen's desk. 'Jane Reddon in Mark's flat.'

'Fontaine,' Stephen said bitterly. 'Is he still about? I'm not sure I would trust him as far as I could throw him. Whatever you pay him he's always looking for a little more on the side, another angle. He hasn't worked for me for ten years, though I have to admit he's a good enough photographer. He'll be up to something. This could have been taken anywhere. How do we know it's Mark's flat?'

'That's where he said he took it.'

'Did he say they were definitely having a relationship?' John asked.

'Not exactly.'

'Right, so as far as I can see you and Mark are pretty much in the same boat,' Stephen said. 'Fontaine saw Jane in Mark's flat; John saw you and Jane leaving the fireworks party. Do you have any other reason for thinking that Mark was Perdita's father?'

'What had you got in mind?'

'My photograph came with a typed message.'

'*Feeling guilty?*' I suggested.

'No,' Stephen said sharply. 'Why do you say that?'

It wasn't something that I had necessarily planned to reveal but it seemed I had backed myself into a corner.

'It was the message I got.'

'Was it?' Stephen said. 'Mine was *Feeling wealthy?* Are you sure that this isn't some sort of elaborate joke? You give yourself the most incriminating message to throw people off the fact that it's you who is doing all this?'

'I think it's a bit more sinister than that,' John said. 'It looks as though somebody wants to stir things up. Perhaps we should all come clean. The message I got was *Feeling lucky?*'

'And are you?'

'If Jane Reddon is Perdita's mother the answer is yes. I couldn't get near her. Which is just as well as I wouldn't want to take on any more financial obligations. I nearly didn't find the note in the pile of bills in my hallway.'

'I'm not sure all these notes aren't just a blind,' Stephen said. 'Whoever sent these notes is after me. *Feeling wealthy?* How much do they want?'

John looked puzzled.

'Stephen thinks it's a plot to extract money from him,' I said. 'He's about to go into partnership with some born-again Americans – Borkmann Industries. They wouldn't welcome an illegitimate daughter.'

'Borkmann,' John said. 'Didn't they fund that crusader film? I imagine they could be difficult to deal with.'

He was about to say something else but he was interrupted by a discreet knock at the door. Brown had returned.

'Excuse me Mr Angell, but the video conference will start in five minutes.'

'Thank you Brown,' Stephen said. 'I'll be with you shortly.'

The door was pulled to.

'This shouldn't take long,' Stephen said. 'Billionaires have shorter attention spans than ordinary men and Thomas Borkmann is no exception. They'll offer ten million less and we'll agree to disagree and decide we need to talk further tomorrow. I'll remain as stiff upper lipped as I can while they tell me it's the best deal of the century and I would be a fool to renege on it. In fact I probably don't need to speak at all but just shake my head. That should do unless they've got something else as a lever. When I come back we need a plan to deal with Perdita and this photograph.'

'I think I could do with a drink,' John Hazlitt said after the door closed. 'I imagine Stephen won't mind.' He hovered over a collection of malt whiskies laid out on a sideboard and started comparing bottles.

I got to my feet and looked out of the mullioned windows. On this side of the house the land slipped gently down to an idyllic water meadow where colour-coordinated cows were grazing contentedly. It was more like a dream of England than England itself.

Silence settled upon the two of us interrupted only by the sound of liquid being poured into a glass and a contented sigh behind me. I wondered how many hours I had spent with John in Cambridge dreaming about the future. Stephen was one of Europe's leading entrepreneurs. Peter was beloved of children everywhere. Mark had been a musical genius. John had made a fortune in banking. I had invented a fictional detective whose powers seemed in near terminal decline. I wasn't doing too well in the pecking order.

'Do you see Rosemary these days, or Jonathan?'

'Since we were divorced we don't meet up much. Rosemary prefers it that way. Jonathan, perfectly rightly, thinks I'm to blame for the break-up and takes his mother's side. I haven't seen him for five years. Rosemary's family tend not to acknowledge me, which is understandable. Not that it's a great wrench – I never liked them.'

'Apart from that?'

'I do have one or two other mouths to feed and I'm a little short of funds at the moment.'

'Must be difficult.'

'It's not good. I need to go abroad for a bit. There are some people it would be better to steer clear of for the moment – creditors mostly. It's all a bit tricky. Just at the moment in my circle everybody owes everybody and nobody can pay. But there might be a way out.'

John was gathering breath to deliver the details of his plan when the door opened. Stephen looked much calmer than when he had left.

'Have they signed?' John asked.

'No, but they will. They'll be a bit hesitant about it but they'll pay top dollar for Picture Screen as long as they don't get handed any additional negotiating cards to play. At the moment they don't seem to know anything about Perdita. But I need to cover that angle off. One thing my people can do is to go through the company records and see if they hold any details on Jane Reddon. Given that one of our candidates for fatherhood is dead and the other one can't remember anything about the period in question we need more reliable witnesses as to what might have happened.' Stephen held up his hands. 'No offence David, but that's the way it is.'

'There may be another way out of this that might benefit us all,' John said. 'I've got a proposition.'

'Which is?' Stephen said.

'Before I get to that,' John said, 'does anyone know where Peter is?'

'Why?' Stephen asked.

'Because he's part of this, all of us in the photograph are. We've all been put in the frame haven't we? I'd like him to be on board as well.'

'He's hardly going to object if David and I agree is he?' Stephen said. 'If there is a herd to be followed Peter will be there. He's filming next week so he's preparing today. It's his best chance for a long time of getting Mr Musgrave and Chorley back on a regular television slot. But why don't you tell us what you have in mind? We can sort Peter out later.'

I felt like protesting for a moment but I was sure Peter would go along with what we agreed unless, remarkably, he had developed a sudden taste for social responsibility. He and Lorna had never had children. I wondered if either of them had ever wanted them.

'It's simple enough really. I'm Perdita's father,' John Hazlitt said.

'What?'

'I'm Perdita's father. Why not? I'm intending to go abroad. Once I've disappeared you can embellish my character with all sorts of favourable or unfavourable characteristics depending on what you think would be most helpful at the time. Perdita gets a father, albeit an absent one, but at least has the certainty. Peter and the two of you avoid awkward questions, sign the deals and save the marriages or do whatever you want to. I can leave a note regretting my absence that you could give to her. Problem over.'

'But you could be tripped up on the detail. The story could come apart. Think of the consequences of that.'

'There aren't any consequences David. I'm not going to be here to answer any questions. I'm not going to be here to do a DNA test. As I said I need to get out of the country for a bit. If you're right about Jane Reddon being

Perdita's mother then the only strong links we're aware of between the five of us in the photograph and Jane are you, David, and Mark. Mark's dead. There's nothing he can tell Perdita. If it's you, you can't tell her anything either because you don't remember anything. What does she gain from that? Meanwhile the Borkmann people are looking for any way they can to put the squeeze on Stephen. That's a hook that can be removed. If you need a story it was like this. Jane Reddon and I met after she got a job with Stephen. I was wildly attracted to her and the feeling seemed to be mutual. I wanted very much to go to bed with her but I was married with a young child and I thought I should resist. Unfortunately I wasn't strong enough and we started an affair. It was an affair of the body and the mind. That would give it some integrity wouldn't it? How would it go? Ah yes. I hadn't properly known what love was until we came together. But conscience got the better of me and I said we must break up, because of my wife and child. But then she found she was pregnant and came back to me for help. I forced her away. I've always regretted my cowardice and hope my daughter will forgive me but I don't feel I can meet her. But I've never regretted meeting her mother, only my subsequent actions. There, that's about it. You could believe in that couldn't you? If you embellish the basic storyline it will come to have a life of its own.'

'Very philanthropic,' Stephen said.

'Not entirely. I do have a slight problem. Some debts that need settling.'

'How much?' Stephen said.

'£50k would cover it.'

'Just a moment,' I said, 'aren't we rushing in to this? I mean don't we need to think about how Perdita might feel?'

'She's not my daughter,' Stephen said.

'Nor mine,' John added.

'There you are then,' Stephen said. 'As things stand it's most likely you or Mark. Mark's dead and you say you can't remember anything about it. It's not a great deal for the girl, is it?'

'What about Peter? Supposing he's Perdita's father. Supposing he wants to acknowledge the fact?'

'OK,' Stephen said, 'we'll find out what Peter thinks. But I want a backstop if this story starts to run. It should help Peter stop panicking as well. Somebody put the five of us in a frame for some reason or another. They're after something. If it comes up I want to have an answer to give. I need an insurance policy now if this Perdita story breaks. If John wants to provide one I'll take care of the finances.'

'Not a problem. Have we got a deal?'

'I think we have,' Stephen said, 'you admit to being Perdita's father if the story breaks. Otherwise you say nothing.'

'And the 50k?'

'You can pick it up in the next couple of days.'

'Notes?' John asked.

'Anything you like.'

I should have said something but I was counting down the months. If Perdita had been born on the 5th of August nine months before would take us to the 5th of November

'Are you happy with that David?' Stephen said.

I nodded.

TWELVE

SUNDAY 5.30PM – 11.00PM

I LEFT STEPHEN AND JOHN sorting out the precise details of the funding of Perdita's parentage. I spent an idle ten minutes in the Great Hall researching the genetic history of the Hayter-Molyneuxs and wondering what I had just agreed to. I was about to join the last of the retreating lunch guests wending their way back to their cars when I had a sense that I was being watched.

I turned round. Frederick St James was looking down from the gallery above. He was just as menacing as he had been when Francesca's aunt had pointed him out at lunch. If anything he seemed taller standing up. I was sure he had been observing me for the whole time. I raised a hand in friendly farewell that he ignored.

On the way back to London the returning weekend traffic clogging up the roads gave me an opportunity to think. By the time I got back to the house I had a list of things to do assembled in my mind. Always check your facts, as Tom Travis would say, particularly the ones that don't seem to need checking.

According to Wikipedia Thomas Borkmann, Stephen's prospective business partner, was the 213th wealthiest billionaire in the world with numerous companies and interests in media and scientific research. He was also a Republican and an advocate of intelligent design. That seemed enough, even for Tom Travis. Besides I didn't have time to read the other 123,000 entries.

I couldn't find any reference to Picture Screen but then Stephen had every reason to keep his product secret until he had finalised a deal. Scrolling down the futuristic websites I found that Angell Industries had connections with Taiwa Biomedical Engineering, which had managed to convert brain activity in humans into images. The resultant pictures were somewhat fuzzy, but the coverage seemed to hint at step changes in image quality down the line. It was all rather long term and I logged off.

I went down to the kitchen for something to eat. The answering machine's light was set resolutely on red. Nobody had been in contact in my absence. I needed some company and a drink.

Jerry was in the annexe of his house listening to music pouring out of two vast speakers that he had bought from a specialist hi-fi dealer, equipment that had been state of the art twenty years before. Jerry maintained that they hadn't ever been equalled in technical terms. For some reason he was only offering green tea rather than something stronger.

'How's Faith?' I said.

'How do you mean?' he said in a waspish tone.

'I just wondered how she was.'

'I'm sure she's fine.'

'Have you spoken to her?'

'I expect she'll be busy at the moment. Have you spoken to Kate?'

'Not since this morning. I told you about that.'

'So you did. How was Rainbridge?'

'Interesting,' I said. 'I need to mull things over. If you're around tomorrow I can give you a better picture then.'

I had been going to give a briefing on the day but Jerry seemed immersed in his own thoughts. I wondered if he had some inkling that Faith might know what he had been up to and he was working out a story to tell her. I accepted a glass of white wine but Jerry kept resolutely to green tea. After twenty minutes I left.

As I walked back the long way round on the road I reflected that Jerry's relative silence had led me to keep my own counsel on John Hazlitt's proposition which, at least, provided some sort of permanent solution to the Perdita problem. I did, after all, have other matters to concentrate on, such as finishing *Murder is Equal*.

The house seemed empty without Kate and the boys and I resisted the temptation to pour myself a nightcap. Instead I made a leisurely approach to bed to wait for sleep to claim me. I could make a list and divide my life into the positives and what? Not so positives? Perdita was now a problem shared although not necessarily a problem solved, whatever John Hazlitt might be prepared to do. I needed to work out something to say to Perdita in the morning and I wasn't convinced that I had anything like a satisfactory story to tell.

At least the plot of *Murder is Equal* was resolved. Crispin Cruickshank should never have trusted Isabelle and let her get close to him. She had spun a web of deceit around him.

And Jerry? There wasn't a great deal I could do if he wasn't going to acknowledge what had happened. Perhaps there was nothing I could do anyway. Intervening in the relations between husband and wife is hardly ever to be recommended.

Anyway I had other problems to sort out. There was the mix-up with my agent on the new novel I had apparently written. I couldn't think how it could have occurred. I had been about to phone but perhaps there might be something to be gained from going to Coles & Hunter's offices. It was only a short tube journey and turning up in person, albeit casually, to help sort out the mistake, might give me the moral high ground and a bit more breathing space on delivering the next in the Tom Travis series.

And there was something else I should have remembered that was more important than all the other considerations put together. I had a feeling I knew something that would help explain what was happening. But I couldn't think what it was. I eased myself off the bed and walked into the bathroom and looked in the mirror. But the man there just looked confused.

It reminded me of a trivial incident when I was leaving Rainbridge Hall. I was about to get into my car when I saw a balding man approaching through an avenue of trees that snaked off from the main drive. Between us a blue Audi S5 Cabriolet convertible lay open to the elements. John Hazlitt had obviously arrived after the end of the storm and didn't seem to be making any concession to his professed financial circumstances.

'Nice car,' the balding man said looking at the Audi. 'But a bit too young for me. Do you know the grounds? You can get right down to the river. It's a fine walk.'

'Indeed,' I said enthusiastically with the bonhomie that affects strangers who meet with connections they don't understand.

My new friend gestured towards Rainbridge Hall. 'They've done a lot of restoration in recent years. I hardly recognise it. To be truthful I haven't been here for years. I thought I'd been crossed off the guest list.'

'That's hardly likely.'

The man stretched out his hand.

'I'm not sure we've been introduced,' he said. 'I'm David Knight.'

'What an interesting name,' I found myself saying.

'Really?' my companion beamed. 'I suppose it is, most people think that it's derived from the Middle English "knyghte". Chaucer I suppose, a "true and parfait knyghte".'

'Hard to live up to.'

My companion laughed.

'Yes, yes, you're probably right,' he said after a moment's reflection, 'although hopefully not impossible. But I don't think we've met and I don't know your name.'

'John Hazlitt,' I said, after a moment. I didn't quite know why.

PART TWO

Monday,
Tuesday,
Wednesday

*Appearance – noun – the way that someone
or something looks or seems*

THIRTEEN

MONDAY 7.00AM – 11.00AM

WHEN I WAS FULLY AWAKE and had treated my brain to a large caffeine intake and my body to a leisurely breakfast it seemed easy enough to get onto the tube and travel up to North London to resolve the misunderstanding on *Murder Unseen*. Being gracious about the mistake and providing optimistic noises on the timing of the production of *Murder is Equal* seemed a sound plan to keep my agent Debbie and her personal assistant, Angie Bates, on side.

It was only when I got out of the tube at Camden Town and was walking the last few yards to the offices of Coles & Hunter that I began to have doubts. The whole excursion looked like substitute activity for resolving a more serious problem – what it was that I was going to tell Perdita; or Kate for that matter. I was contemplating retreat when I heard a voice behind me and turned to see Angie.

'I really like the new book,' she said before I had time to say anything. 'You must be pleased. Were you passing? Come in and have a coffee. Debbie was thinking about a reissue of Tom Travis at some point and I'd like your views on some new covers we're doing for Dennis Blackstone.'

Without waiting for a reply she pushed open the heavy steel and glass door as though it wasn't there and I found myself sucked in to the vacuum behind her as she sprinted up the stairs. I had never understood how she managed to pack so much energy into such a slight frame. The only theory I had on why she seemed able to operate continuously on maximum power was that her constant intake of fruit, nuts and diet Coke meant that she burnt calories at the same speed as she ingested them and didn't have to bother with the tiresome expediency of fat storage that was so contentious an issue for the rest of us.

'What do you think?'

She was in the doorway of what served as the waiting room at Coles & Hunter. The room itself was crowded with newly published works of the agency's clients on shelves that stretched from floor to ceiling. Facing me were several hundred copies of Dennis Blackstone's Mathias Penn series with the ever-fatter sleuth smiling from both cover and spine. I noticed Dennis's surname was in larger type than before as though the single word BLACKSTONE was enough for most prospective purchasers to agree to buy.

'Very eye-catching,' I said.

'He does sell a lot at airports.'

'I'm sure he must.'

Angie giggled.

'Coffee? Or we've got some really nice pineapple or goji berries.'

'Coffee would be good,' I said, 'but I'll pass on the fruit for the time being. About this *Murder Unseen* business...'

'It's not a bad title either. Actually, now you mention it, there was something I meant to ask you. Just a sec.'

Angie disappeared and I took a deep breath. Newly published books have an intoxicating aroma before they slide into their long-term cohabitation with the world's dust. If I had had any works new enough to be included the place might have been heaven. But I hadn't.

Angie was back in the doorway flourishing a pile of papers in her hand.

'You didn't tell us you were going to write a prequel rather than a sequel, did you?'

'No.'

'I told Debbie you didn't.'

'You were right. Is that *Murder Unseen* you've got there?'

'That's what you sent us. I was a bit surprised because you normally email.'

'Can I borrow it for a minute?'

'Of course. I'll get you that coffee.'

Angie deposited the details of my new novel on a small wooden coffee table in the centre of the room and left. I looked at the papers and counted to ten. I had been expecting Angie to confess at any moment that a mistake had been made. But she hadn't. I suppose I had to reveal the error myself. I stretched out an unwilling hand to pick the papers up.

Murder Unseen consisted of a two-page synopsis; a 20,000-word extract that claimed to be the copyright of David Knight; and a letter to Debbie.

'It's white, no sugar, isn't it?' Angie asked from the doorway.

'Yes,' I said. 'Are you sure this is all the stuff I sent?'

'Those are copies. The originals are on file but yes, that's it. I opened the envelope myself.'

Angie was looking at me curiously but that was hardly surprising, as I didn't know what I was talking about. I needed time.

'That offer of fruit is rather tempting now I think about it. I promised Kate I'd go for a healthier diet. You don't happen to have any mango do you?'

'I'm sure we can rustle one up. I need to stock up from the stall round the corner in any case. Back in a sec.'

'Great.'

I picked up the extract as Angie disappeared, opened it in the middle, and started reading.

> Tom draws the curtains in the front room. Outside monstrous flakes of snow are gliding peacefully to the ground dampening the noise of the city. He turns on the standard lamp, which casts a cone of golden light over Rob. Tom bends down. Rob has stopped breathing. Tom feels his heart pounding. He waits and then picks up the sheet of paper on the mantelpiece. He thinks of folding it into three so that it will fit easily in Rob's hand. Then he stops. Such precision is not consistent with the disordered state of mind he wishes the suicide note to suggest.

I fiddled through the papers and found a plot summary. It seemed that Tom Travis had decided that Rob needed to take his own life and had ensured that he succeeded by topping up his consumption of anti-depressants to a fatal level. The woman who is the central motivational force behind Tom's radical new behaviour is subsequently replaced in his affections by the insurance investigator,

Julie Pearson. This was at least consistent with the growing attraction between the two that I had been hinting at in Tom's adventures.

Angie came back into the room with a plate of fruit.

'You've read all of this?' I said.

'Oh yes, I'm hoping to move on from just being Debbie's PA. She gets me to shadow a few of our developing authors. We were getting a bit concerned about your sales, it's such a crowded market, but this seems very commercial, much less of a traditional puzzle, not, well, so *old-fashioned* as your last one. The characters seem to leap from the page now. I passed it on to her straight away. You must be pleased.'

'You don't think the change in Tom is a bit abrupt do you?'

Angie Bates screwed up her face in what I first thought was distaste but which I then realised was her critical pose. It put years on her. She looked at least twenty.

'All authors have doubts but I don't think there is anything that could cause any problems,' she said authoritatively. 'I think you've been very skilful. You didn't go into any personal depth with either of them in the previous books, did you? Just waiting for the characters to arise by themselves I expect. It's like the classic TV series. They always take a season or two before the characters get fully developed and the writing is at its sharpest. You got the outline of the character established but the last few books haven't really coloured Tom in until now. Debbie was saying that we should get the publishers to put some muscle behind promoting it this time. I mean the plot in the first one was really neat, if you like that sort of thing, but this dark-side psychological stuff is so compelling. And with

Tom disposing of Rob Crane so early on you've got the basic tension in the book set up.'

'It's as if I have just read this for the first time,' I said meditatively. There wasn't a flicker of movement on her face. She was waiting for the next pearl of authorial insight. It was obvious she hadn't written this and she didn't know that I hadn't written it either. Perhaps Debbie had cooked it up? Some deranged real life TV programme? I didn't see any cameras.

'I mean is anyone going to accept such an immoral character?'

'Amoral.'

'He's a murderer.'

'But did he do it though? I mean I know he did it, or at least stood by and didn't intervene. But you get the feeling he has a compelling reason.'

'What could ever justify becoming a killer?'

'I thought the flashback scene got us halfway there.'

I must have looked blank.

'The next chapter, when they are thinking of going to bed together and he has that compulsion to tell her what he has done. Sexy scene. Pushes it along.'

'Do you think so?'

'Yes, great.'

I could have said it then. *I didn't write this! What on earth is going on? When did this arrive?* Make it everybody else's problem rather than mine. But that wouldn't be entirely truthful. I hadn't written this exactly, or at least not every word, but I hadn't been far away from some of these sentences either. It was as though someone had taken existing Tom Travis material and adapted it.

'Look, could I get a copy of this? I'm having terrible problems with my computer and I want to make sure that we've all got the same material. I'm not sure I've got a definitive copy of what I sent.' I let my voice slide into lameness.

'Take what you've got there,' Angie said brightly. 'They're my set but the originals are on file and Debbie has her own copy. I can make another if I need to.'

I looked at the letter to Debbie. There it was at the bottom – *David*. It was my signature. The only problem was that I hadn't signed the letter. I started collecting the papers together. I needed time to examine them in detail.

'I've just remembered I've got another appointment. I need to be off. Let me just tuck into this mango.'

I managed to eat the mango and toy with the goji berries. Angie hadn't moved.

'There was one thing I meant to ask you,' she said.

I got to my feet.

'What's that?' I asked. I noticed a metal rod had been inserted into the ceiling in the entrance hall.

'Well, it's whether…'

'No, I mean that thing on the ceiling,' I said but as the camera turned towards me on its long pole I knew what it was.

'Oh that! It's the new security system,' Angie said. 'You see there's sometimes no cover on reception so anyone could get into the building. This way we can see who's coming in. It's sound and movement sensitive and follows any disturbance. It's so clever. Stores everything on a hard disk for three months.'

'That's good,' I said, but without any great enthusiasm. The camera twitched a little to get me in better shot.

'I do need to be going.'

'You need a cover for those papers,' Angie said, 'and I did want to ask you about Rob Crane. I mean I was interested in who was the inspiration for him?'

It was clear that she had somebody in mind, but then she had had rather more time to mull over the options than I had.

'Who do you think?' I said.

'I wondered if it was Mark Ryland.'

'Why do you think that?' I managed to say after a moment. The camera tracked right a millimetre to ensure it had a clear view.

'You knew Mark Ryland didn't you?'

I must have looked surprised because Angie went on 'You're in that book about him, *Other Lives, Other Times*.'

I was, now I came to think about it, but only on a couple of pages, walk-on parts with no lines, my name included only for completeness. The most interesting reference had been '*others in Mark's year included the crime novelist David Knight.*'

'We were in the same year at Cambridge,' I said.

'The same college?'

'That as well.'

'But Mark is the model for Rob Crane isn't he?'

'You probably know better than I do,' I said.

I could see from Angie's satisfied smile that she took my last utterance as a yes.

'I suppose every character has many sources,' she said diplomatically.

'And every book has many authors,' I added.

I wished I knew who the authors of mine were.

'I'd better be going,' I said.

I walked out into the street. The air seemed clammy and oppressive as I walked back to the tube. I didn't have one less problem as I had hoped I would. The whole thing was unreal. I couldn't think who could have written *Murder Unseen*. Then I stopped dead. Perhaps I could.

FOURTEEN

MONDAY 3.00PM – 3.30PM

ELIMINATE THE IMPOSSIBLE AND whatever is left, however improbable, must be the truth. It was one of Tom Travis's favourite Sherlock Holmes axioms. I had spent the tube journey back home trying to argue myself out of what seemed the inescapable logic of the answer to the question of who had written *Murder Unseen*. I went through the evidence again. Who did I always turn to first for a critical view of my writing? Who had motive and opportunity? Who had been urging me for twelve months to cut through my artistic doubt and simply get on with it? Who had suggested I should get Tom to fall for Julie? Who had calculated that at my slowing rate of progress I wouldn't finish any sequel to *Murder is Equal* before I reached state pension age? Who seemed in recent weeks to be continuously trying to prod me into making progress? Who but my wife, Kate?

Although the scene where Rob was murdered was new, some of the other material seemed to be lifted from various off-cuts of Tom Travis adventures that I hadn't for the most part used but kept stored in case they might come in useful. I had certainly once planned to use a character based on Mark Ryland and it seemed that Kate had actually managed to create one in the form of Rob Crane. What astonished me more than anything else was her decision to focus on Tom's dark side.

The doorbell rang.

More irritating still was the enthusiasm Debbie and Angie had shown. I couldn't believe I hadn't said something as soon as I arrived at Coles & Hunter but I hadn't and now an amoral Tom Travis was elbowing his way forward as the salvation of my writing career. I wondered what my loyal fans would think. As I wasn't exactly in regular contact with any of them it would be hard to tell.

The doorbell rang again. As I hurried down the stairs I remembered I had another problem – what I was going to tell Perdita. I opened the door but it wasn't Perdita on the doorstep. Instead there was an angel outside.

His body was normally formed, unremarkable in itself, but his wings were diaphanous, almost transparent, and scarcely attached. There was deep sadness in his eyes. He was a serious angel. And he was not alone. There were a train of attendants around him equipped with poles and banners.

Except that, on closer inspection, they weren't exactly heavenly, or even heraldic, poles and banners. They were black metal, odd-shaped, but functional looking. This was heaven moving with the times.

'Christ, David. Let me in!'

It wasn't a calm angel.

I didn't have time to indicate assent before there was a mass movement of bodies surging into the house.

I managed a retreat in reasonably good order, but retreat nevertheless it was.

'Have you got somewhere we can go? We need to talk.'

The angel talking had lost his wings, which had become detached and were in the hands of his attendants.

'Somewhere private.'

'We can go to the sitting room.'

The angel brushed past me and took up a position half-way up the stairs. The front door closed on the outside world but the mob was inside and pushing forward. I climbed a couple of stairs after the angel to get a measure of the situation. In the hall below, showing varying signs of boredom and irritation, were two men holding white fabric ovals, a woman with a notepad and clapper board, a man with a boom microphone, a woman with a movie camera precariously balanced on her shoulder, and a short person, of indeterminate sex, dressed as a badger.

'And they are?' I hissed.

'The film crew. Except the badger. He's part of the act.'

'I recognised the badger,' I said, 'otherwise I wouldn't have let you in.'

I looked Peter Parchment up and down. He still had a clown's bendy body, innocent eyes, freckles and ginger hair; and he was still getting into scrapes, or so I deduced from the wild look in his eyes. The critics had found the source of his comic style somewhere in the line between Jacques Tati, Buster Keaton and Mr Pastry, with Peter's special skill being the ability to conjure up chaos in the most domestic of settings. My sons regarded him as the straight man for Chorley the badger.

'We're filming,' he said. 'They're on a break for an hour so I thought it was a good moment to talk. If you get them something to drink they'll go into the kitchen and then we'll get a bit of quiet. Can you fix that? Please mate.'

There was a note of panic in Peter's voice that was impossible to ignore. He looked slightly mad, but he might have been winding down from filming five minutes of mounting mayhem as, panic stricken, he attempted to stop Chorley from destroying whatever environment they were currently inhabiting.

'Nativity play, BBC special, big comeback,' Peter said in impressive anticipation of the subsidiary questions that were running round my brain. I descended into the crowd.

'If you guys could follow me,' I said.

I led the way into the kitchen.

'Help yourselves,' I said. 'There's coffee and tea over there. I imagine you're working and probably won't want anything stronger.'

My proposition seemed to attract no great enthusiasm from the majority. By the sink the badger was helping itself to a glass of water.

'Or a glass of wine?' I said. 'Bit early I know...'

'It's after three,' the man with the microphone boomed and everyone but the badger nodded. I emptied the fridge of its bottles of white wine and found a large packet of hand-nurtured crisps and some glasses.

'Got any red?' microphone man said and nodded as I waved to the bottles in the rack by the microwave.

Upstairs Peter had poured himself a large whisky. The white make-up on his right cheek had smudged since I had last seen him. He was gazing at his watch.

'Are you OK?' I said.

Peter thought for a moment.

'Not sure about wrecking the crib so badly. Might have to do that again.'

He sank dejectedly onto the sofa clutching the whisky like a lifeline. His eyes closed. I could hear an increasing hubbub from downstairs and the sound of a couple of corks being drawn from bottles.

I hadn't seen Peter since Stephen's annual fireworks party the year before. Then he had seemed only moderately disorganised and we had spent a happy enough twenty minutes talking over his work on the scripts for the TV special that Stephen's company had lined up for him and my own prediction that I would be able to sign the latest Tom Travis off around the beginning of April. According to Peter, Stephen didn't have anything to do with the day-to-day running of Angellic Entertainment any longer and was totally focused on the development of high-tech consumer products. We had formed a temporary club of comeback artists who had suffered a hiatus in their careers but who were now poised for new triumphs. I'd even managed to have a reasonably civil word with Lorna Trevanian, who had hovered nervously behind Peter for the last few minutes of our conversation but who didn't seem quite so convinced as usual that I was exercising a baleful effect on him.

Peter seemed anything but relaxed today. Waves in the surface of the whisky beat over and against the sides of the glass he was holding as his arm started shaking violently.

'Let me take that for you,' I said.

I put Peter's whisky on top of some loose pages of the novel. The word 'portent' began to dissolve into near transparency revealing the words on the sheet below. I read the sentence as it disappeared. It shouldn't have been 'portent' but 'potent' anyway. I picked the glass up and looked for a more suitable resting place.

'God,' Peter said. 'Christ, Lord.'

There were rising tones of anxiety in his voice even as he descended the celestial scale.

'Easy Peter,' I said comfortingly. 'Calm down, what's the problem?'

'Have you had a *visit*?'

Peter invested the word with all the trappings of doom. It seemed a rather hysterical reaction to the appearance of an attractive young woman whatever she subsequently might have had to say. But then perhaps he had more reason to be concerned about Perdita's words than I had. I felt a guilty comfort in his obvious distress. It seemed that I was no longer the prime candidate to be Perdita's father.

'A visit? As a matter of fact I have,' I said in soothing tones.

'It's ghastly isn't it?'

'It could prove difficult certainly. But there could be some good in it.'

'I can't see any.'

'These things happen from time to time.'

'Do they?'

'Of course they do.'

Peter wasn't convinced despite my reassuring tones. He was staring at me, as though he couldn't understand what I was saying and needed to work it out from whatever expression was crossing my features. It wasn't his customary crisis mode; normally he was on full internal throttle, revving up his engines for an escape to anywhere but where he happened to be.

'I can't accept that.'

His voice was strangled. He seemed to have opted for total denial. I wondered what was upsetting him so much until I remembered that he must have been starting his relationship with Lorna Trevanian around the time that Jane Reddon had appeared. While I might find it difficult to explain extra progeny to Kate, Peter had a much more difficult problem altogether. No wonder he was suffering from existential angst.

'So you think it could be you?'

Peter blinked, looked horrified, and backed away a step.

'No. How could you say that? You've been writing too many detective novels.'

'Not enough as it happens,' I said lightly but Peter was glancing nervously round the room, looking for ways to escape. I edged towards the door. Peter needed to calm down if he was going to put together a story that would convince Lorna in the longer term. He had reached the bay window where he glanced nervously at the outside world.

'We all need to face up to this.'

He considered the proposition warily.

'If you say so.'

'If we can't sort things out between us John Hazlitt has offered to say that he's responsible.'

An odd look, almost sly cunning, was crossing Peter's features.

'Why would he do that?'

'Money. Stephen will provide it. He doesn't want to be in the frame and frankly I don't think I do either. I mean I could have done it for all I know and just not remember because of my memory loss.'

'So it could be you?'

'It's possible. I don't know what I was doing at the time.'

Peter was looking out of the window, measuring the distance to the ground.

'So what's John going to tell them?'

'That it's him.'

'Won't that be difficult?'

'He's thinking of leaving the country.'

'That's not going to help much is it?'

'It gets the rest of us off the hook.'

'So what's he going to say to Addinson?'

'Addinson, who's Addinson?'

'The policeman, the man who came to see me about it.'

'About what?' I asked.

'Mark Ryland's murder.'

FIFTEEN

MONDAY 3.30PM – 4.00PM

'MARK RYLAND WAS MURDERED?' I said. I didn't think I'd misheard but it was worth checking.

'And you might have killed him, you said so!'

Peter had given up his plan of exiting through the window and started his retreat round the room again.

'No, I didn't.'

I tried to sound as calm and matter of fact as I could but I must have been edging forward like some slow-motion stalker. Peter was going up to seventh gear in the looks of alarm that were swirling across his features and had increased the pace of his retreat, albeit a circular one that also threatened to bring him closer to me. He backed into the carefully assembled pile of A4 notes on Tom Travis's cases, eating habits, actions, potential love life and undiscovered flaws, and Tom's life dissolved into anarchy as the individual sheets of paper flew off the table and spread out across the floor.

'Careful Peter!'

It was a mistake to speak. He didn't seem to be

connecting to the fact that my words were relevant to his actions and emitted a high-pitched yelp as though what I had said was a coded Mafia warning. The lower half of his body encountered the solid side of the old leather armchair that had been Kate's father's favourite, but the top half of his body refused to acknowledge this cessation of movement and continued backwards.

Gravity was a different force in Peter's universe. One moment he was heading backwards like a boxer taking a knockout blow to the jaw, and the next he had invented a new sideways limbo-like technique that enabled him to move back to the vertical. As far as I could see his legs and feet were independently controlled throughout the manoeuvre.

He contorted the right side of his body, not to steady himself, but to extract an object from his pocket and transfer it to the palm of his hand. When all parts of his body had reassembled themselves in traditional order he looked round anxiously and then made a lunge towards the so far untroubled pages of *Murder is Equal* on the table.

I didn't know what was going on in Peter's head and whether the cycle of inadvertent destruction that so consumed his life with the badger was doomed to be repeated in real life. As a theory, it was gaining traction by the moment. I needed a moment away. I closed my eyes.

When they opened I saw that the glass of whisky towards which Peter had been accelerating on top of the manuscript pile had not been propelled with its contents to the far side of the room but was retained in Peter's hand. More than that he was raising it to his lips to help him swallow whatever it was that he had managed to remove from his trouser pocket.

'Stay where you are!'

'I'm not moving towards you, Peter. You're moving towards me.'

He stopped and gulped down the rest of the whisky. The expression on his face changed from alarm to existential confusion and then mellowed into an apprehensive grin.

Downstairs music was added to the hubbub in the kitchen and then shrieks of laughter.

'There are people in the house.'

'They're your film crew,' I said.

Peter considered the point and then nodded. 'Yeah, right, right. What were you saying?'

'You said you'd seen a policeman. Add in? Add in something?'

'Add in what? Oh Addinson! Why didn't you say? He collared me this morning when I was leaving the house. I nearly managed to get back inside but I was too slow. Maybe that was OK; Lorna was in the kitchen, so that wouldn't have been good. No, no, maybe it was good that we had what he said we had. What did he say? A private chat. That's what he said, but that's what policemen say, like that Tom Travis bloke you're always going on about. You know that stuff.'

'But I haven't seen a policeman.'

'So that's not why you telephoned? What you were telling Lorna?'

'No.'

'So what were you on to her about?'

'Tell me about Addinson first. You know, the policeman you saw.'

'Oh, him.'

'Yes, him.'

'It was early today. He said he was checking up about Mark Ryland's murder.'

'And why did he think Mark had been murdered?'

Peter looked puzzled.

'Rumours? Information received?' I suggested hopefully but Peter's face remained blank. 'You don't remember what he said?'

'I wasn't concentrating too well. I was worried about Chorley. He's got an ulcer. Not sure how long he's going to last.'

'You must remember something surely?'

'OK, OK. I think he said Mark had been murdered by one of his university friends.'

'But he didn't say why he thought that?'

'No.'

'And what did he ask you?'

'I couldn't tell him anything. I hadn't ever been to Mark's flat, I hadn't seen him in the weeks before he died.'

Peter's voice was dropping to a flat calm. He was now picking his words carefully and thinking about what he was saying.

'He took my number and then he was gone. I wasn't even late for the shoot, well not too much anyway. So there was time to come here. What was it you wanted to talk about anyway?'

'Do you remember this?'

I picked up the photograph from the desk.

Peter looked at it. His hand was steady. After a minute or so he handed it back. It was clearly a tranquiliser that he had taken with the whisky.

'It's a picture that guy we used to know took. Charles Sotherby, that's him. I helped him set up the tripod.

That girl was around as well. That's who John Hazlitt is gawping at.'

'Which girl?'

'She was called Nikki. She had a red sports car.'

'And?'

'She went to study at Yale.'

Peter was definite. I also remembered a black-haired girl called Nikki who had sparkled briefly in our company before her exit. Perhaps an epitaph of Yale and a red sports car wasn't a bad one.

'So you remember this happening?' I said.

'Yes. Why shouldn't I?'

'No reason. I wondered if you'd seen the photograph after he took it.'

'He had that exhibition in the college didn't he? *Cambridge Image* or whatever it was called – but I think that was all individual portraits. There was one of you wasn't there? You know – the one in the chair with you looking like you didn't think you had much more to learn?'

'It was this photograph I was particularly interested in. Have you seen it recently?'

Peter hesitated.

'No.'

'Or got your own copy recently in the post with a message?'

'Lorna does the post.'

'And she hasn't said anything about a photograph?'

'No.'

'I got this in the post with a message but I also had a visit from a young woman called Perdita Green.'

'So?'

'She came to see me on Friday. She's probably on her way to see you as well.'

'Why?'

'She thinks that one of the five of us in the photograph is her father.'

I saw that Peter was searching in his trouser pocket again.

'Never heard of her.'

'I may even know who her mother is.'

'Looks like you've solved it then. I'm sure I don't know her.'

It was uncharacteristic of Peter to be quite so definite in his view.

'I do have another photograph,' I said. 'The person who may be Perdita's mother. I could show it to you.'

Peter's moment of tranquillity was deserting him. He was looking for the door. I took the photograph of Jane Reddon from my desk drawer.

'You really ought to see this.'

'I need to be off.'

'It might be important.'

I held the photograph in front of him.

I didn't know what reaction I was expecting. Peter looked at the picture and gave a slight sigh. Then his knees buckled under him and he slumped to the floor and lay still.

'Peter?' I said, but he didn't move.

SIXTEEN

MONDAY 4.00PM – 5.00PM

THE OCCUPANTS OF THE kitchen greeted Peter's collapse with no particular surprise. There was only a muted pause from drinking as the woman with the notepad, who seemed to be the director, fought her way through the raucous company to inspect her star. Upstairs she helped me deposit him on the sofa and then pulled out her mobile and said that she would telephone Peter's wife to come and pick him up. I gathered it was a routine procedure.

When I went back with her to the kitchen the badger had disappeared but the rest of the crew were continuing to drink purposefully. It took ten minutes to persuade them that perhaps the moment to leave had arrived. By this time they had finished the three bottles of red they had added to the two of white I had provided. Their mutual endeavour had put them in a much better mood and their farewells at the front door were infinitely cheerier than their initial greetings had been.

Then the house was silent again. In the study Peter appeared to be in a deep sleep. I bent down beside him. His breathing was slow and regular. I had a curious sense that thirty years hadn't passed at all and if I looked up I would find myself in my old college room that Peter, particularly in daylight hours, had always had a tendency to treat as an auxiliary bedroom. But there were no dreaming spires outside the window. I looked at my watch. According to the woman with the notepad Lorna would be here in a few minutes. Before she arrived I needed to find out why he had fainted at the sight of the photograph of Jane Reddon. I gave him a gentle shake. He groaned softly. I shook him again.

Objects were spilling out of his trouser pockets. There was a business card from a film company and a grubby folded sheet of paper that turned out to be a bill for a top hat. On the floor next to the sofa was a small crumpled box marked *ASSERTON TABLETS*. Four pills were left in a blister pack that seemed to have been stress tested by rats. According to the label the pills had been manufactured by Hoyte Industries of East Erie Avenue, Philadelphia, Pennsylvania (PA), USA. Quite why Peter was getting drugs from America wasn't clear. After a moment, conscience got the better of me and I stuffed the objects back into Peter's pockets.

I must have pushed too hard for Peter stirred and a minute later his eyes were open and he was sliding himself into a sitting position. After a moment he reached inside his pocket and produced the blister pack. He took a look at the glass of whisky and blinked.

'Could I have a glass of water David?'

Once he had swallowed both tablets down his body shivered a little but his eyes were calm.

'Have you got that photograph?'

I passed him the picture of Jane Reddon. He nodded.

'It's me. I'm her father.'

'Are you sure?'

'It was the month Lorna and I got together. Jane was a temp at Angellic filling in at reception. Lorna had got her the job. I was there for a meeting with Stephen. He was stuck on the M4. I had time to kill and she was only doing the morning shift. She was interested in acting and I knew people who could help her. Lunch seemed good. Lorna was away for two weeks doing festivals. One thing led to another. I didn't know what I was going to do. But then Jane found out that I was with Lorna and it was all off. She dropped me like a brick. What's my daughter like? Does she need money?'

'No, I don't think so,' I said, 'she seems well provided for.'

'So where is Jane?' Peter continued. 'Did she marry somebody called Green? I don't get this. Why hasn't Perdita talked this through with her mother? Why didn't Jane tell me she was pregnant?'

'There could be any number of reasons, I...'

There was a ring at the front door.

'Who's that?'

'It's probably Lorna. Your director phoned her.'

'Why couldn't she mind her own business? What's this got to do with anyone else? You're not going to tell Lorna are you? She mustn't find out about this. You haven't told her anything have you?'

'Nothing specific.'

'I don't want to see her,' Peter said, 'not now. I need to think. But if she knows I'm here. I know...'

He sat on the sofa and slid gently into a horizontal position. He had all the appearance of being unconscious again. Perhaps he was. I hurried downstairs.

Lorna was as thin and willowy as ever. Today the little lines of suffering etched across her brow seemed to have multiplied.

'I've come for Peter.'

I gathered that Lorna wasn't entirely delighted to see me, but the lack of any warmth at all in her tone suggested that Peter was also in trouble. I was used to being in her eternal disfavour, although I wished I knew what it was that I had done to cause the rift between us and justify my role of chief defective male.

'Where is he?'

'He's sleeping,' I said blandly. 'He turned up with his film crew. But they left. He was obviously dizzy and fainted but he seemed to be better. But then he said he needed to rest. He seems to be flat out at the moment. He's upstairs.'

I would have led the way but Lorna was standing in front of me.

'What did you want to talk to him about?'

'It's a long story,' I said. 'I think you should check on him. It would put my mind at rest.'

'He suffers from Enzheimer's Syndrome,' she said as we went up the stairs. 'It's brought on by stress. The body shuts down so the mind can devote all its resources to dealing with the threat. He's really not terribly well. He's got high blood pressure and should avoid anything traumatic. Mysterious phone calls from his friends are not helpful.'

'I imagine filming must be very taxing,' I said doing my best to ignore her critical tone.

Lorna said nothing but I sensed there was another chapter being added to her accumulating dossier of my moral failings. I could feel waves of dislike emanating from her and moving round the house looking for dark creepy corners to nest in.

She was bending over Peter listening to his breathing. It sounded deep and relaxed. She prised open his eyelids. Peter made no movement. If he was faking unconsciousness it was an impressive performance. Lorna got to her feet.

'He could do with sleeping a bit. I suppose it had better be here. Twenty minutes if that is not inconvenient.'

I gathered the inconvenience was hers rather than mine.

'Coffee? Tea? A glass of wine?' I said.

'I'd prefer a glass of water.'

I picked up the nearly empty whisky glass before Lorna had a chance to notice it and went to the kitchen for the water. When I got back I switched on a table lamp to try to dispel the mood of gloom that was enveloping the room despite the sunlight filtering through the windows. Lorna sipped her water, occasionally glancing at Peter.

I sat in an armchair and resisted the temptation to pour myself something stronger.

'You've got children haven't you?' Lorna said.

'Yes. Two boys. Iain and Oliver.'

Lorna looked around the room as though they should be there.

'They're away on holiday, with my wife.'

From the expression on her face Lorna didn't find this story particularly convincing.

'In Norfolk,' I added. 'Staying with some friends of Kate. That's my wife, I'm sure you must have met. I'm thinking of joining them in a couple of days.'

It hadn't been a firm plan up till that point but now it seemed an attractive one.

'Happily married are you?'

It sounded more like an accusation than a question.

'Yes, I think so.'

'You're lucky then.'

'Am I? These things ebb and flow.'

'Do they?'

'I'm sure they do,' I said, 'for most people.'

Lorna nodded in a way that suggested she didn't entirely agree with the judgement and then she spoke again.

'So what was so important that you had to discuss it with Peter urgently?'

'Did I say urgently?'

'Yes.'

'That was probably a bit of an exaggeration. It's just something that's come up.'

'So you're not going to tell me?'

Lorna was subjecting me to an appraising glance like a teacher preparing to fail a pupil in an oral examination.

'I'm sure Peter will mention it to you.'

Lorna looked as though she was going to say something further but Peter happily chose that moment to start muttering. His eyes opened and went wide with alarm.

'We should be moving,' Lorna said rising to her feet.

'There's no rush surely. Peter seems to be tired. You could give him a few more minutes to recover. It's no problem.'

'No,' Lorna gave me a frosty smile and pulled her jacket round herself in a protective gesture. 'We've intruded too much already. It's time to go.'

She managed to get Peter to his feet with an efficiency that suggested that she had done it several times before and within a couple of minutes he was pretty much under his own steam again. I tried to catch his eye but without success.

I opened the front door. A uniformed policeman stood with his hand poised to ring the bell. Peter took a step backwards in alarm but was prevented from retreating further by Lorna.

'I wonder if you could spare me a few moments, sir,' the policeman said. 'There have been reports of a giant rodent in your back garden.'

He seemed a perfectly serious policeman so I let him in. Lorna hurried Peter down the steps and into the street without a backward glance.

SEVENTEEN

MONDAY 5.00PM – 6.30PM

I WONDERED IF ANY OF my neighbours was responsible
for the search for the giant badger. When we had first
entered the garden there had been rustling and movement
in the bushes against the back fence but I had been slow
to react and had anyway no interest in apprehending a
drunken animal. My police companion had ignored the
movement but started a methodical and energetic search
of the garden. Any animal within a hundred yards, that
was not dead, would have been frightened away. We did,
however, find an additional empty bottle of red wine, the
contents of which had recently been under my ownership. I
would have explained more but I was asked no questions.
After twenty minutes the policeman, young and solid,
wrote something in his notebook and left.

Once I had closed the door I had a feeling that I might
have imagined the afternoon that had just passed. I should
have asked for the constable's name and a contact number
to report the appearance of any additional outsize rodents.
Then at least I would have had some tangible proof that

what had happened was real. I switched on the computer.
Lorna had mentioned a condition that Peter suffered from.
I couldn't have made that up -

> Enzheimer's Syndrome – extreme condition where
> the body shuts down its physical activities. The
> extreme form of stress (fear) in Enzheimer's triggers
> the release of hormones, adrenalin and other
> substances. During the stressful event catecholamines
> also suppress activity in the front of the brain
> concerned with short term memory, concentration,
> inhibition and rational thought. In Enzheimer's
> sufferers such circumstances do not enhance the
> individual's ability to react quickly – fight or flight –
> but result instead in physical collapse. The condition
> is named after August Enzheimer, a 19th Century
> German Shakespearean actor who fainted playing
> Antigonus in 'A Winter's Tale', imagining he was
> being pursued by a real bear...

as for Peter's medication -

> the original formulation for ASSERTON tablets
> was trialled by American military forces in Vietnam.
> ASSERTON increases dopamine levels in the brain,
> aiding assertiveness. But the high doses required by
> marines had unfortunate side effects, particularly in
> triggering massively increased heart rates and blood
> pressure, leading to chemical friendly fire...modern
> formulations licensed in the United States but not
> in the European Union are much more effective in
> crossing the blood/brain barrier and trigger only a
> mild increase in heart rate and a correspondingly
> modest adrenalin trigger, a slight squeeze of a rifle
> rather than a burst from a machine gun...

It seemed to go some way to explaining what I had seen with Peter although I couldn't find anything specific on the interaction between ASSERTON and alcohol.

Whatever chemical storms were affecting Peter's brain hadn't altered the fact that he had been absolutely certain he was Perdita's father. But then he was the second person, after John Hazlitt, to acknowledge parenthood. I was reminded that I had once proposed calling *Murder is Equal* 'A Surfeit of Suspects'. Andy Fontaine had photographed Mark and Jane together and obviously believed they were romantically linked. Stephen Angell had suddenly been prepared to fork out £50k at a moment's notice to preserve the fiction that John was Perdita's father. Why? Even if he was a multi-millionaire, and the sum was small change to him, it all felt too abrupt even to fend off the possibility of a collapsed business deal. I felt better for a few seconds. Simply leaving a bonfire party with Jane didn't seem as significant as it had.

The phone rang.

'Hi, it's Perdita. Is anything happening?'

'Oh hi, no, nothing is very clear at the moment. There are some leads but it will take a day or two to sort them out.'

'You don't sound hopeful.'

'Everything is a bit more complicated than I thought it would be.'

As an understatement it was in a class of its own.

'Has something happened?'

Maybe I wasn't too good at disguising the underlying sense of panic that was beginning to grip me. However unreliable Peter was, he had been clear that a policeman had questioned him about the possibility that Mark Ryland had been murdered by one of his university friends.

I had managed to hold the thought at bay while I went through the list of Perdita's potential fathers but now it was bubbling up like over-active lava.

'David?'

I was losing the battle. Perdita sounded positively anxious.

'I'm sorry. It's a friend of mine. He's got some problems with his wife. I was thinking about him.'

The statement was at least half true. Jerry and Faith did have problems. The fact that those problems hadn't registered on my radar for the past few hours was another matter.

'I see.'

I could feel Perdita's brain whirring at the other end of the line trying to put together the fragments of information she was receiving into a reasonably coherent whole. I felt a need to tell her all that had happened but the headlines didn't make any sort of sense. Two of the people in the photograph are definite that they are your father. One of the others, who could be your father, seems to have been murdered.

She was speaking again, with smooth and measured tones; oil spreading across a troubled and choppy sea. 'I wondered if you were any clearer about whether you could be my father...'

It was a perfectly matter-of-fact observation, intended to inject clarity, scarcely a question at all. She had an agenda to follow and she was keeping to it. I saw her at the other end of the line, determined and resourceful.

'I don't think it's likely at the moment.'

'Well that's good in some ways, I mean with your memory loss you couldn't tell me anything about my mother could you?'

There was a jocular note in her voice taking the edge off her remark but I could sense the void underneath what she was saying, the little trapdoor waiting to open under her feet.

'I mean I think I would like to know even if we left it just like that with whoever it turns out to be.' Her tone was now very measured. 'Nobody would need to tell their wives or children. I'd just like to know. Then I can simply move on if that's what needs to happen.'

'Give me a couple more days.'

'Are you sure?'

'Absolutely.'

I managed to inject some authority into the word, exchanged a couple of pleasantries, and put the phone down. I found myself walking round the house. The call hadn't been as I had anticipated. I hadn't known what to tell Perdita but I had thought I would be in control of the situation, albeit in some haphazard way that Tom Travis would never have tolerated. Instead I had had the distinct feeling that far from rescuing some damsel in distress I was part of a plan to make things worse.

I was saved from further reflection by Jerry's arrival. He had reverted to military uniform. He looked tired but enthusiastic.

'These battle fatigues I've been given, tremendous kit. They seem to breathe with you. I've been up to Hendon on the assault course. I didn't think you'd need me. These really are amazing. Heat, water, they stand up to anything. I can write most of the report I've been commissioned to do on how effective they are now. In fact I could do the whole thing if I had a second opinion. Sure you don't want to try them out?'

'No thanks Jerry.'

'They're really state of the art and they say they're even more effective at night. Absorb light, or reflect it, or both I think. It's the material they're made of. The net effect is to make the wearer almost invisible in dim light. We could do it this evening.'

'No, Jerry.'

He looked perplexed by my lack of enthusiasm.

'Sure?'

I nodded.

'Worrying about Perdita and this woman?' he suggested.

'I was thinking about Faith,' I countered.

'Bit early, isn't it? Not even the long shadows of evening yet,' he said.

'*Faith*, not faith.'

'My Faith?'

'Your Faith.'

'What about her?'

'Well, it's not so much about her as about both of you.'

'What about us?'

Now I came to think about it, it didn't seem the right moment to mention the events of Saturday morning in the annexe and Jerry's new girlfriend. His private life was best left private while I sorted out my own.

'It's Perdita,' I said.

'What is?'

'The reason I started thinking about you and Faith.'

'Why?' Jerry said with an edge of uneasiness in his voice.

'I mean facing up to the fact of possibly having another child. I mean I might have committed some rash act all those years ago and now it has come back to haunt me. Who knows what the consequences of any action will be?

I mean any of us might have to face up to the consequences of an action that might have happened in the last few days in many years' time. Any of us.'

'What's that got to do with me?'

From his tone I gathered that Jerry was still in denial about the possible consequences of his actions of Saturday morning.

'Nothing, I imagine,' I said into the gathering silence.

The phone was ringing.

'I'll take it upstairs,' I said. It wasn't that I didn't trust Jerry on anything to do with Perdita but I wished he had been a bit more forthcoming on what was happening with Faith. I didn't know quite what was bugging me about the situation, given everything else that was happening, but something was. All in all it seemed to me that if I could confess to the possibility of having another child, Jerry might reasonably own up to his affair.

'David? It's Stephen Angell. I need to keep this brief. I had a visit from the police today. They'll be calling on you. They want to talk about Mark Ryland.'

'Why?'

'They think he was murdered. They were very interested in yesterday's party. Wanted the recordings from all the video cameras to take away and examine. I nearly said no but they gave me the impression they would come back with a warrant if I did.'

'That's crazy...'

'It's worse than that. They've also got it into their heads that the murderer was one of his contemporaries at Cambridge. I had the photograph of us up on Picture Screen. I couldn't deny who we were particularly as the guy in charge, a man called Addinson, recognised Mark.

He's a Detective Chief Inspector dealing with "cold" cases. He seemed to think the photograph was significant. I didn't feel like telling him the real reason it was there. He also knew that you and John had come to the lunch on Sunday. I said I had a few places spare and as you're both old friends I didn't think you'd mind last-minute invitations. That will square with any information that he gets from people in the office, if he goes that far. Are you happy with that?'

'OK by me,' I said. 'Did he tell you why he thought Mark had been murdered?'

'He wouldn't say anything specific. Although he was anxious to remind me that Mark died in a flat that was on Angellic Entertainment's books. We've still got it. Fred St James found his body when he was checking whether some maintenance work on the boiler had been done. I was in the States. Francesca had flown out to say that she accepted my proposal so I was pretty much in seventh heaven until I got the news. Luckily she had left that morning to see some relatives in Vermont. I had some business engagements I couldn't break, but I got back as soon as I could. Do you remember anything about it?'

'No. It's the black hole in my memory. All I know is what people told me.'

'Weren't you and Mark still close?'

'We may have been. I don't know. I can't remember anything.'

'Hmmh,' Stephen said. 'Good luck with Addinson then. And his questions.'

I put the telephone down. Mark murdered? It didn't make any sort of sense except, I realised with a sinking feeling, that it wasn't entirely nonsense either. I didn't have to go looking too far for one of the reasons the police might suspect that Mark had been murdered. It was on the coffee table – the manuscript of *Murder Unseen*. To the outside world I was the author of a book in which a fictional creation of my own, Tom Travis, murders one Rob Crane, a thinly disguised Mark Ryland. I sat down. I needed to take this slowly. *Assemble the facts in order*, as Tom Travis would say.

The only people I was certain that knew about *Murder Unseen* were Angie and Debbie Hunter. Not that that was entirely reassuring. If Debbie knew, and she was as enthusiastic as Angie had claimed, it was probably embedded by now in Hollywood gossip. Debbie had once advised me that the money in films, particularly in my case, was not getting them made but selling an option, or even an idea, that just might be, but probably never would be, made. Knowing Debbie she would have started that process already.

Why hadn't I denied that Mark Ryland was the model for Rob Crane in *Murder Unseen* when Angie had raised the subject? Why hadn't I told her that I hadn't written the book? I felt like retching. It was a short-odds bet that the source of the Mark Ryland murder rumour was *Murder Unseen* and its author. Kate. My wife.

EIGHTEEN

MONDAY 7.00PM – 8.00PM

ADDINSON CAME AT SEVEN, five minutes after Jerry had left and before I had got my ideas into any sort of order. He was a stocky man with a battered face that looked as though he had spent too long with the villains of the world.

'Mr David Knight?'

'Yes,' I said.

'I wonder if I could have a word, sir. Metropolitan Police. There are some matters that I think you might be able to assist us with.'

I tried to look blank.

'It's about a Mr Mark Ryland sir, the singer. I believe he used to be a friend of yours.'

'He died twenty-five years ago.'

'That's what I want to ask you about, sir.'

'And might I ask who you are?' I said.

'Detective Chief Inspector Addinson.'

Addinson reached into the inside pocket of his jacket and produced an identity card.

'You'd better come in.'

I could see Addinson in the mirror as I led the way down the hall to the kitchen. He was looking intently at the objects on the hall table, and the pictures on the walls. He was trying to learn about the suspect, trying to get the measure of him. If I hadn't been the suspect I might have felt like taking notes.

'I hope this is a convenient time sir? I wouldn't want to upset your working routine.'

I must have looked blank.

'The production of the new Tom Travis?' Addison ventured. 'I haven't missed it have I? I was expecting a new book. It's a little habit of mine. Collecting crime first editions.'

'No, it's been delayed. Might just make the end of the year if I'm lucky. I'm very flattered by your interest but I'm sure you haven't come to talk to me about that. What's this all about?'

'I believe you know a Mr Angell sir.'

It might have been a statement or a question.

'Stephen Angell. Yes I do.'

'And have you seen him recently?'

'I was at a lunch party at his home yesterday.'

Addinson nodded approvingly. I seemed to have got two answers right in a row.

'As it happens I saw Mr Angell earlier today. A fascinating man, if I may say so, very talented, something of a national asset. Did you see that *Horizon* programme? Mr Angell was demonstrating a small implant device that could give you a visual record of your whole life. If you wanted to find out what you had done, you would simply play the record back to the appropriate moment and see what occurred. The rumour is that the Home Secretary was very taken with it. She suggested we should run a trial fitting them to serial offenders, burglars for example, who would have the record available to prove their innocence if they were suspected of further crime.'

'Or to prove they were guilty.'

'It would have that advantage as well sir.'

Addinson seemed to reflect on the point.

'So,' I said, 'what's all this about Mark?'

'We have reason to believe that the circumstances of Mr Ryland's death may not have been entirely straightforward.'

'There was a programme about him on television the other night. It did discuss whether he had committed suicide or whether his death was accidental. I'm not sure it reached any great conclusion except that he was in a very vulnerable state.'

'That's the conventional account,' Addinson said dismissively. 'But there are stories about. Indications that he might have been murdered.'

'Stories?' I found myself saying rather foolishly. I needed to be careful. I had nearly said *novels*.

'Stories,' Addinson said firmly.

I felt I was being asked to react in some way. Addinson was watching me intently. I said nothing.

'So you haven't heard any of these stories about Mr Ryland being murdered?'

'I haven't heard any stories.'

I could be firm on that. I might have read them but I certainly hadn't heard them.

'Anyway what kind of stories do you mean?' I added.

'There's a piece being offered to the Sunday newspapers saying that Mark Ryland didn't commit suicide twenty-five years ago but was deliberately murdered by a friend from his student days at Cambridge. One of those friends is Mr Angell, who you saw on Sunday. Whoever has the piece is asking for a considerable sum given the public figures involved, promising the detail when the story is bought. Apart from Mr Angell there's a Mr John Hazlitt and a Mr Peter Parchment, the children's television favourite. And then, of course, there is you sir.'

'I'm hardly a public figure like Peter,' I said.

'More so than Mr Hazlitt.'

'Not as much as Stephen Angell.'

'That could be debatable sir. I'm sure the Tom Travis novels have a dedicated following. I've rather enjoyed them. I find a good crime novel very relaxing, although not police procedurals sir, they're far too close to home for my liking.' Addinson chuckled. 'No, I suppose I have a taste for more classical crime – locked room mysteries; somebody convicts himself of a murder he didn't commit; a body surrounded by snow with a dagger in its back but no footprints; impossible crimes; that sort of thing. Although I do like them set in the present, not back in the villages and country houses of the Thirties. And I do like a modern sleuth, who is aware of the pressures of life today.'

'I'm rather sorry I gave Tom Travis independent means.'

'It was a lottery win sir. Perfectly justifiable I think, and helpful in giving him the time he needs to spend on his investigations.'

'That's kind of you to say so. It was a bit of an arbitrary device though. And my plots can be a little artificial. None of them reflect real life.'

'You're being too hard on yourself sir. In a crime novel you need to tie all the loose ends up if you're going to have a good read. I mean it's reasonable enough to have a few red herrings, but fundamentally everything that happens has got to be relevant to the story. In real life it's different – all sorts of arbitrary events can obscure what is happening.'

'Is that so?'

'In my experience.'

'I'll bear that in mind. But I mustn't take your time.'

Addison sighed.

'You're quite right sir. I need to get back to the reason I'm here. Do you have any reason to suppose that Mark Ryland was murdered?'

'I've always understood it was an overdose. Whether accidental or as a deliberate action on his part I really don't know.'

'Mr Ryland was taking medication for his depression, sir – amitriptyline hydrochloride to be precise. In moderate doses it combats depression. Taken in sufficient quantities it kills you. An overdose seems to have been the main factor in Mr Ryland's death.'

'That all seems consistent with an accident or suicide.'

'Indeed it does, sir. But there now seems to be a suggestion that his medication was tampered with in some way. As a writer of crime fiction I'm sure you will appreciate that it all could have been relatively simple. The medication Mr Ryland was taking was essentially a poison if taken in sufficiently large doses. All the murderer would have to do was ensure that the doses were increased. The poison was already at hand.'

'Relatively straightforward then.'

'It certainly wouldn't occur in one of your novels. You would be more likely to favour an unusual poison brought in from outside which the murderer would have to get access to. It offers more opportunity for the planting of clues. Unless of course it's some sort of gambit; the murder weapon in full view, like the priceless stamp on a postcard above the fireplace.' Addison sighed. 'But I suppose we'd better get back to business. Do you remember where you were on the 20th January…'

'The year Mark died?'

'Yes.'

'It's a long time ago.'

'I know that sir. But it's a question that I'm asking a number of friends of Mr Ryland. I appreciate you may not know precisely but any information you have will help. Mr Angell, for example, was in the United States on business. He was having a series of meeting with Atlantic Records. I wondered if you could recollect what you were doing? Were you in London at that time?'

'I was house sitting.'

'Whereabouts sir?'

'Kensington.'

'Very pleasant I'm sure sir. If you remember there was a cold snap the week that Mr Ryland died. There was lots of snow, more than a foot one day. It was the only substantial snow that winter. Perhaps you remember it.'

'I'm afraid I don't,' I said.

I explained about the ill-starred game of hockey and the effects of traumatic amnesia.

'So you wouldn't remember if you had gone to Mr Ryland's flat?' Addinson said when I had finished. He suddenly looked rather glum.

'I'm afraid I wouldn't remember if I had or I hadn't. Not in this period. It's a time when I don't remember anything at all.'

'Work colleagues?'

'Freelance.'

'A girlfriend?'

'Not that I remember.'

'Someone else who was living in the house?'

'No.'

'And you don't ever remember going to Mr Ryland's flat? At any other time?'

'No. But I don't remember anything around that time.'

'And how long did all this last?'

'There's a period of six months where I have no memory of what happened at all. Mr Ryland died in the middle of that period.'

'So there is nothing you can add sir?'

For a moment I thought of recounting what Andy Fontaine had told me but it was only for a moment. I wasn't at all sure he would be willing to repeat it to the police.

'No,' I said. 'Nothing at all.'

NINETEEN

MONDAY 8.00PM – 9.45PM

I CLOSED THE DOOR CALMLY and then tried to stop myself retching. It hadn't been a good couple of hours. But then it hadn't been a good day. When I had woken I had been fearful that I might be Perdita's father. Now it seemed I might be a murderer. Worse than that I might not even know it. I didn't believe either that Addinson had asked about my next book by chance. But how could he know about *Murder Unseen*? What did he know that I didn't?

I needed a drink but instead I sat back in front of the computer and typed in my password. KNIGHTFALL. My habitual fear of accidentally deleting something that would one day turn out to be useful meant that I had at least two copies of anything significant. It would take a forensic wordsmith to find the precise documents that Kate had electronically cut and copied her way through, unless of course it hadn't been Kate but myself. Could I have sent the package off in some sort of trance? I had spent enough days looking at endless drafts and simply changing odd words and then printing new versions out and then changing them again.

I flipped through the pages that Angie had given me. The sample chapters that the author, whoever she or he was, had supplied came from the first part of the book. As far as I could see what the writer had supplied was an inverted crime story with the evil deed, Tom's murder of Rob Crane, or as Addinson would no doubt have it, my murder of Mark Ryland, happening pretty much at the beginning in full view of the reader. I flicked through a few more pages. Tom's motivation was anything but clear. The only thing that was perfectly straightforward and clear was the murder itself. It seemed that the book was designed as a *whydunnit?* with Tom's motivation the mystery to be unravelled. I flicked on through the pages looking for an answer as to why he had committed a murder. What motive could he possibly have? As far as I could see there were only hints and allusions to the precise nature of the pressure that Tom was under, intriguing enough in their own way, but only giving enough detail to compel the reader to journey on if they wanted a proper answer.

I wasn't thinking straight.

There was a two-page synopsis. Rather than trying to pick reasons out of a teasing text I could find out what I wanted to know far more economically. Page one skirted through the early actions but didn't quite get to the bottom of Tom's motivation or indeed anywhere near a plausible version. I turned to page two – it was blank.

Angie hadn't included the second page. It was a simple mistake, a rare deviation from the perfection of her normal working life.

The look that Kate and Debbie had given me at Coles and Hunter's Christmas party six months before was suddenly etched in my memory. At the time I had been trying to dodge Dennis Blackstone for fear of being drawn into a conversation about the looming re-issue of all his Mathias Penn titles. Dennis, champagne glass in hand and eyes glinting with achievement, had been more serpentine than ever, a growing counterpoint to his ponderous hero. In the event I hadn't succeeded in avoiding him and had been forced into five minutes of conversation before a genuine Penn fan had arrived to claim Dennis's time and add fulsome praise to my own perfunctory note of congratulation. Even then Dennis had persisted in pursuing a lengthy and solicitous enquiry about Tom's professional welfare. I had been able to respond relatively enthusiastically as Tom had seemed on the point of solving the Cruickshank case although then the eldest nephew, Rupert Cruickshank, and not Isabelle, had been in the frame. I had enquired in turn about Penn's physical health, which, I was told, remained robust. It was when I had finally managed to extricate myself that I had seen Kate and Debbie talking. And that was when they had both looked at me and I was certain that they hadn't been engaged in idle gossip, or pleasantries, but in a discussion of where next for a flagging Tom Travis and his equally exhausted creator.

I looked at my watch. It was time for a glass of something with Jerry. It was time for him to tell me that fiction and fact were two different worlds that didn't meet.

I left the house by the back door. Overhead a succession of planes was flying down to Heathrow in a congealing red sky, and the garden was a slowly darkening green as the sun dropped towards the horizon. It was just another normal day, indistinguishable from all the others.

I thought I heard rustling as I crossed the woodland to the back of Jerry's house but when I looked round I couldn't see any trace of policemen or badgers.

The door to the annexe swung open as I approached. Mercifully Jerry was no longer dressed in military uniform.

'Well?' Jerry said looking me up and down.

'It's a long story. I could do with a drink. Nothing too heavy, I need to keep my mind clear.'

'It had better be white wine then. Given I owe you a favour, and you look as though you need one, one of us ought to stay sober so I'll nominate myself.'

'Fine,' I said.

'No hardship. Once you've gone the first twenty-four hours without alcohol it gets less of a temptation.'

'Temptation?' I said. It seemed a promising noun. Perhaps Jerry was at last going to come clean on whatever it was that had been going on in the early part of Saturday morning. Besides, thinking about Jerry's possible road to Damascus enabled me to stop thinking about my own. Except that now that I thought about it Perdita had her mother's eyes, the eyes that I now remembered so well and not just as part of a dream. Were they eyes to kill for? Perhaps I had been transported by sexual jealousy and disposed of Mark in a fit of rage – or, if *Murder Unseen* was to be believed, in a calculated cold-blooded killing. Perhaps it had been a slow smouldering jealousy that Mark would never have been fully aware of. It wasn't really helping. I needed to focus on Jerry's concrete transgressions rather than theoretical ones of my own.

'It's probably something one shouldn't get into,' I said helpfully in the face of Jerry's studious silence.

Jerry looked blank.

'Temptation that is,' I continued. 'I mean once you give way, once you've crossed the barrier, it can be difficult to climb back, although not impossible of course, whatever the situation, however black it might look. I always think it helps to confide in someone if one ever gets into a situation like that. Share the perspective as it were. Things can seem quite different if one does that. It's a good way of finding a way back. Of course one would need to confide in someone that one was close to. However outrageous something might seem at first sight it can almost never be as bad if it is shared. I mean we all give way to temptation now and again don't we? Some of that is understandable, almost planned by nature; sexual attraction between a man and a woman for instance.'

'You did say a glass of white didn't you?' Jerry said. 'There's a bottle of something in the fridge. Faith and I were going to have it last week but there wasn't the time. You look as though you need it. Hang on, I'll get it for you.'

I was slightly disappointed in Jerry. Perhaps I didn't know him as well as I thought. But then he wouldn't know that I had seen anything. He had been too engrossed in the extraction of carnal pleasure to notice.

'It's Sancerre,' Jerry said.

He was in the doorway of the room, a glass of wine in one hand and what looked like a glass of water in the other.

'That's fine,' I said.

Jerry handed me the wine, took a sip of water, and looked me up and down.

'Who is she?' he said.

'What?'

'Who are you having this fling with? I've been wondering why Kate has been looking so fed up lately. Now I know. Presumably that's why you've given up a week's holiday. Well you had better make sure she's worth it. A younger model isn't always worth a trade-in. Think what your boys would say.'

'Don't be ridiculous.'

'You're denying you're having an affair?'

'Of course I am.'

Jerry looked far from convinced.

'What was all that temptation stuff about then? Are you saying that wasn't about a woman?'

'Not a woman I'm involved with.'

'Who then? Ben Horne?' Jerry said. 'I've always thought he has a roving eye.'

'Not our neighbours.'

'Who then?'

'It was a general proposition, not a particular one.'

'Really?'

'Really. We've all got something to feel guilty about. Why don't we share our secrets? Why don't you kick this off? Tell me something you feel guilty about in relation to Faith. I don't mind how bad or trivial it is. Say something over the last week.'

'There's nothing I've done recently that I would feel guilty about in relation to Faith.'

I waited but Jerry remained steadfast. I hadn't thought he would be such a convincing liar. I wondered how much I understood him at all.

'What did that policeman want?' Jerry asked.

'What policeman?'

'The plainclothes man that arrived just after I left. He was a policeman wasn't he?'

'Yes.'

'So what did he want?'

'He came to tell me that I might be charged with murder in the next few days.'

Jerry thought about what I had said for a moment.

'That's impressive,' he said. 'Why didn't you tell me before?'

TWENTY

'SO THAT'S IT, IS IT?' I said indignantly an hour later. '*I can't remember Your Honour*. That's the best defence you can muster?'

'Given you can't recall anything, it isn't bad,' Jerry said. 'It's difficult to catch you out if you keep to that single statement. Impossible really. You could plead some form of insanity I suppose, and have a new syndrome named after you, but you don't seem mad to me.'

'I'm grateful for your vote of confidence.'

'You need to chill a little and give yourself time to wire it all up as Tom Travis always says.'

'Tom Travis would never suggest *wiring up*. And he doesn't exactly *chill* either.'

'Are you sure? Maybe I'm thinking of somebody else.' Jerry looked pensive. 'Yes, you're right. It's that detective your friend writes about – the fat man. It's convincing when he says it. Anyway that's beside the point. What I'm getting at is that you need to sit back and take an overall view. Sort of Tom Travis-like – even if it's not *wiring*. Just look at all the facts. Tom Travis would agree about that wouldn't he? Ask yourself some questions. Who is this friend who has been in touch with Perdita? Why was she adopted in such mysterious circumstances? Who has got a motive for any of this? How about the common thread being jealousy over a woman? Could that account for Mark being murdered? That's quite good really. Motive is all. I thought you said John Hazlitt had a bit of an eye for the ladies? And you always have had. I mean I know you're happily married to Kate but there's still a certain glint in your eye. Imagine what you would have been like when you were younger and wilder.'

'This isn't a crime thriller Jerry. Not everything that happens is relevant. I don't have to tie up all the loose ends.'

'I'm just saying you need to separate them out. I mean take that photograph of the five of you that just happens to be yours. Are you sure you've never seen it?'

'Definitely not.'

'Positive?'

'Yes.'

Jerry shrugged in a manner that suggested I was not being quite as forthcoming as I might. I didn't like the mistrust that was hovering in the air between us. I had a sense that Jerry thought I might have unconsciously put together the *Murder Unseen* package and that accounted for my reluctance to share his forensic zeal on exploring every possibility of what had happened to the photograph in case I turned up enough evidence to convict myself. We bade each other a tetchy goodnight and I bit my lip when I was about to ask him whether he seriously thought I could have murdered Mark Ryland.

I was about to turn back into Benton Road and feeling for the house keys in my trouser pocket when I was aware of a black shadow sliding along the road behind me.

'David!'

The shadow was a large Bentley purring at walking pace with Francesca Hayter beckoning from the car's rear window. Brown was at the wheel, his face expressionless.

'David, I need to talk to you, it's about Stephen.'

'Now?'

'It's very urgent.'

'Well, as you're here my house is...'

'No, no, we can use the car. Much easier. We can go for a spin round Clapham Common. Do get in.'

I suspected Francesca Hayter normally got her own way. This time wasn't going to be an exception. I walked round to the other side of the car and found Brown had managed somehow to precede me and was already holding the door open.

I sank back into the depths. The seat seemed to mould itself around me and to be raked back more than usual so it was almost like getting into bed. There was the faintest sound of the engine engaging and then the car was gliding away. A glass screen separated the back of the car from the front so that we were in our own private capsule moving through the night. Francesca had a bottle in her hand.

'Would you like some champagne?'

'Thanks.'

An intriguing sensual scent blended into the warm night air. Perhaps Francesca served Bollinger to everyone who got into the car. If she did it would no doubt be a habit that would be remarked upon in her obituary. Or perhaps it was solely for my benefit. She was reaching behind her left shoulder for glasses, arching her body so that she could pick them out by their stems from the little cupboard in which they were stored.

She was wearing very little but that was probably because the gold around her neck glittered best against her bare skin. Her exaggerated action was baring more of her body and accentuating its curves. The white and gold dress that was clinging seductively to at least some parts of her had drawn inspiration from a point somewhere between Hollywood and ancient Greece: Penelope, as played by Grace Kelly. I could discern little wrinkles around her mischievous eyes but that wouldn't have deterred a single suitor from praying that Odysseus didn't return. I wondered how long she had known that even if she hadn't been born with a fortune, she would have had no difficulty in acquiring one. It was quite a performance and I had no idea why it was being switched on for my benefit.

The glasses she had reached for turned out to be silver goblets monogrammed with a delicate intertwined F and S that mimicked the designs on the ceilings at Rainbridge.

'If you could just hold that.'

She gave me a glass and leant forward to pour the champagne. The bottom half of her dress was more sober than the top but slit to the waist to enable a long slim leg to protrude invitingly. I looked into her eyes. As far as I could see she was completely sober.

'You just happened to be passing I imagine?'

'No,' she said, 'not entirely. I've been at a reception at the Abyssinian Embassy, no, that's not right is it? That's what it was called the last time a member of the family went there. Sorry, I'm feeling distracted for some reason, positively breathless. Ethiopian, that's what it's called, the Ethiopian Embassy. One of Stephen's charities was involved. He's still talking to the Americans so he couldn't go.'

'No deal then?'

'Not yet. Soon Stephen says. I hope so. It's putting him under a lot of pressure. I'm worried about him.'

Francesca favoured me with a smile that encouraged mutual confidences.

'These goblets…' I said.

'Stephen designed them. Rather clever I thought, although Brown wouldn't agree. Don't worry, he can't hear. The screen is soundproof. I don't think he likes that either. He hates anything modern, including this car. Stephen insisted we should have it customised and I don't mind the luxury one bit. It's a refreshing change from my childhood.'

'I gather he doesn't much like the Three Graces either.'

'I do have some sympathy with him there. Stephen never got their position quite right. Brown got into a huff about balance and perspective in the garden, that lasted for about a decade, and even I thought Stephen should move them. But Brown had really got under his skin by then and he refused. I hadn't the heart to press the matter. He did install them himself after all. Single-handed, so he maintains, but I'm sure the dreadful St James gave him some help, which may explain how they got to be put where they are. Stephen should have got somebody else to help. The truth is that the man may be fine organising security at rock festivals but his aesthetic judgement is zero. Stephen insisted we went out to see him in the Algarve once. It was quite an experience. At least the boys liked their monogrammed towels. In any event it's not a pressing problem. The yew hedges will need to be replaced in a couple of generations. There will be time to remodel that part of the garden then. I'll leave a note.'

I looked out of the window. The common was gliding by as the car purred onward through the traffic. I must have driven this way a hundred times but the familiar now seemed strange.

'So,' I said, 'you wanted to talk about Stephen. How can I help?'

She was leaning towards me, the hint of perfume in the air was stronger, a scent that might have lingered over crisp white cotton sheets. 'Stephen is upset about something. When he found out they'd invited the wrong David Knight to that lunch party on Sunday he got as angry as I've ever seen him. Stephen doesn't get that angry, at least not about anything as trivial as a party invitation, albeit to one of his oldest and most charming friends. So why was he so intent that you were at the party? Why are all these old acquaintances from Cambridge suddenly top of his concerns?'

'He's probably worried about this deal with the Americans.'

'You know there's something else. It wouldn't do any harm to tell me. I'm devoted to Stephen. I want to help. Anything you say will be between us.'

I took a deep breath. There wasn't anything very much between us as it was. I wondered why she was so anxious to find out what was happening and what she might do to ensure that she did.

'A woman called Perdita Green has appeared. There is a suggestion that one of five people in a photograph is her father.'

Francesca leant back and took a sip of her champagne.

'And how old is this woman?'

'Twenty-five.'

'And you're one of the people that may be the father?'

'Yes.'

'And John Hazlitt is another? He was also a late addition to the lunch.'

'John, Stephen, myself, Peter Parchment and Mark Ryland.'

'And this was out of the blue?'

'Completely.'

Francesca contemplated raising the glass of champagne to her lips but decided against it in mid-transit.

'These things happen.'

I suppose that if one inherits a house with five hundred years of family portraits on the walls where infidelity is obvious, whatever official records say, one is entitled to a measure of detachment. I wasn't sure Kate would have taken it so calmly. She certainly wouldn't if I also told her that she was not the first woman I had chosen to confide in.

'We don't know who the father is at the moment.'

Francesca smiled.

'A little bit of DNA testing would do it surely? Why don't you boys sort it out that way? Just find out who it is and make the appropriate arrangements when you have. I'm sure this young woman would appreciate knowing who her father is, whatever charade is played out in public. I don't think tests take too long to arrange do they? It would resolve matters one way or another. It might just be a mistake. Perhaps none of you is the father? But, well, how about it David? Is it you?'

'I'm not entirely sure.'

'Almost a yes. Do tell me more.'

Francesca looked at me. I couldn't remember being quite so close to a woman with such beguiling green eyes before. My account of the hockey accident and my subsequent memory loss wasn't as precise as normal.

'You're in rather a difficult position aren't you?' Francesca said when I had managed to make it to a reasonably coherent finish. 'Still DNA doesn't depend on memory. It really would be quite simple.'

I gathered from her tone that she regarded the problem as solved. It was probably a traditional Hayter-Molyneux approach. Perdita would be bought off with a parcel of land or some similar arrangement. I was about to say something more when I saw she had a remote control in her hand and the interior of the car was transforming before my eyes. Panels in the partition that separated us from Brown slid back to reveal a flat screen, which brightened into life.

'This might help you as well,' Francesca said.

On the screen a man in swimming trunks was bending over a figure at the side of a pool. The water in the pool was a vivid blue. The man moved to one side to reveal a younger Francesca, eyes bright, seemingly laughing aloud. Francesca splashes in the water but the man has disappeared from view. His face has been hidden and it is not clear who he is.

Now Francesca is running towards a creamy white house with wooden shutters and orange tiles on the roof. Somehow, in the few seconds that have passed, she has lost her clothes. It's like the re-enactment of a Greek myth in which gods and nymphs circle each other for relative favour. Francesca doesn't go into the house but runs into the forest, her long limbs swallowed up by the green of the trees.

The camera pulls back reluctantly from its pursuit and now we're back at the swimming pool. A young woman is floating lazily towards the pool steps. She looks familiar but I can't for a moment think who she is. There is splashing in the water and a figure starts swimming powerfully towards her. It may be the man we've already seen or someone new. It's not possible to tell. The woman is half out of the pool when he reaches her, the water glistening on her body. He pulls her back in. She looks towards us, her hand caressing his neck. She gives him a long and lingering kiss and then turns to face the camera completely unabashed. Then his face becomes visible. I feel an electric jolt of excitement or perhaps alarm, I don't know which, for this is someone I know, or think I know. This is the man I see in the mirror every morning. The woman stares at me seductively and purses her lips into a kiss.

Now she is in a new swirling embrace with her companion. She runs her hand across his muscular chest. I don't remember my body ever being that toned but there's no doubt that it's me.

'I do so wonder what happened to me after I ran into the forest,' Francesca said. 'Sadly I'm not that shape these days.'

'I wouldn't say that,' I said. 'But I'm absolutely certain I was never that fit.'

Francesca laughed. 'You do look rather gorgeous. And who is that with you?'

'I'm not sure I remember,' I said, 'although she does look familiar.' My voice sounds diffident, insubstantial. I wonder if Francesca knows I'm lying or whether she thinks I'm simply being discreet. But I'm not totally sure I am lying. I mean I know who this woman is but I don't remember any of the times I have actually met her. A week ago I wouldn't have been able to give her a name, might not even have been able to recognise the woman of my dreams. But that isn't the case now. This is Jane Reddon.

'Are you sure you don't know her?'

Francesca hasn't been watching the screen; she has been watching me.

'Could you just wind it back? There's something I'm missing. There, stop.'

Francesca has run into the forest. My alter ego has started splashing around the pool with Jane Reddon. It's not clear where we are. Everything is bright, populated with vegetation that would be at home in the south of France. But there is a large building in the background that could be Rainbridge and something in the corner of the frame that looks like a statue. Somebody has taken a lot of disparate elements and decided to put them together.

'There, there's somebody else there, if you could just move back a frame or two I'd like to find out who she is.'

Francesca presses a button on the remote control and we go backward frame by frame. I don't have to say stop because there she is. It's another young woman gazing into the pool. She's in the picture for no more than a second and then she's gone. There is something about her that is familiar and I'm sure if I just had time to think I could remember who she was, but I can't find a name or a memory of what we might have done. It seems that just as I identify one mystery woman, another is fated to appear.

'She is rather beautiful. I can see why you wanted to go back. Who is she?'

'I really don't know.'

'She seems to know you. There was nobody else in the pool she was looking at.'

'Seriously I don't know. She does seem familiar in some way but I simply can't place her.'

'Are you sure?'

'Positive.'

'Broken too many hearts to be able to remember?'

I don't know if she's teasing or it's an accusation. Perhaps it's the latter. The me in the picture isn't quite so adoring of Jane Reddon as he first appears. His eyes flick across to the mystery woman I still can't remember.

'Look, is this computer-generated? CGI or whatever it's called? Somebody has shaved a stone off me at least. Is this something Stephen has done? He showed me a product on Sunday that was all about manipulating images.'

'He is brilliant isn't he? But you're not to tell him I've got this. I'm not meant to have seen it. But when I did I couldn't resist taking it. I shouldn't really be showing it to anyone but you are in it.'

'I'm sorry,' I said, 'I know my memory is faulty, but I'm sure I was never there. Where is it meant to be anyway? It looks like France with a bit of Rainbridge thrown in. I don't know how Stephen could have done it. I can't see how he's made it so seamless, whatever basic images he's using. It's not me, not the real me. What is this?'

'It's very simple,' Francesca said. 'It's a recording Stephen made of his dreams.'

TWENTY-ONE

MONDAY 12.00PM – TUESDAY 1.00AM

'HIS DREAMS?' I SAID.

Francesca nodded. 'Difficult to believe isn't it? He's so brilliant. I don't know how he's done it in the time. Only three months ago he thought it was impossible.' There was a note of awe in Francesca's voice as though she found it difficult to come to terms with the fact that her husband was a genius.

'But how does he do it?'

'He was mapping his brain signals when he looked at an object and developing a way to decode them into an image. He said it was like trying to write a novel with a gigantic Chinese typewriter and thousands of characters but doing it in reverse, and in poor light, but then he hit on something much simpler. I'm not sure I would be able to understand even if he told me but he's got a lot cagier about things recently, particularly now they work. Officially everything is pretty much still fuzzy and indistinguishable. I think he's worried that somebody will steal the process before he has time to get it patented.

He used to have to attach electrodes to his head but now he has a silver helmet with thousands of receptors in it. I think that's why he's so desperate for the money from Borkmann. He needs it to develop this.'

'And would you want access to your dreams?'

'Why wouldn't I?'

'There might be things you wouldn't want to see, or for other people to see.'

'You might be right, but I think most people would be just too curious.' Francesca looked at the golden bubbles in her champagne spiralling to the surface.

'And Stephen doesn't know you have this?'

'No.'

She was subjecting me to another intensive gaze, her green eyes trying to probe into the shadowy parts of my soul.

'So he doesn't know that anyone has seen this?'

'He hasn't seen it. Not this one. No one has except you and me. I came across the recordings when Stephen was away for the afternoon. Most of them were very fuzzy; it was difficult to make out what was going on but two or three of them were very clear. I was transfixed. I had to take one. I wouldn't have looked at them but I'm worried about Stephen. I'm sure he's working too hard and there's something else that has happened in the last few days. So I looked at these and I saw you, and I wanted to find out who these women were and I thought you would know. That's why I'm here. This is what is worrying him isn't it? That's why he is dreaming about them and you. It's not the deal with Borkmann.'

'I'm not sure I can give you any answers at the moment.'

She switched on the radiant appeal function in her eyes.

I hesitated for a moment.

'I'll think about it.'

The car was circling back towards my house.

'Let me out here. I could do with some air. A short walk will help me collect my thoughts.'

Francesca pressed a button in a control panel in her seat and the Bentley purred to a halt.

'We should keep this between ourselves David.'

The green eyes were on overtime and the errant Knight was being signed up to a sacred mission.

I nodded. 'Of course.'

Brown opened my door on cue and a few seconds later the car was purring away. I watched it till it disappeared in the traffic and then I looked at my watch. It was five minutes after midnight. I could have sworn it was much later.

Instead of walking to the front door I headed back towards Jerry's house so I could get into my own through the back garden. Suddenly I didn't want people to know my every movement. I didn't want me to know my every movement. I wanted everything a little less certain. I reached up and slid the bolt on the top of the garden gate back. Then I pushed against the gate but it refused to give. I swore softly. I didn't like the way that inanimate objects had joined the conspiracy against me. I pulled myself up on the frame of the gate and managed to rest my left foot on the top of the fence. One small push and I would be over.

As a plan it had the benefits of simplicity and, until I landed on the other side, it seemed to have worked. Actually I landed rather well and it was only the entanglement with the wild rose on the way down that was a problem.

Once I had got into the house I spent an unhappy few minutes removing spikes from my skin and painfully applying TCP. By the time I had finished the scratches on my face and hands were barely noticeable. I checked the kitchen. There was no glowing green light on the answering machine. Neither Kate nor anyone else had been in contact. I checked my mobile. It had no new messages.

I thought it would be difficult sleeping but as I lay in bed the pain from my lacerated arm slowly ebbed away. My eyes closed. I wondered what Brown really thought about his employer.

I could see Francesca running naked into the trees beyond the villa. What was I doing in Stephen's dream? I walked across the grass but couldn't find the place where Francesca had disappeared into the forest. There was something on the grass under my feet, a round white plastic box of tablets with PUSH DOWN AND UNSCREW written on the lid. I picked it up.

AMITRIP PLUS 200 MG
To be taken until DEAD
With or after food

It was difficult to be sure I had got it right because the moonlight was so faint and I had to hold it close to my eyes. There were a couple of other things on the label:

Mr Mark Ryland
Keep out of the reach and sight of policemen

'What have you got there?' Stephen said.
I hadn't seen him approaching.
'Oh just something somebody has dropped.'
Stephen nodded disinterestedly and looked around.

'Have you seen Francesca? She's lost her clothes and there's quite a chill tonight.'

'I think I saw her go into the woods.'

'If she's gone there it will be hours before she is back,' Stephen said in a resigned tone. 'We'd better have some food while we wait.'

He turned and led the way back up stone steps to a terrace overlooking the woods. There was a large oak table at one end set for a dozen people with bread, olives, charcuterie and salad. On a small table nearby John Hazlitt was counting coins next to a sleeping figure that looked like Peter Parchment.

Stephen was pouring out glasses of red wine.

'Do you know where Mark is? Or Jane? Or your wife?'

I shook my head. I looked round. There was a figure in the evening shadows but I couldn't see who it was.

'Have one of these.'

I put out my hand to take the glass but somehow all that I succeeded in doing was knocking the glass and spilling the wine over Stephen's white shirt. As I looked aghast the wine darkened like congealing blood.

'I'm sorry,' I said.

'It's not a problem,' Stephen said. 'It's a new fabric I've invented. It will just brush off when it's dry.'

TWENTY-TWO

TUESDAY 7.00AM – 9.00AM

I WOKE FEELING RAGGED AT the edges. I rather wished I had Stephen's technology to hand. I might have been able to find out what had happened in my dreams that had left me feeling so tired.

I thought of telephoning Kate but neither of my options of telling her either everything or nothing seemed appealing and I decided to phone once I had worked out a plan. I cooked myself breakfast and managed to consume most of my daily allocation of calories. This left me, or at least my stomach, feeling temporarily contented. Then a ring at the front door jerked me back to the present.

I didn't know who I expected to be calling but DCI Addinson wasn't the most obvious choice for any place in the top three. It was only twelve hours since he had last appeared.

'You've scratched your hand sir.'

'Yes.'

'It looks quite nasty.'

'It was an accident.'

'And you've bruised your face.'

'Same accident. I was climbing over the back fence. The gate was jammed. It was dark and I slipped.'

'Very unfortunate sir,' Addinson pronounced. 'You didn't think of coming round to the front?'

'No, I sometimes come in the back way. I thought I could easily hop over but I was mistaken. I'm not as young as I think I am. Why don't you come in? I'm just in the kitchen.'

I wasn't sure Addinson believed me. He spent a few seconds pondering my actions and then shrugged his shoulders. He had a small laptop in his hand that he put on the kitchen table and opened up.

'If you wouldn't mind looking at the screen sir. There are a few questions I need to ask you.'

There was an underlying note of steel in Addinson's voice. The convivial crime enthusiast who had questioned me in leisurely fashion before was no longer in evidence.

'Fine,' I said. 'What have we got to see?'

The answer seemed to be pictures of me with my car. I had a hand on the door, about to get in. Then a balding man came into view.

'You can get right down to the river,' he said. 'It's a fine walk.'

'Indeed,' I said cheerfully.

Not that I was feeling cheerful now. The footage came from one of Stephen's surveillance cameras at Rainbridge Hall. I hadn't realised they recorded sound as well.

The balding man gestured to something out of shot.

'They've done a lot of restoration in recent years. I hardly recognise it.'

The man was walking towards me. He stretched out his hand.

'I'm not sure we've been introduced,' he said. 'I'm David Knight.'

There was a wobble on the screen that distorted the picture for a moment and mercifully the sound cut out. We chatted amiably for a few seconds and then the sound returned.

'But I don't think we've met and I don't know your name,' the man was saying.

'John Hazlitt,' I said. 'One of Stephen's Cambridge friends.'

'Pleased to meet you, I...'

The balding man stood frozen in time. Addinson must have a remote control. I wondered what he was planning next.

'Do you have anything you want to say sir?'

'About what?'

'About claiming to be Mr Hazlitt.'

'It was a spur of the moment decision. I was embarrassed. This other man had been invited to Stephen's party in error. Nobody wants to know they've been invited to a social occasion by mistake.'

'Indeed not sir,' Addinson said. 'I'm sure your feelings do you credit. Personally I think a *what an extraordinary coincidence* conversation might have done the trick, but perhaps I don't understand the imaginative mind. And why Mr Hazlitt's name?'

'Why not?'

'Why not as you say sir? I suppose if you were trying to mislead Mr Knight for some reason any name would do.'

'Why would I want to mislead Mr Knight?'

'I don't know sir. In the normal run of events *social embarrassment* might be a perfectly reasonable explanation. But this is a murder enquiry.'

'Suspected murder.'

'As you wish. In any event it needs clearing up. Three of the four people who may be involved with Mr Ryland's death happen to be meeting at a luncheon party in Rainbridge Hall. I also understand Mr Parchment would have been there had it not been for a pressing engagement with a film crew. It's *rather suggestive*, as Tom Travis would say.'

'Appearances can be deceptive. Anyway I really don't know where this rumour about Mark Ryland being murdered could have come from.'

'You have no idea?'

'No.'

My not-so-pastoral idyll in the country with the other David Knight faded from the screen to be replaced by Angie Bates and the offices of Coles & Hunter.

'I did want to ask you about Rob Crane,' Angie said. 'I mean I was interested in who was the inspiration for him?'

I didn't feel well. How had the police got this? The sound was nowhere near the quality that Stephen had achieved on his equipment but perfectly intelligible. Surely most CCTV cameras didn't have sound anyway?

'Who do you think?' I said.

'I wondered if it was Mark Ryland?'

'Why do you think that?'

'You knew Mark Ryland didn't you?'

'We were in the same year at Cambridge.'

'The same college?'

'That as well.'

'But Mark is the model for Rob Crane isn't he?'

'You probably know better than I do.'

Addinson stopped the recording.

'How did you get this?'

'It turned up in the course of our investigations sir. We've also got your book sir, or at least the material you've completed.'

'*Murder Unseen*?'

'Yes.'

'Coles & Hunter gave you that without asking me?'

'I'm afraid they had no option sir. I also told them they were forbidden to communicate the fact to you before I had a chance to speak to you personally. I must say I thought I was fortunate to have a preview of the next Tom Travis novel.'

'It's not my next Tom Travis novel. That's called *Murder is Equal*. I didn't write *Murder Unseen*.'

Addinson looked bemused.

'You didn't write it sir?'

'No, not all of it.'

'Not all of it?'

'No.'

'Just some of it?'

'In a manner of speaking.'

'So which bits didn't you write?'

'Not the murdering bits, at least I'm not entirely sure there is a murder.'

'It's fairly clear from the synopsis sir.'

'Is it?'

'Yes.'

'I'll take your word for it.'

'Are you saying you didn't write the synopsis sir?'

'I don't think so.'

'You don't think so?'

'I'm sure I didn't.'

'That's more helpful sir.'

'I mean it doesn't make sense to make your hero a murderer.'

'Possibly not sir, but from what I've read he's in a little more of an ambivalent position than that. Although I agree there's a lot of force in your proposition in general.'

'Well then?'

'Well then what sir?'

'Look,' I said. 'I find this as confusing as you do. Somebody has taken my material and added bits to it, in particular Rob Crane's murder. They've also changed Tom Travis into a murderer, which he isn't.'

'I didn't think he was,' Addinson said, 'at least not before I read this. I would have said he hadn't got it in him. But I wondered if what you were writing was a confession. I'm not a psychologist but perhaps the guilt is just bubbling up through your subconscious. You do seem to have the ability to switch personalities, or at least identities, as you've demonstrated with John Hazlitt.'

'I'm not confessing to anything,' I said but Addinson waved his hands in placatory fashion.

'I'm not saying you are sir, but just supposing you were it would save a lot of paperwork. It could take years assembling the evidence otherwise. The whole process would put you and your family under a great deal of strain. You should think of them and of yourself sir.'

'Why?'

'The thing is,' Addison continued in an avuncular tone, 'there's research that suggests that almost fifty per cent of murderers *want* to confess. The problem is that they get sucked into the legal system before they have a chance to come clean. You know how it is sir,' Addinson's voice was almost jocular, 'lawyers get engaged, the simplest fact becomes open to misinterpretation and challenge. What once seemed straightforward gets changed and twisted. It's a very short step these days from feeling responsible to feeling that one is a victim of circumstances. After a couple of hours with a lawyer whatever has happened isn't your fault anymore. You've been subjected to intolerable pressures that no reasonable person could blame you for submitting to. It becomes clear that you're not the perpetrator of the crime but its victim. You don't want to go down that route sir. It would be undignified for the creator of Tom Travis. Think of your fans.'

'I didn't do it,' I said. 'I...'

'Just a moment sir.' Addinson held up his hand as though he were stopping traffic. 'Let me think. I know it's a natural reaction to deny it but from what you said there's a six-month period when you can't be certain what you did or didn't do. So you can't say you didn't do it.'

'But if that's true I can't say I did do it either.'

A frown crossed Addinson's face.

'That's reasonable I suppose, but tell me, do you have any sort of feeling that it's your subconscious that's telling you that you did do it? I mean if you didn't write this, who did?'

'Didn't write part of it.'

'As you will sir. The part of it you didn't write, who wrote that?'

'I don't know.'

'You don't know?'

'Not for certain.'

'You must have some suspicions.'

'I do.'

'And what are they sir?'

'I need to ask the person concerned.'

'And who is that person sir?'

'It's rather embarrassing.'

'I know matters of etiquette are important to you sir, but please tell me who it is.'

'My wife,' I said.

'So your wife thinks you have murderous tendencies?'

'No, of course not. It's just that I write crime novels. People get murdered in crime novels. That's what happens. I've been blocked on my current book.'

'And the current book you are referring to is what sir? Your other current book? *Murder is Equal*?'

'Yes.'

'And what do you mean by blocked sir? You mean you don't know who to murder?'

'No, I know that. What I mean is I don't know who did it. I mean I know one of them did it but I don't know which one. Actually I suppose I do now.'

'That must be gratifying sir, but getting back to *Murder Unseen*, if we may, does your wife write plots for you? That would be a reasonably well-trodden pathway after all. I believe Mrs Francis did a lot of the plotting for Dick's books. But I understand you could find such a revelation embarrassing. But anything you tell me is in confidence.'

'I'm not saying she provides me with plots. I'm just saying she wrote part of *Murder Unseen*.'

'Then I'm not sure I entirely understand sir. Is your position that you think you didn't murder Mr Ryland because you didn't write the relevant part of the book you've sent to your agent that suggests you did, because your wife wrote it?'

I thought for a moment.

'Pretty much,' I said.

TWENTY-THREE

TUESDAY 12.15PM – 1.25PM

I DON'T NORMALLY SUFFER FROM active panic. I do passive panic, inertia, the sense that one can never change one's situation however hard one tries. But that's not so good when you have the feeling that you might be arrested for murder at any moment, and, worse than that, you have the feeling that it isn't some terrible joke but the long arm of the law working properly for once.

Could you be convicted of a crime you had no knowledge of? It didn't seem a sane idea of justice but why would they let me out if I killed people when I didn't know what I was doing? Why would I let myself out? Aren't we responsible for all aspects of ourselves? What mitigating circumstances could there be? How would it affect my sales?

I opened the front door. I needed to do something, and there was somebody close at hand that knew more about Mark's death than I did.

The skies outside had cleared and the sun was destroying the memory of the rain. A uniformed policeman was walking along the pavement on the opposite side of the road seemingly keeping step. Uniformed policemen weren't common in the area but then, as far as I knew, neither were murder suspects. I needed a plan. I needed to find out more about Mark. I needed to talk to someone who had been around at the time.

As I approached his house Andy Fontaine was emerging through the front door.

'Is Action Man with you?' he said looking round.

I gathered he meant Jerry. I shook my head.

'That's something. You look as though you want a word. If so, you can buy me a pint.'

When we got to the White Hart I thought I could see a policeman's helmet outside. I ducked down out of sight.

'No need to bow. I'll have a pint of bitter thanks.'

I looked round. The bar had a scatter of lunchtime drinkers, predominantly male, hunched over papers or solitary thoughts. A young couple were having an animated discussion in a far corner but their eyes were only for each other. The barman was engaged in a duet of desultory despair about the fate of the nation with a red-faced man drinking a large whisky.

When I managed to get the pints Andy had positioned himself at a table near the door and out of sight of anyone looking in through the window. I pushed back into the corner as far as I could and took a sip of the bitter.

'Very pleasant,' I said.

'That friend of yours isn't turning up is he? The thing is he's a complete prat. I've started imagining I'm seeing him. There was a bloke in military uniform that looked like him, at least from a distance.'

'It could have been him,' I said, 'I wouldn't put it past him to wear military uniform.'

'Yeah, maybe.' He sounded unconvinced.

My new drinking companion was wearing an expensively tailored pink jacket to complement his white shirt and gold chain. He looked tanned and toned. He was following my gaze round the more sombre denizens of the pub, or as the White Hart liked to promote itself, *ale house*.

'You wouldn't know until chucking out time if most of them had died,' he observed.

I nodded. Now I had got to the point I found I hadn't got an easy way in to the subject of Mark Ryland's death, or the flat that he had died in, that wouldn't sound suspicious, particularly if there was any CCTV installed in the neighbourhood. I looked round.

'You avoiding someone?' Andy asked.

It was the same precise tone he had used in his dissenting view in the programme about Mark. He had framed it as a question but it was clear that he knew the answer.

I nodded.

'The fuzz? You didn't seem too keen to be seen when one of them walked past.'

'I...'

Andy leaned forward and put his hands out like a boxing trainer ready to soak up the punches.

'Don't say anything. I don't want to know. Better that way.'

He gave me a benevolent tap on the forearm.

'Anyway,' he added, 'if you want me to answer any questions you need two more of these. And some peanuts. Honey roasted.'

'So what's your question?' he asked when I got back.

'It's what you were saying about Mark Ryland.'

A faint look of unease crossed his face.

'Yeah, Saturday. So?'

'I wonder if you could tell me a bit more about the flat where he died.'

'The flat? What about it?'

'I was trying to remember if I'd been there. I was thinking about Mark after what you said but I just can't remember if I went to that particular flat. I mean it was the standard Victorian conversion wasn't it? Ground floor, sitting room, kitchen, a bedroom at the back. High ceilings.' It was the description in *Murder Unseen*.

'Sounds about right. But you could always check it out.'

'How?'

'Angell Entertainment still owns it. Stephen bought it when he was getting into the music business. It was somewhere he could put up new bands. I'm not sure what it's used for now. But it's much the same as it was, or at least it was the last time I was up in Camden. If you want to check it out, it's Angleford Road, number 27, first-floor flat on the left.'

'Right,' I said.

'If you can get in you can check if Mark's stash is still there. It will be under the doorjamb leading in to the main room, or that's where he always used to keep it. I wouldn't try it though. It'll be past its sell-by.'

'Hardly worth the trip then.'

'If you say so. Look, this trouble or whatever it is you're in, no, no I don't want to know any detail, but is there a woman in there as well? Don't answer that, I can see from your face.'

He shrugged his shoulders.

'I always wondered if that was the trouble with Mark.'

'Women?'

'That woman, the one I showed you the picture of. Are you sure you don't remember her?'

'I can't say one way or the other.'

'Your memory can't be that bad. If you'd met *her* you wouldn't forget. Maybe that was what it was about. I don't see why otherwise. He was on an up with the music. Maybe she tipped him back.'

'His mother always used to say it was an accident didn't she?'

'Well, she would, wouldn't she? Better an accident than suicide or murder. Closure, isn't that what they call it?'

'So where was Mark when you found him? Lying with his back on the floor?'

It was a reasonable proposition. He had been in *Murder Unseen*.

'Yeah, looked like he'd just taken a count of ten.'

'Pity he didn't leave a note or anything then we might have known for sure. Do you want another one of these?'

Andy considered the proposition for a moment and then nodded.

'One for the road,' he said.

When I got back he subjected me to a long appraising stare.

'Cheers,' I said.

'You're a smart cookie,' he said. 'I can see why you write detective stories. All that vague stuff doesn't fool me. You know there's something else don't you? So there was one other thing. Mark did have something in his hand, paper it looked like. I was tempted to look but I didn't. I didn't want to get any more involved than I already was. It's not good breaking into somewhere where there's a dead body. The fuzz don't take kindly to it and I wasn't their favourite anyway. The less you know the less you have to hide. So I left it.'

'So what do you think it was?'

'Your guess is as good as mine.'

Perhaps it was but then I didn't have to guess. In *Murder Unseen* Tom Travis had gently inserted the fake suicide note he had written into Rob's newly dead fingers.

My companion was looking at his watch, all gleaming metal beset with dials.

'There's one other thing,' I said. 'Fred St James, the bloke who found the body. You don't know if he said anything about any note do you?'

'You could ask him yourself. He spends most of his time on the Algarve. Big steel gates to his estate apparently. I've got a friend who lives near him. But he's here now. He comes over in the summer.'

'And you don't know where he lives when he's over, do you?'

'You're sure you want to meet him? He's getting a bit long in the tooth but he's not somebody for a dark night.'

'I'll try the hours of daylight.'

'Yeah, yeah, I'm sure you will. Anyway it's your funeral. When he's over he stays with his mum. She's in her eighties but she spoils him.'

'And you don't happen to know where she lives?'

'Oh I do,' Andy said. 'It's a council flat two roads along from here. Or it was a council flat. She got a discount. Fred bought it for her. I think he only did it as an investment and wanted her to move somewhere more upmarket. But she's still here.'

'Number?'

'Not sure about that but it's on the ground floor, first on the right through the arch, bit of garden outside, you can't miss it. Best of luck. I'll leave you to it.'

He drained his pint and put the empty glass on the table with a contented sigh. Then he sprang to his feet and walked out into the sunshine without a backward glance. For a moment I wondered why he was so eager to be gone.

TWENTY-FOUR

TUESDAY 1.30PM – 2.30PM

ANDY FONTAINE WAS RIGHT. Fred St James's mother's flat wasn't difficult to find. Even though I consciously took my time I managed to be there about five minutes after I left the White Hart. The block was a sturdy brick construction that had risen from the ground without benefit of ornamental detail. Climbing plants cascaded defiantly downwards from a top-floor balcony and an area beyond the railings had been turned into a small private garden.

The door was opened immediately I knocked by a small sprightly woman who looked me up and down. Then she called behind her.

'Fred, you've got a visitor.'

Fred St James was a foot or two taller than his mother and must have weighed about three times as much. He stood behind her, one enormous hand clasped on her shoulder. I wondered if he would recognise me from Stephen's lunch or whether I still had time to make some excuse and slip away.

'Yes,' he said.

I hadn't ever heard a single word imbued with quite such a degree of menace.

'I'm a friend of Stephen Angell,' I said. 'I happened to be passing and I wondered if I could have a word. I meant to speak to you at Sunday's lunch but there wasn't the time.'

Fred St James's expression dropped to the merely menacing and his mother managed to wriggle free from his protective grasp.

'Oh how nice,' she said. 'Frederick doesn't get many visitors. You must have some cake and I'll make a pot of tea, or coffee if you would prefer, or perhaps some squash.'

'Tea would be lovely.'

'I'll go and make it. Fred will take you into the garden room. Fred!'

St James grunted and then retreated a step or two, a gesture that was probably meant as some sort of greeting. Without averting his gaze he beckoned me to follow much like a spider trying to convince that its web isn't sticky. I felt myself being pulled in behind him.

The room that I was sucked into looked out onto the small patch of garden that I had seen from outside. A pair of wooden French windows with shutters, that looked as though they might actually have come from France, had replaced what had originally given light to the room. The walls were covered in an infinitely smooth decorative plaster, a pale muted pink with flecks of gold that had probably been done by an Italian, and the floor was adorned with a couple of Turkish rugs covering large tiles. There was a flat screen television in the corner and a sofa and a couple of armchairs around a coffee table that had a pile of books on it. A large lamp on top of a small wooden cabinet completed the furnishings. It wasn't entirely what I had been expecting.

'It's under-floor heating,' St James said in response to a question I hadn't asked. 'It makes best use of the space. It's too cramped otherwise. But she didn't want to move. Take a seat.'

I sat down on one end of the sofa.

'Very pleasant.'

'It's modelled on a room in the villa. Mum liked it so I sorted this out. You're a friend of Stephen are you?'

'Old college chum. Known him for thirty years.'

'Don't remember you.'

'Our paths may not have crossed recently but I was at the lunch on Sunday. You were…'

'OK, OK. What do you want?'

'It's about Mark Ryland.'

'What about Mark?'

I should have dawdled a bit more on the journey from the White Hart to get my thoughts into order. I wasn't sure quite sure how blunt I should be. Luckily I was interrupted by Mrs St James's appearance, or perhaps she was simply Mrs James.

'Talking about the old days are we? That's nice. I've always said to Frederick that he should invite more of his friends round. He always says he doesn't want to give me trouble but it's no trouble at all. Now Mr…?'

'Knight, David Knight.'

'Now David, what will you have? This is date and walnut but there's some Battenberg outside if you'd prefer that, or you might like both.'

'Well, um…'

'Betty.'

'Betty. This date and walnut looks delicious. In fact it's one of my favourites.'

'Oh good. Frederick, do get some plates! They're in the kitchen. And you can bring the tea through too. That tray is getting too heavy for me.'

St James got to his feet and, with a warning look in my direction, left the room.

'He's such a good boy but I worry about him.'

I felt the feathery touch of her fingers on my arm.

'He's never really found the right girl. Two marriages and no children. It wasn't what I was expecting. I wonder who is going to look after him when he's older. Perhaps there's still time for him to find someone.'

'I'm sure there must be. He's very eligible.'

'Do you think so?'

'Of course. I wouldn't worry.'

St James came back into the room with a tray on which there was a teapot, cups, a milk jug, sugar bowl, plates, napkins and cake forks.

Betty got to her feet.

'I'll leave you boys to chat. I'm so pleased to have met you David, I didn't know Frederick had such nice friends.'

'So,' St James said menacingly when the door closed behind her, 'do you take milk?'

'Just a dash, no sugar, and I'd love some cake. Thanks.'

I ate a mouthful of cake, took a sip of tea, and decided I couldn't put the moment off any longer.

'You found Mark Ryland's body didn't you?'

'That was a long time ago.'

'I wonder when you found Mark did you notice whether he had left a note of any sort? Perhaps it was in his hand or somewhere in the room?'

'I told the coroner everything.'

I didn't feel I was doing too well. St James might

have started by answering a question I hadn't asked, but now he didn't seem able to give a straight answer to a direct question.

'I do understand that there might have been people to protect before – his mother for example. But she's dead now. It doesn't really matter if there was evidence that he committed suicide does it?'

'I've nothing to add.'

'I thought you might, well, have acted for the best at the time. I mean there could have been a note that, say, you might have read or given to someone and then you might have decided that it would only cause distress if it was made public. I'm sure that was the right decision at the time but events move on. If there was a suicide note I'd very much like to know, in confidence of course.'

'I've told you, I've nothing to add to what I said to the coroner.'

'That there wasn't a note.'

'It's a matter of public record.'

'I know but I thought you might wish to reconsider, give some sort of indication.'

'I've nothing to say.'

'So you are definitely saying that there wasn't a note?'

'I'm saying I've got nothing to say.'

I looked at St James. His features were set. He might have been a statue.

'Fair enough,' I said.

Betty arrived after another ten minutes of unexceptional conversation to urge me to consume more cake and, when I said I was full up, to find me a bag so I could take some home.

TWENTY-FIVE

TUESDAY 2.30PM – 3.30PM

I COULDN'T WORK OUT WHETHER what I had been left with was a loose end or a dead end. When I had set out from the White Hart Andy Fontaine's information had seemed a promising lead, the sort of thing that Tom Travis would consider to be a key clue. The only thing I could be certain about was the fictional reference in *Murder Unseen* to a faked suicide note. But I couldn't see any reason why Andy would lie about seeing something in Mark's hand. Which got me to St James. It was clear that nothing was going to persuade him to say anything at all. He was a locked box to which, short of kidnapping his mother, I had no key.

If Andy's information about St James's whereabouts hadn't proved quite as profitable a lead as I had hoped, there was always his other suggestion that I might check out Mark's old flat to see what I could find. It might also prompt my memory to come out of hibernation. I did, however, need somebody who would have some idea of how to get in. Luckily there was an obvious candidate to hand – Jerry.

He was in the annexe.

'I've been thinking about Peter Parchment,' he said before I could introduce the subject of the best way of doing some breaking and entering. 'The fact that he's convinced he's Perdita's father. He certainly seems to have been having an affair with her mother but that's hardly conclusive.'

'So you think there's some sort of love triangle?'

'It has been known to happen,' Jerry said. 'Actually even if you hadn't suffered memory loss you might not know the truth of the matter. *It's a wise child that knows its own father* and all that. So Peter's assumptions, even if they are founded in fact, could be entirely wrong. It's a strange business being a woman involved with two men. In purely monandrous situations for example...'

'*Monandrous*? I did do Eng Lit Jerry but even so.'

'Only having one lover in the same period of time then. Actually it really means only having one husband at a time. Anyway the point to remember is that a woman who is only having a sexual relationship with one man retains fewer of his sperm but during periods of infidelity the woman's orgasm pattern is changed. What happens is that the sperm from the additional lover are favoured for retention in greater numbers raising the chances of the lover's success, as opposed to the husband.'

I would have bet money on Jerry not being able to surprise me. I still suffered an odd jolt when I realised how much technical knowledge he had on any piece of kit he possessed, but I had always thought he was like Sherlock Holmes with immense knowledge of some subjects like cigar ash composition, or, in Jerry's case any gadget known to man, but with no knowledge at all of other swathes of learning. Now it seemed he was also an encyclopaedic reference point on human insemination and its chances of success.

'That's all very well,' I said, 'but the situation with Jane Reddon isn't exactly that is it? It's not a new male intruding on some long established relationship that has lasted years and being favoured by a new orgasmic excitement from the woman concerned is it? Is that the mechanism by the way? More sperm are retained the more satisfying the orgasm achieved? I suppose then a new lover could invade the territory of an old lover and be better received as it were. And you would argue that that situation is analogous to what we've got here, so that Peter is the husband figure and someone else is the new, and favoured, lover.'

'I wouldn't argue anything. You seem to have done it for me. The point is that it would enhance your chances of being Perdita's father. Unconscious motives are important here. Why do you think people get together on the rebound? There's an unconscious fear that they are already pregnant. They want to give themselves a better chance. If they take a lover the chances are that the first sperm will be knocked out of the way.'

'So are you saying that was why Jane wanted to leave the party with me. I'm part of some cosmic war involving millions.'

'You could be.'

'Whether that's true or not I'd just like to be able to remember whether I had slept with her or not. I might not know anything about her motivations, or my motivations, or whether I was the father of Perdita but I would at least know that there was the possibility that I was the father because I had been in bed with her. If I didn't go to bed with her that possibility doesn't arise. Not that I understand what we're talking about.'

'You, Jane, and Peter Parchment,' Jerry said insistently. 'Or if you don't think it can be Peter, you and another. Or if you don't think it can be you or Peter, some other lover.'

'I don't mean that. All this sperm behaviour stuff you've been trotting out. You're not an expert on living things Jerry. You're an expert on hardware. There's no reason why you should know all this. It's not like you.'

'Not like me! You haven't a clue have you David? You don't know what it's like to want children do you? You don't even know how many you have. I imagine apoptosis works perfectly for you doesn't it?'

'Apoptosis?'

'Cell death,' Jerry said witheringly. 'It's programmed into the body. All our cells have a built-in mechanism for suicide when they have divided too many times or some defect appears. You have a lot of specialised machinery built in to ensure a cell can kill itself. It's part of the overall programme and it's essential to keep sperm fit for purpose. Faith and I have been going to a clinic. The whole process is hellishly complicated. You need to create optimum conditions. They thought a new environment for the sperm was needed. Your chances get better if you abandon the normal routines.'

The normal routines? Optimum conditions?

'You don't mean? I mean...Look Jerry, I came round early last Saturday morning. I wanted to talk about Perdita. I thought you'd be up so I came in through the garden and then I thought you were, well...'

'Faith knows all about it,' Jerry said firmly.

'She does?'

'Of course she does.'

'And approves?'

'She suggested it.'

'She did?'

'I've just said so.'

'Fine, fine, that explains it. I was worried for you both. You've always seemed to be so together.'

'You didn't mention it.'

'There didn't seem to be an opportunity. I mean I have had other matters preoccupying me – a long-lost daughter turning up, a possible murder charge.'

'I suppose so,' Jerry said reluctantly.

'To be fair I am under a bit of stress Jerry but even if I wasn't the natural assumption would be, well, recapturing youth and all that. I mean maybe if there had been some other indication that this was some sort of therapy.'

'It's not a therapy,' Jerry said. 'It's an optimum procedure based on scientific evidence. Obviously Faith couldn't do it so it has to be me. But we're certain that we'll improve our chances if my sperm have been exercising so to speak. Next Saturday is the optimum time. But we need to be more like strangers for the greatest chance of success. That's why we're not speaking until it's done. We thought it was going to happen after a couple of years of birth control and when we'd got the house straight but it didn't even though both of Faith's younger sisters had children. We've tried everything and there's no knockout reason why we can't have children. And then Faith saw what it was. We've got too cosy for conception to work easily. In purely monogamous situations females reduce the number of sperm retained but during periods of infidelity they change their orgasm patterns to favour the sperm of the additional male.'

'I'm not sure I'm getting this quite. If you're talking about two men and one woman I can see how you can apply that to Jane Reddon and well...whoever. But for you and Faith it's two women and one man isn't it? I mean you're her husband aren't you and not the other man?'

'It should work both ways round. That's what we've planned. I mean a woman with a new lover always chooses to mate with him when she is close to ovulation. She doesn't know that is what she is doing but that is how it is. Faith and I have got that covered. Next Saturday is the peak moment and if we can condition our unconscious systems we've got our best chance.'

'So there's no role for a partner in all this, observing for instance?' I asked.

I should have kept silent. The colour in Jerry's face was rising to an unhealthy shade of red.

'What sort of world do you live in David?'

It was a good question. I didn't know.

TWENTY-SIX

TUESDAY 8.30PM – 10.30PM

'SO YOU THINK I WOULD do it with Faith as an observer do you?' Jerry said belligerently.

'I told you I saw she was there. I didn't know what to think. We must have been through this a hundred times now. Mind that van.'

'I can't believe you could think that.'

'I didn't say I did think that. I didn't know what to think. Those lights were red weren't they?'

'I don't care what colour they were,' Jerry said. 'What I care about is that this happened three days ago and you didn't tell me Faith was there.'

'If you're in this together Faith could have told you she was there.'

'I've told you we can't speak until Saturday. It's the optimum time for conception.'

'I wasn't to know that. Look we've never really talked about affairs have we? I'm sure some men do but it's never come up between us. I suppose I jumped to the obvious conclusion. I thought you would tell me if you wanted to.

There are speed cameras along here by the way – with film in them. If you could slow down I could find the turning.'

'You can put that map down,' Jerry said, tapping his sat nav with one hand and gesticulating with the other, 'this is accurate to six inches.'

'I don't see the damage anyway,' I ventured. 'If Faith believed what I said then I wouldn't have seen you and you wouldn't have anything to cover up.'

'We haven't got anything to cover up in the first place.'

'I agree you haven't, of course that's right. I shouldn't have been in the garden at that time in the morning but if you had been a little more discreet there wouldn't have been a problem would there?'

'Meaning?'

'I wouldn't have been able to see anything that was happening in an upstairs bedroom for example.'

'I couldn't use one of the main bedrooms could I?'

'Yes,' I said quickly, 'I can see that. It's clear when you spell it out. Look it's getting a bit murky. We could do with some lights.'

'You don't believe me do you?'

'Of course I do now you've explained it. I can see one needs to go to considerable trouble, particularly when one is older, not that you and Faith are particularly old of course, not these days. Do you think that bus is going to stop?'

'You've never liked Faith,' Jerry said.

'That's not true. I just don't know her very well. But there's an obvious explanation for all this.'

'Which is?'

'You said Faith was anxious that you wouldn't be able to go through with this...er...tryst?'

'We're not lovers.'

'Assignation then, no that's too personal a way of putting it, I can see that from your expression, appointment perhaps.'

Jerry grunted as though I might be approaching something he could accept.

'Well then, it's obvious. You probably need to avoid that cyclist though. Faith was concerned that you wouldn't be able to go through with it but didn't want to put you under any pressure. She knew she couldn't contact you before next Saturday but didn't want to put herself under any stress by wondering whether it had happened or not so she thought she would make a discreet check. She recognises the strong bonds the two of you have and was concerned that you wouldn't be able to loosen them even for a moment. That's much the most likely explanation.'

Jerry didn't speak for a moment but the momentum of the car slowed and my heartbeat lessened.

'Probably right,' Jerry said after a few more seconds of deceleration. 'I'll park opposite shall I?'

Without waiting for any word from me he pulled the car sharply into the side of the road.

'Number 27 is over there,' he said.

'Great,' I said. 'Good time. But we're still a bit visible aren't we? Maybe we should wait until it gets dark.'

'If you're going to break in you need to be able to see what you're doing.'

'Good point again but we do need to balance that against being recognised. Give it five minutes, and then we can reconnoitre.'

'It's got a garden hasn't it? We should have brought the battledress. It makes you virtually invisible in vegetation.'

'Yes, good point again, my fault.'

Perhaps I shouldn't have taken up Jerry's offer to accompany me, or, having accepted it, felt obliged to confess all I knew about Faith and his early morning activities. However breaking and entering was likely to be far more Jerry's game than my own and Faith would probably have told him about my appearance in their back garden on her return. All in all there was a case, albeit a slim one, for saying it was probably better to have got it out of the way.

Jerry was looking at his watch again.

'You've had your five minutes. Shall we go?'

Number 27 Angleford Road was a large double-fronted house with a raised ground floor, basement below, two stories above, and a garden at the rear. It had been much the same in *Murder Unseen*.

We seemed to take forever to walk across the road. The house was glistening in the gradually dimming light as though it might be enchanted. 'So which is it?' Jerry asked.

'The flat that Mark was meant to be holed up in? Upper ground floor, the one on the left.'

'How do you know that?'

'It will be the same as in *Murder Unseen*.'

'If you say so,' Jerry said. 'Anyway we need to go through that first.'

'That' was a solid Victorian front door with stained glass panels. Jerry pushed against it.

'Commendably burglar proof,' he said. 'Not that there looks to be much to see,' he added taking a step back and peering through the bay window into Mark's flat. 'One thing for it.'

He pushed the doorbell.

'What are you doing?' I said. 'I didn't say I wanted to get in now.'

'You didn't say you didn't. Anyway leave it to me.'

The young woman who came to the door was dripping and dressed in a towel.

'You're not Geoffrey,' she said accusingly as Jerry took a step backwards.

'True enough,' Jerry said, 'but I need to get into 27C. Angell Industries want to spruce it up a bit and they've asked me and my mate here to give them a quote. As we're here is there anything you want doing?' He gestured towards me. 'Reginald is very good at papering and does a bit of carpentry as well. Cash of course.'

'It's a bit late isn't it?' the young woman said, wiping water out of her eye.

'Last call of the day,' Jerry said authoritatively. 'Look we won't be here long. We'll let ourselves out. Might be a bit of banging but we shouldn't be more than ten minutes or so.'

'You'd better come in then,' the woman said, rearranging her towel and moving backwards into her flat.

'Very kind of you,' Jerry said, peering unnecessarily after her retreating form.

'What are you up to?'

'She's not going to be in a great hurry to come out again is she? Time for us to get in.'

'And how are we going to do that?'

'It's only a Yale,' Jerry said. 'Give me a credit card. It'll take about thirty seconds.'

In the end it was more like a minute but only, Jerry maintained, as he tapped back the doorstop, because he had taken great care that nobody should be able to tell that the lock had been forced.

We stepped inside and I looked up at the ceiling.

'It's a conversion isn't it?'

'You can tell where the new walls have been put in,' Jerry said, switching the light on, 'look, you can see where the moulding stops.'

The flat in *Murder Unseen* had been carved out of an existing building. The front room where Mark and his alter ego, Rob, had died now had a slightly faded Persian carpet covering most of the floorboards. Other than that the room had a large leather sofa and armchair, an ageing television, a coffee table, and a plant-like object with spindly silver arms that turned out to be a lighting system.

'Shouldn't we turn the light off?'

'Do you want to attract attention?' Jerry said. 'Poking around in the dark would strike most people as pretty suspicious. Besides it's easier to look around if there's some light.'

A brief search revealed a bathroom that had been recently refurbished, the grout down the side of the bath white and untouched by mould, the sink gleaming and clean. The kitchen was slightly older but perfectly serviceable.

'It doesn't look as though this place has been used for some time,' Jerry said. 'There's no food at all, not even pepper and salt, nothing.'

The bedroom at the back had a bed with a mattress, an old wooden wardrobe, and a chair. The wardrobe doors were stiff and I had to pull hard to get them open. A couple of wire coat hangers, fearful of asphyxiation, started an involved dance of gratitude but they were the wardrobe's only occupants.

'They look like they're preparing to sell this place,' Jerry said. 'You need to get on to your friend Stephen and find out what's going on. And we ought to finish off what we came to do. If I'm not mistaken it's here.'

Jerry was pointing to a short floorboard under the doorjamb that had been screwed down.

'You wouldn't screw it down would you? Doesn't make for ease of access does it?'

'Depends how permanent a hiding place you want. Besides this has been fixed up. There don't seem to be any loose floorboards in here. Somebody has done a bit of refurbishing recently. Still it won't take long to get this one up.'

Jerry had a small cylindrical object in his hand into which he was inserting a screw head from a selection in the bottom of the object. He gave a grunt of satisfaction.

'Mini drill,' he said, 'Korean. Magnetic bit. Best on the market by a long way. There, see what I mean.'

Jerry placed the four screws he had extracted to one side. They looked shiny and untroubled by the passage of time.

'Brilliant,' I said. 'Clever of you to think of bringing that.'

'I always carry it,' Jerry said. 'Basic kit. Why don't you do the honours?'

Despite the screws being removed the small section of floorboard was tightly jammed against its fellows and it was difficult to get any grip on it.

'Here,' Jerry said. 'Use this.'

'This' was a long thin blade that slid between the floor-boards without difficulty.

'Clever,' I said.

'B & Q.'

'Right.'

I eased the floorboard out. I didn't know what to expect but I sensed that Andy Fontaine hadn't simply sent me on a wild goose chase in search of a long-lost stash of something illegal. There had been more to it than that. There also had to be more to it than that because this was the scene of the crime in *Murder Unseen*. But what had I got? Dust and some screws. What had I been expecting – a suicide note?

'Well?' Jerry said.

'Nothing.'

'Let me look.'

I would have put a reasonable amount of money on Jerry not having a torch with him. I couldn't see where he could possibly store any additional implements about his person. On this occasion it seemed that there was a hidden pocket in the side of his trousers. There was a mirror attachment with the torch as well that I hadn't seen before.

'I think you'll find,' Jerry said after a moment, 'there is something. I need to reach along. Yep. Here, you can take it.'

He handed me a small blue velvet bag with a hard oblong shape inside it. Then he lowered the torch with its mirror attachment back under the floorboards.

'And this,' he said. 'Clever, you wouldn't know there was anything there unless you were conducting a thorough search.'

The second object was a leather pouch with something round inside it that was about the size of a golf ball. Jerry put the floorboard back in place and re-inserted the screws.

'Good as new. No one would ever know. Aren't you going to see what we've got?'

'I think we ought to leave,' I said. 'We could have been followed.'

'Not at the speed I was going.'

'Maybe not,' I said remembering the two sets of newly changed red lights that Jerry had insisted on driving across. 'But I want to get out of here. We can look at these later.'

'Fair enough.'

Jerry suggested that the least suspicious course of action would be to bang the front door shut but I insisted on closing it gently behind us. The woman with the towel didn't reappear and deep shadows were gathering as we walked down the front steps and back across the road to the car. The street light next to the car was flickering into nightly life. Perhaps that was why we didn't see them until we were only a few feet away.

'Mr Knight,' DCI Addinson said, 'and surely this is your neighbour Mr Davis isn't it? This is an unexpected meeting. Might I ask you what you're doing in this part of town sir?'

'It's a free country,' I said.

'Indeed it is sir, and the price of keeping it free is eternal vigilance and, shall we say, co-operation between the country's citizens and the institutions and authorities that are needed to maintain the fabric of any modern state. I like to think that the Metropolitan Police is one of those authorities, and one that citizens can accord respect to. As it happens I'm about to visit 27 Angleford Road where Mr Ryland met his unfortunate end. Mr Angell kindly arranged for us to be provided with the appropriate keys. Police Constable Evans here is accompanying me. Number 27 Angleford Road is across the road here.'

'Is it?' Jerry said. He sounded bemused. It was impressive. For a moment I believed him myself.

'The thing is,' Jerry continued, 'I'm looking for a second

property to rent out. Don't trust the stock market any more or the banks. Mr Knight was helping me. I was saying to him that these houses are too large for what I had in mind and that we should go somewhere else.'

'That explains why you're here then,' Addinson said jocularly. 'Anyway I mustn't detain you any longer than is necessary. I mean people go about wasting police time but it seems to me that a lot of the time it's the other way round.'

'There is one thing,' I said.

'And what is that sir?'

'These murder rumours about Mark Ryland. Can you tell me anything more about them?'

'My information is that Mr Ryland was killed by one of his university, what shall we say, *colleagues*. I was going to say chums but that is hardly appropriate in the circumstances is it?'

'But I understood John Hazlitt was in Geneva the Saturday that Mark was killed. He can hardly be a suspect if he was out of the country can he?'

'You can remember it was a Saturday then sir?'

'I don't remember as such. I found out it was a Saturday afterwards.'

'I'm grateful for the clarification sir. What was I saying? Oh yes, being abroad does have advantages in alibi terms, no question, but only if you can't get back to London easily. I mean there was no way Stephen Angell could have managed it, he was at a dinner at a college in Vermont that Saturday evening anyway. But flying in from Geneva wouldn't have posed anything like the same problem for Mr Hazlitt. And he did make several return trips that year, some of them no more than an overnight stay, so perhaps the picture isn't so clear for him. Anyway best of luck. It's very difficult to understand at the present time I imagine…'

'What is?' Jerry said.

'The property market. Knowing where prices are going to go up or down given the financial circumstances. I'm glad it's not a decision I'm faced with. Still I'm sure there are experts you can consult if you need to and it's not a matter of life and death is it? Goodnight sir.'

Addinson crossed the road.

'We'd better get out of here before he gets to the flat,' Jerry said. 'I haven't a clue what he's up to. Perhaps I didn't play that too well.'

'At least it got us out of the situation.'

'Short term,' Jerry said ruefully.

As the car drew away I experienced an overwhelming sense of relief that I was still free. I had had a horrible feeling that Addinson was going to arrest me there and then. He was toying with me, like a cat with a trapped bird. That was why he had been so forthcoming about John Hazlitt. But what had he got linking me with Mark that was concrete? Surely that was what he would need if he was going to get a conviction after so many years.

'Fingerprints,' Jerry said, 'our fingerprints are all over the flat. I've got some gloves that would have done the trick. I should have thought of that. I'm sorry David.'

'No,' I said, 'that's fine, everything is fine. I liked the property line. Good story to hold off Addinson while we work this out.'

'Right,' Jerry said unconvinced.

The lights we were approaching turned amber. Jerry braked hard.

'No point in cutting corners,' he said.

The traffic streamed across the junction in front of us.

'Glad you told me about Faith,' Jerry continued. 'Best to know I think.'

'I could have put it better.'

'That was always going to be difficult. Actually I did mean to ask you something.'

'Fire away.'

'Do you know you didn't murder Mark Ryland? I can't believe you could, or did, but from what you say Addinson and his sidekick certainly think you did, otherwise what precisely were they doing this evening? And if you can't remember anything that happened in that six-month period, and Mark was murdered right in the middle of it, you can't be absolutely certain that it wasn't you can you? I mean I don't for a moment think it could be you but it struck me that you weren't in a position to clear it up one way or another. If we're being totally straightforward with each other...'

Jerry's voice tailed off into silence. Something odd and darkly red edged across the junction ahead. It was a few seconds before I realised it was a London bus.

I should have replied but instead I stayed silent. What Jerry had said wasn't completely true. The six months of my life that I thought had been cut off weren't totally beyond reach. Some memory of Jane Reddon had been offered up from the black depths and incorporated into my dreams. The photograph that Andy Fontaine had produced had triggered some area in my conscious mind and a little door into one small part of the dark period had opened. So there was one thing I did recollect. And now I realised that it wasn't just one thing but another as well. I had been to 27 Angleford Road sometime in the past. It wasn't the inside of the building that I remembered. That had been clad in new paint and varnish anyway. It was the outside. Although the tree was larger than it had been the outside was unmistakeable. I had stood outside number 27 before. I could see my hand reaching for the doorbell. That hadn't changed, a white button surrounded by a wooden moulding that looked like a miniature beehive seen from above. My finger had pressed that white button in the past. There was something else I was sure about. It hadn't been a happy moment.

'You're right not to answer,' Jerry said. 'It's the only response. I shouldn't have asked the question. I'm sorry. It's not even worth thinking about.'

I muttered something that might have sounded like agreement but I was hardly listening. There was another memory that had been triggered that was engulfing me. I had blood on my hands. It had been bright red. I had tried to wash it off in a dirty grey sink but somehow it had clung to my fingers.

The lights in front of us turned green.

TWENTY-SEVEN

TUESDAY 11.00PM – WEDNESDAY 1.00AM

I TOOK A LONG LOOK at my face in the bathroom mirror. The bruising around my left eye from my collision with the ground the night before hadn't developed into anything and was already starting to fade. As far as I could see there was nothing in my appearance to suggest that I might be a murderer. I bit my lip. A couple of times on the drive back from Angleford Road I had felt like telling Jerry that there were memories welling up inside me that I didn't think were dreams but events that had actually occurred. They were also accompanied by a strong sense of guilt. In the end I had resisted saying anything. A sense of guilt was an emotion that often crossed my mind, mostly for no apparent reason, and I was not inclined to convict myself, at least not on the present evidence, or at least not yet. I could hear Jerry moving about downstairs, growing restless. It was time to go down.

'There you are,' Jerry said when I got into the kitchen. 'What are you going to do with them?'

The blue velvet bag and the leather pouch retrieved from under the floorboards at Mark's flat were lying in the middle of the table.

'We'd better open them.'

'That isn't a foolish move is it?' Jerry asked.

'How do you mean?'

'They could only do us for breaking and entering at the moment. If we open these does it make it any worse?'

'I can't see it makes much difference.'

'Right.' Jerry didn't sound altogether convinced. 'If you say so. We should go ahead then. Here are the gloves. Better late than never. No point in getting your prints all over illegal substances. Why don't you try the leather pouch first? The other one probably has the amitriptyline tablets in it – it's the right shape.'

Whatever was in the pouch had wax paper twisted round it. When I managed to pull the paper away I was confronted with a small brown ball with the colour and texture of an over-fried Scotch egg.

Jerry picked it up and sniffed it.

'It's opium,' he said. 'Probably Spanish in origin.'

'I won't ask how you know.'

Jerry looked offended but managed to restrain himself from launching into an explanation.

'I suppose we ought to keep it,' I said. 'It backs up our story.'

'I thought you said Andy Fontaine was going to deny that he had ever said anything to you.'

'It's his word against mine.'

'Normally I'd go for you,' Jerry said. 'But Addinson has just seen you, well, *leaving the scene of the crime*.'

'So? There's no proof there was any crime.'

'If there wasn't why would we happen to be in the area?'

'We were looking at property, you said so yourself.'

'Even I didn't believe that. Nor will Addinson if they check for fingerprints. You could be digging us into a hole.'

'It's only a significant hole because *you* broke in.'

'*You* suggested we go over to see what we could find.'

'*I* only wanted to look at the outside. And *I* wouldn't have done that if you hadn't introduced me to Andy.'

'*I* wouldn't have introduced you if *you* hadn't been burbling on about Mark Ryland. Anyway it's a result isn't it? Fontaine is nervous about some drugs he might have supplied twenty-five years ago? Really? Is that likely? Maybe he's got a guilty conscience instead.'

'Could that have killed Mark?' I pointed at the opium ball.

'It was amitriptyline pills in *Murder Unseen* wasn't it? Let's have a look at them.'

I felt inside the leather pouch.

'You're going to be disappointed.'

I put a cassette box on the table. The cassette came with a card that listed seven tracks on either side identified by the numbers one to fourteen. Jerry picked it up.

'Chrome. Good quality – looks fine. No mould or anything that I can see.'

'Have you got something we can play this on?'

'There's an old twin tape deck in my garage that would plug into your system somewhere but it would take a bit of digging out.'

'Tomorrow morning then?'

Jerry nodded. 'I could be over around about ten.'

'Perfect.'

When Jerry had left I felt a sense of relief. He had been subjecting me to searching glances ever since we had got back to the house. I took a deep breath. I knew I had been outside Mark's flat before. I had pressed the beehive bell before, I was certain about that. I remembered taking a step backwards and looking up at the entrance portico. Then the memory or dream or whatever it was cut out.

I looked at my watch. It was almost midnight. I walked up the stairs and into Iain's bedroom. Plastic planes were suspended from the ceiling looking for a spare inch of space to land. A half-completed model of a tank was next to the bed awaiting his return, its gun turret resting awkwardly to one side as though it might have just been disabled rather than being in the final stages of construction. I crossed into Oliver's room. A nearly complete set of Tom Travis novels had a position, if not pride of place, on a crowded bookshelf. I straightened the covers on the bed and propped the cricket bat against his desk.

Oliver had taken to asking me, on a more or less daily basis, whether I had had a good writing day. He had started the requests for information at pretty much the time that Kate had abandoned hers. I had initially answered with a policy of complete truthfulness but had taken to using less and less specific indications of progress as time wore on.

I went into the bathroom and found myself looking at the water gushing from the tap and swirling round the basin. I couldn't move. It was hypnotic. The memory was vivid. *I had been scrubbing dull blood from my hands in a sink that was grey with age and neglect*. The blood came in two instalments, the dull blood and then a much shorter sequence of bright red blood. I was kneeling by the body of a young woman. She was lying face down.

Then the picture faded. I turned the tap off and saw the water hurrying away.

I was tired, close to sleep. But when I lay on the bed I found that I was breathless and the inside of the house was humid and oppressive, full of leaden air. There was a sound outside. Jerry was on the landing, flicking sand from his jacket.

'Did you know the ancient Egyptian word for dream is *rswt* which means awakening?'

'No,' I said but when I went back to my room and lay on the bed I knew I couldn't sleep, so I went downstairs but Jerry had left.

I opened the front door and walked down the steps into the cooler night. I must have walked for ten minutes before I realised that I wasn't walking where I had intended but towards Clapham Junction. I thought of retracing my steps and starting again but instead I turned right at the traffic lights and walked up the hill. A young couple, arm in arm, came zigzagging toward me celebrating the start of their relationship. I pulled into a doorway to avoid them.

'Cab sir?'

It was a hopeful voice from somewhere behind me.

'No thanks,' I said.

I turned round and peered through a small hatch into a dingy office equipped with a telephone, a television showing a football match, a table and chair, and a mug of a steaming liquid held in a hand attached to a bulging arm. The arm, in turn, was attached to the ample form of a woman in a tight-fitting dress.

'I'm looking for...' I said and stopped. I didn't know who I was looking for. The woman didn't seem to share my doubts.

'He's upstairs. You need to go through that door there and up to the first floor. He's expecting you.'

'Is he?'

'He wasn't too pleased. You'd think they could have got it round the right way.'

'If you say so.'

The door pushed open to the touch. Ahead of me was a steep flight of wooden stairs. On the landing above were more doors. Behind one a warm golden light illuminated a name on the other side of an opaque glass panel. It was just possible to make it out:

ƧIVAЯT MOT

I knocked, rattling the glass. In response to an affirmative grunt I pushed the door open. The room seemed to be deserted. A desk lamp with a long giraffe-like neck cast a wide cone of light downwards onto the green leather surface of a large and battered wooden desk. On one side of the desk was a large pile of papers parcelled up into bundles. I leant forward. Someone had scrawled across a red cardboard file in large capital letters: CRUICKSHANK CASE VOL. 1.

'Are you the glass man?' a voice asked.

'No.'

My denial was greeted by a theatrical moan.

'I suppose it'll have to wait till tomorrow then.'

There were two further doors in the room, both open, but no sign of the owner of the voice that had greeted me. I looked at the files on the tables.

'They're all to do with the Cruickshank business if you're interested,' the voice continued. 'Personally I can't say that I am. Although I'm sure there is a clue in old man Cruickshank's cabin that I'm missing...'

A tall elegant figure was standing in the right doorway fitting cufflinks into a newly ironed white shirt that had flecks of silver in it.

'Cruickshank was an avid reader of detective stories wasn't he?' I found myself asking nervously.

'There was certainly one in his bedroom on the boat. It was a John Dickson Carr locked room mystery, so this could be a locked cabin mystery, which would mean there are only six possible suspects, the nephews and nieces on the boat at the time. The impossible thing about it of course was that none of them could have done it, not on what we know about how the murder was committed.'

'Don't you think it's most likely to have been Isabelle? She was the only one who had any idea what her uncle's art collection might be worth.'

My companion paused in his exposition and looked thoughtful. I was about to speak again but he held up a hand to stop me.

'Aren't you forgetting Rupert? He had money difficulties – motive. He was on the yacht – opportunity. He was on much worse terms with his uncle than the rest of them and had good reason to suppose that he might be cut out of any re-drafted will – motive squared. And you can't rule out any of the others either, particularly the twins who could have been acting together.'

'I don't...'

'No, no,' he said. 'Not another word. That's final. I don't need to talk about this. I need to think about it. What did you come here for anyway?'

'I may be on a murder charge.'

'Are you sure? I was hoping for something different from murder. I seem to attract it! But that's as may be. You'd better give me the facts. Do keep it as short as you can.'

I sketched in the circumstances surrounding Mark Ryland's death as quickly as I could.

'Is that it?'

'There's also a dream about a young woman but I know who she is now.'

I mumbled on for a few more sentences about memory and the past and found I was not making a great deal of sense. Finally I ground to a halt and my companion delivered his judgement.

'You're not the murdering type. Take my word for it. Is there anything else? I have another appointment.'

'Do I know her?'

'Am I that transparent?'

'A friend of mine mentioned she knew you. Rather an attractive woman. Julie Pearson.'

'You seem remarkably well informed but you're only half right. As it happens it isn't Julie. And I don't think she's mentioned you – Mr...?'

'Knight, David Knight.'

'No, I'm sure she hasn't.'

'No reason why she should.'

'I suppose not. Anyway it's not her.'

'My mistake, I'm sorry.'

'It's not a problem. Actually Claire is a Detective Sergeant in the Met. She'll be off her shift soon unless something has come up.'

His voice had mellowed. He was staring into a middle distance from which I was absent.

'She's really quite something. One of the Wiltshire Moriartys. No money left in the family but brilliant and beautiful. Can't think what she's doing in the police. Do you know her?'

'Doesn't ring a bell.'

He grunted in a mildly disapproving manner at my ignorance and retreated into the room behind him, emerging with a jacket. He looked me up and down and then transferred his attention to the door.

'Perhaps you could answer me one question?' he said. 'How can anyone put glass in a door the wrong way round? Why would anyone think I would want to sit here looking at my own name?'

'It's just a mistake.'

'Is it?'

'They were just looking at things the wrong way round.'

'Were they?'

He didn't seem convinced.

I found myself holding his arm, stopping him leaving.

'I have got another question. Do you know somebody called Rob Crane?'

'No.'

'Are you sure?'

'Absolutely certain. Never forget a name or a face,' Tom Travis said. 'But I've got to go – Claire will be waiting.'

TWENTY-EIGHT

WEDNESDAY 9.00AM – 9.30AM

I WOKE AFTER A FITFUL night's sleep feeling frayed at the edges, exhausted, and bad-tempered. I had hoped for illuminating dreams but none had come. I closed my eyes firmly but there was no warm and untroubled sleep to fall back into and eventually I gave up the effort as too exhausting, stumbled out of bed, dressed and got myself a cup of coffee.

There was a ring at the doorbell. I looked at my watch. It was just after nine, too early for Jerry. It was more likely that the police had decided to return to sample the second half of what I suspected they regarded as a fictional story. Or perhaps the arrest warrant they had for me had just been signed.

For a moment I hesitated. I looked out of the window but whoever it was at the door was hidden from view, ducking out of the rain. *The rain?* I hadn't noticed it was raining. It was the end of a heavy squall that must have been shaking against the house for the last few minutes.

I opened the door. Lorna Trevanian was looking over

her shoulder back down the road. For a moment she didn't seem to notice I was there. Then, as she turned to face me, the slightly wary look on her face was replaced by one of dislike. She was wiping her glasses, and the shoulders of her light mackintosh were dark with water.

'I wanted a word about Peter,' she announced.

'You'd better come in.'

She took a reluctant step across the doorway and left a trail of damp footprints down the hall.

'Let me take your coat,' I said. 'I can hang it here to dry.'

Lorna looked at me as though I might be a mugger on a dark night and took a step back to avoid my outstretched arm. I could see the lines of tiredness etched on her face. Only her eyes seemed to glitter with passion. She took off her coat but clung to her handbag like a drowning woman.

'Why don't you come into the kitchen?' I said to fill the silence. 'Coffee?'

She nodded with the warmth of someone about to be offered hemlock.

I busied myself making the coffee and tried to work out how forthcoming I should be in answering her questions about Peter and Jane Reddon.

'So what's this all about?' I said positively. 'How can I help?'

I picked up a mug of coffee in each hand and turned round.

Lorna's face was as tired and strained as normal but this time she was also shaking a little. The additional movement was explained by the gun she had in her hand that was pointed, albeit with a modicum of imprecision, in my direction. She might miss me altogether but it wasn't an outcome to rely on. The gun was a grey metal semi-automatic that was far too heavy for her. It was the sort of gun, Jerry would tell me, that kept on firing as long as you exerted pressure on the trigger. If the magazine was full she was likely to have fifteen or sixteen chances of killing me. In his cases Tom Travis had never yet been held at gunpoint. The real world seemed to offer a whole different level of threat.

'Could you put that down,' I said.

'You're all the same aren't you?'

It wasn't clear what particular sub-group she was referring to although it was evident that whatever group it was, it was one that was endangered. I also gathered I was a leading member.

'Probably we are,' I said in as conciliatory a tone as I could muster on the rising currents of anger and panic within me. 'But I really don't know what I'm being blamed for.'

'You don't get it do you? It's all a bit of a joke to you isn't it? All boys together?' She shook her head unbelievingly and her arm began to shake increasing her arc of fire by thirty degrees on either side. It was unnerving, like being in front of a drunken firing squad.

'Look, Lorna,' I said in as reasonable tones as I could muster. 'We may not always have seen eye to eye but some people don't. It's just one of those things. I've always been fond of Peter and we've met at parties but there never seems to have been the right moment to talk – that's my fault undoubtedly. We should have made time. We should have talked more in the past. In fact I'm sorry we didn't. We could have got over whatever misunderstanding this is. But really what is all this? You've always been Peter's chief support.'

'Crutch,' Lorna said.

The gun in her hand had stopped wavering from side to side but whatever conversation we were involved in, for whatever reason, wasn't going well. Perhaps she could tell that I was lying, or if not lying, perhaps not quite telling the truth. The truth was that I really couldn't stand her and had spent twenty-plus years avoiding her at parties confining myself to the odd civil word if she happened to appear while Peter and I were talking. She was a perfectly attractive woman, more so when she was younger, but I had never found myself attracted. I was normally perfectly happy to sign up to the nostrum that one should never come between a man and his wife, or to be more precise in Lorna's case, a wife and her man. But that was only an effective principle if one didn't see too much of the wife. If she had made her base a little way away from London and Stephen's parties – the Orkney Islands for example – the whole matter would have been much simpler and unpleasantness much easier to avoid. My view that Peter would have been better advised to marry someone with a sunnier temperament than Lorna wouldn't have been a problem at all.

'Buttress,' I said.

'Prop.'

She made it sound as though Peter would fall over without her. Perhaps he would. Perhaps I wasn't being realistic. He had always needed somebody to be there, dedicated to him. I remembered one night I had spent five hours listening to him speaking only to find out the following morning that he remembered nothing of what had happened or the subjects he had been pronouncing on.

'I don't get it,' I said. 'What is this all about, Lorna?'

I almost sounded angry, in fact I did sound angry. I wasn't at my best. The muzzle of the gun moved up towards my face and then down below my waist.

'Men,' she pronounced.

Although she seemed certain it didn't seem to me to be sufficient reason in itself for her to be here with me now – certainly not with a gun in her hand. I stretched out my arms a little, palms imploringly open, seeking more information but she interpreted my gesture more as one of fatalistic acceptance, to judge from the rather firmer aim she was taking.

It occurred to me that I ought to say something. It was hideously clear that there was more than an element of premeditation in her actions. You don't turn up at somebody's house with a gun in your handbag without some sort of plan in mind. What had she come here to do? It shouldn't be difficult to work out, if I could keep calm and ignore the icy feeling creeping up my body. Except that I wasn't feeling calm any more. I knew why she was here. She was here to kill me. Perhaps she simply thought of it as some sort of judicial despatch.

'This is about Peter isn't it?'

I had meant to sound sympathetic and convey a sense of a problem shared but it seemed to come out more as a challenge that she was fully prepared to embrace. The malevolence of the look on her face increased and there was a marked diminution of the swaying movement of the semi-automatic. Now it seemed to be aimed directly at me.

'You always stick together don't you? Peter sees you and then the next day he disappears completely, but you're not going to tell me where he is are you? Well you've got to tell me. He's ill.'

'I haven't seen him since he left with you yesterday.'

'I didn't ask you whether you'd seen him, I want to know where he is.'

'I don't know. Perhaps he's staying with friends...'

'I've checked everyone. He's not hiding, he's bolted.'

I'd always regarded the fact that my eyesight is good as an advantage. But I could see the knuckles of her fingers whitening as she increased the pressure on the trigger.

'I don't know what you're talking about,' I said desperately.

'Yes you do.'

'No I don't.'

'Yes you do.'

'No I...' I stopped. I didn't want to end my life in the middle of a pantomime exchange. It was too ridiculous.

'So where are they?' she said.

They? Who were they? I didn't know who *they* were.

'Who do you mean?'

I must have sounded mildly plausible. Lorna put the gun down and started rummaging in her bag but her eyes never left me. She put a photograph on the table and slid it across towards me. I was too far away from her and the gun to do anything decisive. I picked the photograph up.

Two young women had been photographed at a party. Jane Reddon was closer to the camera, hair in mid toss, as young and vital as she had ever been. Her companion was more restrained and diffident, eyes lowered, more aware of the intrusion of the camera as a threat, a little less willing to go with the moment.

Lorna hadn't aged well. The surface lines of concern that were just discernible in the photographs had become deeply etched around her eyes. The feelings of displacement and unease had become obsessions.

'You're not going to tell me you don't know who this is?'

'No.'

I thought there was a faint flicker of approval on her features, some recognition that I was co-operating at last, but perhaps I was misunderstanding what she had said. I didn't know why she couldn't ask straightforward questions. I needed to rule out any ambiguity.

'It's Jane Reddon,' I said.

Lorna nodded.

'So where are they?'

She raised the gun a little higher. It was pointing at me again, round about the chest. Her hand was steady. I wondered how good her knowledge of anatomy was and whether she was purposefully aiming for my heart.

'Who?'

'Jane and Peter.'

'I don't know.'

'You don't know where they are?'

'No idea. I don't know where she is. I don't know where Peter is. The last time I saw Peter he was with you. I don't remember the last time I saw Jane.'

It seemed there were quite a lot of things that I didn't know but I put those to one side for a moment. Why was Lorna so certain that *they* were Jane and Peter? And why was she so certain that I would know something about them?

'Jane and I were good friends once,' Lorna said. 'I worshipped her from the day she started with Angellic. She was hoping to stay in the UK. I used to tell her to look at the men in the room and pick out the one she wanted to marry. Then she could stay as long as she liked and trace her roots.'

'Her roots?' I said.

'I imagine you've forgotten everything about her,' Lorna said.

I felt like agreeing but I had recognised the photograph of Jane. Identifying her as the woman of my dreams had come from somewhere. Some part of me knew more than I did about what was going on.

'It seems you have,' Lorna continued. 'You might have made some effort to remember given her circumstances. Her mother died when she was born and her father got cancer. She was put into foster care when she was seven.'

'I don't understand...'

'Her parents had emigrated as newlyweds in the late Sixties. There was no family in Australia and there didn't seem to be much in England either but she remembered her father telling her that he and Jane's mother used to live in Exeter. She thought she might be able to track some of her relations down.'

'And did she?'

'She never told me. But after a time that didn't seem to be the priority it had been. She had got involved with someone. Seriously involved. She wouldn't say who it was so I thought maybe he was married. She seemed happy but then a few weeks after Christmas she disappeared. She was going on a trip somewhere and she said she'd call when she got back but I never saw her again.'

Lorna stopped talking. A shaft of sunlight entered the kitchen. The storm had passed. I noticed my arms were getting heavy from being held in the air and that my heart wasn't beating at quite the manic rate it had been a few seconds before.

I saw that the second hand on the clock on the wall was still ticking so time hadn't stopped as I might have supposed. I watched the hand crawl forward. I felt my shoulders begin to ache. I turned my attention from the clock to Lorna. I wondered what I could have done to create such animosity; I wondered what I should be feeling guilty about.

'It was you, wasn't it?' she said.

'I'm sorry,' I said. 'What did you say?'

'You were the man she was in love with weren't you? You were the man she was infatuated with. She might have had a mild fling with Peter but you were the man she was trembling over. That was what you were phoning Peter about wasn't it? Trying to find a mug to take the rap and look after this daughter who has just appeared.'

'I can't see...'

'Don't deny it. I saw the two of you.'

'When?'

'At Stephen's party. You were sneaking away with Jane. It was obvious what you were up to. If Stephen hadn't had those night-into-day fireworks that year you'd have got away unseen. You're not going to deny it are you?'

'No.'

First John Hazlitt and now Lorna. It would have passed Tom Travis's normal rules on reliable evidence – two witnesses with the same story and neither with a motive for not telling the truth. It was cast iron. I would have liked to share the experience. Then I could have remembered whatever it was that I had done that had so upset Lorna, or whether the feelings of guilt that I had always had about the period had a concrete cause.

But there was something wrong with the present as well as something wrong with the past. If you had a gun in your hand it wasn't your job to answer the questions. That was for the person you were aiming the gun at. Yet Lorna no longer seemed interested in extracting the truth from me. She had made up her mind that she wasn't going to get anything from me.

I could see her fingers whitening as she increased the pressure on the trigger of the gun. I don't know what she expected me to say or do. Perhaps the answer to that was nothing. It might even make the newspapers. *Crime novelist gunned down in kitchen.* Sales might soar. My new novel *Murder Unseen* could be finished by another hand, easy enough as it had been started by one, and published on the back of the publicity. This was ridiculous. I didn't want to die here. No, that wasn't right. I didn't want to die now. *Now* was the point. Not now. I hadn't prepared myself. My affairs were not in any sort of order at all. I wasn't even sure that Kate knew about the cash ISAs and my will no longer reflected my true wishes. Not now.

'It wasn't...' I said.

But I was too late. There was a terrifying roar as Lorna pulled the trigger. *Unusual death of local wordsmith*, I thought, coverage in the local paper, not a plug for anything, literary estate worthless. Why had I let Kate and the children go to the country without me? Not a question that there was too much time to dwell on. Then there was pain as I hit the floor.

TWENTY-NINE

WEDNESDAY 9.30AM – 10.00AM

'YOU'D PROBABLY THINK IT was something other than a bullet hole,' Jerry said.

'What about that one next to the dresser?' I said dabbing at the blood on my lip.

'That's a bit more obvious. It'll need filling. That's not a problem. I've got some stuff that you can colour match that sets in less than ten minutes. I can sort that out. You'd better check there aren't any spent cartridge cases anywhere. Other than that I can't see that there's a problem unless somebody heard the shots.'

'You thought it was a gun backfiring.'

'A car. I thought it was a car backfiring. Are you sure you don't want another brandy. You seem to be shaking.'

'I wonder why my blood isn't clotting. There's another drop on the floor.'

'Just hold the tissue against the skin,' Jerry said. 'You shouldn't be dabbing at it like that. You're just opening the wound. It's a neurotic gesture.'

'I've just dodged six bullets.'

'You fell over backwards and knocked yourself sense-less. There was no dodging involved as far as I can see and no aiming either. She thought the gun was a replica.'

'That didn't stop her pulling the trigger.'

'She was as surprised as you that she fired six bullets but that could easily be done in a panic – one bullet must have gone through that open window by the way as far as I can see – good job it was open otherwise you'd need a glazier.'

'Yes, that was lucky,' I said with as much irony as I could muster but Jerry seemed not to notice.

'And you could have had the television on loudly if any-body asks. An action film. That would explain the sound of shots.'

'Never mind about the sound of shots, how come she had a gun?'

'She found it this morning. She decided to tidy up while she waited for him to come back. This was in the bottom of a props box in the cellar. She thought it was something he had got for one of his shows. Now she thinks Peter's father must have given it to him. Apparently he was in the Special Boat Squadron.'

'Convenient,' I said as another drop of blood hit the floor.

Jerry had picked up the gun and was weighing it in his hands.

'What she says is plausible. He could have kept it as a souvenir. This sort of weapon was used by the...'

'It may have been,' I said, 'but I'm more interested in why she was aiming it at me.'

'She thinks you know where Peter and Jane Reddon are. Peter was talking in his sleep. The gist of it was that he was worrying about what to do about his newfound daughter.

Lorna never suspected there was anything between Peter and Jane. Now she's convinced that Jane Reddon has returned and that Peter wants to go off with her.'

There was the sound of movement upstairs, Lorna recovering, or at least getting to her feet.

'And she's pretty sure that you're helping him. More than that she seems to think you could be Perdita's father and could have murdered Jane.'

'If Peter has just admitted to being the father and is away seeing Jane that doesn't sound too plausible does it?'

'The facts are a bit difficult to square,' Jerry said reluctantly. 'But you do need a plan if people are prepared to come round and threaten you. At the moment it strikes me that you can't see the wood for the trees, or the trees for the wood.'

'Either would be helpful.'

'You could get the police involved.'

'I don't want to see Addinson. He already thinks I'm the prime suspect in this Mark Ryland murder business. The fact that somebody has just tried to shoot me…'

'I don't think she really meant to.'

'Whether she did or not that's what happened.'

'It was an accident.'

'Whether she's claiming she did it accidentally or otherwise won't convince Addinson that all this talk about Mark Ryland's murder is just so much fantasy, even if most of it seems to have been invented by Kate through that ridiculous proposal for *Murder Unseen* that she sent to my agent.'

'Do you really think this murder thing is all down to Kate?'

'It's the only explanation that makes sense.'

I was about to press Jerry for an alternative theory when I heard a footfall behind me. Lorna was in the kitchen doorway. For once she didn't have a suppressed scowl hovering around her features.

'I'm sorry,' she said. It was a reasonably graceful apology only weakened by the gesture she made, which seemed more to indicate the damage done to the kitchen rather than to me.

'You weren't to know that the gun was real,' Jerry said soothingly.

'No. I should never have brought it with me. And I should never have pulled the trigger whether it was a real gun or not.'

'It could have happened to anyone.'

Jerry probably knew hundreds of people with fathers in the services who had kept illegal guns to hide in their attics and cellars. With the equality agenda in full swing there were probably mothers with illegal weapons as well. I didn't know any of them, but then I didn't think it could have happened to anyone. More irritatingly both Lorna and Jerry were looking at me sympathetically.

'I suppose you could have lost your memory,' Lorna said slowly. She was looking me straight in the face, something I never remembered her doing before. Behind her Jerry was nodding encouragingly.

'I told Lorna about your amnesia.'

'Then I suppose I should show you the photograph that was sent to Peter.'

Lorna had it in her hand. There we are again, the five of us, with our varying degrees of attention to the camera and Peter partly hidden towards the back looking conspiratorial.

'It came with this.'

She handed me a sheet of paper. I unfolded it with a feeling of unease that quite swamped the previous giddiness that had been my prevailing physical emotion. Somebody, the same somebody who had raised the question of whether I was feeling guilty, had typed two words in an italic font in the middle of the page:

Feeling Funny?

It wasn't a benevolent question if you were stressing over your television comeback, and whether it made children and university students laugh.

'I think you said that Peter hadn't seen this?' Jerry prompted.

'I deal with all Peter's post,' Lorna said. 'He hasn't got time to do it. Besides he was never very organised about it even when we first got together. It's important that the children get replies and know why Chorley likes sherry trifle so much. It's basic marketing. I consult him on anything important but there are some things that it is better that he doesn't see. He needs to keep as calm as possible.'

'So you're sure he couldn't have seen this?'

Lorna nodded.

'Absolutely. Anything he knows about this comes from talking to you. And he's taken some pills. Otherwise he wouldn't be so confident about sorting everything out. He can't sort anything out at the moment. The film crew were hanging around in Hounslow yesterday afternoon. They don't know anything. He didn't even tell them he wasn't coming. He always does that whatever else happens. Something has happened. He was talking about you in his sleep. You must know something.'

Lorna's tone was becoming strident again. I wondered where Jerry had put the gun. Wherever it was, it wasn't far enough away.

'I haven't heard from Jane Reddon. I can't remember her at all.'

'There you are then,' Jerry said soothingly.

'Just a moment,' Lorna said. 'If you can't remember any-thing about the six months when Lorna was with Angellic, how did you recognise her in the photograph you showed to Peter?'

'I remembered her from a dream. I didn't know it was her until a photographer called Andy Fontaine showed me her picture.'

'So you dream about her, but you can't remember anything about her in real life?'

'I know it sounds strange but you have to trust me.'

Lorna looked doubtful. For once I had some sympathy with her. Mine wasn't the most plausible story I had ever heard.

'Conscious memories and dreams are on different wiring circuits in the brain,' Jerry said authoritatively. 'It's a bit more complicated than that but that's pretty much how it works.'

'I see,' Lorna said. 'But just because you can't remember anything it doesn't mean that you can't be the father of this girl, whatever she's called.'

'Perdita.'

'Perdita. That doesn't mean that you're not her father.'

'No, of course not,' I said.

'If you'd known you were the father you would have told Peter wouldn't you?'

'Of course but I simply don't know whether I am or not.'

Lorna was looking at the floor.

'It could be Peter. I knew there was something going on. I was away for a couple of weeks setting up a festival in Cornwall. It could have happened then. When I got back he was a bit like a deflated balloon. He said it was a gig where his new material had gone flat. It seemed reasonable enough and I left it at that. It never crossed my mind that it could be Jane.'

Lorna looked up. This time a watery smile was caressing her features.

'You will tell me if he contacts you won't you?'

'You'll be the first to know.'

'I'd better be going. He may be trying to phone the house.'

'Can I run you anywhere?' Jerry asked solicitously.

'No, no, I'll get the tube. It's the quickest way home.'

Outside the world to which Lorna was returning was sunny but she didn't seem to notice. I watched her walk away down the road and then went back to the kitchen. Jerry was looking out of the French windows into the garden.

'I didn't know you were an expert on the brain.'

'I'm not. I made it up.' Jerry gave a complacent shrug of his shoulders. 'We wouldn't have been able to convince her otherwise.'

'I'm not...' I said.

'What?'

'Oh nothing.'

But it wasn't nothing. My critical faculties might be blurred by Jerry's advocacy of a misunderstood woman and mild concussion but they hadn't been blunted altogether. There was something, probably a great deal of something, that Lorna wasn't telling us.

THIRTY

WEDNESDAY 10.05AM – 11.00AM

'I THOUGHT I WAS PRETTY good as the victim's friend,' Jerry said five minutes later putting a freshly brewed jug of coffee between us. 'It certainly got Lorna out of her shell.'

'Maybe her normal reserve was broken because I was on the floor moaning. Surely I'm the victim anyway? What do you have to do these days to put yourself into the category? She fired six bullets at me.'

'But not intentionally,' Jerry said. 'She was pointing what she thought was a toy gun at you and when she pulled the trigger she found it was a real one. Because it was a semi-automatic it didn't stop firing. It must have been a hell of a shock. I'm surprised she took it as well as she did.'

'What about me? It was a hell of a shock to me.'

'Not quite in the same league. You must have had at least a couple of minutes to prepare for it. When she started firing you probably found your predominant emotion was more relief than anything else. There wouldn't have been anything of the same intensity of shock of the unexpected.

She must have tremendous reserves of mental strength. I suspect that's the first time she has let her emotions about Peter show.'

'I knocked myself out.'

'I'm not sure you were totally unconscious. You went quiet for a bit but that gave me the chance to talk to Lorna. Anyway you've finally managed to stop bleeding. If you clean yourself up a bit nobody is going to notice.'

'I'll take your word for it.'

'You should have one of these biscuits,' Jerry said. 'I haven't had a chocolate finger in ages. There were some in the cupboard. Do have one. You're looking a bit pale. It'll get your blood sugar up.'

Jerry was trying to be helpful but his actions had just given me another problem to solve. I needed to replace the fingers before Kate got home to avoid her coming to the conclusion that I had abandoned my vow to give up chocolate until Christmas.

'Do you think Jane Reddon is behind this?' Jerry continued brightly. 'Maybe she doesn't like men. Perhaps you abandoned her, forcing her to get Perdita adopted. I mean, when I say you, I don't necessarily mean you *singular*, more you *plural*. Maybe you all let her down in some way. I was thinking about the messages you all got with the photographs. The ones to John Hazlitt and Stephen Angell are pretty much on the edge as well. *Feeling lucky?* Not if he was about to have his whole life wrecked by gambling debts. *Feeling wealthy?* Not if this American deal collapsed. *Feeling funny?* Not if the television deal didn't work out. *Feeling guilty?* Well, come to think of it, that's a little more pointed isn't it?'

'Or abstract.'

'If you say so,' Jerry said reluctantly. 'Anyway Peter is a strong runner in the fatherhood stakes by his own admission. Maybe you're off the hook.'

'I wouldn't bet on it.'

Jerry raised his eyebrows

'You'd better explain.'

'Perdita was born on the 5th of August. Using the usual nine months as a guide that takes us back to the 5th of November as the likeliest moment of conception.'

'That's rather too neat isn't it? Anyway that isn't right. The average length of conception is 280 days. That's 40 weeks. You're a week out. Besides the only thing that we know for certain is that you were seen leaving a party with a woman who happened to conceive a child around the same time. It's circumstantial evidence, if it's evidence at all. Peter Parchment must be the leading candidate. He's convinced Perdita is his child. He wants to take responsibility for her. It's really quite noble.'

'I'm not so sure.'

'Why for heaven's sake?'

'It's the timing.'

'What timing?'

'Lorna's trip to Cornwall.'

'What about it?'

'It was at the end of July.'

'So?'

'She was convinced that any affair had taken place when she was away and that it was over by the time she returned.'

'Could have been a final fling.'

'I don't think so. Peter couldn't have hidden it from her if she was around. She must have been away. Anything that happened with Jane is at least three months earlier than the date Perdita was conceived. Whatever was happening in Jane's life at that time had nothing to do with Peter.'

'So where is he?'

'Somewhere trying to summon up the courage to face Lorna I imagine. Look, I need to phone Kate. If she comes clean on this *Murder Unseen* business there's a chance that I can get Addinson off my back. Did you say you had the tape deck? We'd better find out what is on that cassette.'

'I'll get it. Back in fifteen minutes or so.'

When Jerry had gone I found my hands were shaking as I picked up the phone. Perhaps I should tuck into the chocolate fingers to get my blood sugar up.

'Kate?'

'David. You always seem to call when we're about to go off somewhere. How's the book darling? If it's not going too well why don't you come down for the rest of the week? The boys miss you. You can bring it with you if you like. There's a summerhouse in the garden – well more a shed actually, but it has got power. You could use that. You might find it relaxing to be seen practising your trade. I'm sure William and Anne would be sympathetic to your artistic needs.'

There was an edge to Kate's voice that suggested that William and Anne might easily exceed her own levels of support.

'Sounds very attractive,' I said as breezily as I could. I found my shoulders were shaking as well as my hands. 'But the book really is going very well except that something has cropped up that I need to ask you about. You remember you were talking to Debbie at the Christmas party. The thing is somebody has sent in an outline for a new Tom

Travis book to my agent.' I paused. 'Not unhelpful in some ways, but it's causing a bit of confusion. It was nothing to do with you was it?'

It was time for Kate to own up. Perhaps a wry laugh and some collapse of her position on the moral high ground that would pave the way for my news about the other concerns that had crowded in upon me since Friday evening.

'What are you talking about David?'

My stomach contracted. Kate hadn't spoken at once, that might have left some room for doubt. Here there was none. Kate hadn't had anything to do with the production of a new book. I couldn't think why I had ever imagined she could be the author in the first place. I stumbled on through some of the detail on *Murder Unseen* but it seemed fantastic even to me.

'Are you sure it isn't a misunderstanding?' Kate said after three or four minutes of torture. 'Or perhaps Debbie is trying to gee you up, or that assistant of hers, the one young enough to be your granddaughter – Angie isn't it? She's a bright girl. She might have done something. You're more than a bit late on delivering the book. They were worried enough six months ago. Debbie said you were in danger of losing your visibility and the more you do that the more it's going to be difficult to sell the new Tom Travis for anything approaching a reasonable amount. Perhaps this is their way of encouraging you to get a move on. Good for them if it is.'

I didn't feel well. I've never been very good at dealing with shock waves crashing through my brain. I wasn't sure that the floor below me wasn't going to give way. I had been walking on a surface that wasn't real.

'David? Are you still there?'

'Yes.'

'Look, darling, perhaps you need to get away from the book for a bit. Why don't you have a real break down in the country for a couple of days and then reassess where you are with Tom Travis. Then you can sort out whatever this is with Debbie and Angie. Do come. You could get here this evening.'

I couldn't work out what Kate was saying for a moment. Then I realised that it wasn't a breakdown in the country she was talking about but a break *down* in the country although perhaps she was nearer the truth than she knew.

'David?'

'I need to finish things off here.'

I wondered if I had got my sentence the right way round. Perhaps events would finish me off rather than the other way round.

'If you must,' Kate said in a resigned tone. 'Anyway Oliver wants to talk to you. Don't be too long. We've got to leave in five minutes.'

I would have said something more about messing things up and how sorry I was but Kate had gone.

'Dad,' Oliver was saying, 'you really do need to come. We can't get two decent sides for the cricket match without you.'

After some intensive negotiation overcoming Oliver's aversion to having a girl in his team I managed to organise two sides that were reasonably balanced. I could hear Kate calling in the background, unwilling to countenance further delay.

'I saw a woman reading one of your books on the beach Dad. She wasn't too old.'

'That's great.'

'I've got to go. Bye Dad.'

I got up and looked out of the window. Rain was beginning to sweep in again, rattling against the windowpanes, another unseasonable squall. Something was staring me in the face but all I could see was the outline of my head reflected in the glass, faint and insubstantial.

CHAPTER THIRTY-ONE

WEDNESDAY 11.55AM – 3.00PM

I WONDERED WHY I HAD been so certain that Kate had written *Murder Unseen*. For the tenth time in the hour since we spoke I lined up the other possible authors that made any sort of sense. Kate had admitted that my lack of progress on Tom Travis had been discussed at the Coles & Hunter Christmas party. That gave me three potential authors – Kate, Angie, and Debbie Hunter herself. But I had already ruled out Angie and it clearly wasn't Kate. And, if I was being realistic, it wasn't something that Debbie would have either the time or inclination to do herself. So the benevolent hypothesis for *Murder Unseen* – that the production of the book had been intended to get me to buck my ideas up in relation to Tom Travis – had disintegrated into dust. If that were the case then the unfortunate and unintended consequence of the book's production – that it was the source of the rumour that Mark Ryland had been murdered – was far less easy to deal with. If the book no longer had an identifiable author there was no one to parade in front of Addinson to demolish the edifice of suspicion that the book provided the foundations for.

It also cast the whole matter of the book's production and the motives surrounding it into a far murkier light. Perhaps whoever had written it had been attempting to bring a real crime to light. I swallowed hard. It was a convincing enough argument or, at least, better than anything else I could come up with. I needed another plausible suggestion on authorship to give to Addinson.

There was a sound in the doorway. Jerry had a silver cassette deck in his hands. The fifteen minutes he had promised had turned into more than an hour.

'Needed a bit of adjustment,' he said. 'I've checked it out and it's ready to run. It will play both sides automatically and then repeat until you stop. It's good for another twenty years at least. Dolby noise reduction of course and there's an unusual feature...'

'You can give me the full spec later. Do you want to hear this?'

He locked at his watch.

'Not for the moment. I need to get the battle kit in order.'

'Could you look one out for me? It might come in useful.'

'Good move,' he said enthusiastically. 'You look better by the way. You're only a bit pale. Did you say you expected Perdita back?'

'Sometime in the next hour or two.'

'Excellent,' he said for no particular reason I could discern. But he seemed happier on a full war footing. His father had served with the Gurkhas in the war-torn jungles of Borneo in the Sixties, an outstanding feat of arms that no one now seemed, according to Jerry, to know anything about. Jerry himself had wanted to join the regular army but for some reason had not been able to.

He plugged the deck into the rest of the system, tapped the metal casing and gave the deck a last appreciative look. I heard the back door close and then the only sound in the house was somebody breathing faster than normal who turned out to be me.

I pressed the play button and sank into the armchair. I didn't have another plan to hand or at least one that had any comprehensive approach to the growing list of problems that were affecting me. I needed to step back for a couple of minutes and let my unconscious mind mull them over.

I leant further back in the chair and closed my eyes. It took a bar or two for me to be distracted from my portfolio of pressing crises but not very much longer. I needed to know whether this was old material. But while it was indisputably Mark, these weren't songs that I had heard before. Andy Fontaine had been certain that Mark had been working actively on new songs and had had access to a recording studio. He was right. What I was listening to was the lost album.

His notes were different from everybody else's. It wasn't simply the way he played his guitar, or the strange tuning, it was that the music conjured up a world that was as far away as possible from the shiny mechanical clamour of the present. He was breathing summer into a quiet room lit with flecks of sunlight.

There was another element I hadn't encountered before. The music and Mark's words were no longer distant and recessed but advancing much closer than usual. It was a more acute yearning, a desire for the particular, the personal, something that might give happiness in the physical world, but that being physical and particular, might also be taken away. There was someone else in these songs. Two people together, falling together, being together. Mark had written a series of love songs.

There was just Mark and his guitar until right at the end of the second side there was something more, a woman's warm voice, and then silence. The tape reversed and the songs started again and it became a moment out of time until we got to the end again and the woman's voice. I don't remember how long I listened or how long the tape played backwards and forth but suddenly there was sound in the room breaking over the music, like a turbulent wave appearing on a calm sea.

'David!'

Jerry was in the doorway looking agitated. There was a note in his voice that I hadn't heard before. It was panic, unreasonable blood-curdling panic.

'We've got a problem.' Jerry gestured behind him.

'Which is?'

'It's Peter Parchment.'

'Peter? What about him?'

'He's dead. He's in the garden.'

'What do you mean dead? How can he be dead?'

'It's simple. He's been murdered.'

PART THREE

Wednesday (later),
Thursday,
Friday (early)

Appearance – noun – an act of becoming visible

THIRTY-TWO

WEDNESDAY 3.00PM – 4.00PM

JERRY WAS POINTING AT something halfway down the garden behind the raised vegetable bed. When I got to where he was standing I couldn't make out what I was looking at for a moment. A large animal was lying dead on the path. It was only when you blinked that you saw that the animal had a knife stuck in its back and that it wasn't an animal but a man in an animal costume. Peter had changed places with his sidekick and was dressed as Chorley the badger.

I bent down. Chorley's black and white striped head was hanging forlornly off the rest of the costume exposing Peter's face. His features were blank, already relaxed into a death mask. I swallowed hard but it didn't help. Peter was dead. The life that had intertwined chaotically with mine was over. I didn't understand. This wasn't another scrape to be extricated from, no sudden flight to take; just death in a suburban garden.

So why had he been killed? Why had somebody taken his life away? There was no sense in it at all. Peter didn't have enemies, didn't have an ounce of malice in his body. He just had problems. He always had had. But this was one mishap he wasn't going to be able to get out of.

I straightened up. I needed to breathe. Why would anyone want to murder him? And why do it in this mocking fashion? Then it struck me like an icy wave. There were answers to the questions that were swirling round my head. There was someone who could make sense of this. *Me*. Peter was here like this, dressed like this, because of *me*.

'It is Peter isn't it?'

I nodded.

'We ought to…' Jerry made abstract movements with his hands as though he was trying to sculpt a plan out of air.

Jerry might have no idea of what had happened and no idea what to do but I wasn't at such a disadvantage. Not that that made me any happier. If anything I felt worse. I knew why Peter was dressed in a Chorley costume and had a dagger in his back, although of course it shouldn't be a dagger but a kitchen knife with a black handle. I bent down over the body for a closer look. It was a kitchen knife with a black handle.

'We ought to call the police!' Jerry started his sentence again and this time managed to finish it.

'No, no, not now,' I hissed. 'And keep your voice down. We don't want to be overheard.'

I looked around. Calling the police would be easy. That was what I was meant to do. I was meant to let myself be sucked into a terminally compromising situation. But there might be a way out if only I could keep calm. The trees above the body were in full leaf blotting out the sky. Clematis was running riot against the fence competing for space with a rampant wild rose and endless shoots of ivy. I'd told Kate I would hack order back into the area when I'd finished the book but at least I could use one piece of inactivity to my benefit. As far as I could see this section of the garden wasn't overseen at all.

'But...' Jerry was shrugging his shoulders.

'There's something going on here,' I said firmly. 'I need to check a few things before we let anyone know what has happened – anyone at all. But we need to be careful. Have you got any, I don't know, rubber gloves?'

'White latex?'

'Perfect.'

Jerry gave me a look that hovered around the quizzical and then shrugged his shoulders. 'I've got some somewhere. I'll get them.' He looked at Peter's body and then nodded reluctantly. 'Good plan.'

In another moment he had gone. Tom Travis would have told me this was a crime scene and it wasn't good policy to touch the body. But then he wasn't the chief suspect in the cases he investigated. I knew I shouldn't deposit DNA and fingerprints everywhere but there were things I needed to know. I took another deep breath to stop myself retching and tried to hold the chill invading my body at bay. Then, with a muttered apology, I started undoing the Velcro fastenings on the fake animal fur.

Under the Chorley costume Peter was wearing a blue John Wayne cowboy shirt and casual black trousers. He had always liked John Wayne. But he would never have dressed as Chorley voluntarily. He had always maintained that dressing like his comic stooge would bring him bad luck. Chorley, he had been at pains to assure everyone, was as real as you or I.

I pulled Peter up and propped the top half of his body against the wooden side of the raised flowerbed. I could feel my heart pounding but I had to go on. The knife had been plunged in to Peter's back up to the black handle. I hadn't been too precise in my description in *Killing Spree* but it was an unmistakeable match.

Tom Travis's second outing after *Death of a Socialite* had seen him involved with a travelling theatre company putting on *A Midsummer Night's Dream* in Cornwall. The director, Julian, had been keen that his cast surrendered their personal identities to the collective good, ostensibly seeing the play as a revolutionary text. He had also been conscious that a breaking down of bourgeois constraint would help his own libidinous intentions. His plan for sexual conquest had additionally depended on a certain use of disguise. This had enabled him to achieve his objective, but his actions had also had the consequence that he had ended up stabbed on stage after filling in for the actor playing Bottom.

The early drafts of *Killing Spree* had an ass's head to disguise Julian's identity. But it hadn't been credible that even someone executing a spur-of-the-moment murder wouldn't have noticed that Bottom's lower body had changed from the rugged proportions of the intended victim into Julian's elegant frame. So full costume it had to be, Julian foolishly complicit in the arrangements for his own death, and in the end, as Tom had deduced, the apparently *wrong* victim was the *right* victim, or certainly the intended one.

It didn't take a genius to work out what was happening in front of me. It might be a badger's skin rather than that of an ass but Peter's death was a copy of Julian's. Fiction had become fact, albeit a slightly wobbly version, but near enough for any self-respecting Chief Inspector to notice, let alone a crime enthusiast like Addinson. Somebody out there didn't like me. No, that wasn't right. Somebody out there hated me. Suddenly I found it difficult to breathe and I could feel my heart beating faster.

Peter. I needed to focus on Peter and how he came to be here with a knife stuck in his back. I was sure of one thing. Whatever had happened to him had been deliberate. Addinson wasn't investigating rumours of murder any longer. This was a real one. I took another deep breath, not the sort of thing Tom Travis would do, and found a new noise was irritating me. It was the sound of grinding teeth – my own.

'Sorry Peter. Horrible habit. Really must get it under control. The trouble is that I'm in a bit of a scrape. You understand don't you? Don't quite know what to do. Can't run away exactly, nowhere to go. Just need to see what you've got.'

Peter's trouser pockets revealed a set of house keys, a wallet with credit cards, receipts, and a crumpled wad of banknotes, mostly twenties. There was also something else in his back pocket, a battered cardboard carton and a couple of pills left in their blister packing. The last time I had emptied Peter's pockets his medicine of choice had been ASSERTON tablets. Here he had apparently changed to Amitrip Plus 200 Mg, but that didn't surprise me. Peter and I knew that they weren't his pills of choice. These were the pills that Mark Ryland had overdosed on. I put them in my jacket pocket. Somebody had planted them on him. I needed to work out why.

There was a faint sound. I turned. Perdita was be-hind me, quite motionless. I didn't know how long she had been there and if she had seen me rifling through Peter's pockets.

'It's Peter Parchment. He's been murdered. It's horrible. I can't think how anyone could have done that or why anyone would want to kill him. I was looking for clues.'

I sounded anything but convincing but Perdita wasn't paying too much attention to what I was saying. As I watched a couple of tears ran unhurriedly down her face on parallel tracks, one from each of her eyes. As far as I could see they kept perfect pace with each other. She dabbed at her face and took a step forward.

'I ought to have a look.'

'Are you sure you want to? I mean I knew Peter. It's easier for me.'

'It's what I'm trained to do.'

She was taking a pair of gloves out of her handbag. They looked like the same form of white latex that Jerry had gone off to get. For once he was being upstaged. I wondered why he was taking so long. Perhaps even his immaculate logistic systems had collapsed under the strain.

Perdita wiped away her tears in an orderly manner and started examining Peter's body. After a minute or two she looked up. She was white-faced but otherwise calm.

'Have you called the police?'

'No.'

'There's something a bit odd. It would be good to get an expert medical view.'

'I don't think I can do that. I'm pretty sure I'm being framed. If Peter is found here I'm certain to be arrested.'

'Why?'

'I'm already a murder suspect according to the police. Peter's body just happens to be in my garden. He's been murdered in the same way that a character I invented was. You won't have heard of him but whoever did this had.'

'It's Julian Swift in *Killing Spree* isn't it? I read it last week. I suppose it is pretty similar.'

'It's more than that. It's pretty much identical, or as identical as DCI Addinson would need. We need to get Peter's body out of here.'

'What's that?' Jerry had finally returned brandishing a couple of pairs of white latex gloves produced from a canvas bag he was holding.

'Perdita and I were discussing what was the best thing to do with Peter. Although I can't understand how he got here in the first place.'

'Just a second,' Jerry said. 'Perhaps we know more than we think. I left your house about one o'clock. I went through the garden and out by the back gate. There was nothing here then. I found Peter at four. So his body was dumped in the garden sometime after one o'clock and before four. But maybe we can narrow it down further? You were in the house. Did you come out in the garden? Did you hear anything?'

'I can't help much. I remember starting to listen to the tape when you left but I dozed off. I was aware of it playing – it was on auto-reverse – but I don't remember anything much but the last few tracks and you coming in, Jerry.'

'So you were asleep most of the time?'

'I must have been.'

'You don't sleepwalk do you? People can do all sorts of things while they're sleepwalking can't they?'

'I'm sure they can Jerry, but I woke up with a stiff neck, not grime on my shoes or blood on my hands.'

Jerry was shifting from foot to foot. It was a habit he had, normally a sign that he was about to leap into action. Perhaps he was as anxious to move Peter's body as I was.

'We need to move him,' I said.

'All in good time David.'

'Time isn't on our side. What happens if Addinson and the police turn up?'

'I'm sure we can cope.' Jerry's was reaching inside the canvas bag. I wondered what he had brought with him. Something to throw over the body to hide it would be useful.

But what he took out of the bag was Lorna's automatic. That explained why he had been so long finding the gloves. I supposed it was sensible to hunt the automatic down especially if there was any chance of Addinson and his colleagues appearing but that didn't quite square with the fact that it was now aimed in my direction.

'You need to be careful with that Jerry. If Lorna is right it's got a faulty safety catch. You need to make sure it doesn't go off accidentally.'

'I know what I'm doing.'

'Well don't point it at me, or Perdita. It's an accident waiting to happen.'

The gun was steady enough in Jerry's grip. The only trouble was that it was still pointed directly at me.

'Jerry, I...'

'Please put your hands up David, above your head, and don't make any sudden movement.'

'Very funny Jerry.'

'This isn't a joke David. Hands up. We can end this farce now.'

THIRTY-THREE

WEDNESDAY 4.00PM – 4.30PM

'ARE YOU SERIOUS JERRY?'

'Just move back a bit David. Now take your jacket off and put it on the table and then put your hands up and move away.'

I did as I was told. Perdita was to my left, immobile. Jerry moved forward, picked up my jacket and examined the contents of the pockets. He pulled out the Amitrip packet.

'I took them from Peter.'

'He takes these pills does he?'

The truthful answer would be that I didn't think he did. In fact I would have bet money that he didn't. But that didn't seem to help me very much.

'Can I sit down?' I said. I gestured towards one of the garden chairs. 'Whatever we need to discuss we should be comfortable shouldn't we?'

It wasn't a bad option. I could see the reasonableness of the suggestion creeping into Jerry's soul.

'OK.' Jerry gestured toward the chair and I lowered myself into it, in as untroubled a manner as I could.

I was sure it was more difficult morally to shoot somebody sitting down, and, if that were the case, it must be even more difficult to shoot somebody sitting who is also relaxed.

'So.' I spread my hands expansively. 'Peter's dead. That's a shock for all of us. I was trying to find out what had happened. That's why I searched the body. The pills were in his trouser pocket. But what is this all about? Why are you holding a gun on me?'

'Somebody murdered Peter Parchment. You seem to be the prime suspect.'

'I'm being framed. This is a plot. In fact it's good news. I might have had some doubts as to what I had done in the past with my memory loss but that's not a worry any longer. I can't have done anything wrong because I'm being set up.'

'You'd better explain that.'

'Somebody is trying to implicate me in these murders. Mark Ryland dies of an overdose and suddenly I've written *Murder Unseen* in which Tom Travis, my alter ego, kills a character based on Mark by giving him an overdose. Peter's death has been arranged so that it mirrors the circumstances of Julian Swift's death in *Killing Spree*. Somebody is trying to suggest that when I murder someone I have to draw attention to it in a fictional way or that murders I commit are based on fictional ones that I have already created. Maybe they think they can convince me it's my subconscious wanting to draw attention to itself, or probably myself. Maybe they think they can convince me that I did do it and that secretly I want to be arrested.'

'That would be complicated even for one of your plots,' Jerry said. 'I don't believe a word of it. There's a far simpler explanation.'

'Which is?'

'One: you wrote *Murder Unseen*. Some strange ghost writer coming on the scene and being able to pull off your style and fool your agent isn't plausible.'

'I told you it could have been Kate.'

'I thought you said it wasn't Kate.'

'I'm not saying it was. I'm just saying it could have been.'

'And it could have been you.'

'Why would it be me?'

'Because you're involved in this up to your neck. These Amitrip pills you have. We've only got your word for it that you found them on Peter. Overdoses seem to be your chosen *modus operandi*.'

'But if I had killed Mark in that way and I wanted to announce it why on earth would I wait for twenty-five years?'

'Because you got hit by a hockey ball. You didn't remember what method you had used. You didn't even remember you had killed Mark. But now it's bubbling up in your subconscious and you need to face up to what you've done.'

'And dressing people in animal fur before killing them with kitchen knives is my way of doing it, is it?'

Jerry thought the point over and then nodded.

'You're right. If in doubt always take the simplest explanation that meets with the facts,' he pronounced seizing on Tom Travis's second favourite maxim. 'Now I think about it there's a simpler explanation of what all this is about. Peter heard the rumour that Mark Ryland was murdered. He discovered something that implicated you. You lured him here on the pretext that a face-to-face discussion would sort the matter out. He got here and you realised that he had conclusive evidence against you. So you knifed him.'

'Having a Chorley costume to hand I suppose?'

'That was a piece of improvisation. Peter and his film crew, one of them dressed as Chorley, have already been here. You had a policeman here searching for a giant rodent didn't you? I imagine whoever was playing Chorley dumped the costume to escape police attention. You found it and used it to disguise his body.'

'And why would I need to disguise his body?'

'You were moving it somewhere. You've already reported the existence of a giant rodent to the police. They're not going to turn out again for another wild goose chase. Besides I have access to the garden and you needed some explanation. If I was suspicious you could spin the *Killing Spree* story and maintain that you were being set up. Either way you had everything to gain by dressing Peter in a Chorley costume. You were just using what was to hand, to make something simple look complicated.'

'So I persuaded Peter to get into costume – something he would never have done – and then I knifed him. Is that likely?'

'The knife didn't kill him.' It was a new voice, Perdita's. 'There wasn't enough blood around the entry wound. In fact there was hardly any blood at all. He was dead when the knife was plunged into his back. He was also wearing the Chorley costume. The tear in the fabric is too small for the knife to have been pushed back out through the costume.'

'So what did kill him?' Jerry said tetchily.

'That's not quite so easy. It could be a seizure of some kind, or a heart attack, or poison.' Perdita seemed to be weighing the options as she mentioned them. In time I was sure she would have a charming bedside manner. Just at the moment I found it rather chilling.

'But don't you see,' I said, 'I'm being stitched up. Somebody has decided to make me the Clapham murderer. Peter's body was in my garden. The knife would call attention to the fact that a murder had taken place, imitating the method in *Killing Spree*. The post-mortem would then establish that Peter had died of something else.'

'Could it be an overdose of Amitrip pills that caused this?' Jerry interjected looking at Perdita.

She nodded. 'If he'd taken enough.'

'Then it would occur to Addinson that the administration of an overdose was my accepted way of killing, as in *Murder Unseen*.'

'Difficult to disagree with,' Jerry said. 'Particularly with the pills in your possession.'

'I got them from Peter's pocket.'

'So you say.'

'It's the truth.'

'It may be, but shouldn't we get back to the obvious?'

'Which is?'

'You killed him. Perhaps it was an accident. Perhaps you didn't mean to. But it was you who killed him.'

'I was asleep.'

'You were in the garden with Peter's body. The tablets had been administered. You had already disguised him in the Chorley costume. Then you realised I was likely to be back in the garden before you could complete the removal of the body. So you got a kitchen knife and stuck it in his back so you could fall back on the *Killing Spree* story. It fitted in with this farrago of some twisted criminal genius trying to get you to admit to a murder you couldn't remember committing. That's hardly likely is it?'

'I don't see what is so unlikely about it.'

'Somebody writes a book to frame you for Mark Ryland's murder, kills Peter, dresses him as Chorley, stabs him in the back with a kitchen knife, and then dumps him in your garden. Not to mention steals a photograph that only you can have and starts sending it out all over the place. Who is this person and why are they doing this? I thought you said it was Kate?'

'It's not her.'

'So who is this criminal mastermind who is after you?'

I couldn't think of an answer but then Jerry wasn't expecting one. I needed to cling on to the fact that I, at least, was sure I was being set up and wait for help to arrive, although where that help was coming from I was hard pressed to know.

'Case closed!' Jerry pronounced.

'I'm not sure that's right.' Perdita had a reasonable, balanced tone to her voice.

'Why not?'

'Well for one thing I don't believe that David can be a murderer.'

'I'm not sure that's going to stand up in a court of law,' Jerry said dismissively. 'So what's the other thing?'

'Peter has been dead for some time. Rigor mortis has set in and he's much the same temperature as his surroundings despite being in that costume. This sort of stiffness would take twelve hours or more to build up as he's been insulated. I mean I really don't know but I would say he's been dead for a minimum of twelve hours and possibly up to twice that. If I had to guess I'd say he died late last night, probably before midnight.'

THIRTY-FOUR

WEDNESDAY 4.30PM – 5.00PM

'SO?' JERRY'S VOICE HAD risen by an octave. The gun was now veering in irritated fashion between Perdita and myself.

'The point is that David has had at least twelve hours to dispose of Peter's body. It doesn't make much sense if he's done nothing for eleven and three-quarters of them and just improvised in the last fifteen minutes. Additionally if I'm right and Peter was killed yesterday evening David may have an alibi for that time.'

'He has,' Jerry said reluctantly after a moment. 'He was with me.'

'Can anyone but you vouch for that?'

'The police.'

'So?' Perdita said.

Jerry seemed inclined to continue to argue with himself but the gun in his hand completed its final irritated loop and he shrugged his shoulders.

'Jerry?'

'Put your hands down David, you look ridiculous.'

'That's hardly my fault. You don't expect one of your best friends to hold you up at gunpoint.'

'You could be in league with someone.' Jerry looked nervously at Perdita. 'What about all that other stuff that only you could have done but that you claim you know nothing about? What about the photograph? Charles Sotherby gave you six prints, and you have five left, so one of them is missing. That's the one the copies were made from. Yet you can't remember what happened to it. You don't remember commissioning the photograph. You can't even remember seeing it. This wasn't in your dark period or whatever you call it. Surely you can remember something.'

'As it happens I do remember doing something with Charles, but I can't remember what it was specifically. One thing I am sure about is that I've never seen that photograph before it arrived.'

'That's hard to believe.'

'It happens to be true.'

'I might be able to help on the photograph.'

Perdita had been shifting her glance between us like an anxious tennis referee waiting for a long-fought point to finish.

'So you saw David posting the copies of the missing print off did you?' Jerry said belligerently before she had time to speak further.

'No, but I do know who has the sixth print.'

'Who?'

'Peter Parchment.'

'How do you know that?' Jerry's voice registered disbelief.

'He had it in his house. I saw it when I was with Lorna.'

'That makes sense,' I found myself saying. 'I suspect Peter has had his print for thirty years. I think I gave it to him.'

Jerry looked apoplectic.

'That's convenient. You've just worked this out now have you?'

'My memory is coming back a bit. It's probably all these blows to the head I've suffered. The consultant said that could happen. The thing is I hadn't thought about Peter in connection with the photograph before. Suggesting the link has brought it all back. I can explain what happened.'

'This had better be good.'

I stumbled through the explanation a bit but managed to get out a fairly coherent account. Charles Sotherby had delivered the photographs to me thirty years before in the envelope that Jerry and I had found in the loft. He had put them in a letter holder I kept for incoming mail on the mantelpiece above the gas fire. I had opened the envelope but had been interrupted just as I was about to discover what its contents were. Peter had been at the door. Then John Hazlitt and Mark had arrived. Peter had asked if I minded if he took one as I had lots. I had agreed without realising what he was talking about. He must have tucked the flap of the envelope back in. When I got back I put it into a box to deal with later, and then never dealt with it at all. Although I've had it in my possession I'd never seen the photograph until it had arrived with Perdita.

Jerry accepted the explanation with a certain amount of reluctance. 'And the photograph and letters? Who sent those out?' He asked as I finished.

'I can answer that,' Perdita said as the silence was becoming threatening. 'Lorna sent them.'

'Why on earth would she do that?' Jerry said.

'There were things she knew about the photograph of the five of you. She told me that Peter had had it up in the flat in Hackney that they shared before they moved to their present house. Jane was round one evening when Peter was out. This was near the time she disappeared. She told Lorna that her love life had become complicated and she was pregnant and that she didn't know what was for the best. The one thing she was certain about was that she was going to have the baby and that she would never give it up. Lorna was trying to find out who was involved but all that Jane would say was that the father of her child was one of the men in the photograph but that it wasn't Peter. A week later she was gone and Lorna never saw her again.'

'So why was she telling you this?'

'We were talking about my mother. The Greens left me a note in the event of their deaths saying that I had been adopted. I think they meant to leave it at that. But that wasn't the only lead as to who my real parents might be. I was clearing out the wardrobe in their bedroom when I found a bag that was filled with clothes for a newborn baby – me I imagine. I was laying them out on the bed when I came across this.'

Perdita opened her handbag and pulled out the amber necklace that she had worn the first time I had seen her.

'It came with a box on the back of which someone had written a name and a telephone number. It wasn't my adopted mother's handwriting. The London codes had changed but it wasn't difficult to work out what the number should be. So I rang and asked for someone called Lorna. It was Lorna who answered the phone. When we met the next day she looked at my mother's necklace and at me and told me I was Jane Reddon's daughter. She also told me that one of the men in the photograph was my father.'

'But why send out the photographs and those notes? Why not just ask?'

Perdita looked sheepish. 'I'm sorry. I shouldn't have gone along with it but Lorna didn't think I would find out who my father was just by asking. She thought it was a boy's club that I was trying to break into, full of secrets. Then she said she had a plan. She would send out the photograph with cryptic messages to all of you. She wanted to create some tension, as if somebody already knew the truth of the matter. If I were to follow up quickly then I might be pushing at an open door if you had all been softened up. I didn't entirely like the idea but I went along with it. And now it's led to this.'

'You're hardly to blame.' Behind Perdita Jerry's features seemed to have been affected by some emollient anti-ageing cream. A similar expression had played on his face when he had been sympathising with Lorna after she had tried to shoot me. His hormonal problems with Faith seemed to be making his moods very changeable.

'So Peter never got a letter?' I said.

'No. Lorna wanted to keep him out of this as far as she could. She just made it up when you asked her, but by then everything had gone wrong.'

A Friend of your Mother – that was how Lorna had signed the letters. I supposed she had been a friend of Jane Reddon until she had found out that Peter had also not been immune. But when Jane Reddon had told her that Peter couldn't be the father of Perdita she had been telling the truth. He couldn't be, the timing was wrong. Whatever fling Jane might have had with Peter had finished at least two months before Perdita could have been conceived. My suspected liaison with Jane on the other hand, the exit from Stephen's fireworks party, was set to optimum timing and Lorna had been a witness to my apparently scurrilous departure. It was easy enough to see why I had become the villain in her eyes.

I wondered what had upset her most, the fact of Peter's continuing affection for Jane, or his obvious enthusiasm at being the father of a child. For a wild moment the thought that she might have killed Peter in some murderous act of revenge crossed my mind. But whoever had dressed him in a Chorley suit had acted in cold blood. Whoever had put him in the garden knew precisely what they were doing and the effect they were trying to create.

I looked at Perdita but she didn't meet my gaze. I had a feeling that there was something I hadn't got to the bottom of. Suddenly I could see the gun in Lorna's hand again. It was pointed at me, and the hand that was holding it was beginning to shake. There was some other reason for such hatred, not just Perdita and my apparent bad behaviour to Jane.

'So what does Lorna think happened to your mother?'

'She thinks she was murdered.'

'What?'

'My mother told her that she would never give me up. She was quite adamant about it. According to Lorna she wasn't a woman who changed her mind. And she never said goodbye to Lorna. She said she would and she always kept her word. But she didn't. She just disappeared and nobody heard of her again. So Lorna thinks she's dead. She thinks it must have been under suspicious circumstances because I disappeared as well.'

'People disappear all the time and for a thousand reasons,' Jerry said authoritatively. 'Jane changed her mind and decided it was better for you to be adopted. She didn't say goodbye to Lorna because she couldn't face her. Then she went back to Australia. It's much the most logical explanation.'

'I don't think that's right,' Perdita said. 'I don't know whether my mother was murdered or not. It's just that I'm sure she's dead. But I can't think about that now. We need to do something about Peter.'

'We can't just leave him here,' Jerry added. 'We need to find a place for him while we decide what to do. That's what you want isn't it David?'

Tom Travis wouldn't have hesitated. A plan would have sprung fully formed from his lips but then I would have spent some months preparing it on his behalf.

'We should cover him up at least. Move that black tarpaulin over him,' Jerry continued. He draped the material over Peter but looked unconvinced by his efforts. 'We could do with something else.'

'If you're not going to get the police or an ambulance it would be better if you could keep him as cold as possible,' Perdita said.

'That can be fixed,' Jerry said. 'But let's just cover him up properly first. I'll check if there is anything we can use out front.'

He returned ten seconds later empty-handed. He looked agitated.

'We're not going to have a chance to move the body.'

'Why not?'

'It's Addinson. He's walking down the road. He'll be here in a couple of minutes.'

'Then I'd better go and head him off.' I uttered the words with something of the insouciance Tom Travis would have mustered in a similar situation. In fact the lines probably came from one of the early novels.

'I should take those latex gloves off first,' Perdita said.

THIRTY-FIVE

WEDNESDAY 5.00PM – 5.30PM

BY THE TIME I HAD got the gloves off and walked round the side of the house through the garden gate Addinson was approaching the front door. Behind him, at the end of the road, was a police car.

'Mr Knight!' Addinson called when he saw me. I tried to look surprised.

'Are you coming to see me?'

'If you have a moment sir.'

'Always happy to help the police,' I said, 'particularly on such a pleasant day.'

'I'm sorry to have to trouble you again sir. But there are a few questions I need to ask. Could you spare me ten minutes?' Addinson was speaking jovially, inviting my confidence.

'Shall we go through to the garden?'

'Very agreeable sir. Why don't you lead on?'

As we entered the garden Jerry emerged from the French windows to the kitchen but there was no sign of Perdita.

'And Mr Davis.' Addinson sounded surprised. 'Good after-noon to you sir.'

'I'm on holiday,' Jerry said sharply.

'Of course you are, if you say you are, sir.' Addison seemed to add the *sir* as an optional extra. 'I thought you were looking at property yesterday but of course that isn't incompatible with you being on holiday. Not at all. Please excuse me going on like this. It's just an old policeman's habit of weighing statements one against the other to look for flaws. I just can't stop myself. Even my wife complains. I'm something of a dinosaur in that I'm afraid. It's not modern police work. It's very much the application of science on serious cases these days – a fingerprint here, a thread of DNA there. Then perhaps a bit of psychological profiling. I must say I do find that bit interesting. What motivates us? What makes us do things? Fascinating stuff. But you don't want to hear me rambling on about police work do you?' Addinson chuckled. 'I mustn't take your time sir. It is Mr Knight I've come to see.'

'I was thinking of making some tea,' Jerry said improbably. 'Would you care for a cup?'

'Thank you sir. Milk, one sugar. Nothing Chinese unless that's all you have.'

Addinson contemplated the wire mesh chairs and table that nestled invitingly enough on the patio. Jerry disappeared indoors.

'We try to keep the garden as leafy as possible and blot out the city,' I said. I was finding the expressions on his face difficult to read. It was like looking at some fast-moving weather map and trying to work out the probability of rain.

'Indeed you do sir,' Addinson said. 'It's certainly private here. And that was a very agreeable offer of refreshment. I imagine you and Mr Davis are close friends.'

It was half an observation and half a question.

'Friends and neighbours. I'm sure proximity has something to do with it. It's good to have somebody to share a pint with who doesn't live too far away.'

'It must be sir. I must say I've always found it difficult that nobody I know shares my enthusiasm for crime fiction. My wife will only read literary novels. She does sometimes ask me what I think when I finish a book but doesn't always wait for a reply.' Addinson permitted himself a rueful grin. 'Still we need to get to business.'

'Shall we go inside?'

Addinson contemplated the suggestion as though it were a particularly weighty philosophical proposition and then nodded.

In the kitchen Jerry was pouring water from a kettle into a teapot. Addinson engaged in some mild pleasantries while cups and saucers were produced and I wondered whether he would notice there was a bullet casing under the dresser. Curiously it didn't seem the greatest problem I had to face. I was confident a fairly straightforward lie about research for a new Tom Travis novel would do the trick. Gunplay in London didn't seem so improbable as it once had. Eventually Jerry made an excuse and left. Addinson waited for the kitchen door to close before he spoke again.

'It's about Mr Parchment.'

'What about him?'

'Do you know where he is?'

'No,' I said after a moment's consideration. 'Why do you ask?'

'I had some more questions for him sir. But he doesn't seem to be contactable at the moment.'

'That's rather alarming. I know his wife Lorna is worried. She was here earlier today but I thought, although I didn't like to say, that he might be avoiding her for some reason. But you may have talked to her already.'

'Indeed I have sir. I understand you told her that you don't know where Mr Parchment is. I just wondered if that was entirely correct. You might have some obligation to Mr Parchment that you felt you had to honour.'

'I really don't know anything that could be helpful. I'm sorry.'

'Not at all, sir.' Addinson was beaming. 'But, as I'm here, I do have another question. I'm still confused about why you would want to impersonate Mr Hazlitt.'

'As I said I was merely trying to avoid social embarrassment at Rainbridge Hall by the use of a harmless stratagem.'

'And you're sure about that are you sir?'

'Yes.'

Addinson didn't seem to share my certainty.

'And there's that CCTV footage at Coles & Hunter,' he continued, 'Rob Crane being the model for Mark Ryland.'

'It was a moment of hubris.'

'Hubris sir?'

Addinson seemed baffled.

'I mean Angie Bates was there. We all try and impress the young don't we? I mean she is an attractive young woman.'

'Oh, right sir. I thought for a moment you were talking about it in the Greek tragic sense – excessive pride and defiance of the gods.'

'Look,' I said, 'I admit that I may not have been totally straightforward in some matters.'

'I believe you sir, but of course that means I can't believe a lot of what you have already said.'

'I appreciate that's a difficulty but I can assure you I'll tell the truth from now on.'

'A new beginning?'

'If you want to put it like that.'

'So who do you think wrote *Murder Unseen*?'

'I'm not at all sure.'

'I thought you said you were convinced it was your wife sir?'

'I may have toyed with the idea but I was wrong.'

'You seem very clear about that now sir.'

'I am. I asked her.'

'And she said that she hadn't written *Murder Unseen*?'

'That was the gist of it.'

'So she couldn't have misunderstood what you were saying?'

'I'm clear she didn't write *Murder Unseen*.'

Addinson looked for a moment as though he was going to push the point further but seemed to change his mind.

'Well, that's fairly clear sir. And you don't know who else might have written it?'

'No.'

'And you're sure about that?'

'Yes.'

'That would seem to be that then.'

Addinson got to his feet and strolled out into the garden where he stopped and looked around.

'Very nice sir, and such pleasant surroundings. An English garden, what better place to look out on? One feels like strolling round it. But I must press on. I've got a team in Angleford Road, Mr Ryland's old flat. I need to find out if they've turned anything up. So I mustn't detain you any longer sir. Do thank Mr Davis for the tea. I'll see myself out.'

It was when I was breathing a sigh of relief that Addinson turned back. 'Oh there is something else. I had a report there was an incident here on Monday evening. Apparently there was a giant animal of some kind in the garden. I understand there was a complaint and a constable was sent round to investigate. It rather intrigued me sir. I wonder if I could check out where it might have been.'

Addison's tone might still be jovial but the last few minutes had only been a prelude to the main act. He knew perfectly well where Peter's body was.

I followed him down the garden path. I wondered if I could manage to echo his surprise when he pulled back the black tarpaulin. I thought I might. The fact that there was a body there wouldn't be a surprise to either of us. I wondered if I had any cards to play after that. In the past hour I had managed to coat Peter in liberal instalments of fingerprints and DNA. Whoever had planned this couldn't have hoped for more. Addison had been toying with me. Perhaps he had even wanted to offer me the chance to confess. Not that that mattered any longer. There was no way that I would be a free man once Peter's body was revealed. The next few hours wouldn't provide any respite either. Addinson's people would also have found my fingerprints at Angleford Road. I was finally stuck in the middle of the web with nowhere to go.

Addinson stopped to admire the garden. He was a couple of feet beyond the tarpaulin and didn't seem to be aware of it. But then, as though he had noticed something, he bent down and pulled the edge of the material back.

He gave an exclamation of surprise. It was curiously realistic.

I moved to his side and looked down. The insects were scrambling for cover in the unwelcome light but there was nothing else there. Or at least there was no body, and no Chorley costume.

Addinson turned to me. 'I would have thought it would have been here sir, if anywhere, but it seems to have gone.'

'There are other places in the garden if you want to check.'

'I don't think there is any need for that sir. I'm not sure I want to go in for a wild rodent chase. But if you happen to find it do let me know.'

THIRTY-SIX

WEDNESDAY 5.40PM – 6.30PM

'SO?' I SAID. 'DOES ANYONE know what's happening?'

I looked at Jerry and Jerry looked at Perdita.

'I thought I ought to move Peter's body,' Perdita said. 'So I dragged it through the gate at the bottom of the garden and into next door. You were being set up. I contributed to that by going along with Lorna's plan. I don't know whether it was the right thing to do.'

'Well, if you hadn't, I'd be trying to remember the name of my solicitor by now. But we'd better get it back. The relations with our neighbours are a little tense since the boys started playing cricket in the garden. Discovering a body in their garden could seriously damage them further. We need to put it somewhere safe and out of sight. The police could come back at any moment.'

'I'm pretty sure I've got the answer to that.' Jerry chimed in. 'You know the chest freezer that Faith didn't like, the light blue one.'

'The one with the bad karma? And the hideous colour? I thought you got rid of that.'

'It's at the back of the garage until I find a suitable recycling centre, or that's what I told Faith. It's got decades of life in it. It's German and far more reliable than anything on the market today. It would have been criminal to throw it away.'

'But what on earth would you use a freezer in a garage for?'

'That's not a bad question under normal circumstances but it does happen to be empty and it's six foot long. I've just turned the power back on. It won't take long to chill down.'

We both looked at Perdita.

'It's not a bad idea,' she said. 'But how long do you actually want to keep the body?'

'Not beyond Friday, say forty-eight hours. That should give me time to see if I can get anything out of Stephen and John. They're the only leads I've got left.'

'I'd better take a look at it then,' Perdita said.

'The garage door is open. Help yourself.'

Jerry watched her walk away. 'Resourceful. Did you notice she didn't need to ask where I lived?'

'She's been doing her homework on us.'

'So do you think she's told us everything now?'

'Pretty much. But neither of you has to go on with this. You should both pull out now. It's crazy to get involved.'

'You should tell that to Perdita. I'm not going to let you do this on your own David. You could easily foul everything up. Besides I shouldn't have pulled that gun on you. I can't believe I thought you had anything to do with Mark's murder, or with Peter's. But it seemed to be the only explanation of what was going on.'

'Don't blame yourself. It was what everyone was meant to think.'

It was also what most people would end up believing unless I could find some sort of defence against whoever was setting me up and had tipped off Addinson on where to find Peter's body. Although, now I came to think about it, I did have the beginnings of an idea.

Perdita came back and gave us a thumbs-up. Jerry and I picked up Peter as best we could. He seemed curiously insubstantial. Eventually we managed to lower him gently into the freezer swathed in blankets. Then we closed the heavy, last-a-lifetime, metal door over him.

I went back to my house and picked up the *Murder Unseen* package that Angie had printed off for me. Normally there's nobody as vague as the author about what precisely has happened in a book. So many scenes have been revised and deleted that he or she can never be quite sure what has gone and what remains. Proust wouldn't have had a clue as to what had actually happened in *Temps Perdu* without skimming back to find out which of the many versions of a scene he had settled on. And then he would find that he hadn't managed to express the exact emotions that he had meant to. But I wasn't in quite such difficulty. *Murder Unseen,* in its current form, was infinitely shorter, and I knew there were scenes I hadn't written.

> Tom looks around the Junior Common Room. A tall undergraduate in the far corner of the room gazes out of the window, idle and unmoving. Otherwise the room is deserted, the morning lull when the studious are departing to lectures or working on their essays and the idle have not yet emerged into the day. It is the ideal moment for a refutation of the nonsense he sees pinned on the notice board in front of him and he raises his green pen. Halfway through his first sentence he

finds the ink exhausted and reaches for the second
pen, one-third of his task completed...

It wouldn't be a secret, at least to anyone in the photograph, that the author of the green ink refutations was one
David Knight, undergraduate, possessed at the time of a
tiresome and irritating certainty and a desire to refute any
argument that threatened to be in opposition to the truth.
It was a habit I had abandoned before the end of my first
year and almost forgotten.

I sat down. It wasn't difficult to work out who had put
together my and Tom's murderous future. I was amazed
that I hadn't worked it out before. The fact that I had
used green pens to scrawl refutations on college notices
would have been known to anyone who had been around
in the college at the time, but only one person knew I had
bought three pens.

I couldn't see how he had done it or what his motive
might have been. But I knew who it was. John Hazlitt
had always been good at pastiche. He was also a serial
inventor of imaginary facts, the creator of a mysterious
river in Kazakhstan that only existed in Wikipedia and the
reference books of the world. And now he had turned his
talents to linking me with a Tom Travis whose mind was
set on murder. The question was why?

I needed to connect it up. The four of us in the
photograph with Mark Ryland that Lorna had despatched
just happened to be the same people that Addinson had
identified as Mark's potential murderers. Lorna had been
convinced that Jane had been murdered, and probably by
me. But her actions had been entirely separate from the
production of *Murder Unseen* and the growing rumours
about Mark's death.

I also realised that what I had found familiar about Perdita the first night she had appeared, other than her eyes, was the amber necklace she had been wearing. I had seen it before. Then there was my memory of blood on my hands and a young woman dead, and being outside Mark's flat. I tried to make the events fit together but I had a feeling that something was fundamentally wrong, like finding you have a jigsaw with too many pieces. Maybe that was it. There were too many pieces for everything to fit together. I needed to remind myself that this wasn't a Tom Travis mystery where everything would fall neatly and improbably into place. Real life wasn't a story where everything had an allotted position. I needed to connect only the pieces that fitted, and discard the rest.

So why was John acting as he was? The production of *Murder Unseen* hadn't been done on the spur of the moment. It had been a meticulously planned operation designed to suggest that I had murdered Mark Ryland. Now I thought about it, I had talked to John about my memory loss and told him far more than anything I had ever said to Kate. So he would know that I had no recollection at all of what had happened for a six-month period and I was there to be set up as a murderer. Indeed he seemed to believe that I could be manoeuvred into accepting that I had actually killed Mark. If he could invent imaginary rivers and mountain ranges there would be no difficulty in inventing a murderer. The question was why? The most obvious answer was that Mark's real murderer thought that he or she was in danger of being found out and needed to find someone to act as a fall guy.

The circumstances of Mark's death had always been a fertile ground for conspiracy theorists, particularly since his posthumous rush to fame. I had read through some of the stuff on the net when I had been searching for a subplot for *A Grave Mistake*. It seemed that for once the wild imaginings there were getting near the truth. Somebody had got on to something that was too close for comfort. John had murdered Mark and thought that the matter was over, but had found out that the case might be opened up and the suspects were limited to the four people in the photograph with Mark. He had three possibilities for diverting suspicion but one was ruled out immediately. Stephen had the perfect alibi of being away in America. That only left Peter and myself. Peter was never likely to seem as plausible a murderer as a crime writer who spent his whole life inventing murderous activities, and who might increasingly be unable to tell fact from fiction. Throw in the fact that I didn't remember anything from the time in question and I could pretty much be relied on to convict myself.

I telephoned John's number and got a bored-sounding woman who was vague about his whereabouts. I tried his mobile.

'John, it's David.'

'David. Fire away.' He sounded breezy, cheerful, as though everything on his horizon was sunny. Perhaps it was. Perhaps he didn't know that the Chief Inspector had already come and gone empty-handed.

'Something has come up. We need to talk.'

'I'm a bit tied up.'

'It's urgent.'

I thought for a moment that the line had gone dead but then John spoke again. 'Are you around tomorrow? I'm in Brussels at the moment but I've got a meeting in the Strand tomorrow morning. I could get in a bit earlier and we could have a coffee. I need to pick something up at Waterloo. Say nine there?'

We wrapped up the details and the line went dead. I wondered whether I had made the right move in suggesting a meeting or whether there was any right move to make.

Perdita was in the doorway looking sheepish.

'I'm sorry I didn't tell you everything when we first met. Lorna was insistent that sending out the letters was the only way to do it but I shouldn't have let her persuade me. I've been talking to Jerry. I didn't know Lorna was coming here. I had no idea about the gun. If I had known I would have told you.'

'Not a problem. But I do need your advice on something. It's Lorna. What do we tell her about Peter?'

'I've just got a message from her. She's gone to stay with her sister. She's convinced that it's something serious. He has never been absent this long. I'm not sure telling her that he's been murdered is going to help her if we don't have a better explanation of what actually happened. Besides she needs to rest before she can face up to more bad news. Jerry said you had a plan and you could sort this out by the weekend. I don't think we need to do anything until then.'

'I'm trying to pull a few threads together.'

'I'm sure you'll do more than that. I'd better let you get on with it. I can see you're thinking.'

Perdita's faith buoyed me up for a few moments but then I started wondering if Lorna had been right and Jane Reddon had been murdered, and whether the murderer might strike again. Perdita also seemed certain that her mother was dead.

I took a deep breath. I knew for certain that John Hazlitt was the author of *Murder Unseen*. I had a plausible motive for why he might want to frame me. I couldn't quite work out how he had done it but that was secondary to the fact that he had.

I also wasn't sure that Stephen had been as forthcoming as he might have been. The £50,000 he had been prepared to pay John simply for admitting, if needed, to being Perdita's father would bear a few more questions.

Jerry came in.

'Worked it out yet?'

'I think I'm getting somewhere but I won't know until tomorrow. It might be a good idea to go to Rainbridge tonight. There are a few questions I need to ask. Good a time as any.'

'Right. And, as it happens, I've got something for you. You'll love this.'

Jerry dropped a chunky iPod into my hand.

'Guess what that is.'

'It's an iPod classic isn't it? With more than enough memory for any song I've ever heard?'

'That's what you might think it is.'

'That's what I do think it is.'

'Great. The thing is that it's disguised as an iPod but it's really a bug detector. A *Soundsweep 900X*. Best in its class. Super slim. Given your CCTV appearances recently I thought you would like to know when you were being recorded.'

'Is it complicated?'

'It will beep when it finds something. The screen will tell you what it has detected.'

'Thanks. I'll take it.'

'I thought you'd like it. And are you sure you don't want to try this as well?' He had military battledress under his arm. 'You'll be virtually invisible. That could be useful.'

'I was thinking of making an understated appearance. Nothing more than a spontaneous visit – as I happened to be passing. Coming in dressed for the outbreak of war sort of ups the stakes as far as I can see.'

'Suit yourself,' Jerry said unconvinced. 'You do need to master these *Soundsweep* controls though. Let me run through them.'

I should have listened but my mind was elsewhere. If I had paid attention events might have been different.

THIRTY-SEVEN

WEDNESDAY 7.45PM – 9.00PM

THE SHADOWS CAST BY the evening sun were mellow and warm. Rainbridge Hall basked contentedly in the evening light. It was too civilised a welcome for a man who two hours before had helped place the body of his dead friend into a freezer.

I stopped under the square portico that framed the main entrance and found myself hesitating like a disadvantaged tradesman. It was difficult to know whether I should come out directly with my suspicions about John or lead into the subject in a more gentle fashion. More than that it was difficult to know what I should say about Peter.

I was contemplating a tactical retreat to get my thoughts into order when the great door swung open with only a faint sigh from its oiled hinges.

'Mr Knight, sir, good evening.'

Brown was in the doorway. I could also hear voices somewhere in the recesses of the house.

'To what do we owe this pleasure sir?'

'I happened to be in the neighbourhood. I wondered if Stephen was in. There are some matters I need to discuss with him.'

'Mr Angell is not in residence sir. I'm afraid he has been called away to London on business.'

'Will he be returning this evening?'

'Not for some hours sir. I shall of course ensure that Mr Angell is made aware of your visit immediately he returns.'

A mask of deep regret covered Brown's face. He was poised to close the door as smoothly as he had opened it when there was another voice echoing in the entrance hall.

'David, how nice you could come.'

Brown's mask permitted itself the faintest flicker of surprise before changing to a more welcoming look of greeting.

'Please excuse me sir, I was not aware that you also had an appointment with Mrs Angell.'

'I'm afraid I wasn't clear.'

'My fault entirely sir.'

Francesca, radiant in a black cocktail dress, was moving unnecessarily quickly towards me. Further down the entrance hall Blenkiron, who had managed to pour himself into a close-fitting dinner suit, was glowering after her.

I would have said something else placatory to Brown for my unplanned arrival but at that moment Francesca engulfed me. I felt my body begin to surrender under the unexpected tactic and wondered how long my mind would take to regain control. Then she started whispering in my ear.

'You're here for a private chat. If Blenkiron makes another pass at me I'm going to knee him in the balls. That wouldn't be good for Anglo-American relations or

Stephen's deal. God, we should never have given up the colonies. Come and have a drink.'

Francesca was propelling me towards Blenkiron who had dropped anchor below a picture of one of the more dissolute of the Hayter-Molyneux males, who, while sharing the American's lascivious look, had the advantage of being several stones lighter.

'Hank,' Francesca said, 'you have met David Knight haven't you? He's one of Stephen's oldest college chums and such a darling. And we do have so much to discuss don't we David poppet? I'm so sorry I forgot you were coming. I know how precious your time is. David is always so busy writing it's nearly impossible to get hold of him and there's some urgent advice I need on the gardens. Did I tell you he was a horticultural expert? We were talking at Chelsea and he's got such brilliant ideas that I invited him down to go over the garden plans with me. I'm so sorry. We'll have to postpone our little evening together. I was so looking forward to it but you do see how things are don't you?'

A less determined man than Blenkiron would have buckled underneath such an aristocratic onslaught of charm. But it was clear that he had never read Henry James on the compromises necessary between the new and the old world, and the term *horticultural* had baffled him as much as it had surprised me. For a few seconds he stood resolute and unbending. It was only when Brown mentioned that the Montecristos were laid out in the billiard room that he showed any inclination to relent in his determination not to be deprived of Francesca's company. Even then he attempted to extract a promise from her for a timed meeting the next day.

'Creep,' Francesca said, when he had finally been per-suaded to move on. 'I hope the second Mrs Blenkiron takes him for all he's worth. I can't see anyone wanting to stay married to him much after the arrival of his annual bonus. Hopefully Borkmann will sign tomorrow morning and then I can simply ignore him. I need a drink and some fresh air. Let's go out to the terrace.'

Five minutes later Francesca had armed me with a gin and tonic to support her own and we were looking out at the dimming light over the river that bounded the gardens on the west side.

'So I don't suppose you are going to tell me why you've come all this way to see Stephen are you?' She favoured me with the Hayter-Molyneux look designed to unpick men's souls.

'I don't think I can.'

Francesca sighed theatrically. 'I suppose that's an advance on there being nothing wrong at all. Perhaps you're right. There do need to be secrets between husbands and wives if one is going to have any sort of civilised life. Although perhaps you and your wife...'

'Kate.'

'...Kate, tell each other everything that's important.'

A week before I might have answered yes. Now I had rather a long list of *important* matters that I hadn't told Kate.

'You do look serious,' Francesca continued before I had time to think of an answer. 'It's rather attractive. Do you base this character you've created, this detective, Tom Travis, on yourself? I think I should read one of your books. Stephen seems to like them and he doesn't usually read detective novels. He's got a complete set in the library.'

Tom Travis always maintains that keeping silent and letting a suspect talk is the best way of eliciting information from them. I had a feeling that Francesca was reading the expressions on my face and getting just as much information that way.

'So,' she continued, 'I'll assume one of the matters you are here about is this young woman, Perdita. Personally I wouldn't get too concerned about that. A fling in one's youth is not the most heinous of crimes. Besides it's a long time ago. It can hardly be so important now. But it would be good to get it sorted out, however you do it. I'm sure it's putting an extra burden on Stephen. He's looking tired again like he did a year ago. I thought he'd come out of it, particularly over the last six months with this deal approaching but something has really got to him over the last few days.'

'That's a pity,' I said. 'He's a very talented man.'

'Yes,' Francesca said, 'I suppose he is. He's certainly the most distinguished inventor the Hayter-Molyneux family has ever welcomed to its ranks. But he needs to ease up.'

Francesca was looking down from the terrace to the green sward of lawn that sloped gently down to the distant river. Cone-shaped yew trees gradually led the eye symmetrically forward as they had done for the last few hundred years. I wondered how many times the scene had been played before, the vulnerable heiress with only twenty or so generations of the family to support her. It was an entrancing picture. I didn't know how she and Stephen had met and how they had managed to end up married. For a moment I wondered whether there could have been any circumstances in which I might have ended up in the same position.

I saw a movement in the corner of my eye. At the other end of the terrace an indestructible granite figure was performing a curious zigzag walk like a sailing boat tacking into the wind. On his current rate of progress he would be alongside us in ten minutes or so.

'You know the redoubtable Frederick St James don't you?' Francesca said. 'I was hoping he'd retire but I suppose he is useful on occasion and most of the time he's in Spain. He's doing a security check for Stephen. I think we should leave him to it. Let's go inside.'

We took sanctuary in the gun room, far enough away from the billiard room for there to be little chance of encountering Blenkiron, even if he were to wander out in search of Francesca. I established that Stephen would be at Rainbridge the following evening to sign off the deal with the Americans. Francesca pumped me for more information about what was happening about Perdita but finally accepted that nothing of any substance was going to be forthcoming.

'Still,' she said finally, 'even if you can't tell me what you and Stephen are up to I'm sure you can work out who the women in Stephen's dream are. I really would like to know.'

'I'm not sure entirely.'

'Then perhaps you ought to see it again.'

'That could help.'

'And you'll tell me who they are?'

'Yes.'

I hadn't necessarily meant to agree but I wanted to see the images again.

'Then come with me.'

She led the way down a long thin corridor into the oldest part of the house.

'Here we are. My own little hideaway.'

Francesca's retreat was a small, almost circular, room. A flat screen television nestled below a mullioned window through which a final shaft of sunlight was ebbing away. Opposite the television was a low comfortable couch scattered with cushions and inhabited by a rag doll with long plaited locks who was propped next to a low wooden table with a lamp, a bottle of malt and two heavy glass tumblers. In front of the couch was a pile of books and magazines. On the wall was a photograph of a stunningly beautiful girl, Francesca entering adulthood. Next to it was a black and white study of two young boys who had inherited her good looks – Francesca's sons.

'I used to come here when things went wrong when I was a child. It's still somewhere to get away. Stephen is claustrophobic so I've never managed to tempt him here much. But the boys always used to like to come to watch videos.'

I would have said something but there was a strange beeping emanating from somewhere close at hand.

'What's that?'

'I think it's me.'

I felt in my jacket pocket. A red light was flashing from the *Soundsweep* in time with the beeps. The makers of the *900X* obviously catered for inattentive users of their products. Jerry, now I thought about it, had given me copious instructions on the need to run it on the vibrate setting only to maintain the advantages of the camouflage casing he had added.

'I must have turned it on accidentally,' I said. 'Just a second I'll...'

'No,' Francesca said. 'Let it run. Why is it doing that?'

You didn't need to be an expert to answer. The lights on the display were pulsing out a message: *BUG DETECTED*.

'It's something over there.'

The screen now showed a black dot moving through concentric rings. It was a simple enough matter to position the dot in the centre of the target area. When it got there the *Soundsweep* was in front of a pair of three-pin power sockets in the wall. Francesca took it from my hand and put her finger at right angles across her lips. Then she pointed back the way we had come and I retraced my steps down the long thin corridor.

A couple of minutes later she reappeared and led me down some steps into a modern-looking room furnished as a small cinema. She checked the *Soundsweep* and then gave it back to me.

'Nothing here anyway, although I wouldn't put it past Blenkiron to have bugged the whole house. St James can deal with that later. It seems to be an occupational hazard with the Americans. Still it does mean that we shall get to see you on the big screen.'

The big screen wasn't big by cinema standards but a flat panel that must have been a hundred inches across. A neat row of low, luxuriously padded seats was lined up in front of it.

'Brown actually likes this,' Francesca said. 'It's about the only one of Stephen's improvements that he appreciates. But then he loves war films, the Second World War in particular, although quite why I wouldn't know. Do sit down. I'll run it for you.'

There we are – a fictional David Knight, Jane Reddon, Francesca, and another mystery woman – all in Stephen's dream. It's his eyes we are seeing events through.

So everything tells us something about his interpretation of events. So why is Francesca running away and why has she lost her clothes? What else is there that I should be noticing? What am I missing?

'The woman in the pool is Jane Reddon. She's Perdita's mother. She used to work for Stephen's companies but nobody knows where she is now.'

I sound calm, almost disinterested.

'Can you pause it there?'

The picture is frozen. It's the final mystery woman in a dream that Stephen has made up for himself, or his unconscious has made up for him. Perhaps there isn't much difference.

I know who this is as well now. This must have been before she dyed her hair.

I hadn't seen Nikki Lawrence for thirty years. She had been loitering outside K staircase waiting for Stephen, who was already thirty minutes late, much to her annoyance. It must have been towards the end of their relationship. Then her hair had been a lustrous chestnut brown. I had suggested that she could spend her time in the more amiable surroundings of the Eagle and we left a message pinned to his door. An hour and a half later, when Stephen still hadn't appeared, I had accepted her offer of a lift to London. She had dropped me off in Camden Town. We had seen each other a few times but it was a mild flirtation that hadn't become serious, more the easy relationship of people who are drawn together by chance. In this case chance had come in the form of Stephen's overlong meeting with a bank manager who had been reluctant to lend money to his fledgling company.

'So who is it?' Francesca said. 'I promise not to tell.'

'It's a woman called Nikki Lawrence. She must have dyed her hair. That's why I didn't recognise her. She married Kenneth Templeton the lawyer.'

'Oh him,' Francesca said. 'I think I met him once. Rather a bore. So who was she when she was Nikki Lawrence?'

'She was around in our second year at Cambridge. She knew Stephen. I also went out with her a couple of times but it wasn't serious.'

'Wasn't it?' Francesca's eyes glittered dangerously.

'It was just a friendship.'

'I almost believe you. What about Stephen?'

'I really couldn't say for certain. I...'

'You don't need to answer that. I can see it in your face.' Francesca pressed the controls and the picture in front of us disappeared. 'I'm glad I ran away from you. You boys are so competitive. It wouldn't be good to give you too many conquests.'

Brown was in the corridor when we went back to the main part of the house. As we approached he gave some sort of subtle sign, like a signalman changing the points on a railway track, that propelled Francesca to one side and into a short conversation with him.

I looked at the inscrutable face of one of Francesca's female ancestors. She also refused to give anything away.

'I probably ought to be going,' I said when Francesca emerged from her huddle with Brown. 'But I wouldn't want to expose you to Blenkiron.'

'Brown has introduced him to the last of the 1970 claret and emphasized how priceless it is. He's about to take another bottle in. That should ensure he's no trouble.'

I thought she was about to say something else but she didn't. She sounded bright enough for any normal woman but I sensed her mood had dimmed and she had switched over to reserve power.

Brown opened the great door and I walked into the night. When I got into my car I tried to work out what had accounted for her change of mood. She hadn't been pleased to find a bug in the Rainbridge sanctuary she had had from childhood. She hadn't been pleased to find her husband's dreams were inhabited by past lovers, at least one and possibly two. Perhaps Stephen's payment to John Hazlitt was intended to do more than simply protect him from moralistic American businessmen.

I sensed that Francesca had been perfectly content that husbands and wives should have a box of secrets that they kept locked. I suddenly felt that I hadn't done too well in helping her open her own. Perhaps it should have stayed shut.

THIRTY-EIGHT

WEDNESDAY 9.00PM – 10.30PM

THE TRAFFIC WAS LIGHT on the roads back to London but the sky was streaked with red, not so much shepherds' delight as a pollution haze that edged ever closer to looking like blood.

I should have been worrying about Peter's body and how I was going to tackle John Hazlitt. Instead I found myself going over and over Stephen's dream. Francesca clearly thought that both Stephen and I had had love affairs with Nikki Lawrence. She might even think the same about Jane Reddon.

I had been increasingly certain that Mark was Perdita's father but I didn't think he was the only candidate and not simply because of Francesca's suspicions. Tom Travis had also been whispering in my ear about motive. The murderer always had to have a motive. Why kill Mark? The best answer I could come up with was jealousy. I pulled the car into the side of the road. There was one person who might be able to tell me more.

The downstairs lights in Andy Fontaine's house were

on. I hesitated but then I knocked on the door. After a few seconds it swung reluctantly open.

'I could do with a word Andy, if you've got a moment. I wouldn't call if it wasn't important.'

He looked me up and down and didn't seem to be able to make up his mind.

'It's a bit late for a chat.'

'It's a favour for Mark.'

'He's dead.'

'It's his reputation I'm thinking about. Being on the up. What you were saying on the TV programme. Lift off, escaping out of the atmosphere. Everything you've said about what he was like before he died. I might be able to prove you right.'

His hand hovered on the door but then he pulled it open. 'Well, me and you then, the optimists' club. You'd better come in.'

There was a bottle of something that had once been fizzy on the table in front of the television and a couple of glasses.

'Andy?' It was a woman's voice from upstairs.

'Just a friend. Give us five.' He turned to me. 'Well? What have you got?'

'It's about Mark.'

'You said. What about him?'

'The woman you gave me the photograph of. I know who it is. She's called Jane Reddon.'

'Jane Reddon. Yeah. Sounds right. She was certainly called Jane something. What's all this about?'

'I've got some recordings Mark made when she was around. Enough tracks for a new album.'

'You have been a busy boy.' The expression on his face

darkened. 'Is Angell involved in this?'

'He doesn't know anything about it.'

'Keep it that way. He'll crap all over it if he gets a chance.'

'I'd rather not involve him but he may have an interest. Why do you hate him so much?'

'He's all gloss isn't he? He's the man for the shiny future when everyone records everything and shares it with all their friends and we all stand about with our bite-sized reactions. Did you know Angellic manufacture 30% of the surveillance cameras in this country? So everything is recorded and captured. So what? He should have stopped trying to control everything and given Mark some air. Then he might have realised he had a genius on his hands. He just wanted Mark out on the road so he could maximise his profits. But that is enough about him. What do you want precisely?'

'Mark was talking about a new album. He had you lined up for the artwork. You know he wanted you to do it. I've got the songs. I just wanted to know if you're in the game if I can put something together.'

'Maybe. But it's late in the day. Pity. It could have been another *Other Days*, except that you don't get much room for art with a poxy CD case. People don't understand relative size these days. It's not Google Earth, you just can't change the scale up and down if you want anything good.'

'I was thinking about a vinyl edition, double sleeve. I know someone in the business if we can get hold of the rights. These songs have got a special feel – romantic, lyrical. I think Jane Reddon was the inspiration for them. We could use a picture of her on the album. Maybe a picture of them together, inside.'

'You might have to get her say-so, but that could work. Yeah, that could work.'

He was looking enthusiastic. I wondered how much more froth I could pile on top of the daydream I had created before it started to blow away.

'I'm not sure there's anything with both of them but you never know. I'll see what I've got. They're upstairs.'

I looked round the room once he had left. One side of the fireplace had been fitted out as shelving for large photographic books, the other as storage for CDs.

'There we are.' Andy said when he returned. He pushed the empty bottle and glasses to one side and put a small loose-leaf photo album in front of me. 'Artist and muse.'

Mark and Jane are back-to-back facing away from each other in black and white, head and shoulders in view, the left side for Jane and the right for Mark. They have solemn expressions on their faces as though they might be preparing to interpret some serious classical work and don't know to what depths that will take them.

'Good effect.'

'Yeah, yeah, I'm pleased with it. Much better than face to face. They didn't particularly want to do it that way but I persuaded them. There are a couple more of them together but those are more like snaps. Otherwise it's just him or one or two of her.' He was flipping through the album.

'Did they want to keep it quiet?'

He looked up.

'What do you mean?'

'I'm sure the songs I found are about her. I think they were together.'

'If they were it didn't last for long.'

'She used to work for Angellic didn't she? In fact I think I heard somewhere she used to be involved with Stephen.'

'No way. She wouldn't be the sort for Stephen, not when she got past that surface gloss at least. She was more your type. Are you sure you're not thinking about yourself?'

I shook my head.

There was movement upstairs.

'Look I'd better be going Andy. Thanks for your time. Could I have one of these?'

'Both together? Yeah. Take one of the snaps of the two of them as well.'

As I was about to leave Andy placed a restraining hand across the front door with the calm authority of a commissionaire who suddenly finds his queue is facing the wrong way.

'See St James?'

'Yes.'

'Helpful was he?'

'No.'

Andy's features twisted into a bitter smile and then went blank.

'Didn't think he would be. Watch out for him though. He'd do anything for Stephen. You wouldn't want to tangle with him or any of his friends.'

THIRTY-NINE

WEDNESDAY 10.30PM – 12.00PM

JERRY APPROACHED AS I WAS getting out of the car.

'So?'

'Stephen wasn't there but I can see him tomorrow. I had an interesting talk with Francesca.' I gave him the details. 'And then I called in to see Andy Fontaine. He gave me these.'

'Just a second.' Jerry got a small credit card from his wallet and switched it on. A small beam of light illuminated the photographs.

'We could go inside.'

'In a moment,' Jerry said scrutinising them. 'Well, well. Mark and Jane. So they were together at one point.'

'Seems like it.'

'So that bit is solved is it? We know it can't be Peter so it has to be Mark. So if he is Perdita's father where does that get us?'

'I'm not entirely sure he is.'

'Are you going to explain that? Just because Stephen has dreams of an imaginary *you* flirting with an imaginary

Jane doesn't mean anything does it?'

'I think there's somebody else. Something happened with Mark. Something happened to Jane. There must be somebody else involved. There's other stuff as well. I don't know why I didn't think of it before. Who arranged for Perdita to be adopted? Who put up the money? That's who we've got to find. It might have been Peter but he would never have been able to keep it from Lorna. Anyway it's not him. And it can't be Mark because he died before Perdita was born.'

'Then it's John Hazlitt isn't it? He's a banker – he would have access to the funds. Isn't he a womaniser? Didn't he write *Murder Unseen*? Isn't he in the photograph? He and Mark have a fight over Jane. He needs to get rid of him. So he fakes Mark's suicide. He's in touch with Jane. If Mark is dead she'll probably turn to him in what look like tragic circumstances. He needs to keep her close for some reason so that the truth doesn't come out. Was he married at the time?'

'Yes.'

'There you are then. He provides financial support for Jane. The baby is adopted. Jane goes back to Australia to start a new life. He carries on his life untroubled. That's logical enough isn't it?'

'I can't see anything wrong with it at the moment.'

'There you are then. Get him to admit it when you see him tomorrow and it's plain sailing.'

'I'm not sure it's as easy as that,' I said. 'Why should he admit it? If it's him he's just dumped a body on me. He also seems to have an alibi for the day that Mark was murdered. He claims to have been in Geneva. I'm not sure Addinson has checked it through and it's not a cast iron alibi like Stephen's, but at the moment I'm Addinson's prime suspect, not John.'

'Take it in stages then. Just get him to admit that he wrote *Murder Unseen* then at least you've got something to say to Addinson. I could wire you up for sound if you like.'

'What if he doesn't admit it?'

'We've always got Peter's body. He's bound to have left some trace on it.'

'So have we. So has Perdita.'

'That's a fair enough point,' Jerry said reluctantly. 'Let me think about that. Besides there's something else I wanted to talk to you about. Perdita.'

'What about her?'

'She shouldn't be here – however much help she is. What's going to happen to her if Addinson mounts a raid in the next few hours? They're going to find DNA traces or fingerprints or something for all of us but they'll be concentrating on you and me rather than anyone else. They're not going to be worried about stray traces from other people they can't easily identify. If she's not here there's no reason to link her with what is going on. Nobody has seen her with us. If she disappears now she can get out of this if it all goes wrong.'

I thought about what Andy Fontaine had said. It might not simply be the police who came calling. Whoever had moved Peter's body might not be averse to taking more direct measures.

'You're right,' I said. 'She needs to leave as soon as possible.'

'So you agree?' Jerry sounded surprised.

'Yes. Let's go inside and talk it through with her. And you can turn that light off. You're wasting the battery.'

'It's not battery powered. It's...'

'When we've got a bit more time Jerry.'

'It's really quite interesting...'

Perdita was sitting in Jerry and Faith's spotless kitchen that flecks of dust and grime did not frequent because of the lack of company. She was wearing the amber necklace.

I put the photographs of Mark and Jane on the table.

'They look happy together,' Perdita said.

I took the photograph from her. She was right.

'There's something we need to discuss,' I said.

When we were finished we went outside to look at Peter. Until I lifted the freezer lid I hadn't really seen the point of those late Shakespeare plays where people come back to life.

'No worse than being in a morgue,' Perdita said. 'Better if anything. Jerry has managed to adjust the temperature controls. He's more chilled than frozen. I shouldn't worry about it David. There's no good place to be if you're a corpse.'

It wasn't one of those points you could argue with. We went back into the house. Jerry had transferred Mark's last album onto Perdita's iPod.

'They're good songs. More than good. And about your mother.'

'I'm looking forward to hearing them.' Perdita smiled, a slightly wan smile that strengthened into courage at its edges.

'And you're all right about leaving?'

'If that's what you want. I need to see Lorna anyway. I can help her cope with Peter being missing. Just let me know what's happening.'

'If you have to tell her...'

'I think she knows that Peter is dead. The circumstances don't have to be revealed until you've had time to sort things out. It's better if she knows precisely what happened.'

Perdita sounded confident that it would soon be resolved. I called a taxi. As we waited she fidgeted with the amber necklace that I knew I had seen before.

'It suits you. Did Lorna have any idea who gave it to your mother?'

'Lorna thought the man she loved had given it to her.'

'And who did she think that was?'

'She didn't know.'

The doorbell rang. It was the taxi. Jerry excused himself saying he had some equipment to prepare. We walked down the hall to the front door.

'Call me when anything happens.'

'Will do. It will be me or Jerry.'

Perdita stopped when the front door opened and turned to face me.

'You're lucky to have Jerry. Whatever all this has to do with you and me, it has nothing to do with him.'

'He always wanted to get into the army like his father but never could. Perhaps this is the next best thing.'

I stopped. I might have arrived at the explanation for Jerry's cavalier attitude to danger but I found I had another problem.

'Is anything the matter David?'

'No, no,' I said. 'I was reminded of something. It's not important.'

I opened the door and helped load Perdita's bag in the back of the taxi and then watched it disappear down the road.

Then I let what I had remembered flood over me. I knew one of the places I had seen the amber necklace before. I could see it under the glass in the elegant jewellery shop I was in. It was a shop in an arcade. It was being taken out and put in a box on a glass counter and I was putting something on top of the glass. It had a big orange A on a green background. Access – my new credit card. I had paid for Perdita's mother's necklace with my flexible friend.

'We're getting down to the meat of it,' Jerry said confidently when I went back inside. 'If you can crack John Hazlitt it should all fall into place.'

'Do you think so?' I said, unconvinced.

FORTY

THURSDAY 7.45AM – 11.00AM

I WAS TROUBLED BY THE endless series of evasions I had employed to keep Lorna from finding the body. Peter also appeared, a newly calm man who had some difficulty in believing he was dead, and who went to great pains to write out instructions that I needed to pass on to Chorley. I wasn't sure that was going to be easy because of the pressing mass of children outside waving their little crutches in the air. Then I found myself bending over Mark's body counting out pills before I saw that St James was behind me holding a noose. Then I woke up.

I brewed myself some coffee and then called Jerry to see if there had been any developments but apart from an early morning police car on an emergency call – which I hadn't heard – it had been an untroubled night. I forced myself to concentrate on John Hazlitt. I couldn't see how he had done it or guess what his motive might have been but I knew for certain that he was the author of *Murder Unseen*. He was the only person who could have known the detail that had been included.

I looked at my watch. His train would already be on its way to Waterloo. In forty-five minutes he would be crossing the Hungerford footbridge on his way to an appointment in Covent Garden. He had half an hour free to snatch a coffee and discuss whatever it was that was on my mind.

My eyes blinked in the bright sunlight as I emerged from Embankment tube. The day was heating up and the clouds were dissolving in a blue sky. The river sparkled. I walked out across the bridge against the flow of people hurrying to office life. I got to the opposite bank of the river and our agreed meeting place. Then I saw him approaching. He waved a hand in greeting.

'David! Good to see you. Coffee? What can I get you?'

He was dressed in an expensive grey suit, the sort of cloth that even Francesca might run through her fingers in admiration. His silver cufflinks gleamed in the sunshine. An immaculately knotted tie, pink and blue interweaved diamond shapes, complemented a shirt of mellow creamy whiteness. Only his briefcase, a bulky box-like object, struck a jarring note against the overall symphony of elegance.

'Cappuccino,' I said. 'But why don't we sit outside? Here, let me look after your case.'

'That's no trouble.'

'No, no,' I said. 'It's crowded in there.'

For a moment he seemed reluctant to agree but then put the briefcase down beside the shiny aluminium legs of the table.

I slid the briefcase towards me with my toe when he went inside. It looked as though it was new. I could see John through the glass window, third in the queue.

The briefcase would be hidden from him. I reached down. I spun both locks to quadruple zero and prayed. They opened. He hadn't changed the combination from the default setting. I looked inside.

Stephen had provided his promised £50,000 in £50 notes, red and seductive beneath their protective wrappers. As far as I could see there were twenty bundles – £2,500 a time. Except these weren't slim bundles but thick ones. There weren't fifty notes a time, more like five hundred. I took a deep breath. Stephen hadn't coughed up £50,000 but £500,000. I closed the briefcase and slid it back to its original position.

'Have you seen Peter?' I said when John returned.

'No. I thought Stephen was going to contact him after our little talk about Perdita. Haven't either of you spoken to him? He's probably got the wind up about this murder business and has decided to hide out somewhere.'

'So you've seen Addinson?'

'He dropped in for a few words. Seemed to think somebody had polished poor old Mark off. There wasn't much I could say to help him. I probably should have paid more attention but I was out of the country when Mark died – working in Geneva.'

'That's convenient.'

'Doesn't harm.'

'Did Addinson say why he was so convinced Mark had been murdered?'

'He wasn't terribly forthcoming, no. But policemen never are, are they?'

'He didn't mention a book did he? *Murder Unseen*?'

'No. Should he have done?'

'It's a Tom Travis novel.'

'So? What has that got to do with Mark's death?'

'You've never heard of *Murder Unseen* then?'

'Was it the one before *A Grave Mistake*?'

'It's not actually something that has been released yet. Or finished.'

'I'm not following this. Look, I need another coffee. I meant to order a double espresso anyway. Then you can explain about this *Murder Unseen* business. Can I get you another?'

'No, I'm fine.'

John disappeared back into the coffee house. For a moment when I had first mentioned *Murder Unseen* I thought he might have been going to open up. But a moment later it was clear that he wasn't going to be forthcoming. I imagined he was rehearsing additional lines of denial while he waited for the coffee. Whatever he was going to say everything was taking too long. There was a good chance that I wouldn't be a free man by the time Kate returned if I didn't act fast. I picked up the briefcase and started walking back towards the footbridge across the river.

I was halfway towards the bridge when John emerged. He checked the briefcase was really gone and sipped his espresso before setting off after me. I hurried my pace a little and he also speeded up but the gap between us remained a constant. He had worked out there was nothing he could do that would prevent me from getting to the bridge first. I went up the first set of steps, and then the second. I was heading out over the river. I perched the briefcase on the top of the handrail and then pushed it a little more over the edge and closer to the muddy water below.

'What are you doing David?'

John was edging towards me.

'Just stay there,' I said. 'This could easily end up in the river. It might bob down to the sea but it strikes me as being quite heavy and liable to sink. I'm not particularly eager to find out which, but I will if you get any closer and don't answer my questions.'

'David, do be reasonable, just bring that case back onto the bridge and then we can talk.'

'I think we can talk as we are.'

'This is crazy.'

'It may be. Do you want to tell me about *Murder Unseen*?'

'I told you I had no idea what you were talking about.'

I let the briefcase slide further out over the side of the bridge.

'Don't do that.'

'I'm not planning to drop it but my hands are really quite slippery and I do need some information.'

'OK, OK. *Murder Unseen*. Yes, I wrote it. I admit it. Give me the case.'

'I can't do that just yet. I need to know a lot more.'

'What?'

'Why did you send *Murder Unseen* to my agent?'

'I didn't.'

I let the case slide a little.

'That's the honest answer. I didn't. I may have written *Murder Unseen* but I didn't send it to anyone.'

'So who did?'

'Stephen.'

'Stephen?'

'Do be careful, you nearly let it go.'

'Tell me more.'

'Just keep your hand steady! Stephen said you were suffering from writer's block. He thought you needed a helping hand. He said you'd failed to deliver the next novel to your agent and your career was going downhill. He wanted to give you a jolt, a wake-up call. He had an idea for a new Tom Travis book that he thought would spark you into life and he wanted somebody to write up a package for him. He said he thought I could do it.'

'And you agreed?'

'I had a cash crisis and Stephen was willing to pay the money upfront. It got me over my immediate problems. I couldn't see any particular harm in it, but, if I'm honest, I didn't think about it too much. I needed the money.'

'And the business about Perdita, and you being her father?'

'Stephen needed an alibi for some reason. Perhaps his wife wouldn't be too keen on finding out there was a daughter in the family. Perhaps it was fear of what the Americans might do if they found out. Whatever it was he didn't want to be in the line of fire. You were there when we talked about it. What do you think? In any case it was an opportunity. I'd thought the money he'd paid me for *Murder Unseen* would see me through but my luck hasn't been good. I needed another cash injection to stay afloat. The people who had taken on my debts don't tolerate delay.'

I looked down. The water was still flowing out to the sea. Below on the concrete island that supported this bit of the bridge someone had thrown a broken umbrella. It lay uselessly on its back, its spokes twisted and rusting, like the discarded carcass of an animal.

'£50,000 is a lot even to provide cover on Perdita.'

'Not if you're Stephen. Small change. Lost in the rounding.' John sounded as confident as only a banker can when talking about zeroes.

'And how much was he in control of the plot in *Murder Unseen*?'

'I'm not sure I remember.'

'I think you do.'

I let the case slip a little.

'OK, OK, David. He gave me the details on the body and the flat and Tom's actions. He also had a lot of what looked like your draft material for the Tom Travis series. He said I should use it wherever I could so what I produced was as near to an original David Knight as it was possible to get. I don't know where he got it. I didn't ask. I thought he was in cahoots with someone, perhaps Kate, perhaps your agent. Anyway it was a lifeline I couldn't refuse. I'm sorry if I couldn't tell you but what's the problem?'

'Addinson has seen the book. It seems to be one of the main reasons he thinks Mark was murdered and I did it.'

'I don't get it. He's not going to mount a murder investigation just because you've written a book is he?'

'You wrote it.'

'On Stephen's instructions. He was just trying to help you. Or that's what he said.'

'So how much did he give you for writing *Murder Unseen*?'

'£25,000.'

'And £50,000 for admitting, if necessary, to being Perdita's father.'

'Yes.'

'So why is there £500,000 in the briefcase?'

John took a step backwards.

'So you've looked?'

I nodded. I loosened my grip on it slightly.

'This detective stuff seems to suit you,' John said, the look of dismay on his face replaced by a smile. I wondered how he managed to do it, but not why he seemed so fascinating to women. 'You're not going to drop that are you? I really can't tell you anything else. Except that if he's willing to pay £500,000 there really is something he doesn't want you to know. I guess it must be *Murder Unseen*. I really don't know anything else. There was an opportunity and I took it. I didn't ask any questions. And if you don't want another dead man in the photograph I could really do with that briefcase. There are some people I need to pay off. Please.'

I lifted it up over the railings and gave it to him.

'Thanks,' he said. 'How did you know that I wrote *Murder Unseen* by the way? I thought I'd got your style pretty well.'

'The bit about the green pens. You were the only person who knew I had bought three. You were in the shop with me.'

'Ah,' John said. 'Yes. I suppose it's obvious enough. It's the detail that trap us.'

'And the weekend Mark died? Where were you?'

'I told you, Geneva. I can prove it. It was a bankers' conference and I was speaking at it. There was no way that I could have got to London and back on that day.'

'Fair enough. And that's the truth is it?'

'Absolutely. And thanks.' He indicated the briefcase. 'This is a game changer.' There was a familiar bounce in his voice. I had heard it before.

'Who is she?'

'You're certainly on form David. You won't know her. We're thinking of living in France.'

'And this is serious?'

'I'm always serious David.'

'So which cradle have you raided now?'

'I've given that up. I'm in a more soulful mood these days. In fact there's not much of an age gap at all.'

'It's not Nikki Templeton is it?'

'Nikki Templeton? Nikki Lawrence? No. Why would you think that?'

'Just a hunch.'

'Well, it's not her. I haven't seen her for thirty years. Is she still on your mind? Some women can linger can't they? And you were going out with her at one stage weren't you? Didn't you snaffle her off Stephen?'

'Hardly. Besides it was a friendship, nothing more.'

'That's not what I heard.'

'Seriously.'

'If you say so.' John looked unconvinced. 'Did you find out what happened to Jane after you whisked her away from Stephen's party by the way? Beneath the surface gloss she was a very serious girl. Did you tell her about all those didactic messages you used to scrawl on notice boards? I always thought the two of you would have a meeting of minds. Do you remember? Do you know where she is?'

'No.'

John Hazlitt looked at his watch and touched the briefcase to check that it was still there.

'Then I need to get a move on. It's not a good idea to be late paying your debts.'

FORTY-ONE

THURSDAY 11.00AM – 2.30PM

I BOUGHT ANOTHER COFFEE AND sat looking at the river. Stephen couldn't have murdered Mark but, given what John had said about *Murder Unseen*, he was in prime position to have got rid of Peter, and possibly Jane Reddon. And, if he couldn't have murdered Mark, he had in the presence of St James a proxy assassin. It was getting simpler. But I needed to stay free. Peter's body had to be moved before Addinson arrived with search warrants and Stephen's trap started closing around me again. There was only one place to take the body – Rainbridge Hall.

'Sounds very much the best plan,' Jerry said when I got back to the house. 'Shock Stephen into confessing.'

I hadn't expected him to agree so readily. I had been hoping that he would come up with suggestions for improvement to something that just as easily could be characterised as being full of holes.

'There's no sense in you getting mixed up any further in this,' I said, 'things could easily go wrong.'

'You're not going to be able to move Peter's body by yourself are you? And in case you're forgetting I did hold you up at gunpoint.'

'That's been a fairly common occurrence for me recently. I'm getting used to it.'

'Sorry about that. But it reminds me that's the second favour I owe you. Besides my fingerprints are all over this – literally. So let's get on with it.'

'You don't want to talk to Faith?'

'We're meant to be keeping our distance and dismissing each other from our thoughts to keep stress to a minimum. Telling Faith I'm about to move a dead body out of our garage isn't going to do anything for her ability to ovulate. Besides a bit of action should take my mind off things. We need to get you out of this. As it happens I've been doing some research on Rainbridge and its electronic defences. There's quite an interesting bit of kit that I've got that helps you detect how these systems are wired up. If we treat it like a military operation they can be vulnerable to...'

'Sounds great,' I said before Jerry could get into a full technical briefing. 'We need to get on top of that. It could be make or break.'

'Right,' Jerry said. 'Right. Have you any idea who's likely to be around?'

'Stephen, Francesca, Brown the butler, some domestic staff, a large American called Blenkiron. Oh and Frederick St James who used to be Stephen's chief fixer from his rock festival days. Apparently he still lends a hand now and again. Must be in his early sixties but I wouldn't tangle with him. Seems to be made of teak. Nice mother though.'

'How do you know?'

'She gave me a piece of cake to take away when I met her.'

'That's OK then.'

I left Jerry sorting out tactical possibilities and retreated upstairs. My unfinished masterpiece *Murder is Equal* lay in a neat pile of A4 sheets. I must have tidied them after Peter's attempt to inject a new randomness into the events in the book. Just at the moment I couldn't remember who the murderer was.

The last consultant I had seen about the accident, the most senior, and the most vague, had said that they really didn't understand how memory returned or why it didn't. A particular stimulus could trigger a recovery or indeed sometimes a blow on the head might reverse what a previous blow had caused. I might recover all my memory or nothing at all and it might be a slow process or come in a rush. The only thing I might do to help speed up the process was to run any bits of returning memory actively through my mind at intervals to help the connections between them reappear.

I could remember kneeling down by the woman. There was blood on my hands. She had been lying on her front.

I knew I had been outside Mark's flat. I could remember the detail. I could remember looking up. I could remember feeling guilty.

I was sure I had seen Jane wearing the amber necklace and I was now certain that I had bought it.

I could remember Jane's face close to me.

The phone was ringing.

Kate's voice came as a shock.

'William and Anne send their love. They're looking forward to reading *Murder is Equal*. So you'd better get a move on. Their niece is staying over this evening to look after the children and we're going out to the Cross Keys. According to William it does the most amazing fish. He's still salivating about some pan-fried turbot he had when he and Anne were last there. I'm sorry you're going to miss it but I'm sure we'll go back the next time we stay.'

'Sounds great.'

'Are you all right darling? You don't sound quite yourself. At least you won't be putting on the pounds.'

'There's a lot going on.'

'Must be the life of the mind. I'm sure you can use much more energy thinking than people ever imagine. Doesn't the brain use a quarter of the energy the body produces? I'm sure it's probably a lot more in your case. Don't worry the book will get done.'

I didn't know why Kate was being so reassuring. I had had the strongest feeling when she left that she never expected the book to be finished at all. That was why I had thought that it was she who had written *Murder Unseen.* Perhaps she and William and Anne had been to a pub at lunchtime.

I could hear excited voices in the background – the boys and the three Watson children. I had a sense that if I were suddenly to disappear nobody would remember that I had ever been here at all. There would be no trace left. Perhaps that wasn't such a bad fate if I didn't know what I had done.

'There's one thing I did mean to ask you,' I said. 'I was wondering – I know it sounds crazy, but do you think I could be capable of murdering somebody? Do you think I've got it in me?'

'Don't be ridiculous darling. You're not the type. Never in a million years.'

'You're certain about that?'

'Of course I am. But why are you asking me this? Have you got a problem with the book?'

'I was just wondering what people might be capable of if they got into extreme situations, or they suffered from memory lapses and didn't know what they had done.'

'It's not a bad subject for a plot but don't you think you ought to finish *Murder is Equal* before you go on to anything new? I told William that any of the six Cruickshank nephews and nieces could have done it and he said that was precisely the sort of mystery he liked. He wants everyone in the game until the final twist at the end. I thought you said that was sorted. It's Isabelle isn't it? That's a good choice. I never liked her.'

'The problem is that I don't quite see how she could have got into Crispin's cabin unless he opened the door for her. He would never have done that given that he knew one or more of them were trying to get rid of him after the rock incident.'

'You just need to choose one of them darling. Isabelle could have disguised herself as someone else. Didn't she resemble the great love of his life that he let get away and that was why he had such ambivalent feelings about her?'

'The love of his life looked like the twins.'

'Did she? I suppose you're right. Well, even better, one of them could be in two places at once since they're identical. Dennis Blackstone used triplets in that Mathias Penn you gave me. What was it called – *Crime Seen*? That was an incredible plot. Perhaps there really are three of them and one of them was separated off at birth, although that would a bit of a copycat of what Dennis did, good as it was.'

'That still doesn't get them, plural or singular, into Cruickshank's cabin.'

'A hairpin for picking locks? You could make it an antique one. Give it to Rupert if you like, I always thought he was the only other person capable of doing it. Anyway just make a final decision. I thought you had anyway. It doesn't really matter which one of them it is as long as it is a surprise. All they've got to do is to get into Crispin's cabin and outwit Tom. Actually I have been wondering about that as well. There's rather a high level of attrition among his clients isn't there? I mean they wouldn't keep walking through his door if he can't protect them would they?'

'That's because he solves the most difficult cases.'

'Then he should solve this one. I though you said he had. It must be Isabelle or Rupert. You can always toss a coin if you're not sure. When you've done that you'll be free of all of it. And for the next book you should take my advice. Talk to some policemen. The plots will come to you rather than you having to go to them. Anyway I must go. The boys send their love.'

'I'm sorry this is taking so long. Please forgive me.'

'There's nothing to forgive darling. Just get the book done and a film contract and I'll forgive anything and everything. But I must dash. See you on Saturday. Bye.'

I put the phone down. I had given *Crime Seen* to Kate in the confident expectation that she would find the identical triplet plot laughable and Mathias Penn cliché-ridden. Instead she had lapped up the plot and suspended critical judgement.

In normal circumstances Kate's attitude, however modified by alcohol, would have caused me intense irritation.

Now it seemed a problem that had already passed, a pinprick to be ignored, something that should never have had any importance at all. It was also reassuring that she didn't think I could do anything really bad. It wasn't so reassuring that the evidence to hand didn't exactly seem to support her assertion.

FORTY-TWO

THURSDAY 5.30PM – 8.45PM

THE S-MAX WAS AT the front of the house gleaming innocently in the sun. I managed to help Jerry lift
Peter into the back without thinking too much about
what I was doing. Our only witness was a young woman
talking animatedly into a mobile phone as she walked
by with a pram and child. She looked as though she
had too many concerns of her own to be bothered
with any of ours although the child favoured us with a
suspicious frown.

'So?' Jerry said as I climbed in beside him in the front
of the car. 'Ready?'

'You don't need to come you know.'

'We've been through that. Yes I do.'

'Why?'

'Well in addition to everything else you're not insured
to drive this.'

'That's not exactly our most pressing problem. Stop
now and I can say that you didn't know what you were
getting involved in.'

'Addinson is going to conclude that you did all this by yourself is he? If he arrests you he's certainly going to do me as an accomplice. I don't want that, certainly not before Saturday. Besides you're not going to be able to move Peter's body on your own. It's stiff. And I owe you one. So this is a joint venture. Let's turn our mobiles off. We don't want to be traced remotely. I'm starting the car. A3?'

I nodded. The S-Max pulled smoothly away.

I dropped into a sort of waking reverie, as we moved through the suburbs, vaguely aware of the drift of early evening traffic glistening in the sunshine. Then I saw Jerry was glancing anxiously into the rear mirror.

'There's a police car behind. It's been there for a bit.'

I looked round. The car was about thirty yards adrift, neither gaining nor losing distance. I glanced into the back of the S-Max. Jerry had put all of the seats down. In addition to an oversized badger there were two sets of military uniforms, a small metal equipment box, a crowbar, a trowel, a bag of ready-mixed exterior filler and what looked like the butt of a gun. In fact it didn't look like the butt of a handgun, it was the butt of an automatic, and an automatic I recognised. Time had slowed down so much in the moments before Lorna had pulled the trigger that every detail of the gun she had been using was engraved in unmistakeable detail on my mind.

'I didn't think it was safe to leave it in your house,' Jerry said following my eyes and causing the S-Max to swerve. 'The safety catch really is very faulty. I wouldn't touch it if I were you. Particularly if you have to lean back to reach it. There's not much of a chance but it might go off.'

Jerry sounded eerily matter of fact.

'We're being followed by a police car and we've got a gun on board,' I said as slowly as I could. 'How do we explain that when we get stopped?'

Jerry looked in the mirror.

'If you can distract them for a minute when they pull us over I'll hide it under Peter's body.'

'You could take this a bit more seriously.'

'I don't need to. They've moved into the outside lane.'

The police car slid level and for a moment we were travelling side by side, now one car edging into the lead, now another. The policewoman in the passenger seat, a hard-faced blonde with pinned-back hair, gave me a long cold look as though computing what cocktail of offences I could be brought to book for. As we drove down the hill the road started undulating so that for a moment it seemed we were more like boats bobbing up and down at sea.

'Can't you slow down,' I said, 'I'm being given a visual third degree over here.'

'I don't think we should do anything unusual,' Jerry said. 'We don't want to attract any more attention to ourselves than we need to. Just look a little more relaxed if you can. Bear in mind the bruising below your eye makes it look as though you've been involved in a fight. I'm pretty sure I've got something that would disguise it though. Remind me when we stop. It's thinning out up ahead anyway. They'll soon be past.'

They were. Or at least in real time they were. In my memory they seem to be there forever, a policewoman's cold official eyes looking at me, waiting for me to confess.

'So,' Jerry said once the police car had disappeared into the distance, 'I need to know your thinking on this. The whole package.'

I wasn't sure Jerry's consultancy mode was the most helpful one he could have adopted in the circumstances but he was a volunteer rather than a pressed man and needed to be humoured. I needed some method of getting my thoughts straight in any case.

'We're a team.'

'Good, good.' Jerry nodded encouragingly. 'What sort of team?'

'A united one.'

'Yeah, yeah, sorry about pulling a gun. Freaky moment but I didn't really mean that. I meant more what's our plan? What are our roles?'

'Stephen must be behind all this. John wrote *Murder Unseen* on his instructions. *Murder Unseen* is why Addinson is becoming convinced I'm the Clapham poisoner. Dumping Peter's body in the garden of my house was a blatant attempt to incriminate me. It was what you assumed had happened, and what anyone would have assumed.'

'I jumped to conclusions.'

'Which were there to be jumped to. Most people would have done the same. I wasn't entirely coming across as a reliable witness. Anyway, as far as I can see, it probably goes something like this. The knife didn't kill Peter. Any half-decent autopsy would have established that beyond question. So the police would have to find another cause of death. Peter had Amitrip tablets in his pocket but as far as I know he didn't take that medication. Perdita seems to think he had a seizure or a heart attack. Given my preferred modus operandi, outlined in *Murder Unseen*, of poisoning my victims to death by getting them to overdose on drugs leading to a heart attack, it's pretty clear what they are going to conclude has happened, and who they might be looking to as the culprit. The fact that I say I'm being framed is not going to convince them otherwise unless I have some evidence to back it up.'

'Good analysis. So what are we going to do?'

'We take Peter's body to Rainbridge and confront Stephen.'

'So we're using the body as a bargaining chip?'

'More a lever. I need to shake Stephen's confidence. He's only happy when he's in control. I reckon if we can get Peter's body up near to the house we're in business. It's the shock value.'

'Good. Makes sense. Do we have a plan B?'

'Do we need a plan B?'

'We could use it to foolproof plan A,' Jerry said reasonably.

'Sounds helpful. Any ideas?'

'We could dispose of Peter permanently.'

'Why would we want to do that?'

'No body, no murder, no conviction. However strong the evidence is against you if there is a body, there's no evidence if there isn't one.'

'But whoever dumped the body on me is going to know.'

'They're not going to tell anyone are they?'

'No, that's a fair point,' I conceded, 'but what about Lorna?'

'What's Lorna got to do with this?'

'It's not exactly closure if we just dispose of Peter's body is it? I mean no funeral or anything. She seems convinced he's dead but unless his body turns up it's all a loose end. It's not, I don't know, *dignified* is it?'

'Yes,' Jerry said after a moment. 'I see what you mean. Tricky. But if we just deliver the body to Stephen what happens if he just denies everything. It's the same problem you would have had with John. We could do with a plan C.'

'Or a better plan B, or A come to that.'

'Maybe a hybrid.' Jerry sounded confident.

'You'd better explain.'

'Well suppose you tell Stephen we've got Peter's body and we've put it back on his land but we've hidden it so he doesn't know where it is. If he's dumped the body on you in the first place he'll know you're telling the truth and may confess or whatever you expect him to do. If he hasn't there's no body around if he calls the police.'

'It's not going to be that easy to hide a body.'

'I've got an idea about that. Consider that covered off.'

'So where is this hiding place?'

'Probably better you don't know.'

'Why?'

'One, it's just a hunch I have. It may not work. Two, if you don't know, they can't force the hiding place out of you can they if, I don't know, this guy St James tried to beat the truth out of you. There wouldn't be anything you could tell him.'

'That's logical,' I said. 'Good point.' Actually I had a suspicion that the plan was flawed in some way and would have said something else but I found I was distracted by a vision of a greying sink where I was washing blood off my hands.

'Then we've got a plan,' Jerry said.

'Yes, although there are a lot of surveillance cameras round the house. We need to bear that in mind.'

'Not a problem,' Jerry said confidently. 'But I do need to do a small reconnaissance once we get there. I'm not sure we should leave the body in the car while I do. I've had a look at maps of the area. There's what looks like a derelict boathouse near a pub. It's on the main road that runs round the estate. It looks like a good place to get into the grounds anyway unless you've got a better suggestion.'

'Sounds as good as anything.'

'Here we are,' Jerry said half an hour later. 'Looks sober to me.'

'Sorry?'

'The duck,' Jerry said, 'it looks sober to me.'

I looked to where he was pointing. On the pub sign an expressionless mallard was perched immobile on the edge of a landing stage by a river, seemingly indifferent to the grey-brown countryside that some anonymous artist had consigned it to.

'It could be stoned. Look at its eyes.'

The Drunken Duck Inn, in contrast, was bustling with life. Trestle tables were set out at front and back of the building and an aromatic billow of smoke was rising from an open-air barbecue that promised, according to a newly chalked board beside it, a variety of sausages, burgers and salads. Ahead of us the long narrow car park, already half full of vehicles, stretched away to a dark wooden building close to the water's edge.

'So that looks like the boathouse,' Jerry said driving towards it.

'Must be. Are you sure we should park so close?' I said.

'If anybody sees us they'll assume we came to put something in the building, which is what we'll be doing. Why should we want to lug it any further than we need to? That would be suspicious.'

There was one other problem I noticed as Jerry backed the S-Max as close as he could to the wire fence that separated the Drunken Duck's car park from Rainbridge Hall land. A large and rusty padlock secured the gate that led to the boathouse.

'Wouldn't stop a child,' Jerry said confidently.

The lock on the boathouse door proved slightly trickier in that he had to use a bigger metal pick than the one he had first selected.

'Let's do it then.'

'Shouldn't we wait until it gets darker?'

'Best done in daylight,' Jerry said. 'Less suspicious.'

'Fair enough.'

'I've been thinking...' Jerry said as we eased Peter's body in its badger suit out of the back of the car.

But whatever train of thought was in motion was interrupted by a dog emitting a series of bloodcurdling barks. I pushed Peter's legs back into the car and turned round. It was a small hairy golden beast that might have got a part in a remake of *Lassie*. It also seemed set on a direct course for the open hatch of the S-Max. How the dog and its owner had got so close without us noticing them was difficult to understand.

'Evening,' cried its owner above the hubbub. He was a tall grey-haired man who looked as though he didn't believe in discipline. 'Sorry about this. Do stop messing about old girl!' The dog's mouth was open in something approaching a snarl. 'She's not normally like this,' he added unconvincingly as he dragged her past.

'No problem,' Jerry said unconcernedly.

As the two of them made their way towards the Drunken Duck the dog kept looking back suspiciously while its owner kept his eyes rigidly forward and applied corrective tugs to the dog's lead to keep it moving. Eventually the dog abandoned its ill-judged attempt to be a harbinger of justice and started wagging its tail.

We got Peter into the boathouse without too much difficulty. He wasn't as cold as he had been. We found him a temporary resting place between two long wooden rowing boats secured to hooks in the wall of the shed by fraying ropes and poised on the edge of a stone ramp that ran down to the river.

'I suppose this will have to do,' I said unenthusiastically.

'Serves a purpose.'

We closed the boathouse door and Jerry replaced the padlock on the gate. Then we went back to the S-Max and sat in the front seats.

'Could that dog smell something?'

'Maybe it sensed we were behaving suspiciously.'

'Why would it do that?'

'It's probably how we look.'

'So can't it tell we're innocent?'

'It's only a dog,' Jerry said. 'I've never trusted them.'

FORTY-THREE

THURSDAY 8.45PM – 9.15PM

THE SHADOWS WERE LENGTHENING around us. The barking dog was only an echo. I tried to clear my mind.

'Might as well turn our mobiles back on,' Jerry said. 'We might need to message each other once I'm in the grounds.'

'So you're checking out this potential resting place?'

'That and a general reconnoitre.'

'So are you going to tell me about it?'

'Does the name Muller mean anything to you?'

'Does it have an umlaut?'

'I don't think so. Muller the concrete engineer. Well, more of a concrete artist actually, and not just concrete. Quite famous.'

'Never heard of him. Anyway what has he got to do with this?'

'I'm not sure yet. But if you haven't heard of Muller it's going to be a little difficult to explain. Let me just get into Rainbridge and find it.'

'That's not going to be easy is it?'

'I have the perfect kit for it.'

Jerry had the battledress in his hand and was fingering it lovingly.

'Isn't that going to make you more conspicuous rather than less?'

'Not in gloom or darkness. It's specially coated. Incredible stuff! I'm virtually invisible. Give it five minutes until it gets really dark and I'm into the grounds.'

'Surveillance cameras?'

'Shouldn't be a problem.'

Jerry had the crowbar in his hand.

'So what are you checking out?'

'If it's what I think it is, I'll let you know. Let me handle it. Besides you need to work out what you're going to be telling Stephen.'

'And what am I going to be telling him about Peter's body?'

'Say we've got a place to hide it in the Rainbridge grounds where it would never be discovered.'

'Never?'

'Certainly not for a generation or two. I'm pretty sure that's the case.'

I might have pursued the matter but there was an insistent buzzing from my trouser pocket.

'You ought to take that,' Jerry said. 'It might be important.'

It was a difficult proposition to argue against. There were any number of bits of news that might help me steer between the twin peaks of freedom and imprisonment. It was a text:

DAVID
DEBBIE PHONED. U ARE HOT IN
HOLLYWOOD! LOVE MURDER
UNSEEN. MAY OFFER A MILLION.
ONLY DOWNSIDE WILL TAKE TOTAL
CONTROL AND WRITE THEIR OWN
SCRIPT. COULD BE UNRECOGNISABLE.
NEED REACTION. DEBBIE SAYS DON'T
BE PRECIOUS – BEST DEAL THIS YEAR.
ANGIE XX

I wondered how much Hollywood would offer if they knew I might be arrested at any moment. I laboriously sent a text message back:

ANGIE
A MILLION WHAT?
DAVID X

I scarcely had time to let my fingers rest when the reply came through:

DAVID
DOLLARS! AT 0.63991809 $ TO THE £
THAT'S £639,918.09 YOU'RE A STAR!
WHAT DO YOU WANT TO DO?
ANGIE

I spent a couple of minutes trying to work it out. In London Angie might have supposed I was concerned about my artistic integrity and letting Tom Travis be massaged by the Hollywood dream machine until he was unrecognisable.

That wasn't exactly my most pressing problem, although I had an additional concern to add to my list – whether I actually owned all of what Debbie was selling:

> *ANGIE*
> *I'LL THINK ABOUT IT.*
> *DAVID*

It was a feeble response. Perhaps I should just have said yes.

> *DAVID*
> *COOL!! DEBBIE WILL GET YOU*
> *ANOTHER 10%!!*
> *ANGIE XX*

I looked up. Jerry was staring at his phone. He must have been staring at it for some time while I laboriously typed in my side of the conversation with Angie.

'What is it?'

'It's a message from Faith.'

'I thought you weren't meant to be communicating with each other. I thought that was the whole point. Absence makes the heart grow fonder or whatever more crucial function it was meant to perform.'

'It wasn't quite that but whatever it was it doesn't matter now.'

'Why ever not?'

'She's pregnant. My phone was turned off so she had to text me.'

'What?'

'She's pregnant. We're going to have a child.'

'That's great Jerry.'

'Yes.'

Jerry shook his head as though he was trying to wake himself up.

'You had some messages as well didn't you?'

'Nothing much. Hollywood seem to be offering a million dollars for *Murder Unseen*.'

Jerry didn't reply. He seemed to be having some difficulties with his uniform.

'That's back to front Jerry.'

'So it is. Difficult to tell in this light.'

I blinked. The battledress was blending with the darkening background so for a moment he wasn't there.

'You are up for going into the grounds are you? I mean it's big news.'

'Sorry. What was your news? I missed it.'

'Not mine. I mean Faith.'

'Oh that, yes.'

'I'm going up to the house then. I'll go by the road. I should take five minutes to let it sink in before you set off.'

'Yes, perhaps you're right.'

I hadn't seen Jerry so distracted before. Perhaps this wasn't the time to leave him alone with a body in fancy dress and a gun with a faulty safety catch, or, come to that, dressed in military uniform.

'You get on,' he said. 'I just need to pinch myself a few times. I'm sorry what were you saying?'

'It's nothing Jerry. See what you can do. Aim to be back here in a couple of hours.'

Jerry looked at his watch, got to his feet, and slapped his face.

'Right, I'm focused.'

'And you're not going to tell me where precisely you

think we can put Peter's body if we need to?'

'You'll know soon enough. Besides it may not work.'

Jerry seemed to be emerging from his daze and was fitting the crowbar into his uniform without apparent difficulty.

I left with misgivings. Jerry needed to keep his mind on the job but then so did I. I knew this because, a couple of minutes later, I collided with a shadowy form loitering at the side of the wrought iron gates marking the entrance to the Rainbridge Hall estate.

FORTY-FOUR

THURSDAY 9.15PM – 9.30PM

'MR KNIGHT.' IT WAS a southern drawl.

'Mr Blenkiron.'

I disentangled myself and took a step backwards. Blenkiron was eyeing me up and down.

'Are you going to the house?'

'Yes.'

'Then perhaps we could talk on the way.'

I didn't seem to have an option in the matter. He fell in beside me and we ambled up the drive in an awkward crab-like crawl.

'Have you finished your business with Stephen?' I asked.

'Mostly done.'

He didn't sound entirely convinced.

'Excellent.'

'Are you here with more gardening advice for Francesca?'

'That's pretty much sorted.'

'Really?'

'Oh yes, with gardens as extensive as Rainbridge's any planning has to go through many hands. I think Francesca was looking for some pointers for the next hundred years or so. There's quite a lead-time to achieving some effects but there are some possibilities of enhancing the room-like features of the gardens at the back of the house. And that Three Graces statue is a bit out of place – Stephen's one mistake. But anyway the point is you have to grow the walls – that's why it's such a long-term project.'

My shadowy companion nodded. I hoped he was going to leave it at that. I had just about exhausted my horticultural planning expertise.

'That's interesting.' He didn't sound interested. 'So you're here to finish off the hundred year plan?'

'I'm actually here to see Stephen.'

'Business?'

'A private matter.'

'You've known him long?'

'Since university – college.'

'Quite a time then.'

'Yes.'

I wondered when Blenkiron would get round to what he actually wanted to talk about. I quickened my pace as the drive moved up a slight incline but he managed to keep up with me.

'Have you met Stephen's mother?'

Stephen's father had died young and his mother had brought him up with considerable sacrifice, or so Stephen had once told me. She had apparently been a rather shy woman proud of her only child. I hadn't seen her for many years.

'Not recently.'

Blenkiron snorted.

'You buddies?'

Buddies? It was a good question. Could one be framed for murder by someone and not let that fact affect a relationship? But Stephen deserved an opportunity to explain.

'We're friends.'

'Friends huh?'

'Absolutely. I've always admired Stephen and everything he has accomplished.'

Blenkiron stopped in front of me and placed a restraining hand on my shoulder.

'Listen buddy, you need to wise up. Maybe you're popular with Mrs Angell but he ain't your friend. So – if you know anything I should know – remember to talk to me.'

He thrust a business card into my hand, took a step back and gave me a gentle tap on the chest. I put the card into my pocket, resisted the temptation to take a swing at him, and bade him a curt goodnight.

Tom Travis has an irritating store of maxims that he trots out to confound the expectations of whoever he is talking to. Sentiments like *my enemy's enemy is my friend* are never too far from his lips at plot-changing moments. Blenkiron was clearly Stephen's enemy and I hadn't gone more than a few steps before realising that it might have been prudent to take a more emollient line.

A hundred yards further on I looked round. A red glow in the distance suggested that my new American friend had lit a cigar.

When I got to the great door at Rainbridge I had to knock. The door opened after a few seconds and Brown gave a slight bow.

'Mr Knight sir?' Brown's tone suggested he did not appreciate guests turning up unannounced, particularly in the late hours of the evening.

'My meeting with Mr Angell.'

'Ah yes sir, of course. Have you made any arrangements with Mr Angell? I'm afraid I'm not aware of them if you have.'

'Spur of the moment again I'm afraid. I happened to be passing.'

'As is your custom sir.'

'Mr Angell is in, isn't he?'

'Indeed he is sir, but I believe he is occupied with business.'

'It is rather important. Mrs Angell suggested yesterday that this would be a good time if I wanted to ensure Mr Angell was in.'

'Then I'm sure that's a very wise plan sir.' Brown's tone softened. 'If you'd care to come in I will find Mr or Mrs Angell for you.'

'That's fine Brown, I'll take care of this.'

Francesca had appeared behind him dressed in a black cashmere pullover and elegant jeans that would have equipped her to be a cat burglar in the smarter parts of Paris.

'Of course madam.'

Brown took a step back and pulled the door fully open. Francesca looked me up and down.

'Did you say you were here to see Stephen? He should be free in a few minutes. He's signing some papers. Let's go into the library. Would you like something?'

'Water would be excellent.'

'Are you sure I can't tempt you to something a little more celebratory? Stephen is just signing off the deal.'

'I think I should stick to water for the present.'

'Could we have some then Brown? But make it fizzy.'

When Brown had gone Francesca emitted a sigh.

'It's obviously been a bit of a strain,' I said.

'And some. But it's a lot of money. Stephen always said he wanted to make the estate absolutely secure and this will do it. We can even buy some land. There's a parcel beyond the wood that we had our eye on in the eighteenth century but never managed to get hold of. It could be a reward for having to put up with our American visitor. When he's gone we can relax.'

I wondered if Stephen would be so relaxed when he saw me. He might have assumed I had already been arrested.

'Stephen had this room swept for bugs. The rest of the house will be done over the next week,' Francesca said, 'then we'll be free of Blenkiron and his machinations.'

'Excellent.'

'Isn't it?'

It wasn't quite a rhetorical question. Francesca seemed to need me to agree. There was an expectant pause and I could feel her willing me to say yes so we could unite against the common enemy puffing irritably on his complementary Montecristo. Much as I disliked Blenkiron I found that I couldn't quite take up her offer.

'Look David,' Francesca said, 'I'm really worried about Stephen. He's not been himself in the last few days. You will be careful what you say won't you? He needs to unwind. He's just a bit fragile at the moment.'

I might have asked how long the moment had been and whether killing off one of your friends and dumping the body on another wasn't also likely to cause stress, but Brown arrived with the drinks on a silver tray and the door at the end of the library started to open.

'There are a few things to sort out,' I found myself saying. 'That's why I need to see Stephen.'

'Did somebody mention my name?'

Stephen was in the doorway at the far end of the room. I thought for a moment he looked surprised. But whatever emotion had crossed his features had disappeared in an instant and been replaced with a stoical, almost indifferent, expression. It was the sort of look Roman emperors used to adopt before giving the thumbs down signal to some disarmed and hapless victim of the games.

FORTY-FIVE

THURSDAY 9.30PM – 9.50PM

STEPHEN USHERED ME TO a chair in the small study. He glanced at Picture Screen above the fireplace. This time it was split into four, each showing part of the house or grounds. In the top left the library was now empty. His wife and his butler had melted away as soon as he had appeared.

'Francesca said you called last night. I'm sorry I was out. I had to go to London for a meeting. What was it you wanted to speak to me about? Have you got any news on this Perdita business?'

Francesca might consider him fragile but I couldn't see any convincing signs.

'I spoke to John about a book he'd ghosted for you,' I said. 'Or, if you like, for me – *Murder Unseen*. He told me that you'd paid him to write it.'

'Ah.' Stephen stopped. 'He did, did he? I thought we'd agreed to keep that quiet.'

'You don't deny it then?'

Stephen thought for a moment.

'No.'

'Are you going to tell me why?'

'If I must. Shall we start at the beginning? It was a cocktail party at Number 10 last year. I met a crime-writing colleague of yours, Dennis Blackstone, creator of, if I remember rightly, some immobile sleuth called Mathias Penn who was big in Germany and a major contributor to knowledge exports. I couldn't say I was too interested in what your fellow author was saying and had nearly managed to extricate myself from his circle of self-regard when he mentioned your name. He seemed to have a rather competitive interest in Tom Travis and the delay in the next book in the series. When I said we were old friends he felt compelled to embark on a full-blown analysis of your situation. He wasn't too complimentary about your sales but the gist of it was that your character lacked psychological depth.'

'That's rich. Mathias Penn hasn't moved from his armchair for a decade.'

'Clearly you take a mutual interest. But what he said concerned me. I wondered if I could help. I had the books recorded and listened to them. They're agreeable enough, if you speed them up, but I thought there was something in what Blackstone was saying. You do need to give Tom Travis more depth. Then the idea came to me to become a sort of literary agent provocateur to help you get through the writing block you were suffering from. I decided to put together a package for you. I could see what was needed in terms of plot but writing the text was another matter.'

'So you got John Hazlitt to do it.'

'He needed money and I was willing to come up with cash, which seemed important to him. I thought I was doing you both a good turn.'

'You gave him half a million.'

A look of surprise caressed Stephen's features.

'He told you that did he? He's not as discreet as I would expect for a banker. I'm rather disappointed in him. Still, we are where we are. It's very simple anyway. I'd paid him £50,000 for *Murder Unseen*. I agreed £50,000 for him to admit to being Perdita's father if that proved necessary. But it was clear after you had gone that he was in considerable financial difficulty. The extra £400,000 wasn't a problem for me and he did seem to owe money to some unpleasant people. I needed my arm twisted a bit but in the end I was prepared to help.'

'And the increase of £400,000 was nothing to do with keeping quiet about *Murder Unseen*?'

Stephen smiled benevolently. 'It might have come into our discussions somewhere. But you seem to know a great deal about what's going on. Tell me have you found out who sent the letters we've all been getting?'

'Yes.'

'And who is it?'

'Are you going to tell me what happened to Peter?'

'But you know what happened to Peter. He's in your garden with a knife in his back.' Stephen's voice was quite deadpan. He smiled again. 'Or at least he was the last time I heard. But I'm happy to strike a bargain. I'll tell you how he got there if you tell me about the letters.'

'You first.'

Stephen thought the proposition over.

'All right. You remember what happened in *Killing Spree* of course.'

'I do. That was one of the ones I wrote.'

'Well then, you won't find this difficult to understand.

Peter arrived here on Tuesday evening. I don't know how he got past Brown but there he was in the corridor. He was in a high state of excitement. He'd got this notion that Jane Reddon was coming back and the family he never knew he had were going to be reunited. He wanted an advance from me so he could take care of them. His sense of responsibility was touching but what he said came as more than something of a surprise. I tried to reason with him, to calm him down. I told him you were Perdita's father. When he worked out when he had been with Jane and how long after that Perdita had been born the penny dropped. He said he needed to take something and could he have some water. When I got back he was lying face down on the floor. Dead.'

'So you put him in the Chorley suit and dumped him in the garden of my house. Then you stuck a kitchen knife in his back.'

'It was the weapon in *Killing Spree*.'

'How could you do that?'

Stephen scratched his ear as though the answer to my question was not easily available.

'I wasn't comfortable with it but it seemed too good an opportunity to miss.'

'To frame me.'

'If you must put it like that.' There was almost a note of hurt in Stephen's voice as though whatever he had done had been forced upon him. He'd also taken the news that I knew about John Hazlitt much too calmly. Whatever game we were engaged in he was still several moves ahead. More than that I didn't understand the rules. The only thing I did know was that I hadn't needed to threaten to bring Peter's body into Rainbridge Hall to get him to admit what had happened. It was all far too easy.

'There will be something on Peter's body that the police can trace back to you,' I said. 'It wouldn't need much.'

'I doubt it. I did check that Peter had stopped breathing but after that I got St James to organise the rest. He's always had people he could call on for difficult jobs. They're very discreet.'

'The Chorley suit?'

'Peter gave it to me as a souvenir of the first series. He had several even then. It's been in a box for the last twenty years. I'd almost forgotten I had it. Not something anyone will remember. I can't see that I'm in the frame at all. And I'm not saying anything. You can work on St James if you like but you won't get anything out of him. I wouldn't waste your time.'

'I've got witnesses to prove that I couldn't have moved the body into my garden.'

'Friends of yours I imagine,' Stephen said dismissively. 'But never mind that, you were going to tell me who sent the letters.'

'Lorna Trevanian,' I found myself saying. 'Perdita found a contact number for her in some possessions the Greens had kept. She met Lorna who recognised her as Jane Reddon's daughter. Lorna thinks that Jane is dead. Lorna told Jane that the father of her child was one of the five of us in the photograph. The letters were meant to shake us up so we'd be less guarded in helping her find out who her father was.'

Stephen was nodding contentedly. He was always happier with information to hand.

'Well I suppose it did succeed in shaking things up. But I must say you surprise me. I hadn't realised your powers to extract information from people were so great.

That's very impressive. Very impressive indeed.'

Stephen was looking at the screens above the fireplace. He flicked the controller in his hand. The four screens morphed into nine.

'So are you going to explain? Why you want to frame me for Mark Ryland's murder? Or for Peter's?'

Stephen had stopped tapping the ends of his fingers. He was more relaxed than he had been. I wasn't.

'Peter hasn't been murdered. He appears to have been murdered – which is quite different. As for Mark, it seemed like justice. What I wanted to do was to jog your memory, enable you to catch up with what happened. I thought I ought to persuade you to own up to Mark's murder.'

'Why would I want to do that?'

'Because you killed him.'

'How do you know that?'

'You told me.'

FORTY-SIX

THURSDAY 9.50PM – 10.30PM

'DON'T YOU REMEMBER?' STEPHEN'S voice was full of encouragement as though a simple effort would unlock the depths of moral turpitude in my soul.

I shook my head. It seemed to move the jigsaw pieces of memory closer together. The consultant had said that apart from blows to the head stressful situations might act as a spur to the recovery of memory. He hadn't said what extreme stress would do but it was clear it would do the same, only more quickly. I was kneeling down with blood on my hands next to the young woman. But this time the memories didn't cut out abruptly. Now I could see that she was lying face down in the snow. There had been snow outside Mark's flat. The two memories were of events close together. The snow in London that year according to weather records had only lasted a week. I looked at Stephen.

'What did I tell you?' I said.

I remembered pressing the beehive bell outside Mark's flat.

'When I killed Mark,' I continued. 'What did I say?'

Stephen's face had assumed a Buddha-like serenity. He wasn't going to answer, at least not yet. I found I didn't mind. It was coming back to me. I hadn't managed to get in. It was the outside of Mark's flat I remembered, not the inside. I hadn't been able to make him hear. That's why I had peered through the window. That's why I had stepped back and looked up to see if there were signs of life in the building. I hadn't detected any. That was why I had gone away.

'I mean did I say he had a note in his hand?'

'A note?' The look of beatific complacency on Stephen's face dissolved a little around the edges before moving back into place.

'You remember in *Murder Unseen* when Tom Travis is standing over Rob's body. Rob has this fake suicide note in his hand. John told me you asked him to put that in. Why? There wasn't a suicide note found when Mark's body was discovered. Everything else in the book matches the known circumstances of Mark's death. It had to be like that to hide the one great fictional addition – my presence. So why change anything apart from adding me? There's only one answer – you didn't. There *was* a note in Mark's hand.'

'It's a minor detail, nothing more,' Stephen said wearily. 'It's not going to stop Addinson arresting you. Anyway, if you weren't there, you can't know anything one way or another can you?'

'I don't have to know. Mark had another visitor later that evening – Andy Fontaine. He broke in. It's easy enough as it happens, if you get past the front door, it's just a Yale lock. He finds Mark dead and with a note in his hand. He dislikes involvement with the authorities so he leaves the note untouched, exits as soon as he can, and leaves someone else to alert the police. The person who reports finding the body is Frederick St James. At the inquest there's no report of any suicide note, or any note, fake or real. I asked St James what he remembered but he was remarkably reluctant to say anything one way or another.'

'Fontaine isn't exactly a reliable witness. And if you know it's a Yale you've been inside the building. Why do that if you're not guilty?'

Stephen didn't seem concerned. But then he didn't have any need to be. Addinson wouldn't be basing his case against me simply on *Murder Unseen*, but on moving Peter's body, leaving Mark's flat decorated in my fingerprints and DNA, and my inability to tell the truth on any CCTV recording.

'Did I say I'd actually got into the flat? I mean when I confessed to you.'

Stephen smiled. 'Mark called you.'

'That doesn't answer my question.'

It didn't but it was a trigger that opened another door. Mark *had* called me. He had sounded desperate. I said I could be with him in an hour, perhaps a bit less.

The blizzard had started before I left the house, sweeping in from the Arctic. I had planned to travel by rail but services were grinding to a halt in a white blanket. Metal shutters were being pulled across station entrances. I managed to get on a bus and for a time made adequate, if not rapid, progress. When the bus finally became stalled in the traffic, I reckoned I was no more than a mile away from Mark's flat if I could cut through the side streets. That was when it happened.

Not that I saw it. Indeed I hardly heard what happened either. What should have been a shrieking of brakes was a grumbling, muffled slide. When the lorry had crushed her there had been a distant thumping sound and only the faintest of cries.

When I looked round, giant snowflakes were still dropping slowly and serenely down but the air was clearing. I had bent over the woman lying in the snow. I could see when I got to Mark's flat that I still had traces of blood on my hands. I had knelt down and leant forward to touch the body. That was why my hands were covered in blood. But I had done more than that. I had turned the body slightly and looked at the woman's face.

I can see it again now. It's a young woman who is quite dead but it isn't Jane Reddon. I look up. The driver of the lorry, his face whiter than the snow itself, is forever stumbling towards me but there's nothing he or I can do.

I spoke to a policewoman who told me I wasn't a witness because I had seen nothing of the accident itself. And then an ambulance arrived and I found myself in a down-at-heel pub trying to scrub the blood off my hands in a greying sink filled with cold water.

Then everything is blurred. I found myself in streets I didn't know which doubled back on themselves at every opportunity. I was more than an hour later than I should have been when I got to Mark's flat. I rang the beehive bell. I knocked on the door. I rattled the window. I couldn't find anyone in the building to let me in. Eventually I left.

Back in the present Stephen was saying something but I couldn't work out what it was or how much time had passed.

'Mark,' Stephen repeated. 'You never told me what he said in this call he made to you. And as you don't remember we shall never know.'

But now I could recall what Mark had said. The memory was flooding back. He'd had a terrible row with Jane. She was pregnant but she couldn't be sure who the child of her father was. He'd called her a whore and been completely unreasonable and forced her away when she had needed him most. Half an hour after she had gone he'd tried to call her to tell her how wrong he had been but she had disappeared. He was afraid that the link between them was broken, and could never be mended. He didn't know what he was going to do. That was why I had set out to see him, afraid of what might happen, and what he might do to himself.

'But I do remember now.'

My words were uncertain and halting.

'That's convenient,' Stephen said unbelievingly.

Before I could say anything further the phone rang on Stephen's desk. Even from where I was I could detect Blenkiron's low-pitched drawl.

'If you must,' Stephen said a few seconds later and then put the phone down.

'I'm afraid I have a conference call with our American friends,' Stephen said. 'It should take only take ten minutes but apparently it has to happen now. They're terribly impatient people.'

Stephen ushered me from the room as the internal bolts in the door locked home with an idle flick from the electronic card in his hand. Far from looking agitated by our conversation he looked calmer than ever.

When he had gone I walked along the corridor. There was no one who looked soulful enough to be Mark. There wasn't a comic Hayter depicted on the walls, a stand-in for Peter, some fantastical lord prone to excesses of exuberance and despair before dismissal by an unappreciative goddess of fortune. Only John Hazlitt might have slipped into the tweed suit of a late 1920s squire on a Scottish moor looking forward to the good times to come.

I should have been feeling better. I'd spent twenty-five years worrying about what had happened in my six months of darkness. Now I knew that I hadn't done anything wrong. But then I knew that, whatever I did, I would be convicted of a murder I didn't commit, and which hadn't happened in the first place. I wondered how I could face the boys or Kate. I reached into my pocket for my phone. How could I put it?

> *BEING FRAMED FOR TWO MURDERS.*
> *DIDN'T DO EITHER AND PRETTY SURE*
> *NEITHER WAS A MURDER ANYWAY.*
> *THEY JUST APPEAR TO BE. THE POLICE*
> *ARE AFTER ME BUT I HOPE TO SORT IT*
> *OUT. ALL TO DO WITH MEMORY LOSS.*
> *WILL EXPLAIN. LOVE DAVID.*

As a message to convey the fact that I was feeling slightly crazed it worked on most levels. As the coherent account that I had tried to assemble of my predicament and appeal for understanding and sympathy it didn't seem to score so well. I read it again, shook my head, thought about starting afresh, and then found I had pressed send. There was a message from Jerry:

> *IT'S THE MULLER! LOOKING GOOD.*
> *TWENTY MINUTES SHOULD SORT IT*
> *FOR CERTAIN!*

which suggested he, at least, was making some progress and then a response from Kate:

> *WONDERED WHERE YOU WERE. BUT JUST GOT A TEXT FROM TOM TRAVIS! SOUNDS THRILLING. INSPIRATION OBVIOUSLY IN FULL FLOW. BUT DON'T FORGET TO DO THE ENDING BEFORE YOU MOVE ON. LOOKS LIKE MISSING THE HOLIDAY WAS WORTH IT. BACK SATURDAY A BIT LATER AROUND SIX. BOYS SEND THEIR LOVE. KATE XX.*

I could hear voices somewhere in the house, slightly raised as tension was released. It sounded as though Stephen's meeting was breaking up. I felt a sense of despair. How on earth was I meant to reply to Kate's text? What on earth was Jerry up to? How was I going to handle Stephen? Then I had a revelation.

I had at last got the proper ending for *Murder is Equal*. Crispin Cruickshank hadn't met his end by another hand, but had killed himself in suspicious circumstances to create the appearance of murder. His intention all along had been to create an atmosphere of permanent unease among his six nephews and nieces that would ruin their lives. He was taking revenge on the family he so much disliked through their grandchildren. There never had been a murder. I wondered why Tom Travis hadn't been able to work that out for himself.

At the end of the corridor Blenkiron was giving Stephen a congratulatory slap on the back. It looked like the deal with Borkmann Industries had finally passed all its stages and just for a moment Hank was Stephen's best buddy, if not his friend.

Quite where I ranked in Stephen's affections was more problematic. Stephen knew that I hadn't killed Mark. More than that he probably wouldn't have cared too much if I had.

Then it struck me. Framing me for Mark's murder was simply a way of achieving some other end. Whatever had prompted him to enlist John's help on *Murder Unseen* a year before had had nothing to do with Mark's death but had been caused by something else altogether. And about that I knew nothing at all.

FORTY-SEVEN

THURSDAY 10.30PM – 11.00PM

STEPHEN WAS BACK BEHIND his desk in the small study. He had a slim control pad in his hand and was pointing it at Picture Screen. The photograph of the five of us faded from view and the screen split into four separate images offering coverage of anything moving outside the house; ghostly happenings in the thin white light of the moon.

'So David? Where do you go from here?'

'I have a feeling we're both involved in this.'

'Do you? And why is that?'

'My memory has come back. I know I didn't have anything to do with Mark's death. You can't fool me into thinking I did.'

'It's not you I have to fool exactly. The police will do just as well.'

'But you wouldn't want Peter's body found on your land would you?'

Stephen paused dramatically but that was all that his pause was for – drama. 'That's a fair enough point,' he said.

'The police might feel they had to treat me like a suspect. They might find a trace of antique Rainbridge dust under Peter's fingernails and start asking questions. As it happens there's no possibility of that.'

'Why not?'

Stephen looked at his watch. 'The body has been moved from the boathouse. About ten minutes ago. It should soon be off Rainbridge land and in transit.' Stephen shrugged his shoulders. 'Who knows where?'

'Presumably you do.'

'It will be somewhere safe. I must confess I'm glad you brought the body back. I couldn't have foreseen you meeting Addinson in North London at the time Peter died. My whole scheme could have backfired horribly. What I had planned was tortuous enough without that sort of difficulty. It was far too spur of the moment. Anyway perhaps Peter's body will reappear. He needs a proper funeral.'

'Did the cameras pick us up?' I said with some surprise in my voice. Jerry had seemed certain that the CCTV couldn't cover that part of the estate.

'The boathouse is out of range. It was purely fortuitous that somebody saw you and was public-spirited enough to report the matter.'

'Was it a man with a dog?'

Stephen smiled. 'I couldn't possibly say.'

I pointed to the screen above the fireplace.

'Are they infrared as well? Can they see in the dark?'

'The system operates in all conditions. It's movement sensitive.'

There was activity on a number of screens. St James was walking down the terrace at the back of the house cradling an object in his arms that turned out to be a shotgun.

I saw a flash of something beside a yew hedge but even as the camera zoomed in it was gone. If it was Jerry he had been right about the military kit he was wearing. It made him almost invisible in the watery moonlight.

Stephen moved another control and the screen split into nine, this time showing scenes inside the house as well as those in the gardens. Brown was walking through the great hall with a cocktail on a silver tray. He went into the small corridor with the Zoffanys and disappeared from view.

'Brown seems to work late.'

'He's always available if Francesca is in residence. And the other staff are away tonight.'

'So you called St James in?'

'It's always helpful to have an extra pair of hands.'

'Does he need a shotgun?'

'Some of my commercial competitors don't exactly play by the rules. It's as well to be prepared for anything. St James is checking the surveillance systems. It's good to be able to verify comings and goings.'

'So there'll be a record of Peter's visit?'

'As it happens, no. The system here does permit a certain amount of what would one say? *Editing* I imagine. Not that anyone would be able to detect that anything had been done.'

Stephen emerged from behind the desk.

'Would you care for a drink David? You were always something of a connoisseur of malt whisky weren't you? Let me offer you something I think you'll like.'

He had a collection of decanters on a sideboard. He seemed lost in thought for a second and then poured two glasses in a leisurely fashion. He offered me one, sat in an armchair and gestured toward the seat opposite him.

Behind him Jerry had appeared on the middle right screen. He was near the statue of the Three Graces. The semi-invisible figure I had seen before and thought to be him had been a phantom of my imagination. His battledress did have the effect of making him slightly blurry at the edges as though anyone watching him might feel they had drunk too much; but he hadn't blended into his surroundings. He was still very much there. Perhaps the military didn't have to cope with moonlight in battle situations.

He had been taking something out of one of his pockets and was weighing it up in his hands. For the uninformed observer it might have been difficult to judge precisely what he was trying to decide. It wasn't a problem for me. The object in his hand was the automatic that both he and Lorna had threatened me with. I had a horrible sense that he was gearing up for action, eager for an opportunity to play out the military fantasies of his youth and justify his purchase of the reprinted Commando comics in his study.

'Oh did I tell you?' Stephen said conversationally. 'DCI Addinson. He's on his way here. I was quite surprised he was willing to come at such a late hour.'

In the top left screen St James had abandoned his attentive care of the shotgun and now held it ready for action. After a moment he set off and moved out of the picture. I could have worked out in which direction he was going but just for a moment my mind was elsewhere. There was something else I didn't understand.

'Addinson?' I said. 'How did you know I met Addinson the night Peter died?'

'He must have mentioned it.'

'Why would he do that?'

'We were speaking about you,' Stephen said. 'Yes, that's right. I said I was expecting you here and he ought to come down. That's when he told me about the meeting. It came as something of a shock. I think he was trying to get a reaction out of me. I suspect he thinks we may be in league in some way. Anyway no doubt he'll explain everything when he arrives.'

'We need to sort a few things out before that.'

'Do we?'

'Of course we do. Why don't we start with Perdita? She seems to have turned into a fine young woman. I wonder who put up the money for the Greens? But I know the answer to that. It wasn't me. It couldn't be Mark. John might once have been the leading candidate given his womanizing tendencies but it seems he's out of the picture. It wasn't Peter. There's not really anyone left but you Stephen.'

He considered the point and then nodded.

'I suppose there's no harm in telling you. It's very simple. Jane arrived in Angellic's offices one night. It was a Friday, quite late. I was collecting some papers for the weekend and preparing to lock up. She had a newborn baby with her. She was distressed. I thought she might be suicidal. She told me the father of the baby wouldn't have anything to do with it. She had to give it up but she didn't want it taken into care. St James turned up. He had an answer to Jane's problems. He knew a couple that were desperate to adopt a child but didn't stand any sort of chance of doing so. George Green was an accountant who had got into dodgy company and had done a couple of years inside. He and his wife wanted to make a new start in a new place and they were desperate for a baby, but they were never going to be able to adopt with his record.

With a little money to help them on their way they offered a discreet solution to Jane's problem.'

'So you've been funding Perdita all these years?'

'It seemed the right thing to do. Jane had worked for Angellic. She was in trouble. She needed help. She found she couldn't cope with the baby without support and so she decided to give it up. I was in a position to help. I put the scheme in place and then one day she simply disappeared.'

'And you never told Francesa?'

'We were engaged to be married and I was suffering a little competition from her childhood sweetheart, Ronald Williams. Announcing that I was supporting another man's child didn't seem to be very diplomatic. Besides, given the circumstances, it was better that as few people as possible knew about it.'

'So is that what all this *Murder Unseen* business is about? Neglecting Mark? Neglecting Jane?'

'That's quite a lot isn't it?'

'Look I can remember what happened now. Mark phoned me. I went to see him but I couldn't get there in time. It was snowing heavily and there was an accident, a young woman had died. I was delayed. I was at least an hour later than I should have been. When I got there he didn't answer the door. He must already have been dead.'

'As you say David,' Stephen said with a dismissive wave of his hand. 'It must be so helpful that your memory is returning just at the right moment. What do you think of this by the way?' Stephen indicated the glass of malt in his hand.

Behind Stephen, St James had started moving purposefully forward in a direction, as far as I could see, that would take him to the Three Graces. Unfortunately Jerry had reappeared again at the side of the statue looking at a device that he had in his hand, probably his GPS system, but paying no attention to anything around him.

'Very pleasant,' I said.

Stephen nodded in appreciation of my sound judgement. The camera on Jerry was motionless as he tried to compute his exact position on earth to the nearest millimetre. There was still a shimmer to the outline of his body but he was nowhere near blended into the darkness around him. St James was still advancing shotgun in hand. Their screens were next to each other so that it seemed in a moment they might touch. Stephen was looking at his watch, counting off the seconds till Addinson arrived and seemingly unaware of what was happening behind him. I needed to make sure that he didn't look round.

'But you know what I say about Mark must be true.'

'I don't know anything of the kind.'

'At least you know that I didn't get inside the flat. Mark left a suicide note didn't he? That's what St James found. That's what Andy Fontaine saw. That's why you asked John to put it into *Murder Unseen*.'

'If that's what you want to think.'

'So did Jane say I was the father?'

'She wouldn't say who it was.'

I didn't understand. We were a man short. Jane had been talking about being torn between two men when she had spoken to Lorna. She had said that Perdita's father was one of the men in the photograph. It hadn't been Peter and, unless John Hazlitt was a stupendously skilled liar, it hadn't been him either. It wasn't me. That only left Stephen and Mark. That made much more sense of Stephen's philanthropy.

Jerry was tapping away at the base of the statue with the chisel. On another screen I could see that St James had heard something. I looked back at Stephen. The obvious explanation was probably the best.

'So,' I said, 'why couldn't Perdita have been your child?'

'Because she's your daughter David.'

'I don't think so. In fact I know she's not.'

Behind Stephen, on a split screen, two versions of Jerry were glancing around in every direction but the one from which St James was approaching him.

'Do you?' Stephen sounded unbelieving.

'You had an affair with Jane, didn't you Stephen? That's the only thing that makes sense of this.'

'So what if I did? I grew fond of her to the extent of thinking that I should give up Francesca. But that wasn't going to happen. There was somebody else – you, David – and I realised that we were drifting apart and there was nothing that I could do about it. So I proposed to Francesca. Then Jane told me she was going to have my child but she didn't want to be with me. It seems she must have been in love with someone else – you again David. But by this time you'd conveniently forgotten that you'd ever been with her at all hadn't you? Selective amnesia is so helpful.'

'It wasn't me Stephen. It was Mark.'

I stopped. I had brought Andy Fontaine's photograph of Mark and Jane with me. I could talk about the tape of love songs. There must be something that I could say that would convince him.

On the screens above the fireplace Jerry was continuing to tap away at the stone base of the Three Graces. Above him the long slim legs of the nymphs were motionless in their frozen dance. On the screen next to him St James had reappeared, shotgun at the ready. As the screens were separate there was no way of being absolutely sure the events were connected and there must have been at least a one in ten million chance they weren't. Stephen was following my gaze. For a moment something seemed to cause a flicker of disquiet to cross his features but whatever it was passed away in an instant.

'We need to do something about those two,' I said. 'They could get hurt.'

'He's trespassing. He's dressed in combat gear and is obviously up to no good. St James has every reason to shoot him.' Stephen seemed disinterested. 'I suppose he has something to do with you?'

'He's a friend of mine, Jerry Davis. He's checking out the grounds. He's trying to find a place to put Peter's body. Get St James to stop him now and bring him back to the house before there is an accident. Tell him he needs to be careful. Jerry has a gun with him – probably in a pocket in his trousers.'

Stephen considered the proposition and then muttered some words into the control pad. St James was in the same frame on Picture Screen before Jerry realised he was there. A gesture from the shotgun persuaded him to hand over Lorna's automatic and in another moment, on another screen, they were progressing back to Rainbridge Hall. Jerry had his hands held above his head. It was all very neat. I felt a sudden chill shake me. I'd averted a shooting but at the expense of offering up my last card.

FORTY-EIGHT

THURDAY 11.00PM – 11.30PM

JERRY WAS BEING LED back to the house under the watchful eye of St James. I had the sense again that Stephen had some wider plan in train and that there was nothing I could do to stop it. He was speaking again, his voice flat and matter of fact, as though he was reading out his testimony in a court of law.

'Jane was pining for you. That's why she wouldn't come back to me. You left the fireworks party together and Perdita was conceived. That was what changed everything. You lost your memory and when Jane came looking for support you didn't remember anything that had happened and discarded her, or maybe you did remember and rejected her anyway. So she can't face up to looking after the baby and does a flit.'

'So this isn't about Mark? This is just about Jane?'

'Mark was perfectly capable of killing himself. He didn't need help.'

The note of finality in Stephen's voice was pure ice. We'd finally hit bottom. He didn't care about Mark.

This was all about Jane. This was what paying John Hazlitt to write *Murder Unseen* and moving Peter's body and making it look as though he had been murdered had been about. I'd abandoned the woman he loved. This was the indictment that stood against me. I was responsible for what had happened to Jane and should expect vengeance.

'We need to sort this out,' I said as though somehow I still had a say in events, and reason still had a place in the world. 'Look, I should have brought the tape of Mark's last songs with me. Whatever crisis happened between them, he was in love with Jane. Fontaine can tell you they were together. There had a row about who Perdita's father might be. When he phoned me the day he died he was distraught. He'd said something to Jane that had destroyed everything. He had been on an up and then he found his new world was as fragile as his old one and cracking into pieces. He was at his most vulnerable. That's why he took his own life.'

Stephen was fiddling with the controls on his remote, seemingly uninterested in anything I had said. I was missing something. I tried to clear my mind but then another flood of memories came back to me. There was the smell of burning magnesium. The fireworks were blazing gold and silver. It was Jane who had suggested we leave the party. John had given me a sideways appraising glance before turning his attention back to a pretty woman next to him. Lorna Trevanian, between odd checks to ensure that Peter was still with her, was clearly wondering what was happening. The look on her face was interested but not unfriendly, the last time she had managed to look at me without the beginnings of a scowl crossing her features.

Jane and I left. We went to the basement flat in the house I was looking after and I opened a bottle of red wine. I didn't quite know what I expected but it seemed she wanted advice. She had a choice to make between two men. It took me a couple of minutes to come to terms with the fact that I was neither of them and that what she wanted more than anything else was someone to listen. I said I would favour my heart rather than my head. We must have fallen asleep. It was a bitterly cold night, the first advance of the cold weather that would lead to the sudden heavy snow a few weeks later. I remember waking, suddenly feeling warm. We had wrapped a blanket around us as we sat propped up against the sofa. Her face was so close to mine that it was difficult to see who she was. Then I must have dozed for she was gone and there was only the sense of something luminous being taken away.

I remembered about the amber necklace as well. Jane was wearing it on Piccadilly. The street was bright with Christmas lights. She said she was very happy.

Mark and I had bought it the day before. I was the only person he knew in Kensington who had a credit card. It was something she had seen and that he wanted to give her. It glowed with inner gold like she did. But he hadn't got enough cash to hand and he needed to get it that day.

It was Peter who told me that Mark was dead. Angellic Entertainment's offices had been agog with the news. I tried to telephone Jane but she wasn't answering. I tried to find her but she had disappeared. Then a hockey ball hit me and I couldn't remember anything concrete of what had happened at all and I was left only with fragments that inhabited my dreams.

I looked up. Picture Screen had split into nine. Jerry was approaching the hall under St James's care. Francesca and Brown were still deep in conversation. A transit van was pulling out of the main gates. Blenkiron had moved off camera, the glass of fine red wine he had been drinking empty and discarded. On the far perimeters of Rainbridge a small deer, no bigger than a dog, strayed momentarily into camera range and then trotted peacefully away. There was no sign of Addinson.

The pictures dissolved back into one – Francesca and Brown talking together with an assorted array of Hayters behind them. One camera tracked in and Francesca's eyes became ever more luminous and deliquescent. Then a picture of a rotund, cherubic man in rustic jacket and waistcoat replaced her. He was seated on a bench with an improbably square cow with thin legs on one side and Rainbridge Hall on the other.

'Thomas Styles,' Stephen pronounced. 'It's not often you get a picture of Rainbridge staff although I'm sure that Francesca has something lined up for Brown. Styles drained the fields by the river and put the estate on a proper business footing. He's said to have saved the family from bankruptcy.'

'I suppose the American millions will carry on the good work.'

'They were transferred to the family trust funds a few minutes ago. That was something I had to ensure was done. Excuse me a second.'

Stephen winced and patted his stomach protectively. Francesca had said he had been suffering from stress. Perhaps he had an ulcer.

'Do you think you could get me some water David?' He gestured to a carafe next to the whisky decanters.

I walked across the room. My face was reflected in the thick sheet of glass that had been laid protectively on top of the drinks cabinet. I looked rather more real than I felt and had to steady myself. Then I poured some water from the decanter into a heavy glass tumbler and handed it to Stephen. He took it gingerly as though the weight of glass and water combined might be too heavy for him.

He took some pills from his pocket and weighed them in his hands, as though deciding whether to throw them into the air to see if a pattern propitious to the gods might be revealed. Rejecting the notion after a long scrutiny he swallowed the pills in one go.

'That's good about the estate,' I found myself saying. 'I'm sure Francesca will be pleased. But we do need to sort out our story before Addinson arrives.'

'Our story?' Stephen's tone suggested the problem was more abstract than practical. 'I wonder what that amounts to. Perhaps we feel sad about the people we never were.'

It was rather a nebulous starting point for the problems we were faced with. On Picture Screen a car had arrived at the main Rainbridge gate. It had a blue flashing light.

'DCI Addinson seems finally to have made it,' Stephen said.

'Are you going to tell me precisely why he's here?'

'I said I had information for him about Mark Ryland's murder but that I would only talk in person. It's disappointing that I had to call him here. Francesca shouldn't be involved in any of this. Finding Peter's body in your garden should have been enough. Any expert would dismiss the possibility that the knife had killed him and conclude that death had been brought on by other means. By these, for example.'

Stephen put a small packet of pills on the desk in front of him – Amitrip Plus 200 Mg.

'It shouldn't have taken Addinson long to deduce that it seemed that you had used your normal murder method, the modus operandi for killing Mark. Dressing Peter in a Chorley suit was just an attempt by your subconscious to draw attention to your actions.'

'As far as I can see you panicked.'

'That's a little harsh. Although I must admit I didn't expect you to move Peter's body. But Peter's whole life was chaotic. Anything involving his death was bound to be the same. But I needed something else other than *Murder Unseen* to finally convince Addinson you were the murdering kind.'

'You still do.'

Stephen looked up. 'You may be right. Let me try this one on you. If you had been in close attendance to my own death and I was found to have died from Amitrip poisoning Addison might think that that put the whole matter beyond reasonable doubt.'

'But you're not dying.'

'As a matter of fact I am. As it happens I've just taken some Amitrip pills that won't do me any good at all. It could be suicide but I think the police will conclude it's murder. There will be one or two helpful clues. Your fingerprints are on this glass and the decanter and the glass top I imagine. You could wipe the objects clean of course but that would be almost more suspicious. Dead men don't really go around destroying evidence.'

My brain was in some sort of denial of the present. There must be something that could be picked out of what Stephen had said and used against him but all it could come up with was the clue that Tom Travis could use to deduce what had happened in the Crispin Cruickshank murder in *Murder is Equal*. Everything in the locked cabin had been wiped clean by Crispin himself to conceal the fact that no one had been with him. It solved the only remaining problem that I had with the book but that wasn't what I should have been concentrating on. It was displacement activity of the most abject kind.

Stephen was polishing the packet of Amitrip pills with a cloth that he had produced from his desk drawer. Then he put the packet back on top of the desk.

'Game, set, and match,' he said contentedly.

FORTY-NINE

THURSDAY 11.30PM – THURSDAY 11.50PM

THE POLICE CAR WITH its blue flashing light was still at the estate entrance gates. It would be there for a few minutes more because its path forward was blocked by a large black Mercedes that had come roaring out of the night and managed to collide with it. I had no doubt that the driver was Blenkiron and that he was over the limit. I doubted if Addinson would simply let him drive off. Even a DCI needed to have some explanation for the crumpled front wing of a police car in his possession. He would need to fill in several forms which, in turn, would involve extracting details from Blenkiron who, I sensed, would take some time to become fully co-operative. He could also claim he was driving on private land rather than the public highway. Addinson would need to take a few minutes to sort the matter out. He wouldn't know that he was on the way to finding Stephen's dead body, to all appearances a victim of murder. It gave me an opportunity I shouldn't have had.

A look of irritation crossed Stephen's face at this unexpected development. For a man who had always liked to be in total control this turn of events must be more than irksome, given the limited time he had to live. If he hadn't been trying to frame me I would have been sympathetic.

In the penultimate chapter of each of his adventures Tom Travis outlines what has happened before announcing who committed the murder, or murders. If you look at the disquisition on his methods that I included in *A Grave Mistake* you'll find that one of the key concepts is the moment when Tom and the murderer both know as much as each other. Revealing the identity of the murderer is like the scales of justice balancing.

This wasn't quite like that, not only because there wasn't a murder or a murderer, but also because Stephen's actions were based on a simple miscalculation – that I was Perdita's father. I might appear to be but I wasn't. Our scales were distorted. There must be another reason why he clung to the delusion. I had seen his dream. I should be able to work something out.

That dream. I'm frolicking in the pool with Jane. That's clear enough. Then there's Nikki glimpsed for a second in the bushes. I can explain that as well. Stephen thinks I'm somehow instrumental in her leaving him. That makes sense, or at least it's consistent with what he thinks about Jane. And then Francesca is running away from me and I suppose that's consistent as well, except that somehow it's not me she's running away from but someone or something else.

It's something else. It's something Stephen has only permitted himself a sideways glance at. It's something I've seen elsewhere, something I've seen in the last few minutes, those long limbs frozen in stone – the statue of the Three Graces.

The police car was still at the main gate, its blue light flashing in the night. I had a minute or two, time that would fall outside any plan that Stephen had made.

'I was thinking about Jane,' I said.

'And?'

'She's dead isn't she?'

'I don't know. I haven't seen her since she bolted.'

'Yes you have.'

'Why do you say that?'

'Because you killed her.'

It wasn't anything like a shot in the dark. Perdita was convinced that her mother was dead, as was Lorna. Jerry had been tapping round the bottom of the Three Graces statue in an effort to find somewhere to put a body but he might just as well have been trying to find where one had been put. Stephen had never agreed to move the statue despite Francesca's wishes. The statue was something he avoided looking at in his dreams.

'That's nonsense.'

'Why did you kill her and put her body under the statue of the Three Graces? That's where she is. That's what I shall tell the police.'

I looked up at the CCTV feeds. Addinson was still at the gates to the Rainbridge estate, engaged in an argument with a burly figure. Jerry was in a cell-like room with a heavy wooden door examining the lock. Francesca and Brown were in a huddle. Francesca was gesturing with her hands, the outline of some master plan for Rainbridge for the next century or two.

'It was an accident,' Stephen said slowly. His breathing was shallower than it had been. 'Angellic had a flat in Camden for visiting bands. She was staying there. We were in the kitchen and I was trying to reason with her. Both of us were tense, more tense than usual. Perhaps it was because the baby was crying and wouldn't stop. She was preparing some food for the baby and had cut her finger and I was trying to help her but she pushed me away and then she slipped. She fell backwards and cracked her head against the edge of the kitchen work surface. It was stone and had sharp edges. I thought she'd knocked herself out but her body was twisted and she was dead.'

'The baby was with you?' I had a sudden image of a baby crying and then suddenly becoming aware that something terrible had happened. This was why Perdita knew her mother was dead.

Stephen nodded. 'I needed to get rid of the body but I wanted something dignified for her. We were just about to install the Three Graces as a birthday surprise for Francesca. It was a good resting place.'

'It's a Muller design isn't it?'

Stephen looked surprised. 'Yes, it's by Muller. The plinth is hollow. It was the ideal place to dispose of a body. The whole area was already roped off. We only had to wait until it was dark. It should have been easy enough but it started to rain. That made the whole process much more difficult. We couldn't get the statue to where I had planned.'

I looked up at the CCTV feeds. Even though St James had locked Jerry up he still had his shotgun at the ready. He must have been the extra pair of hands that Stephen had used to help bury Jane under the Three Graces.

I took a deep breath. I reckoned I had everything covered if I could just get my thoughts in order. I had thought I had too many pieces to complete the jigsaw but it was now clear that everything did centre on Jane Reddon and her death. What had been confusing was that the whole matter had had two separate starting points. Stephen had commissioned John Hazlitt to write *Murder Unseen* more than a year before as part of a longer-term plot to make it appear that Mark Ryland had been murdered and that I was the man responsible. Stephen's scheme was about to come to the boil when Perdita had appeared searching for her father and Lorna had persuaded her to send out the photographs of the five of us.

The sudden arrival of the photographs must have been a great shock to Stephen and threatened his master plan. That was why he had started acting on impulse and used Peter's death to make it appear that he had been murdered. When that had proved impossible he had cooked up a new version of the scheme by framing me for his own death. For a moment it all seemed to hang together but then I began to feel the ground shifting below my feet. There had to be sufficient motive and there wasn't.

Arranging for *Murder Unseen* to be written hadn't been undertaken on a whim but had required considerable resources and planning. Something had happened a year ago that had triggered the process. But I had no idea what that was. I didn't have a jigsaw with too many pieces but one with the key pieces still missing.

I looked up at Picture Screen. Addinson seemed finally to have disentangled himself from the clutches of Blenkiron and his car. He would be at the front door in a few minutes and this time he would find me with a dead body. The best defence I had was that I knew where another body was. I was pretty sure I was right about that but it wasn't enough. I wasn't off the hook at all. I might just get arrested for three murders rather than two.

FIFTY

THURSDAY 11.50PM – FRIDAY 00.10AM

THE INCONGRUOUS, TOM TRAVIS had maintained in *A Grave Mistake*, after much prompting from me, *is very rarely that. The deeper one's understanding, the more matters are likely to appear congruous*. So why had Stephen bothered to show me a picture of a rotund, cherubic man in rustic jacket seated on a bench with an improbably square cow with thin legs and Rainbridge Hall in the background? Thomas Styles had saved Rainbridge from bankruptcy and in the last few hours Stephen had secured its financial future for the next hundred years. There was no way he would want that to be upset.

'I can't see any advantage in a body being discovered under the Three Graces,' I said. 'Perdita is convinced her mother is dead. I can't think that digging up her mother's remains is going to add anything. At least she can be told Mark is her father and she can have the love songs. That's the best legacy. There's no need to drag Rainbridge into this. Think of the field day the papers would have with Francesca and your sons. But if we're to keep it like that I do need to know what happened a year ago. Why did you get John Hazlitt to write *Murder Unseen*?'

'Thirteen months ago,' Stephen said slowly, 'I had a meeting with my doctor. I've got liver cancer. It was in its early stages but still untreatable. I was told I only had a couple of years to live.'

'You're going to have to tell me more if you don't want Jane's body exhumed. Better to leave everything orderly.'

I thought for a moment I had gone too far but Stephen simply nodded. 'It seems I've underestimated you David. I should have been more robust in defence of your deductive abilities in my conversations with your crime-writing peers. The reason I was seeing my doctor wasn't because I was feeling ill. It was because of something else altogether. A few days before I had been trying out a new surveillance microphone. It was meant to be able to work anywhere. I'd asked St James to wire it up in some remote part of Rainbridge where the walls were thickest. When I came to test it I found I was listening to a conversation between Francesca and her childhood sweetheart, Ronald Williams. It seemed my eldest son Edward and Emma Williams were getting too close and the relationship needed to be stopped, as they were half-brother and half-sister.'

'I don't understand.'

'Ronald Williams is Edward's father.'

'What?'

'It's not quite what you might think,' Stephen raised his voice with an obvious effort. 'It wasn't simply an affair. It seems that any Hayter heiress looks for certain qualities in a husband in addition to mutual attraction. An entrant to the family has two essential functions – to provide wealth and offspring. From the time that Francesca and

I married there has always been a strong cash inflow from my businesses. This deal I've just done cements the position. The estate now has more land than at any time since the sixteenth century. As for my second obligation I thought that had also been fulfilled but I was wrong.'

Stephen shifted uncomfortably.

'Francesca had been unhappy that she wasn't getting pregnant. It seems it is a Hayter-Molyneux custom not to go beyond two years of marriage without having an heir on the way. She got Ronald Williams to step into the breach. I gathered it was a traditional family approach. If there hadn't been the problem with the young people I'm sure neither of them would have mentioned it again. As far as I could tell the secret was only known to the two of them. The conversation was very matter of fact. The same thing happened with my younger son. The boys have similar features.'

I thought back to Sunday. Clearly word of what had occurred had not extended to the elderly aunt who had expressed surprise at Francesca's opposition to the match between the young people. It also explained Francesca's moment of dismay when the device that Jerry had given me had detected the bug in the room that had been her childhood retreat. That must have been where she and Ronald Williams had had their ill-fated conversation.

'That was why I was seeing my doctor. I went for a series of medical checks. It turns out that I've never been able to have children. The cancer was just something else they found.'

'And Francesca? Didn't you think...'

I let the words trail away into silence. I wondered what I had intended to say when I started the sentence. Stephen wouldn't be the first, or the last, man to find himself in this position though.

'I wouldn't want Francesca to know that I found out,' Stephen said. 'I'm sure she acted with the best intentions.'

Addinson's car was moving gingerly forward. There wouldn't be too many minutes before he arrived. I didn't have much time.

'I certainly wouldn't tell her,' I said. 'If Peter died of a heart attack the only problem I have with Addinson is his fixation that I murdered Mark. If there had been a suicide note that would have been easier...'

'Like this one?' Stephen's words were coming more slowly and he reached into his desk with difficulty. After a few seconds he produced a sheet of paper that he pushed towards me:

It's cold and I can't hear the music anymore.
You were unlocking the trap but now
everything is so much worse. The snow is
falling and soon there will only be whiteness.
Forgive me. I'm sorry I can't go on but it
hasn't worked. It's too late. I'm so sorry.

Mark

'Was there anything else? An envelope? A name?'

'He hardly needed to address it to me did he? I'd spent the best part of two years trying to coax him back into some sort of activity and given him a free flat to live in. No wonder he wanted to apologise.'

'This wasn't meant for you. This was for Jane. She was his muse as well as his lover.'

Stephen shook his head slowly. 'I don't believe that David. I would have known.'

'Why? Who knew that Jane had started an affair with you? Jane kept that from Lorna. She didn't tell anyone she was going out with the boss. Why should she? It would have been odder if she had. Given that you had Mark under contract why would she tell anyone about her new relationship? She would have been afraid it would get back to you.'

Stephen had been shaking his head but he stopped. For a moment I thought it was exhaustion. Then he looked at me.

'You'll say nothing about the Three Graces? Nothing to Francesca?'

'Nothing.'

Stephen nodded and picked up the Amitrip pills. 'Give these to Brown. He'll know what to do with them.' He wasn't looking at me any longer but at something beyond. 'There's nothing to concern you. I have a plan for all eventualities. Peter will reappear tomorrow without a knife in his back and not dressed as Chorley. There will be a friendly GP to say he died of a heart attack. He won't notice that anything else is amiss. If Addinson still has questions about Mark he'll find a convenient entry in my diary detailing an eccentric plan to dislodge your writer's block. Brown will know where to find it. I imagine John Hazlitt will be able to back all that up if he needs to. St James will confirm that he found a suicide note with Mark's body and that I asked him to suppress it to spare the family's feelings. The rumours that Mark was murdered are simply rumours. They really are quite insubstantial. I should know. I started them.'

'And the pills you've taken?'

'There are a couple of other things mixed in with the Amitrip. It wouldn't be particularly easy to detect it unless you're looking for it. The overall effect should be a bit like taking hemlock. I'm getting numb from the feet up, which is reassuring. It seems painless.'

I looked up at Picture Screen. Addinson's car had stopped outside the front entrance to the hall. Jerry was selecting another implement from a selection of lock-picking tools. Brown was talking earnestly to Francesca. St James was polishing the barrel of his shotgun.

'There must be some antidote.'

'It's too late for that.'

'Francesca?'

'We said goodbye a few hours ago. I don't think there's anything to add. The family will look after themselves.'

'I ought to get someone.'

'There's really no time.'

'And how am I going to explain your death?'

'Suicide. In my case I'm only bringing the curtain down a bit early. Choose my own moment. There was a Hayter-Molyneux who did much the same at Waterloo. He managed to get his gambling debts written off. I'm not sure the modern temperament is quite so suited to such gestures but I'm sure Francesca will understand. Better to determine one's own fate. If I stay around things will come to light. I wouldn't want that. I wouldn't want the boys to start digging up the past. This way everything can stay as it is.'

'So it's all simply been the appearance of murder rather than murder itself?' It hardly seemed a sufficient explanation. 'Is that it Stephen? Just some mad jealousy?'

It probably isn't good form to berate the dying but Stephen seemed prepared to answer the question although his voice was growing quieter.

'I did love Jane, David. You have to believe that. Some mornings when I wake up there are a few seconds when I don't remember she's dead. But what happened wasn't an accident. It was murder. I hit her as hard as I could. I was angry. I meant to kill her. I've had to live with that for all these years. And then I found out that Jane couldn't have had my child at all. And I thought I had someone else to blame and that was you.'

On Picture Screen the surveillance of the house and grounds dissolved into the picture of the five of us. It's the last flick of the control that Stephen will make. He's stopped breathing. I look up. We stand in various poses. John is looking to one side distracted by something he has seen – probably a woman. Peter is partly hidden but even then looking to ensure he has a means of escape. Mark looks into the distance to a land beyond the camera lens. Stephen and I look firmly into the lens and I seem to be waiting for something to happen while he seems eager to grasp the future and mould it to his purpose.

I could imagine the portrait of Stephen that would one day grace the Rainbridge walls. It would appear, for a century or two at least, to be very modern. There would be no murky background further coloured by age but a shadow-free present and Stephen would be calm, learned, but with a distant look in his eyes, as though his mind was preoccupied with lofty scientific matters. Perhaps Francesca would have some of the estate, now stretching ever further towards the horizon, painted in behind him. Or it might be some retrospective family portrait; the technocratic squire with the beautiful heiress and their family. Or perhaps the picture was already done and hanging in some more private room upstairs. Whatever was done, or would be done, would give the appearance of a loving husband and wife. Perhaps the loving husband and wife part was true enough. Their marriage, at least to outward appearances, had been better than most.

I got the controls and turned the picture off. The five of us faded from view.

I took a deep breath and picked up the Amitrip pills to give to Brown.

ACKNOWLEDGEMENTS

I USED TO THINK WRITING was a solitary business. With *The Appearance of Murder* I realise how much the efforts of others in reading and commenting on various versions have improved the final readability and construction of the book.

Thank you therefore to my wife, Caroline, for her creative ideas and suggestions for improvement and also to everyone else who has helped shape the book including Caroline Aldridge, David Bickel, Fiona Clarke-Hackston, Caroline Haynes, Mike Hope, the late and sadly missed Mary Jacobs, Alice Leonard, Diane Summers, Jane White, and Charlotte Wightwick.

There will be some characters such as the neo-Fascist politician, Lombardo, or the ageing Polish refugee, Katya Gombrowicz, of whom only readers of early drafts will have knowledge. In the book you have before you Faith develops no feelings for the unworthy Italian and Katya does not have to intervene, implausibly, to restore David and Tom's flagging deductive abilities.

I am also grateful for the professional input of my proofreader Catherine Best; to John Chandler of Chandler Book Design for the internal design; and to Victoria Nightingale for the cover design.

Some of the technological developments in the book are a little ahead of what is possible outside a laboratory but all are based on current research activities. As far as I can see, from the specialist literature, Faith and Jerry's experiment in conception is soundly based. As for Enzheimer's Syndrome, I am beginning to develop early symptoms but this may simply be nervousness about the reaction to this book.